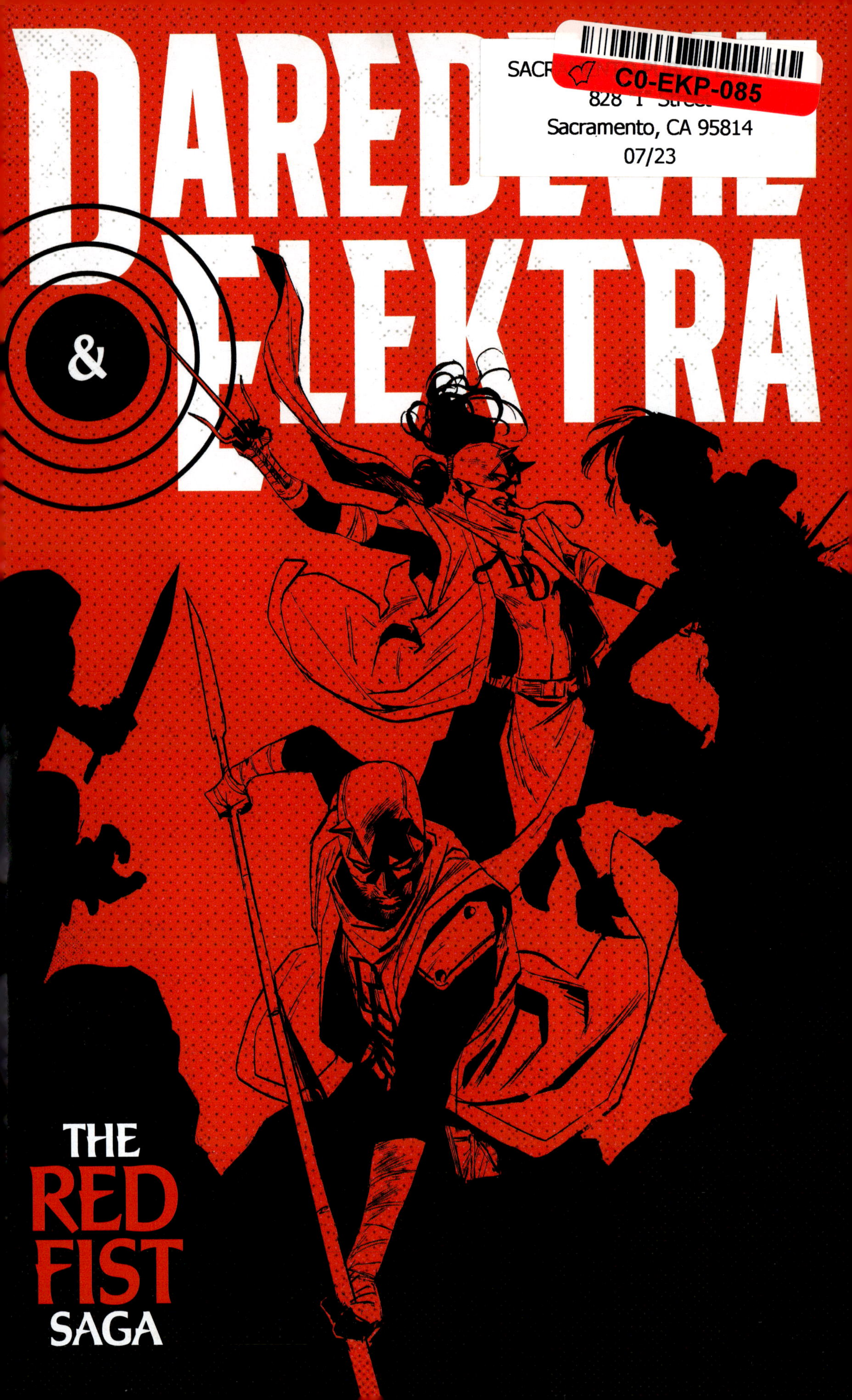
DAREDEVIL
&
ELEKTRA
THE
RED
FIST
SAGA

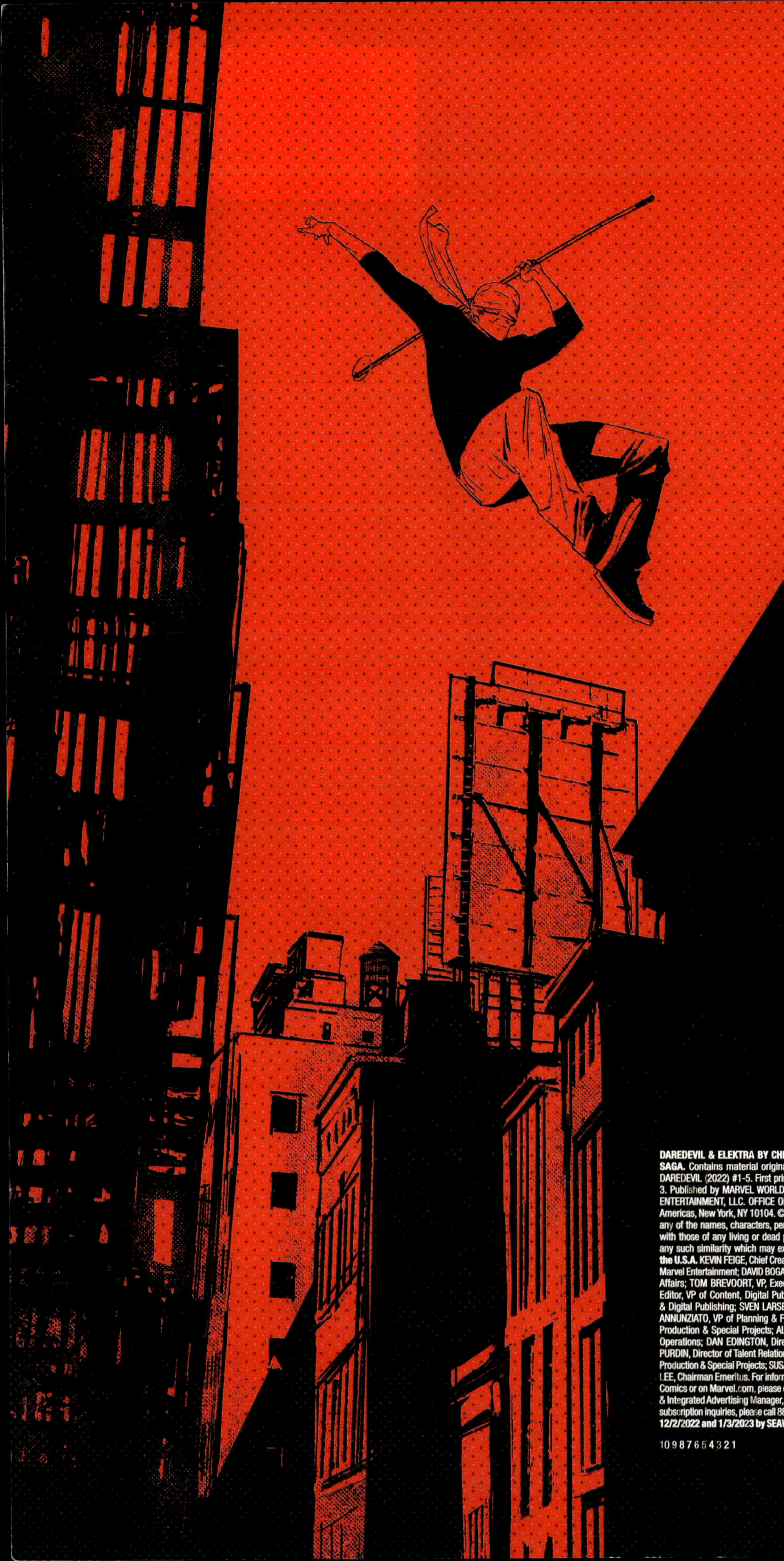

JENNIFER GRÜNWALD
COLLECTION EDITOR

DANIEL KIRCHHOFFER
ASSISTANT EDITOR

MAIA LOY
ASSISTANT
MANAGING EDITOR

LISA MONTALBANO
ASSOCIATE MANAGER,
TALENT RELATIONS

JEFF YOUNGQUIST
VP PRODUCTION
& SPECIAL PROJECTS

ANTHONY GAMBINO
BOOK DESIGNER

JAY BOWEN
SENIOR DESIGNER

DAVID GABRIEL
SVP PRINT, SALES
& MARKETING

C.B. CEBULSKI
EDITOR IN CHIEF

DAREDEVIL & ELEKTRA BY CHIP ZDARSKY VOL. 1: THE RED FIST SAGA. Contains material originally published in magazine form as DAREDEVIL (2022) #1-5. First printing 2022. ISBN 978-1-302-92611-3. Published by MARVEL WORLDWIDE, INC., a subsidiary of MARVEL ENTERTAINMENT, LLC. OFFICE OF PUBLICATION: 1290 Avenue of the Americas, New York, NY 10104. **Printed in the U.S.A.** KEVIN FEIGE, Chief Creative Officer; DAN BUCKLEY, President, Marvel Entertainment; DAVID BOGART, Associate Publisher & SVP of Talent Affairs; TOM BREVOORT, VP, Executive Editor; NICK LOWE, Executive Editor, VP of Content, Digital Publishing; DAVID GABRIEL, VP of Print & Digital Publishing; SVEN LARSEN, VP of Licensed Publishing; MARK ANNUNZIATO, VP of Planning & Forecasting; JEFF YOUNGQUIST, VP of Production & Special Projects; ALEX MORALES, Director of Publishing Operations; DAN EDINGTON, Director of Editorial Operations; RICKEY PURDIN, Director of Talent Relations; JENNIFER GRÜNWALD, Director of Production & Special Projects; SUSAN CRESPI, Production Manager; STAN LEE, Chairman Emeritus. For information regarding advertising in Marvel Comics or on Marvel.com, please contact Vit DeBellis, Custom Solutions & Integrated Advertising Manager, at vdebellis@marvel.com. For Marvel subscription inquiries, please call 888-511-5480. **Manufactured between 12/2/2022 and 1/3/2023 by SEAWAY PRINTING, GREEN BAY, WI, USA.**

10 9 8 7 6 5 4 3 2 1

DAREDEVIL & ELEKTRA
THE RED FIST SAGA

CHIP ZDARSKY
WRITER

MARCO CHECCHETTO
(#1-2) &
RAFAEL De LATORRE
(#3-5, "THE ISLAND" & FLASHBACKS)
ARTISTS

ALEX MALEEV, PAUL AZACETA, PHIL NOTO, CHRIS SAMNEE, KLAUS JANSON, MIKE HAWTHORNE, JOHN ROMITA JR. & **SCOTT HANNA**
#2 GUEST ARTISTS

MATTHEW WILSON
COLOR ARTIST

VC's CLAYTON COWLES
LETTERER

"THE HAND"
ANN NOCENTI
WRITER
CHIP ZDARSKY
ARTIST
VC's CLAYTON COWLES
LETTERER

"MINI MARVELS"
CHRIS GIARRUSSO
WRITER/ARTIST/LETTERER

MARCO CHECCHETTO & **MATTHEW WILSON**
COVER ART

TOM GRONEMAN
ASSOCIATE EDITOR
DEVIN LEWIS
EDITOR

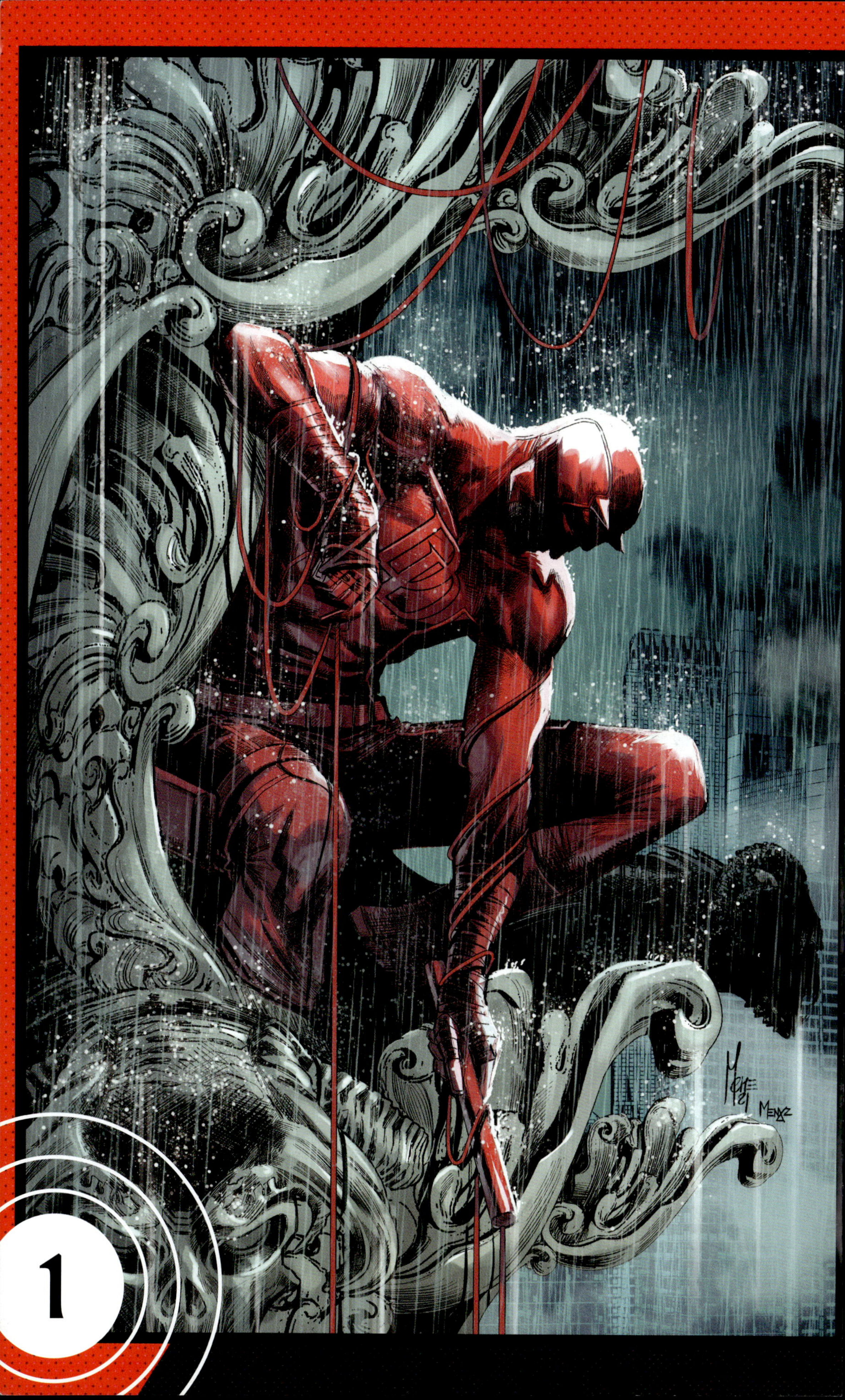
1

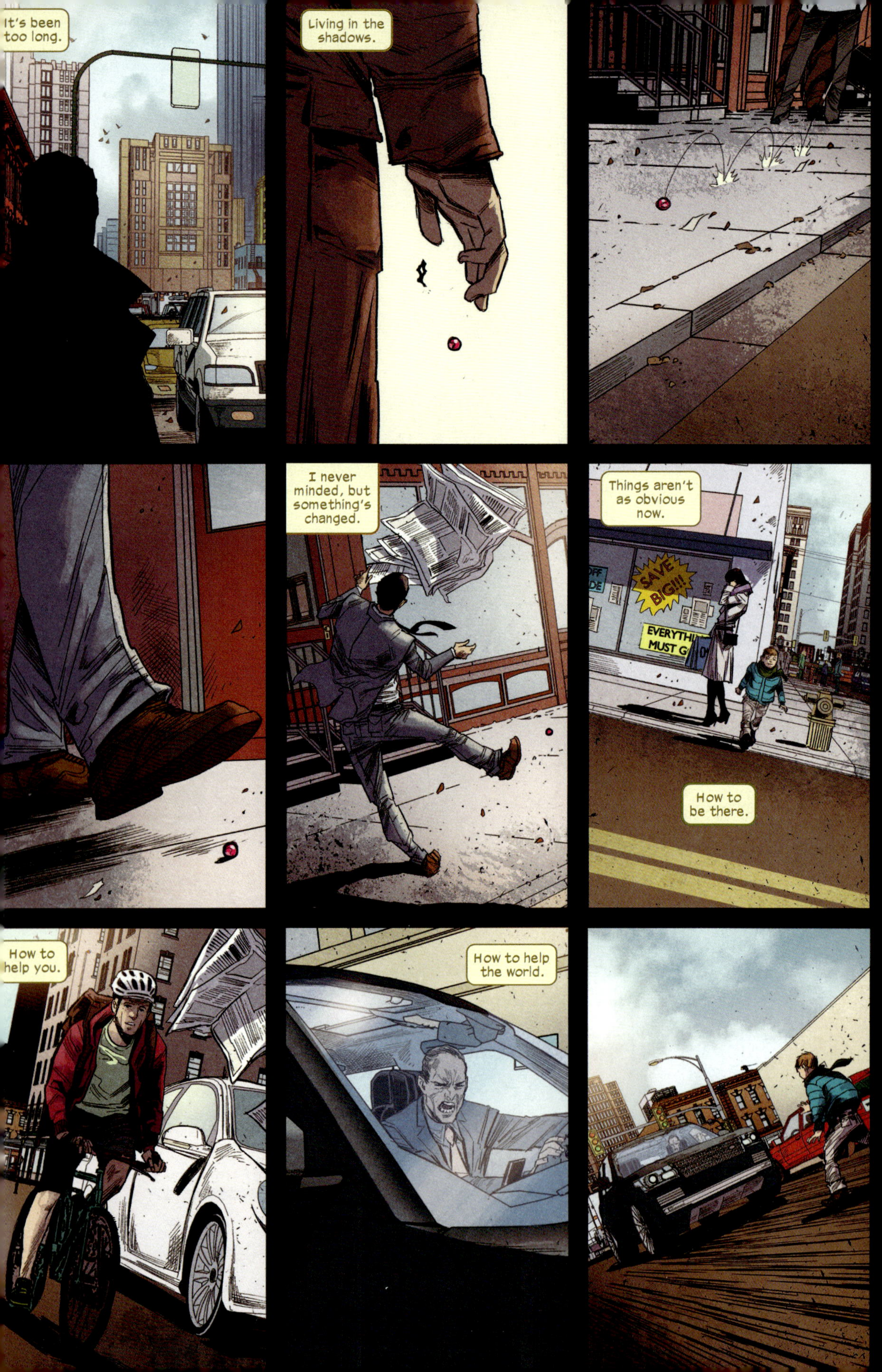
It's been too long.
Living in the shadows.
I never minded, but something's changed.
Things aren't as obvious now.
SAVE BIG!!!
How to be there.
How to help you.
How to help the world.

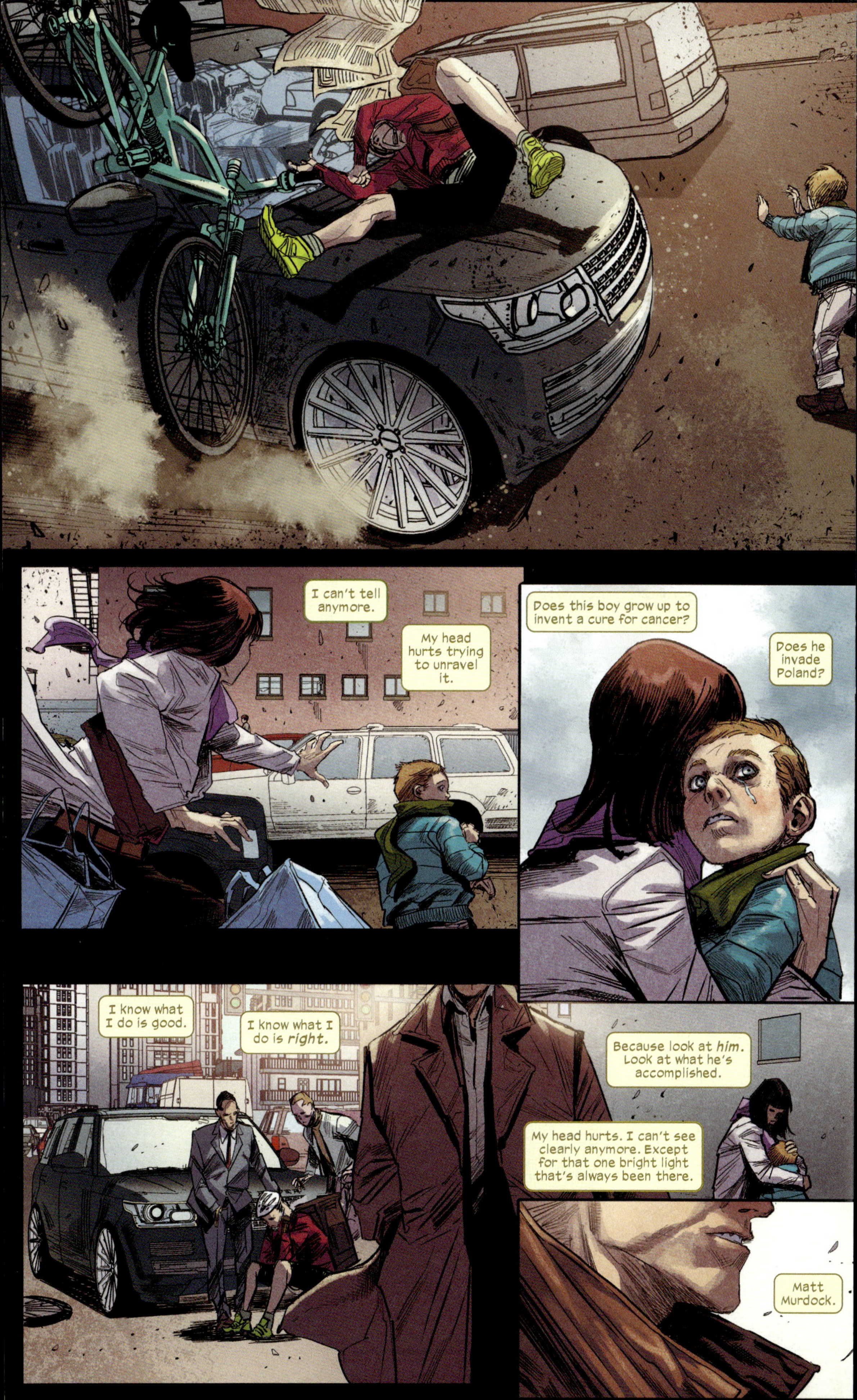

I can't tell anymore.
My head hurts trying to unravel it.
Does this boy grow up to invent a cure for cancer?
Does he invade Poland?
I know what I do is good.
I know what I do is *right*.
Because look at *him*. Look at what he's accomplished.
My head hurts. I can't see clearly anymore. Except for that one bright light that's always been there.
Matt Murdock.

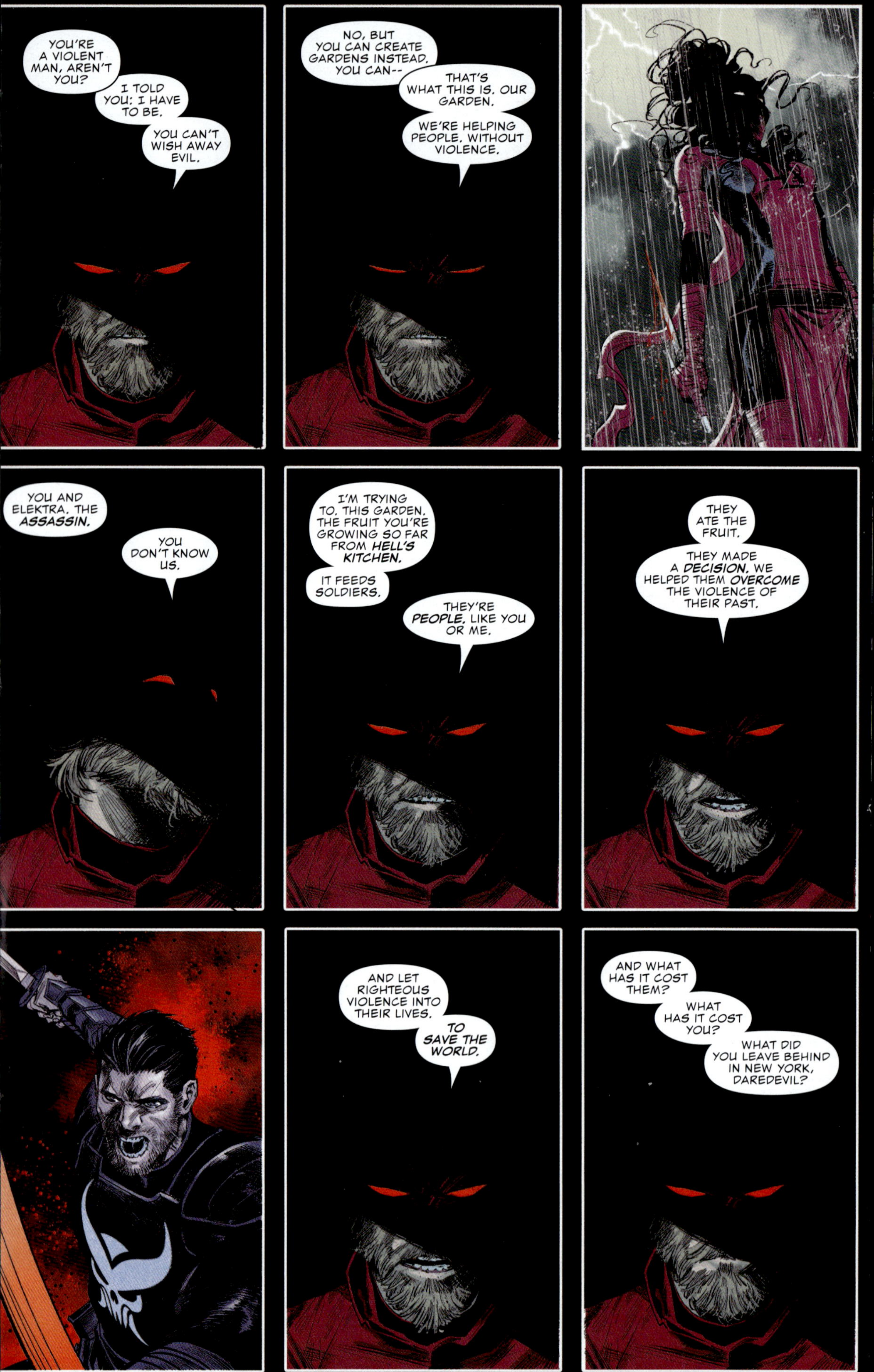
YOU'RE A VIOLENT MAN, AREN'T YOU?
I TOLD YOU: I HAVE TO BE.
YOU CAN'T WISH AWAY EVIL.
NO, BUT YOU CAN CREATE GARDENS INSTEAD. YOU CAN--
THAT'S WHAT THIS IS. OUR GARDEN.
WE'RE HELPING PEOPLE. WITHOUT VIOLENCE.
YOU AND ELEKTRA. THE *ASSASSIN.*
YOU DON'T KNOW US.
I'M TRYING TO. THIS GARDEN. THE FRUIT YOU'RE GROWING SO FAR FROM *HELL'S KITCHEN.*
IT FEEDS SOLDIERS.
THEY'RE *PEOPLE,* LIKE YOU OR ME.
THEY ATE THE FRUIT.
THEY MADE A *DECISION.* WE HELPED THEM *OVERCOME* THE VIOLENCE OF THEIR PAST.
AND LET RIGHTEOUS VIOLENCE INTO THEIR LIVES.
TO SAVE THE WORLD.
AND WHAT HAS IT COST THEM?
WHAT HAS IT COST YOU?
WHAT DID YOU LEAVE BEHIND IN NEW YORK, DAREDEVIL?

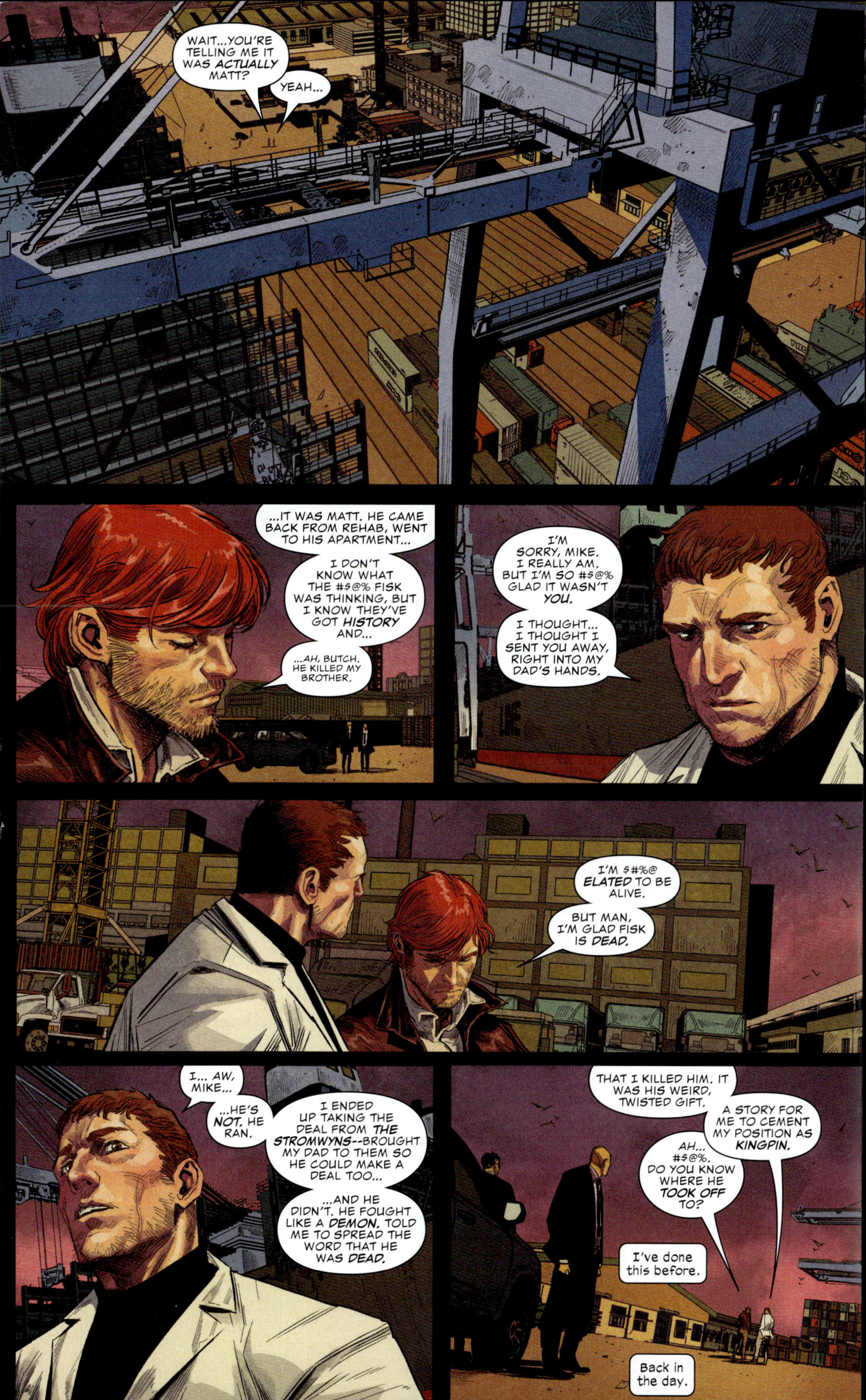

WAIT...YOU'RE TELLING ME IT WAS ACTUALLY MATT?
YEAH...
...IT WAS MATT. HE CAME BACK FROM REHAB, WENT TO HIS APARTMENT...
I DON'T KNOW WHAT THE #$@% FISK WAS THINKING, BUT I KNOW THEY'VE GOT HISTORY AND...
...AH, BUTCH. HE KILLED MY BROTHER.
I'M SORRY, MIKE. I REALLY AM. BUT I'M SO #$@% GLAD IT WASN'T YOU.
I THOUGHT... I THOUGHT I SENT YOU AWAY, RIGHT INTO MY DAD'S HANDS.
I'M $#%@ ELATED TO BE ALIVE.
BUT MAN, I'M GLAD FISK IS DEAD.
I... AW, MIKE...
...HE'S NOT. HE RAN.
I ENDED UP TAKING THE DEAL FROM THE STROMWYNS--BROUGHT MY DAD TO THEM SO HE COULD MAKE A DEAL TOO...
...AND HE DIDN'T. HE FOUGHT LIKE A DEMON. TOLD ME TO SPREAD THE WORD THAT HE WAS DEAD.
THAT I KILLED HIM. IT WAS HIS WEIRD, TWISTED GIFT.
A STORY FOR ME TO CEMENT MY POSITION AS KINGPIN.
AH... #$@%. DO YOU KNOW WHERE HE TOOK OFF TO?
I've done this before.
Back in the day.

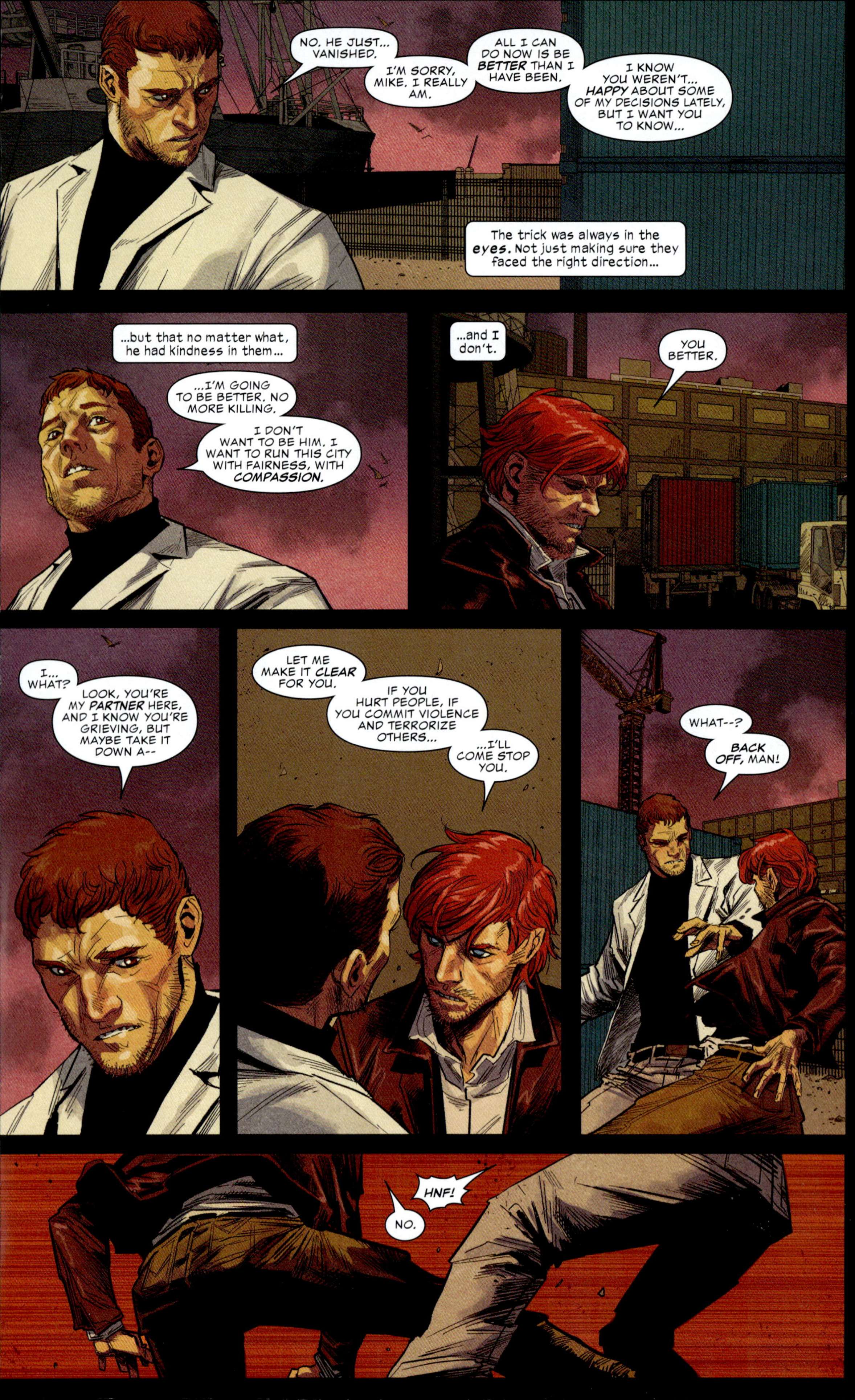
NO. HE JUST... VANISHED.
I'M SORRY, MIKE. I REALLY AM.
ALL I CAN DO NOW IS BE BETTER THAN I HAVE BEEN.
I KNOW YOU WEREN'T... HAPPY ABOUT SOME OF MY DECISIONS LATELY, BUT I WANT YOU TO KNOW...
The trick was always in the eyes. Not just making sure they faced the right direction...
...but that no matter what, he had kindness in them...
...I'M GOING TO BE BETTER. NO MORE KILLING.
I DON'T WANT TO BE HIM. I WANT TO RUN THIS CITY WITH FAIRNESS, WITH COMPASSION.
...and I don't.
YOU BETTER.
I... WHAT?
LOOK, YOU'RE MY PARTNER HERE, AND I KNOW YOU'RE GRIEVING, BUT MAYBE TAKE IT DOWN A--
LET ME MAKE IT CLEAR FOR YOU.
IF YOU HURT PEOPLE, IF YOU COMMIT VIOLENCE AND TERRORIZE OTHERS...
...I'LL COME STOP YOU.
WHAT--?
BACK OFF, MAN!
HNF!
NO.

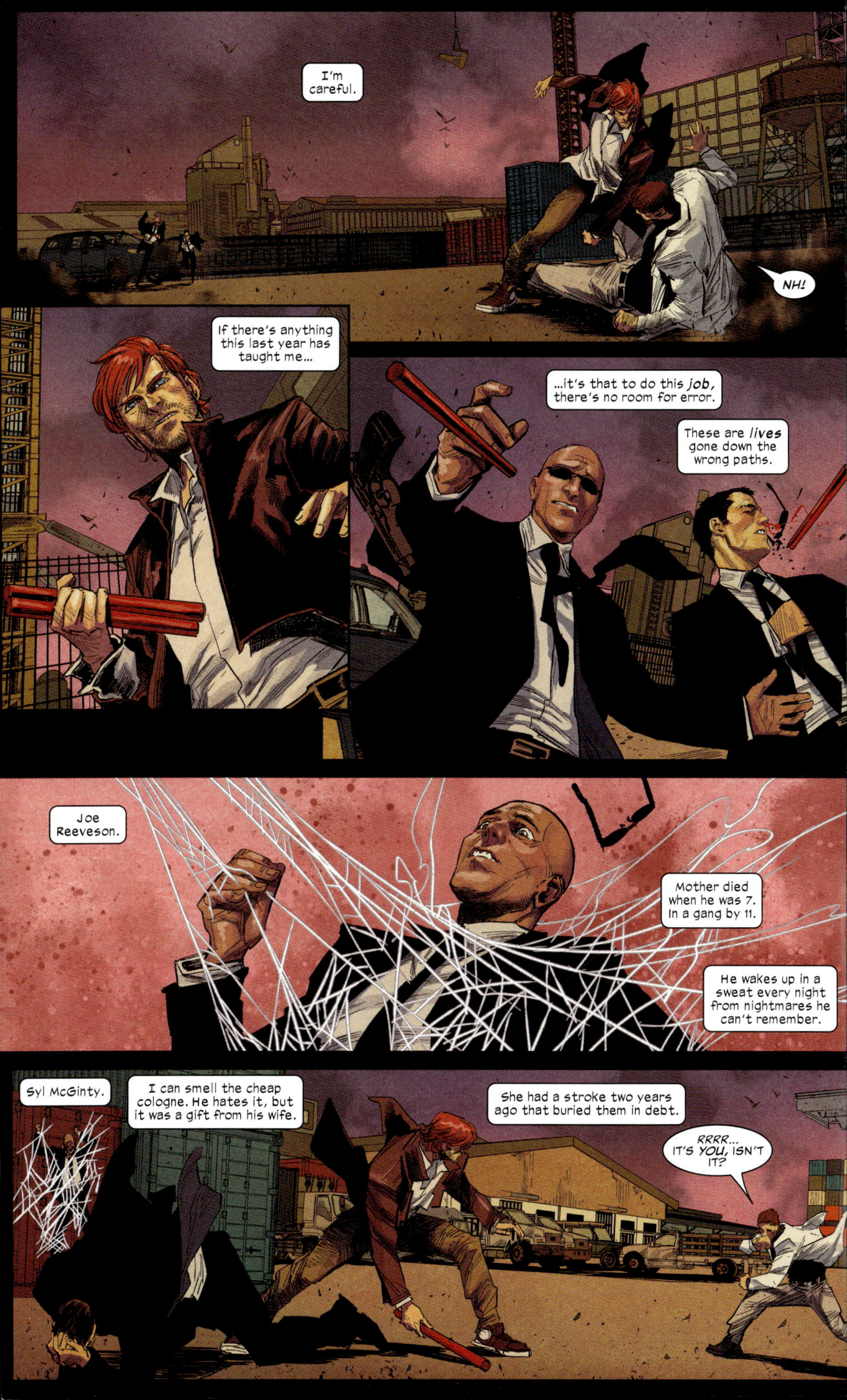
I'm careful.
NH!
If there's anything this last year has taught me...
...it's that to do this *job*, there's no room for error.
These are *lives* gone down the wrong paths.
Joe Reeveson.
Mother died when he was 7. In a gang by 11.
He wakes up in a sweat every night from nightmares he can't remember.
Syl McGinty.
I can smell the cheap cologne. He hates it, but it was a gift from his wife.
She had a stroke two years ago that buried them in debt.
RRRR... IT'S *YOU*, ISN'T IT?

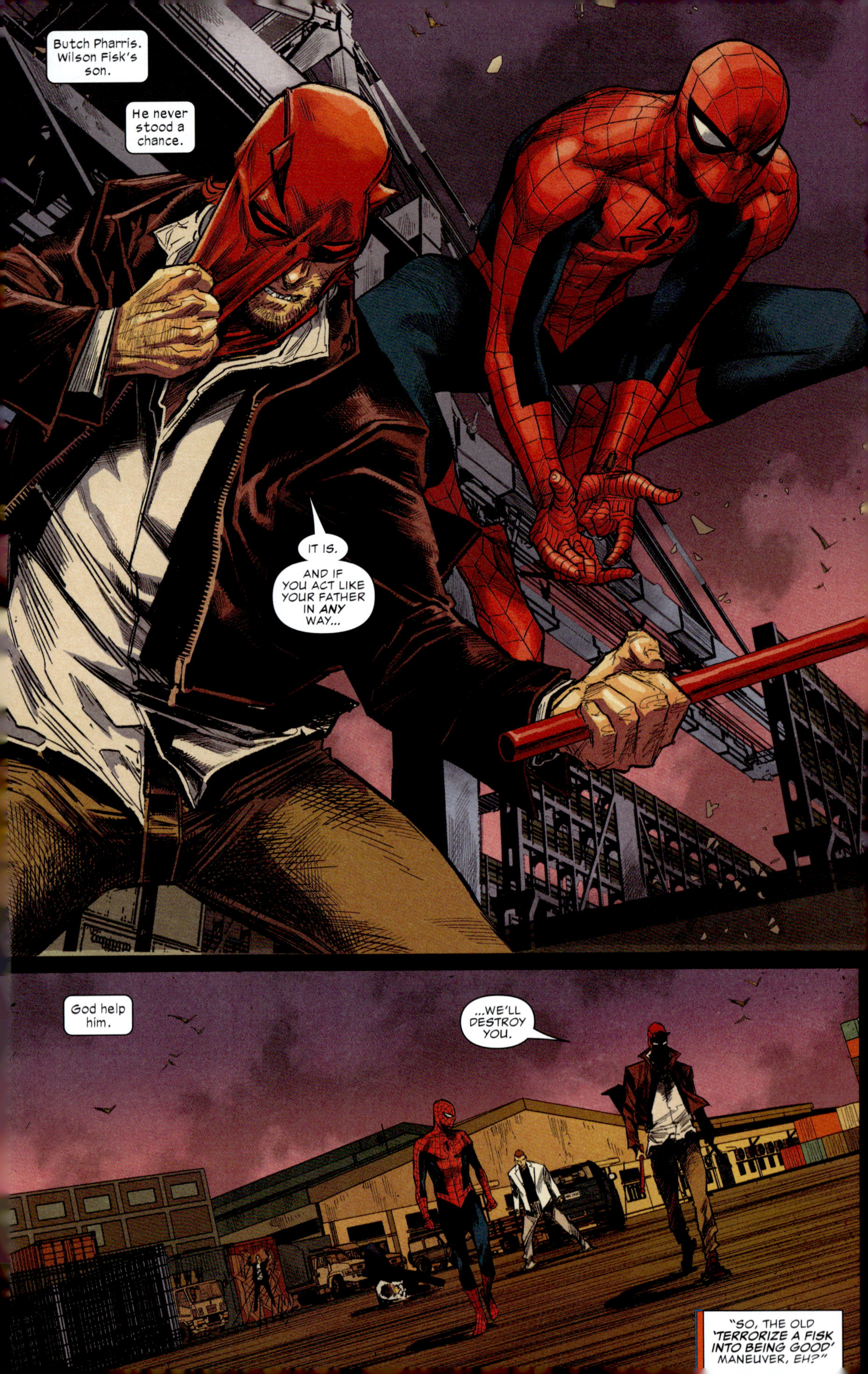
Butch Pharris. Wilson Fisk's son.
He never stood a chance.
IT IS.
AND IF YOU ACT LIKE YOUR FATHER IN ANY WAY...
God help him.
...WE'LL DESTROY YOU.
"SO, THE OLD 'TERRORIZE A FISK INTO BEING GOOD' MANEUVER, EH?"

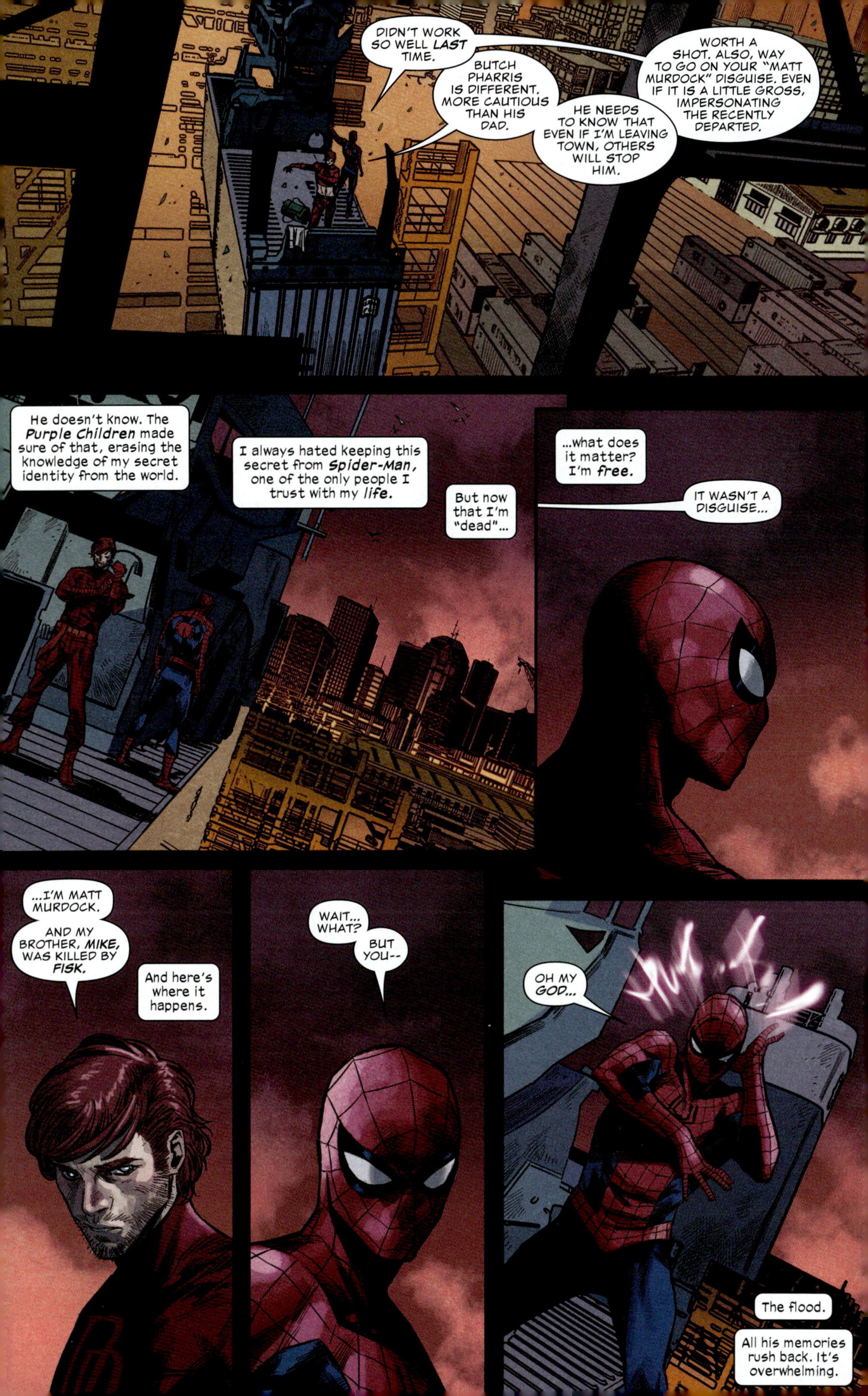
DIDN'T WORK SO WELL LAST TIME.
WORTH A SHOT. ALSO, WAY TO GO ON YOUR "MATT MURDOCK" DISGUISE. EVEN IF IT IS A LITTLE GROSS, IMPERSONATING THE RECENTLY DEPARTED.
BUTCH PHARRIS IS DIFFERENT. MORE CAUTIOUS THAN HIS DAD.
HE NEEDS TO KNOW THAT EVEN IF I'M LEAVING TOWN, OTHERS WILL STOP HIM.
He doesn't know. The Purple Children made sure of that, erasing the knowledge of my secret identity from the world.
I always hated keeping this secret from Spider-Man, one of the only people I trust with my life.
But now that I'm "dead"...
...what does it matter? I'm free.
IT WASN'T A DISGUISE...
...I'M MATT MURDOCK.
AND MY BROTHER, MIKE, WAS KILLED BY FISK.
And here's where it happens.
WAIT... WHAT?
BUT YOU--
OH MY GOD...
The flood.
All his memories rush back. It's overwhelming.

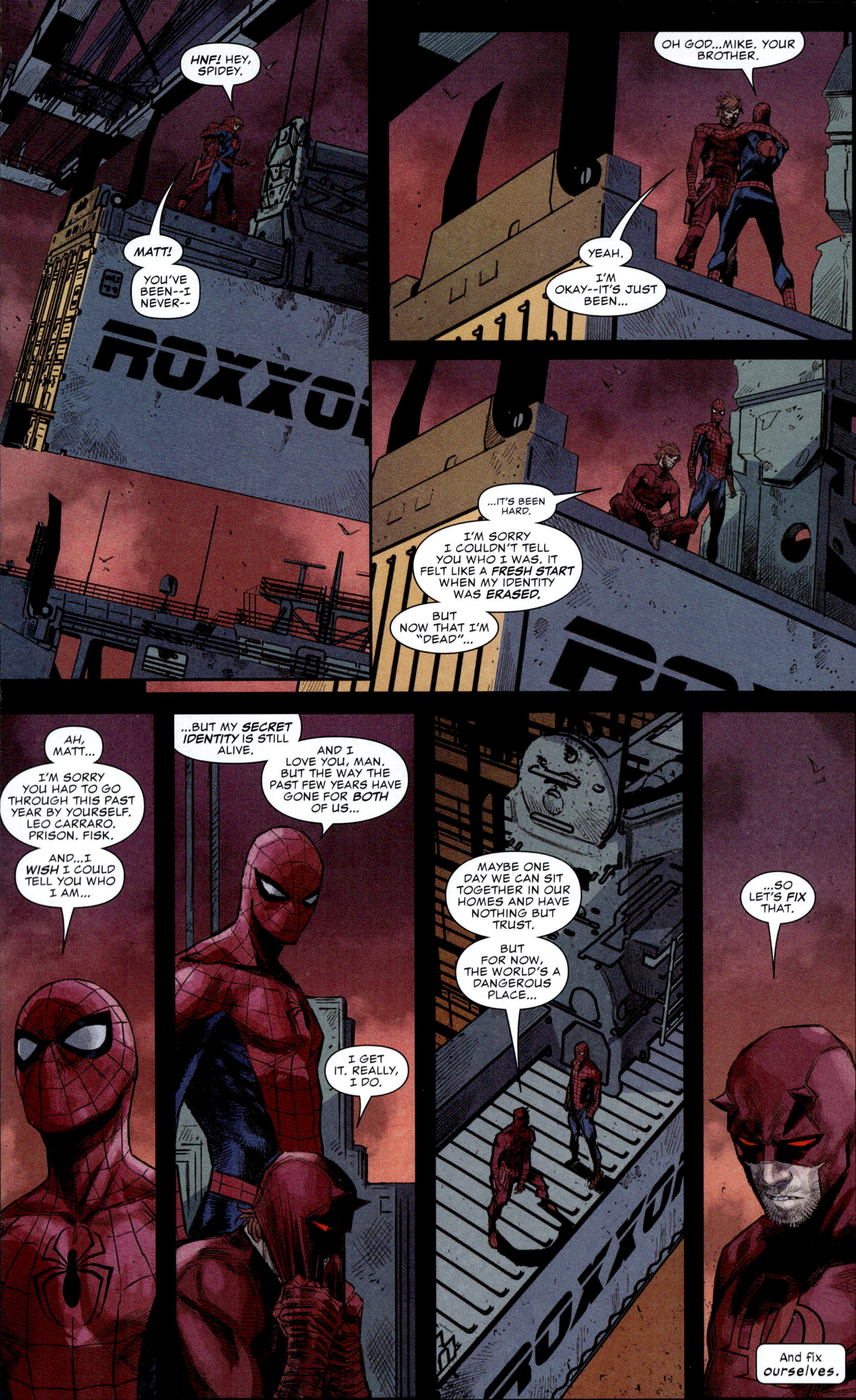
HNF! HEY, SPIDEY.
MATT!
YOU'VE BEEN--I NEVER--
OH GOD...MIKE. YOUR BROTHER.
YEAH.
I'M OKAY--IT'S JUST BEEN...
...IT'S BEEN HARD.
I'M SORRY I COULDN'T TELL YOU WHO I WAS. IT FELT LIKE A FRESH START WHEN MY IDENTITY WAS ERASED.
BUT NOW THAT I'M "DEAD"...
AH, MATT...
I'M SORRY YOU HAD TO GO THROUGH THIS PAST YEAR BY YOURSELF. LEO CARRARO. PRISON. FISK.
AND...I WISH I COULD TELL YOU WHO I AM...
...BUT MY SECRET IDENTITY IS STILL ALIVE.
AND I LOVE YOU, MAN. BUT THE WAY THE PAST FEW YEARS HAVE GONE FOR BOTH OF US...
I GET IT, REALLY, I DO.
MAYBE ONE DAY WE CAN SIT TOGETHER IN OUR HOMES AND HAVE NOTHING BUT TRUST.
BUT FOR NOW, THE WORLD'S A DANGEROUS PLACE...
...SO LET'S FIX THAT.
And fix ourselves.

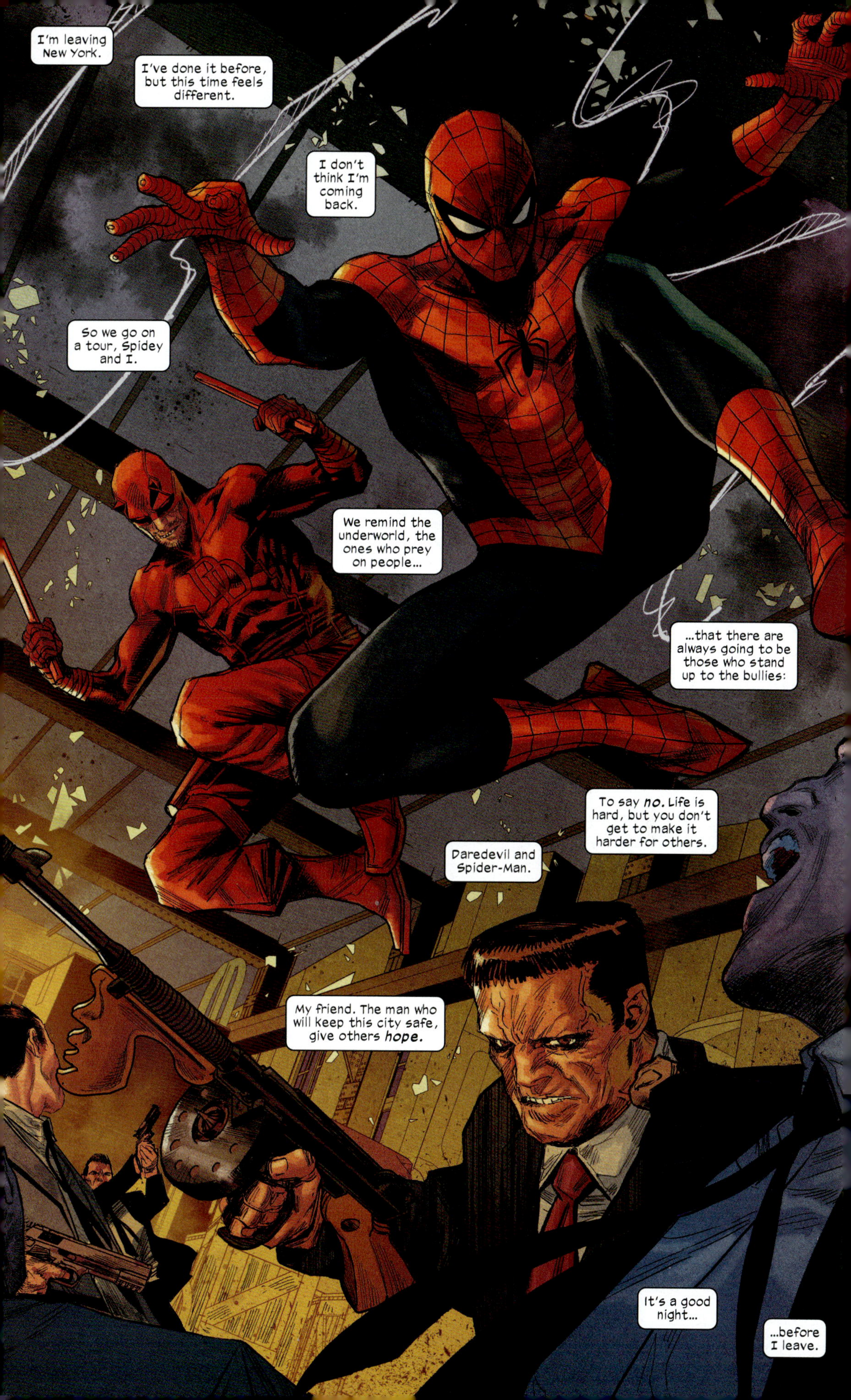
I'm leaving New York.
I've done it before, but this time feels different.
I don't think I'm coming back.
So we go on a tour, Spidey and I.
We remind the underworld, the ones who prey on people...
...that there are always going to be those who stand up to the bullies:
To say *no.* Life is hard, but you don't get to make it harder for others.
Daredevil and Spider-Man.
My friend. The man who will keep this city safe, give others *hope.*
It's a good night...
...before I leave.

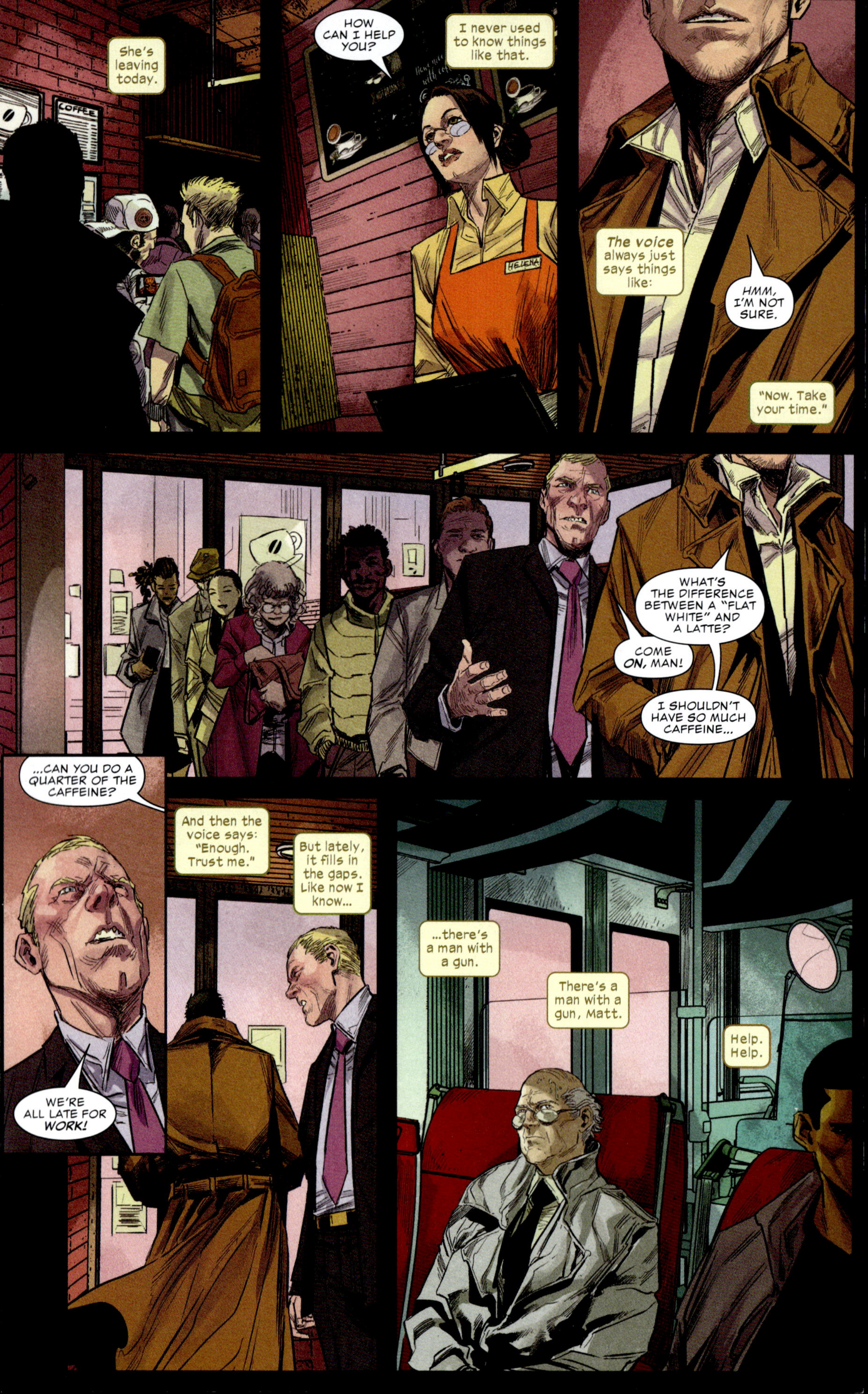
She's leaving today.
HOW CAN I HELP YOU?
I never used to know things like that.
HELENA
The voice always just says things like:
HMM, I'M NOT SURE.
"Now. Take your time."
WHAT'S THE DIFFERENCE BETWEEN A "FLAT WHITE" AND A LATTE?
COME ON, MAN!
I SHOULDN'T HAVE SO MUCH CAFFEINE...
...CAN YOU DO A QUARTER OF THE CAFFEINE?
WE'RE ALL LATE FOR WORK!
And then the voice says: "Enough. Trust me."
But lately, it fills in the gaps. Like now I know...
...there's a man with a gun.
There's a man with a gun, Matt.
Help. Help.

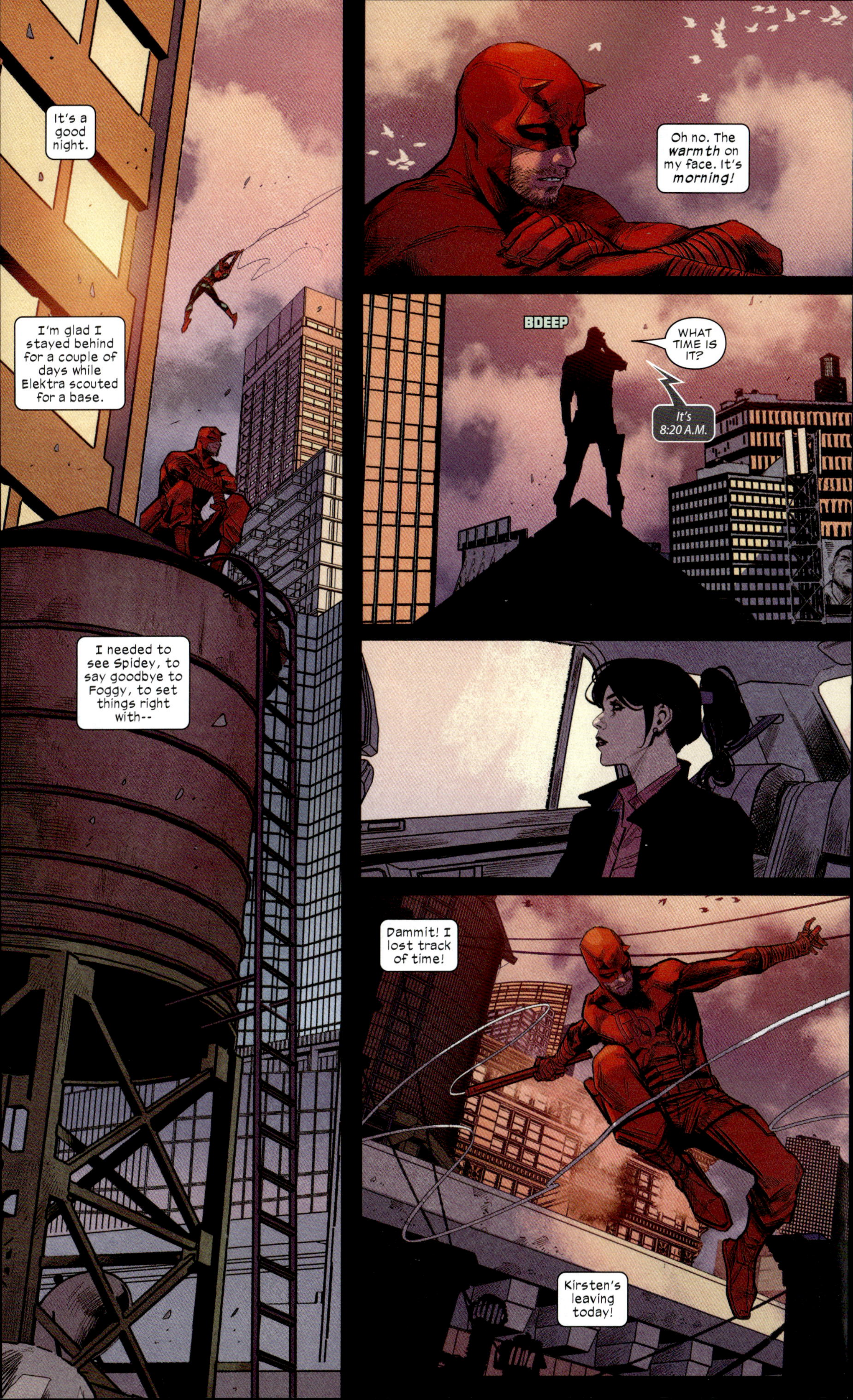
It's a good night.
I'm glad I stayed behind for a couple of days while Elektra scouted for a base.
I needed to see Spidey, to say goodbye to Foggy, to set things right with--
Oh no. The warmth on my face. It's morning!
BDEEP
WHAT TIME IS IT?
It's 8:20 A.M.
Dammit! I lost track of time!
Kirsten's leaving today!

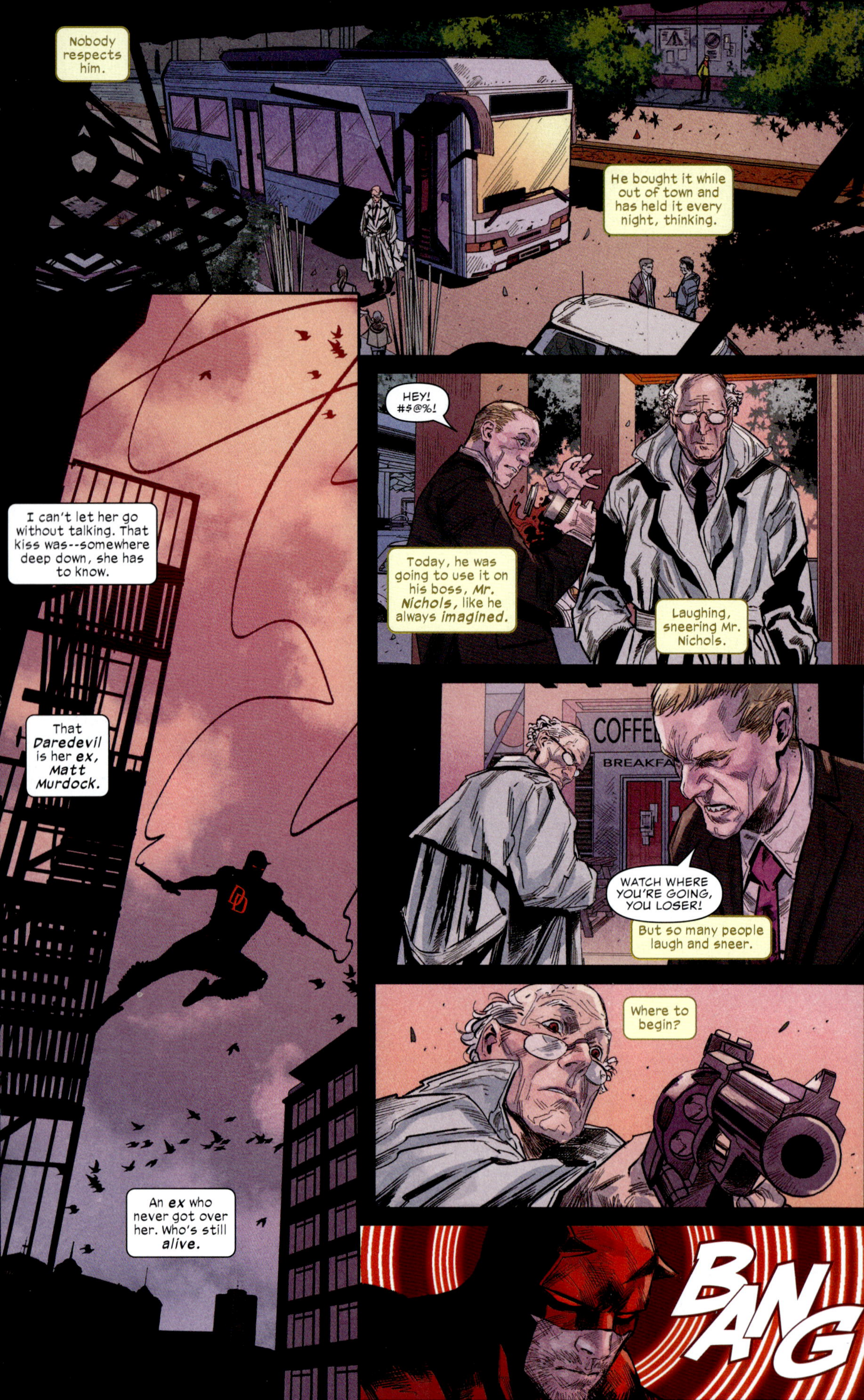
Nobody respects him.
He bought it while out of town and has held it every night, thinking.
HEY! #$@%!
Today, he was going to use it on his boss, Mr. Nichols, like he always imagined.
Laughing, sneering Mr. Nichols.
COFFEE
BREAKFA
WATCH WHERE YOU'RE GOING, YOU LOSER!
But so many people laugh and sneer.
Where to begin?
I can't let her go without talking. That kiss was--somewhere deep down, she has to know.
That Daredevil is her ex, Matt Murdock.
An ex who never got over her. Who's still alive.
BANG

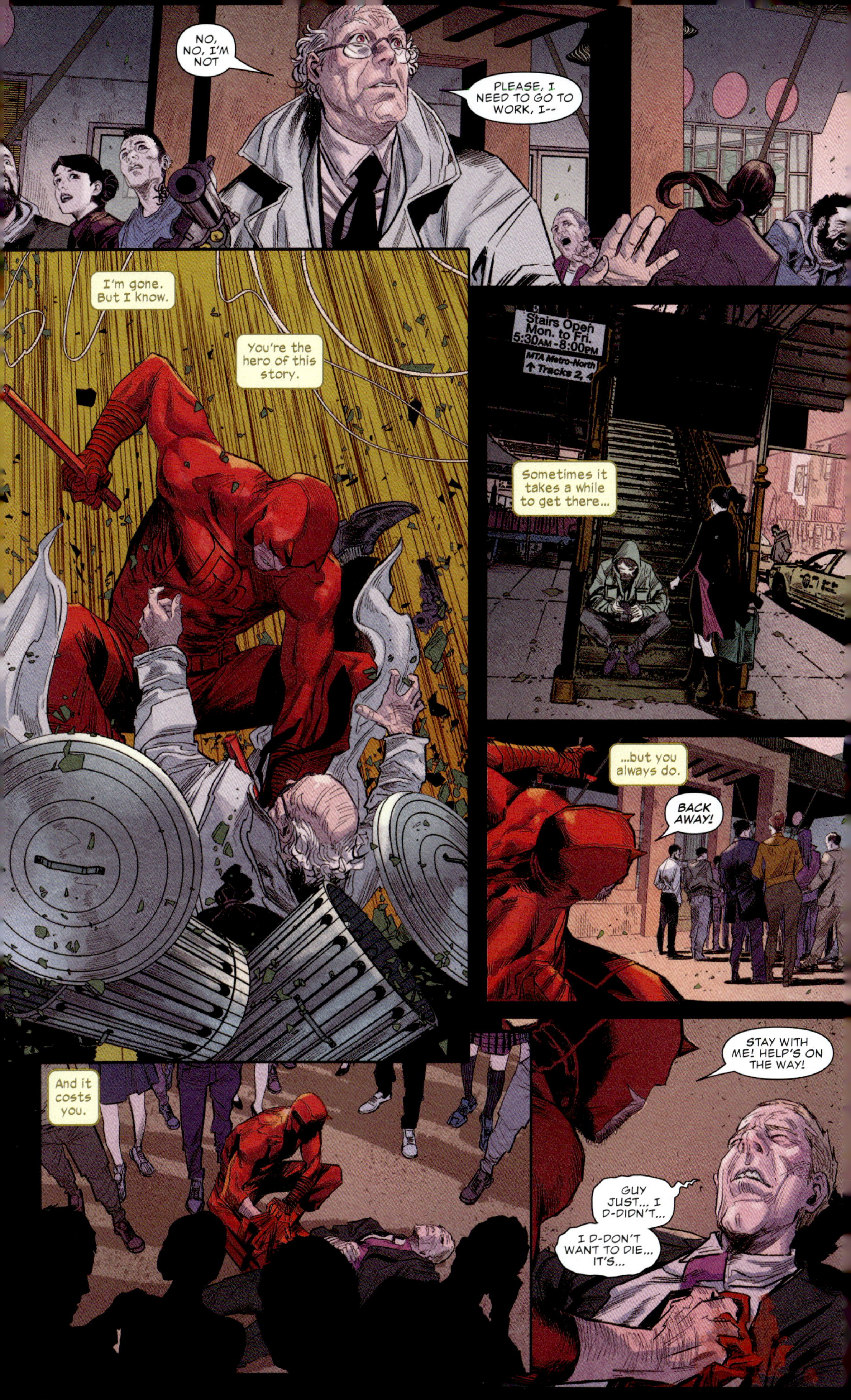
NO, NO, I'M NOT
PLEASE, I NEED TO GO TO WORK, I--
I'm gone. But I know.
You're the hero of this story.
Stairs Open Mon. to Fri. 5:30AM-8:00PM
MTA Metro-North Tracks 2, 4
Sometimes it takes a while to get there...
...but you always do.
BACK AWAY!
And it costs you.
STAY WITH ME! HELP'S ON THE WAY!
GUY JUST... I D-DIDN'T...
I D-DON'T WANT TO DIE... IT'S...

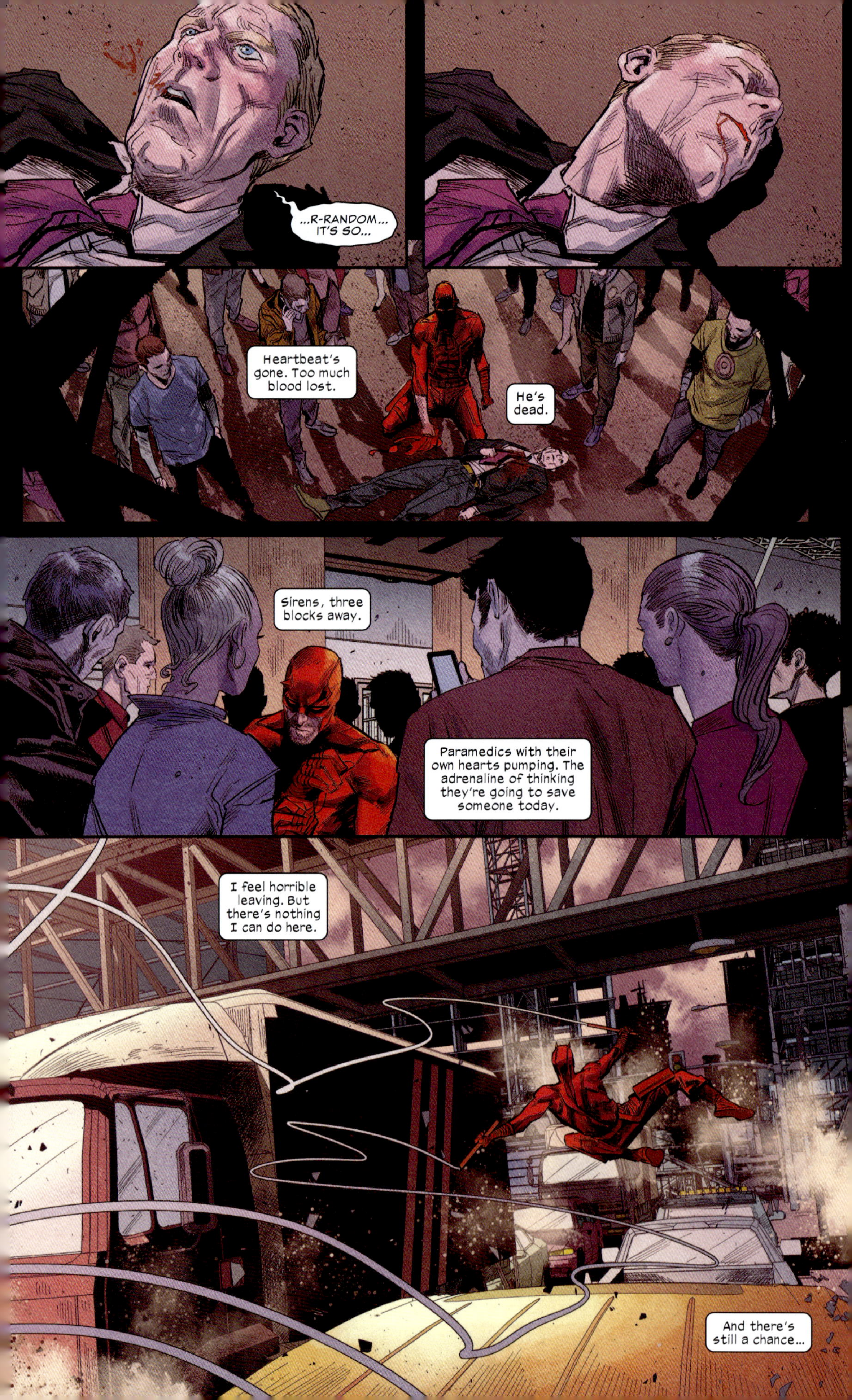
...R-RANDOM... IT'S SO...
Heartbeat's gone. Too much blood lost.
He's dead.
Sirens, three blocks away.
Paramedics with their own hearts pumping. The adrenaline of thinking they're going to save someone today.
I feel horrible leaving. But there's nothing I can do here.
And there's still a chance...

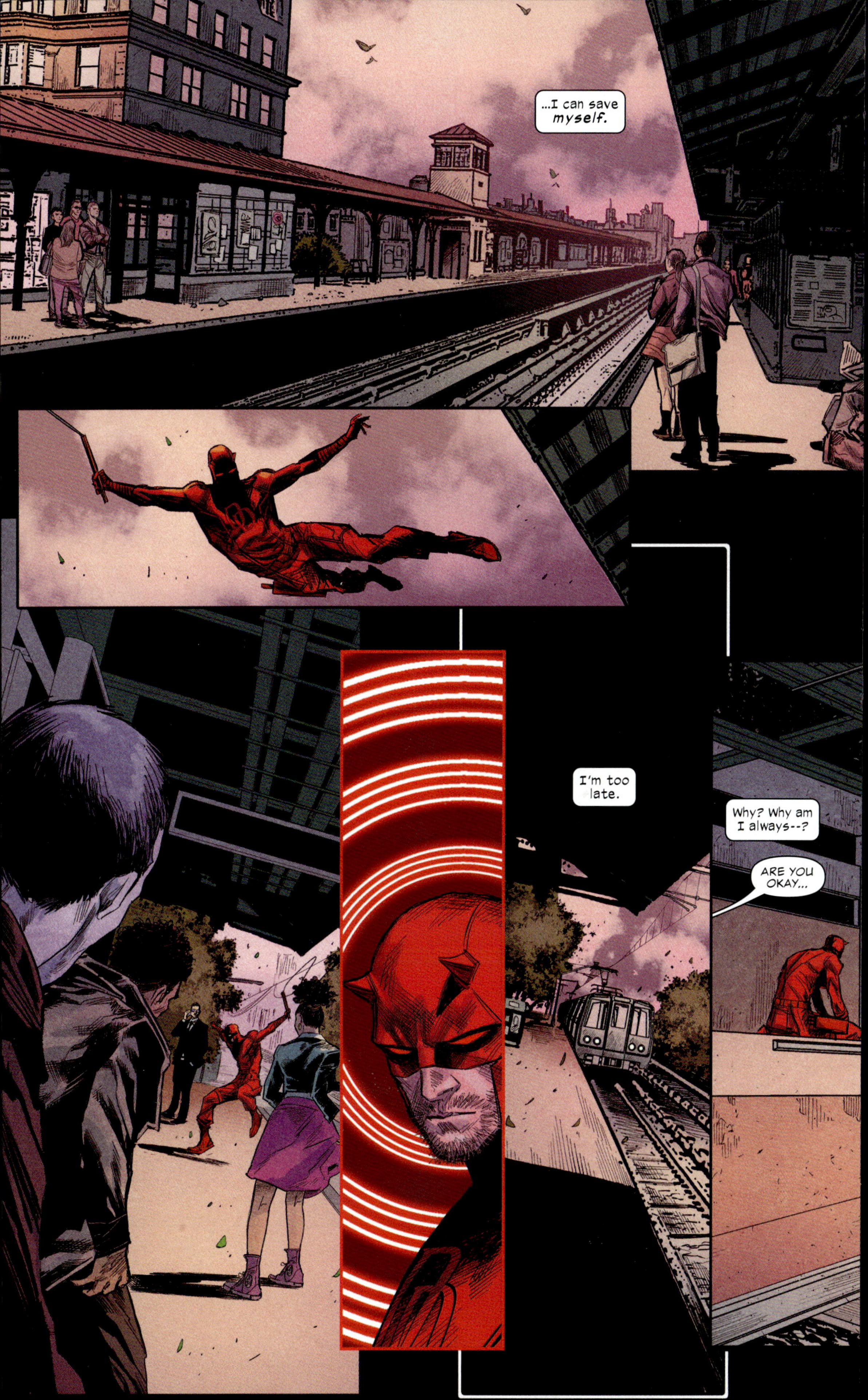
...I can save myself.
I'm too late.
Why? Why am I always--?
ARE YOU OKAY...

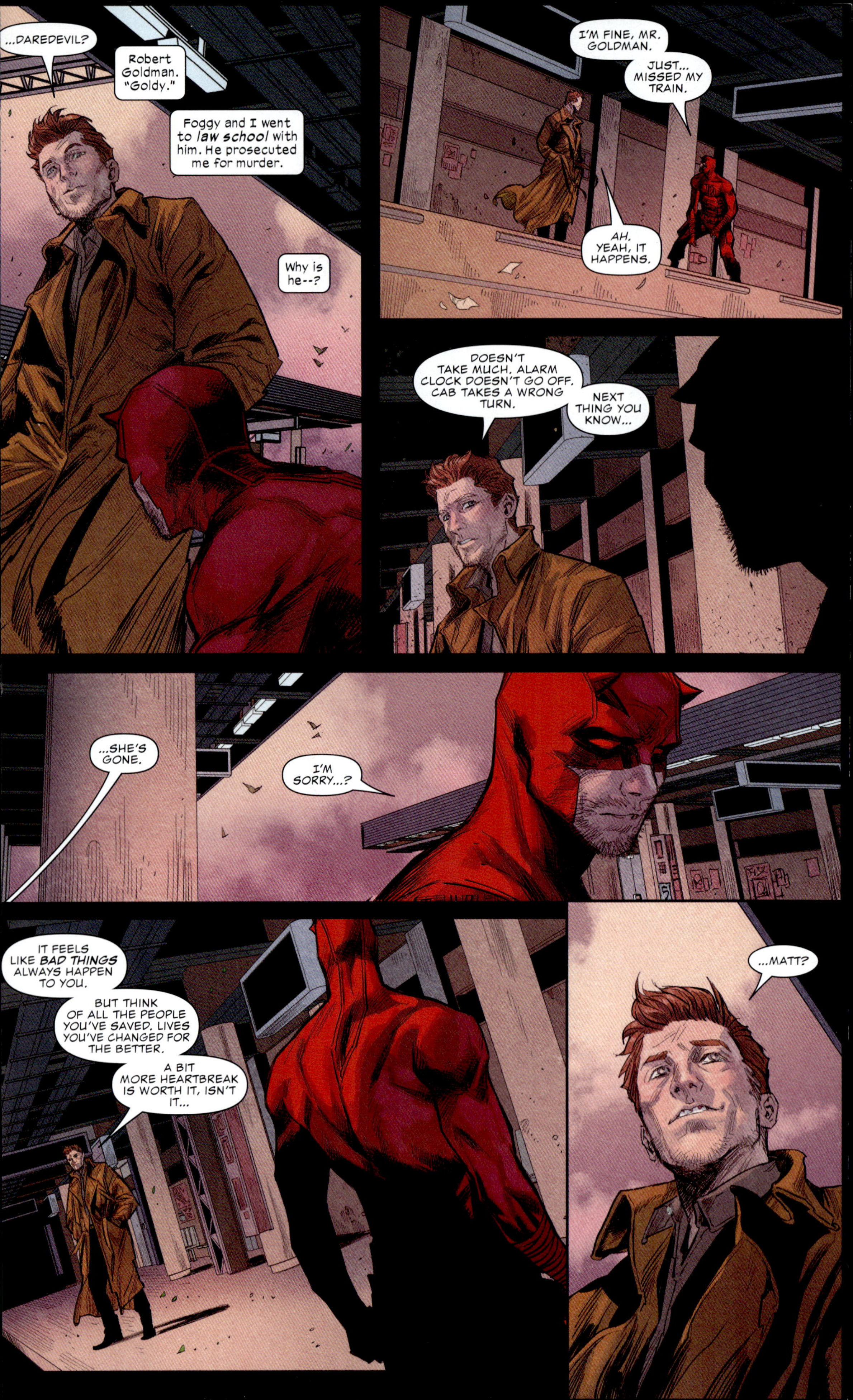
...DAREDEVIL?
Robert Goldman. "Goldy."
Foggy and I went to law school with him. He prosecuted me for murder.
Why is he--?
I'M FINE, MR. GOLDMAN.
JUST... MISSED MY TRAIN.
AH. YEAH, IT HAPPENS.
DOESN'T TAKE MUCH. ALARM CLOCK DOESN'T GO OFF. CAB TAKES A WRONG TURN.
NEXT THING YOU KNOW...
...SHE'S GONE.
I'M SORRY...?
IT FEELS LIKE BAD THINGS ALWAYS HAPPEN TO YOU.
BUT THINK OF ALL THE PEOPLE YOU'VE SAVED. LIVES YOU'VE CHANGED FOR THE BETTER.
A BIT MORE HEARTBREAK IS WORTH IT, ISN'T IT...
...MATT?

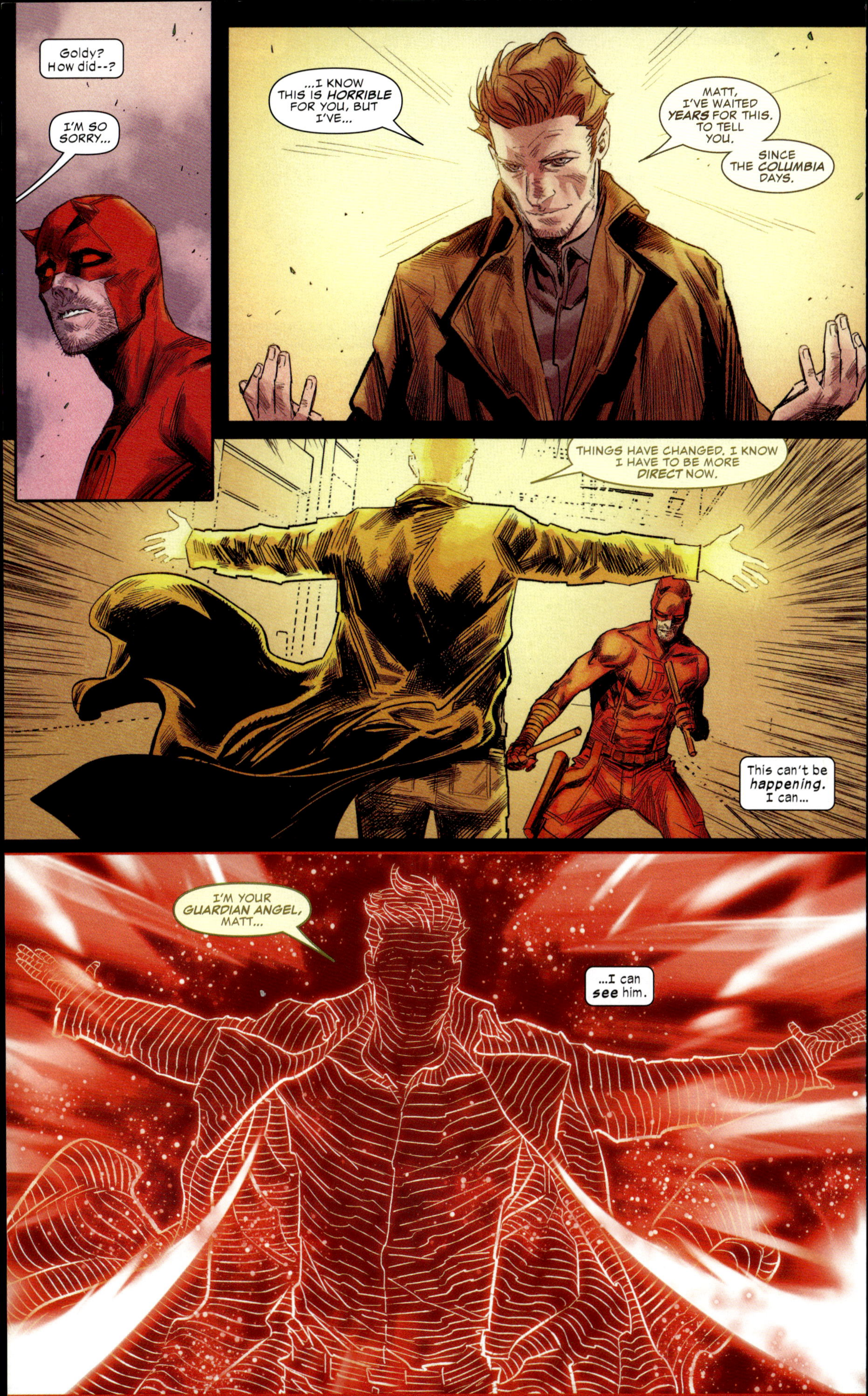

Goldy? How did--?
I'M SO SORRY...
...I KNOW THIS IS HORRIBLE FOR YOU, BUT I'VE...
MATT, I'VE WAITED YEARS FOR THIS. TO TELL YOU.
SINCE THE COLUMBIA DAYS.
THINGS HAVE CHANGED. I KNOW I HAVE TO BE MORE DIRECT NOW.
This can't be happening. I can...
I'M YOUR GUARDIAN ANGEL, MATT...
...I can see him.

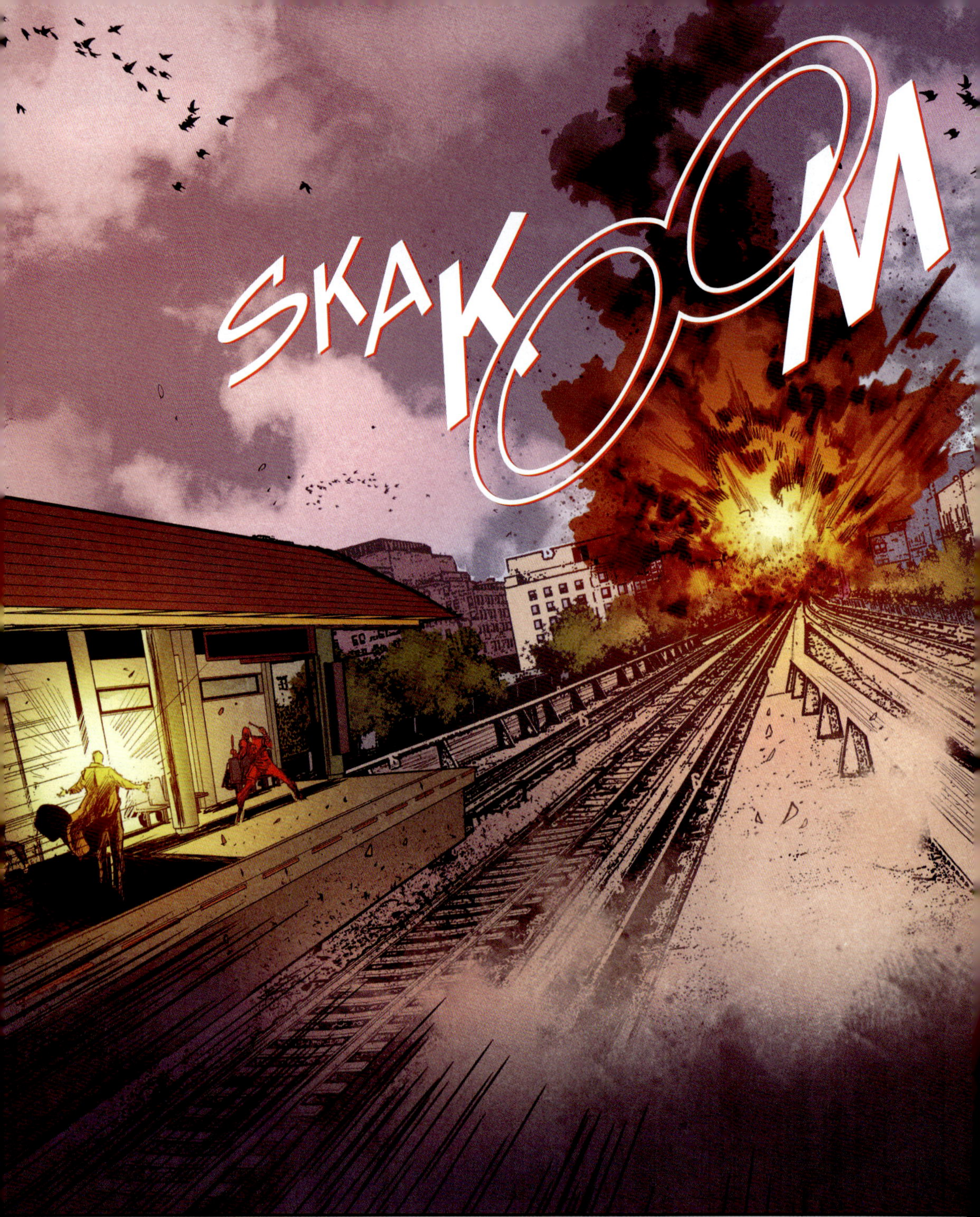
SKAKOOM

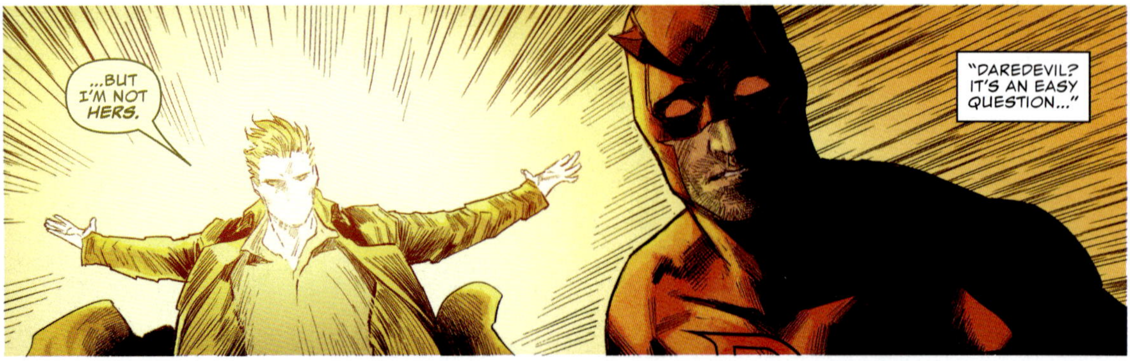
...BUT I'M NOT HERS.
"DAREDEVIL? IT'S AN EASY QUESTION..."

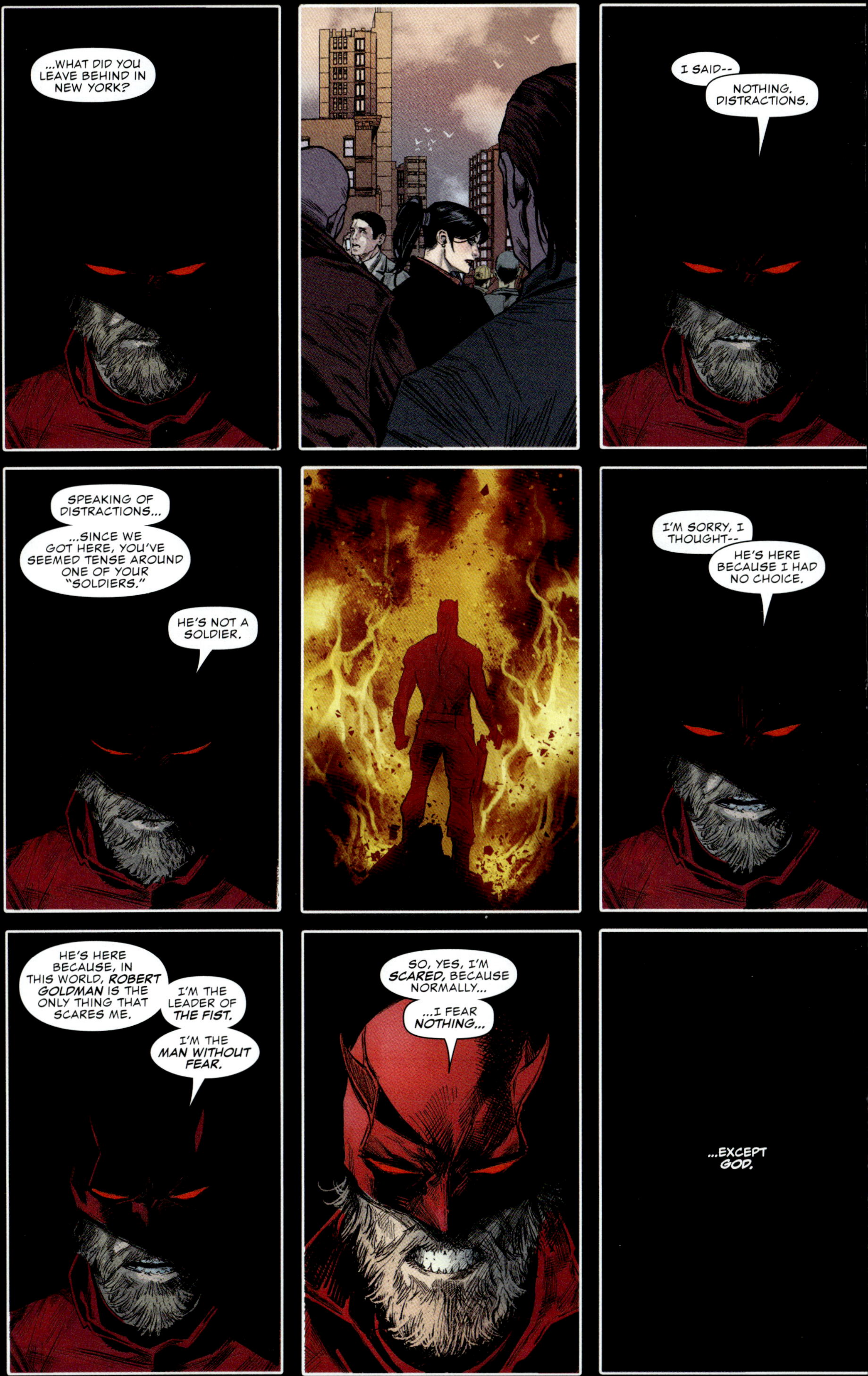
...WHAT DID YOU LEAVE BEHIND IN NEW YORK?
I SAID--
NOTHING. DISTRACTIONS.
SPEAKING OF DISTRACTIONS...
...SINCE WE GOT HERE, YOU'VE SEEMED TENSE AROUND ONE OF YOUR "SOLDIERS."
HE'S NOT A SOLDIER.
I'M SORRY, I THOUGHT--
HE'S HERE BECAUSE I HAD NO CHOICE.
HE'S HERE BECAUSE, IN THIS WORLD, ROBERT GOLDMAN IS THE ONLY THING THAT SCARES ME.
I'M THE LEADER OF THE FIST.
I'M THE MAN WITHOUT FEAR.
SO, YES, I'M SCARED, BECAUSE NORMALLY...
...I FEAR NOTHING...
...EXCEPT GOD.

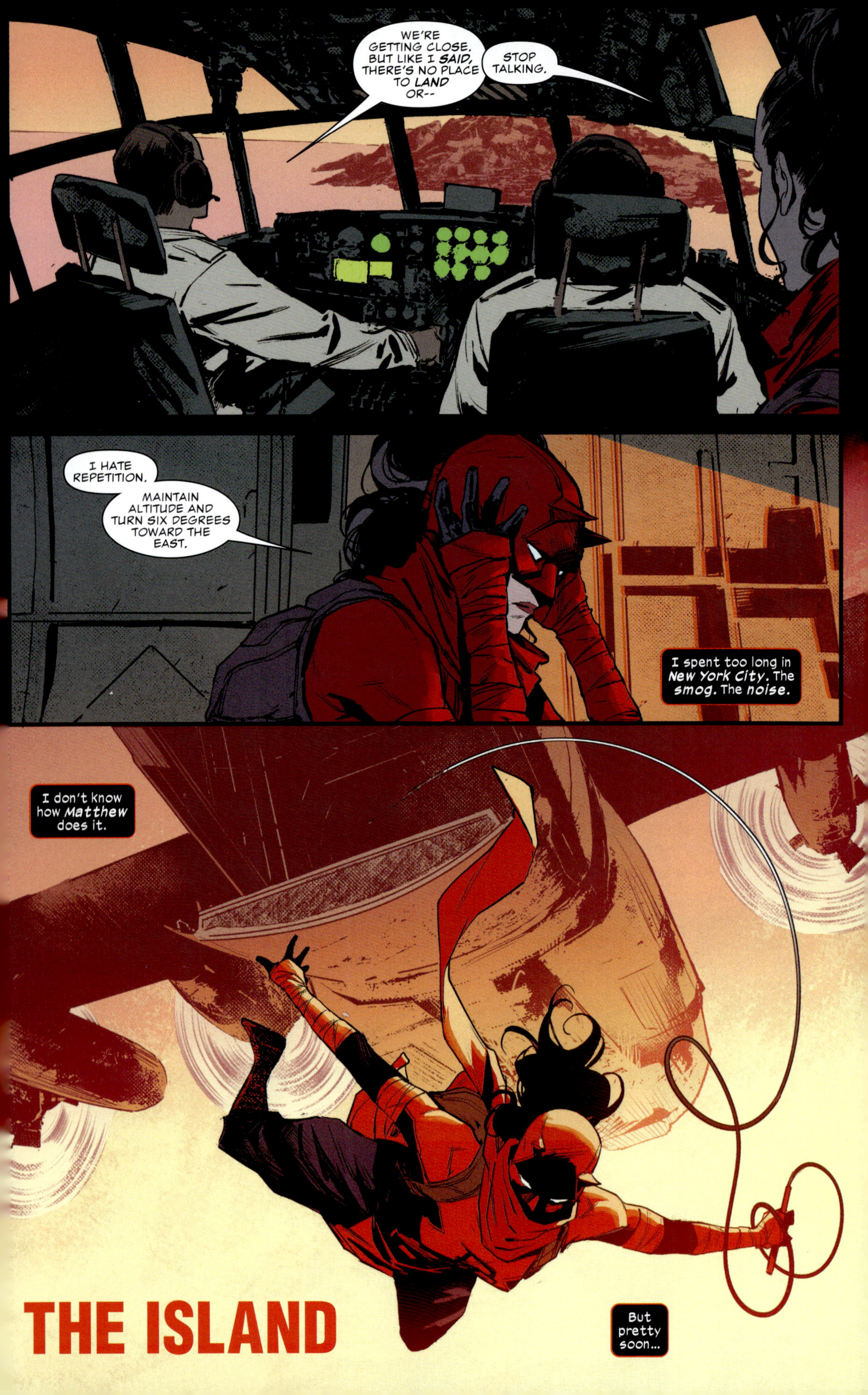
WE'RE GETTING CLOSE. BUT LIKE I SAID, THERE'S NO PLACE TO LAND OR--
STOP TALKING.
I HATE REPETITION.
MAINTAIN ALTITUDE AND TURN SIX DEGREES TOWARD THE EAST.
I spent too long in New York City. The smog. The noise.
I don't know how Matthew does it.
But pretty soon...
THE ISLAND

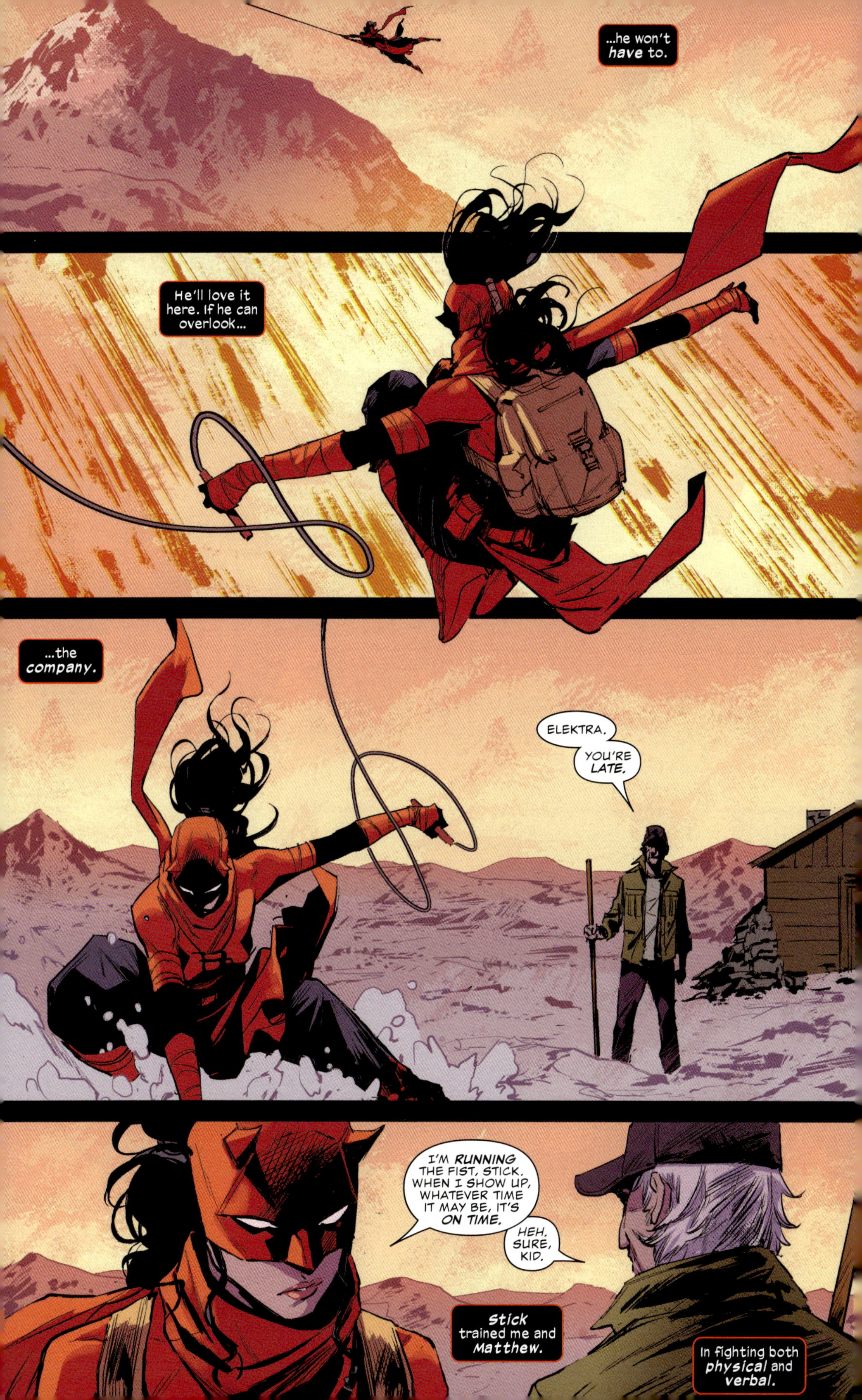
...he won't *have* to.
He'll love it here. If he can overlook...
...the *company*.
ELEKTRA.
YOU'RE *LATE.*
I'M *RUNNING* THE FIST, STICK. WHEN I SHOW UP, WHATEVER TIME IT MAY BE, IT'S *ON TIME.*
HEH. SURE, KID.
Stick trained me and *Matthew.*
In fighting both *physical* and *verbal.*

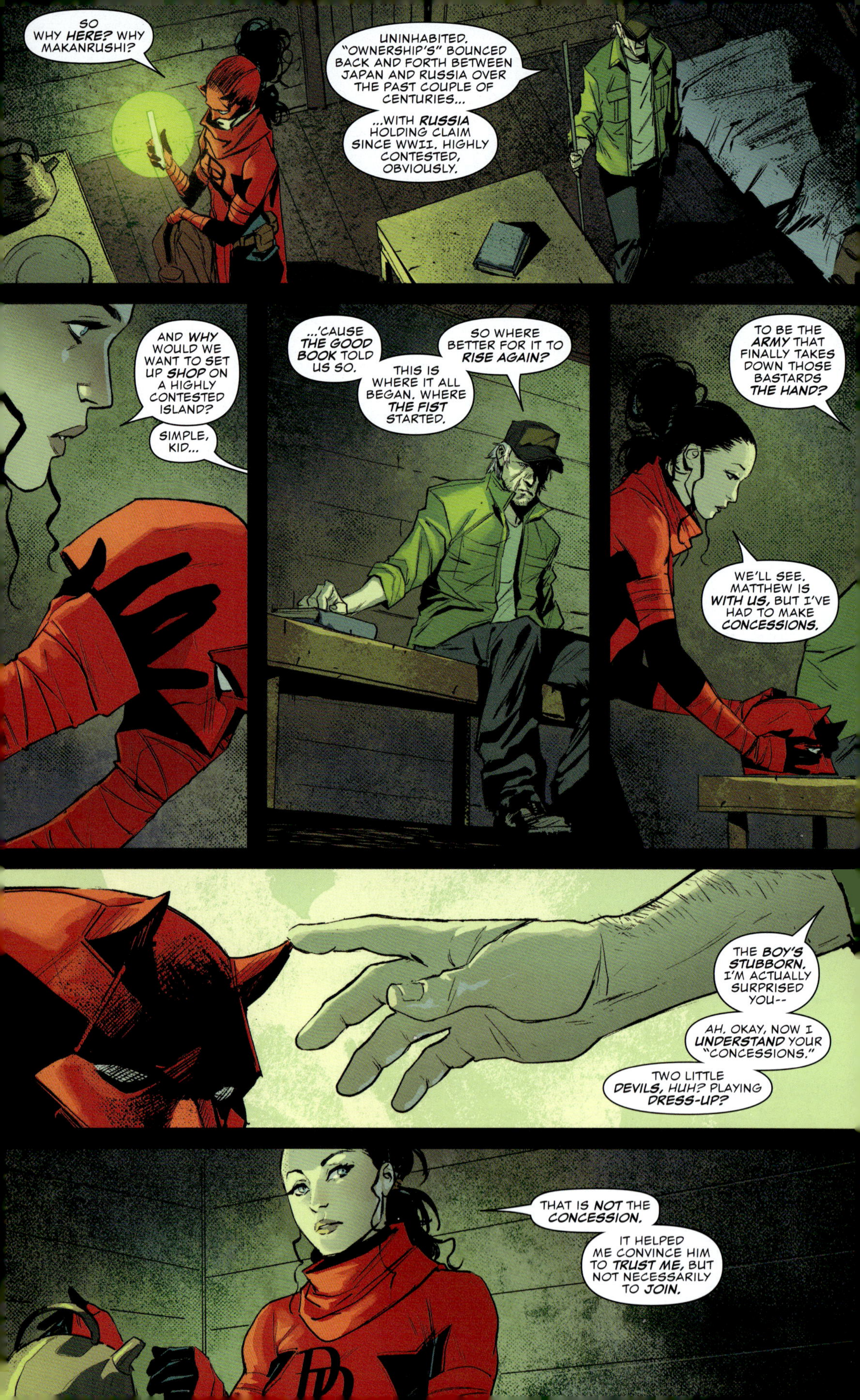
SO WHY HERE? WHY MAKANRUSHI?
UNINHABITED. "OWNERSHIP'S" BOUNCED BACK AND FORTH BETWEEN JAPAN AND RUSSIA OVER THE PAST COUPLE OF CENTURIES...
...WITH RUSSIA HOLDING CLAIM SINCE WWII. HIGHLY CONTESTED, OBVIOUSLY.
AND WHY WOULD WE WANT TO SET UP SHOP ON A HIGHLY CONTESTED ISLAND?
SIMPLE, KID...
...'CAUSE THE GOOD BOOK TOLD US SO.
THIS IS WHERE IT ALL BEGAN. WHERE THE FIST STARTED.
SO WHERE BETTER FOR IT TO RISE AGAIN?
TO BE THE ARMY THAT FINALLY TAKES DOWN THOSE BASTARDS THE HAND?
WE'LL SEE. MATTHEW IS WITH US, BUT I'VE HAD TO MAKE CONCESSIONS.
THE BOY'S STUBBORN. I'M ACTUALLY SURPRISED YOU--
AH. OKAY, NOW I UNDERSTAND YOUR "CONCESSIONS."
TWO LITTLE DEVILS, HUH? PLAYING DRESS-UP?
THAT IS NOT THE CONCESSION.
IT HELPED ME CONVINCE HIM TO TRUST ME, BUT NOT NECESSARILY TO JOIN.

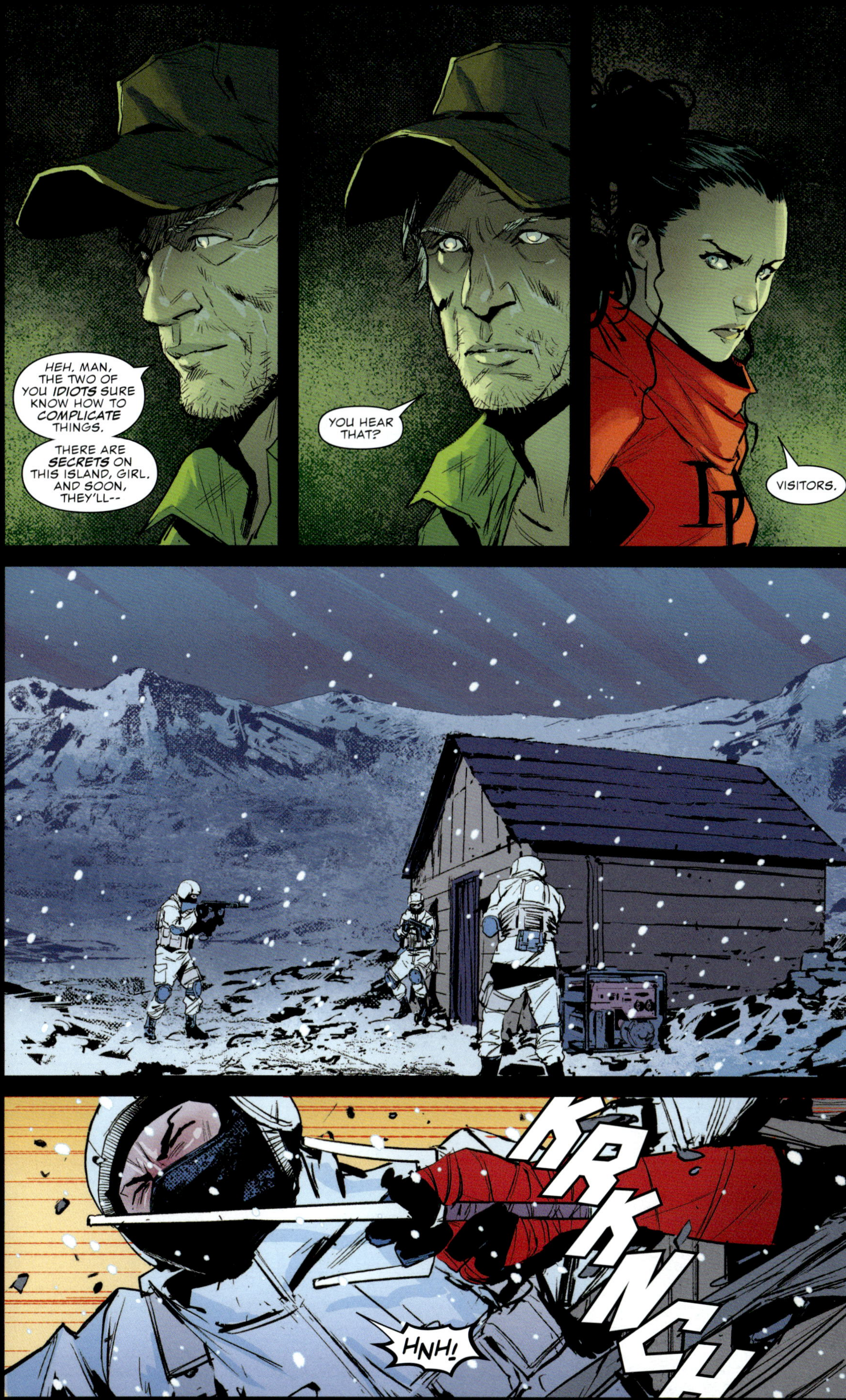
HEH. MAN, THE TWO OF YOU IDIOTS SURE KNOW HOW TO COMPLICATE THINGS.
THERE ARE SECRETS ON THIS ISLAND, GIRL. AND SOON, THEY'LL--
YOU HEAR THAT?
VISITORS.
KRKNCH
HNH!

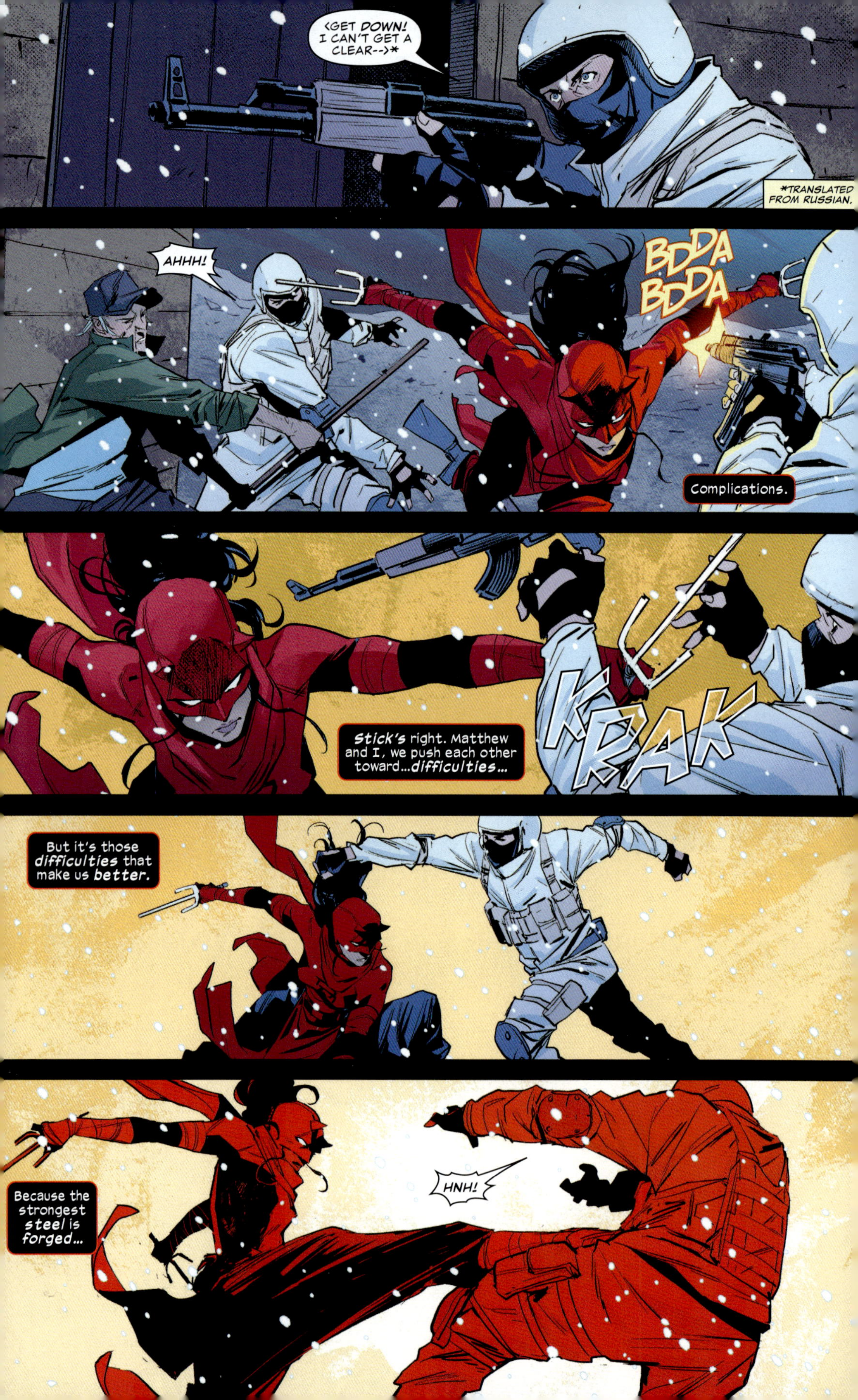

<GET DOWN! I CAN'T GET A CLEAR-->*
*TRANSLATED FROM RUSSIAN.
AHHH!
BDDA BDDA
Complications.
Stick's right. Matthew and I, we push each other toward...difficulties...
KRAK
But it's those difficulties that make us better.
Because the strongest steel is forged...
HNH!

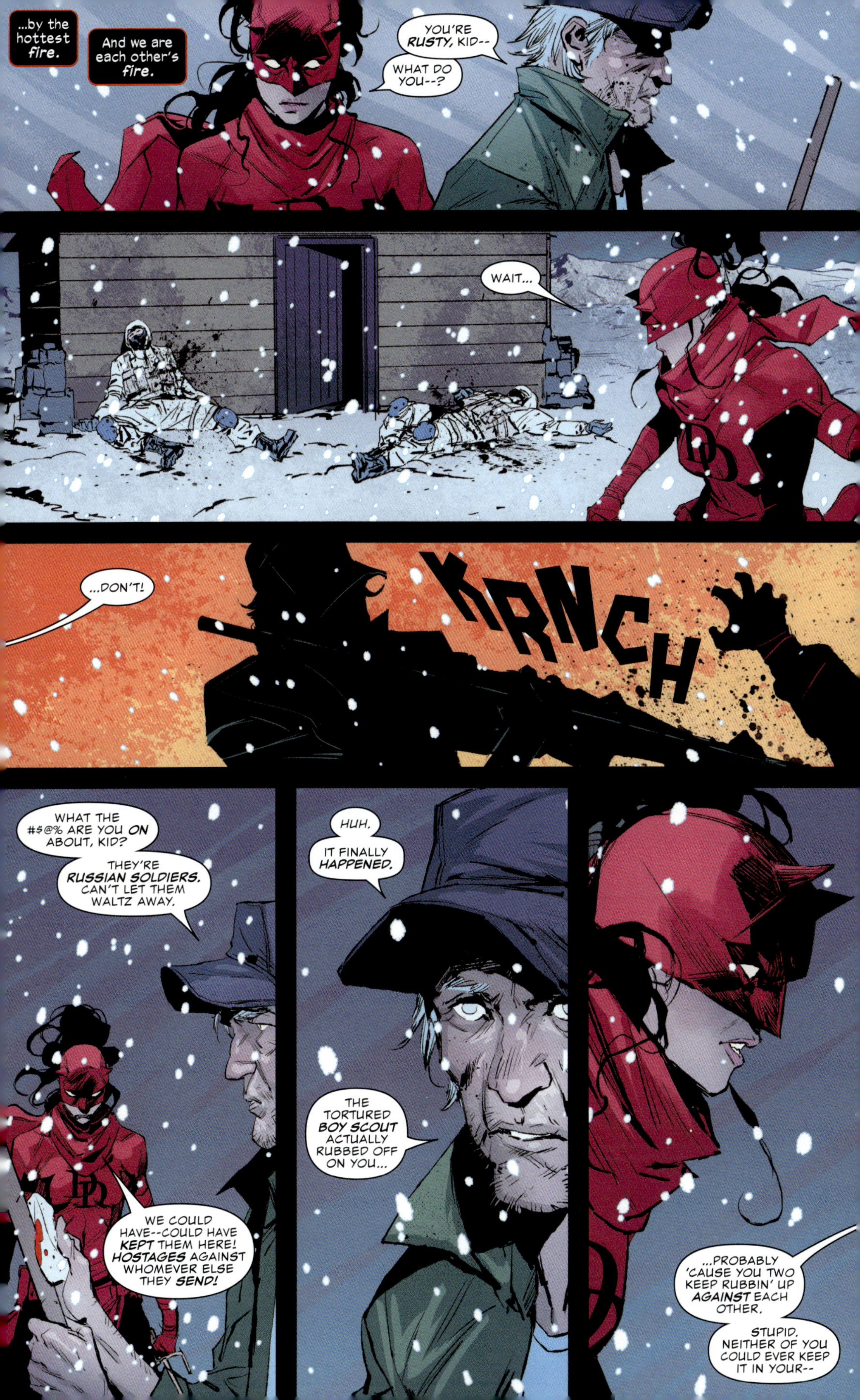

...by the hottest fire.
And we are each other's fire.
YOU'RE RUSTY, KID--
WHAT DO YOU--?
WAIT...
...DON'T!
KRNCH
WHAT THE #$@% ARE YOU ON ABOUT, KID?
THEY'RE RUSSIAN SOLDIERS. CAN'T LET THEM WALTZ AWAY.
WE COULD HAVE--COULD HAVE KEPT THEM HERE! HOSTAGES AGAINST WHOMEVER ELSE THEY SEND!
HUH.
IT FINALLY HAPPENED.
THE TORTURED BOY SCOUT ACTUALLY RUBBED OFF ON YOU...
...PROBABLY 'CAUSE YOU TWO KEEP RUBBIN' UP AGAINST EACH OTHER.
STUPID. NEITHER OF YOU COULD EVER KEEP IT IN YOUR--

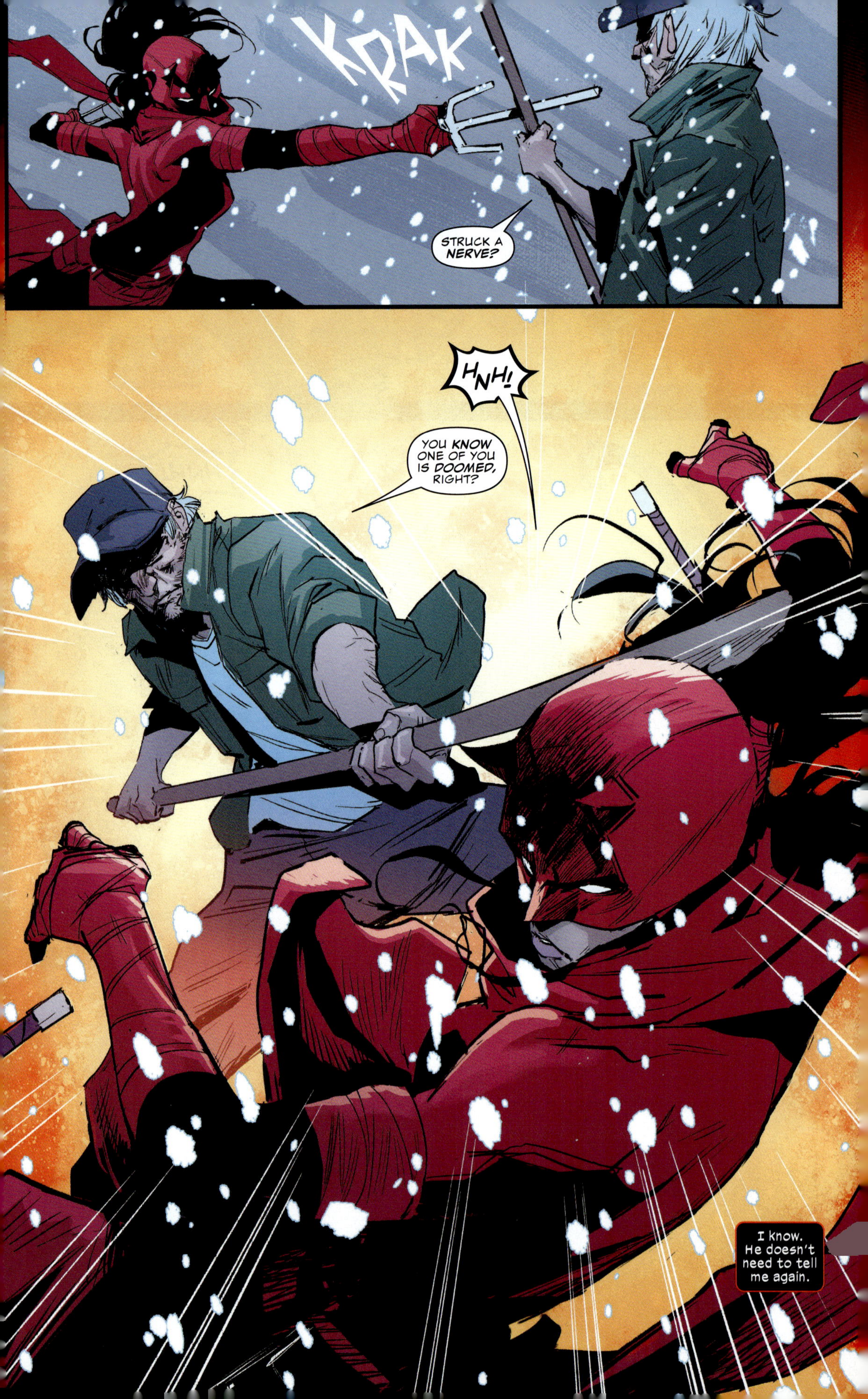
KRAK
STRUCK A NERVE?
HNH!
YOU KNOW ONE OF YOU IS DOOMED, RIGHT?
I know. He doesn't need to tell me again.

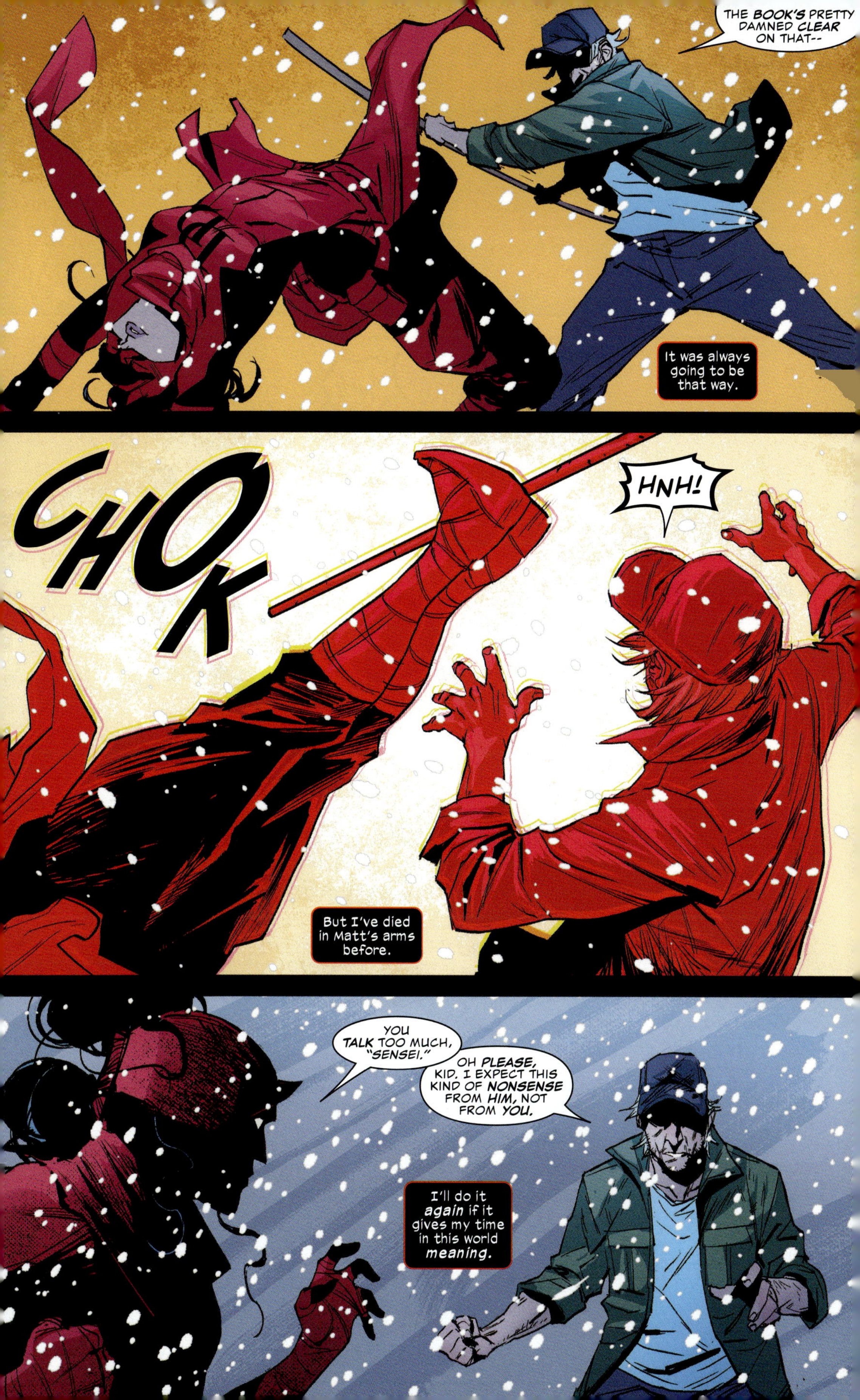
THE BOOK'S PRETTY DAMNED CLEAR ON THAT--
It was always going to be that way.
CHOK
HNH!
But I've died in Matt's arms before.
YOU TALK TOO MUCH, "SENSEI."
OH PLEASE, KID. I EXPECT THIS KIND OF NONSENSE FROM HIM, NOT FROM YOU.
I'll do it again if it gives my time in this world meaning.

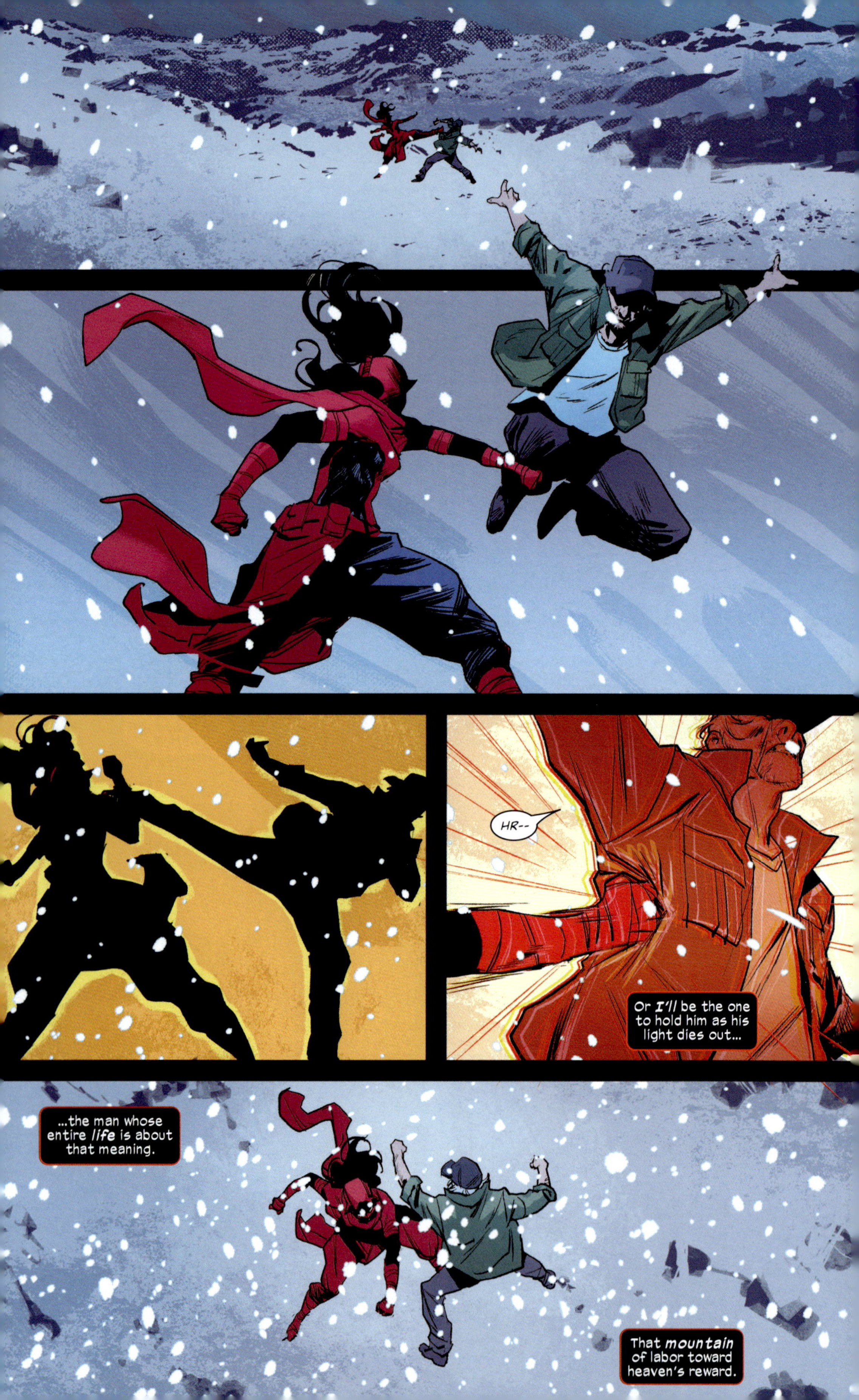
HR--
Or *I'll* be the one to hold him as his light dies out...
...the man whose entire *life* is about that meaning.
That *mountain* of labor toward heaven's reward.

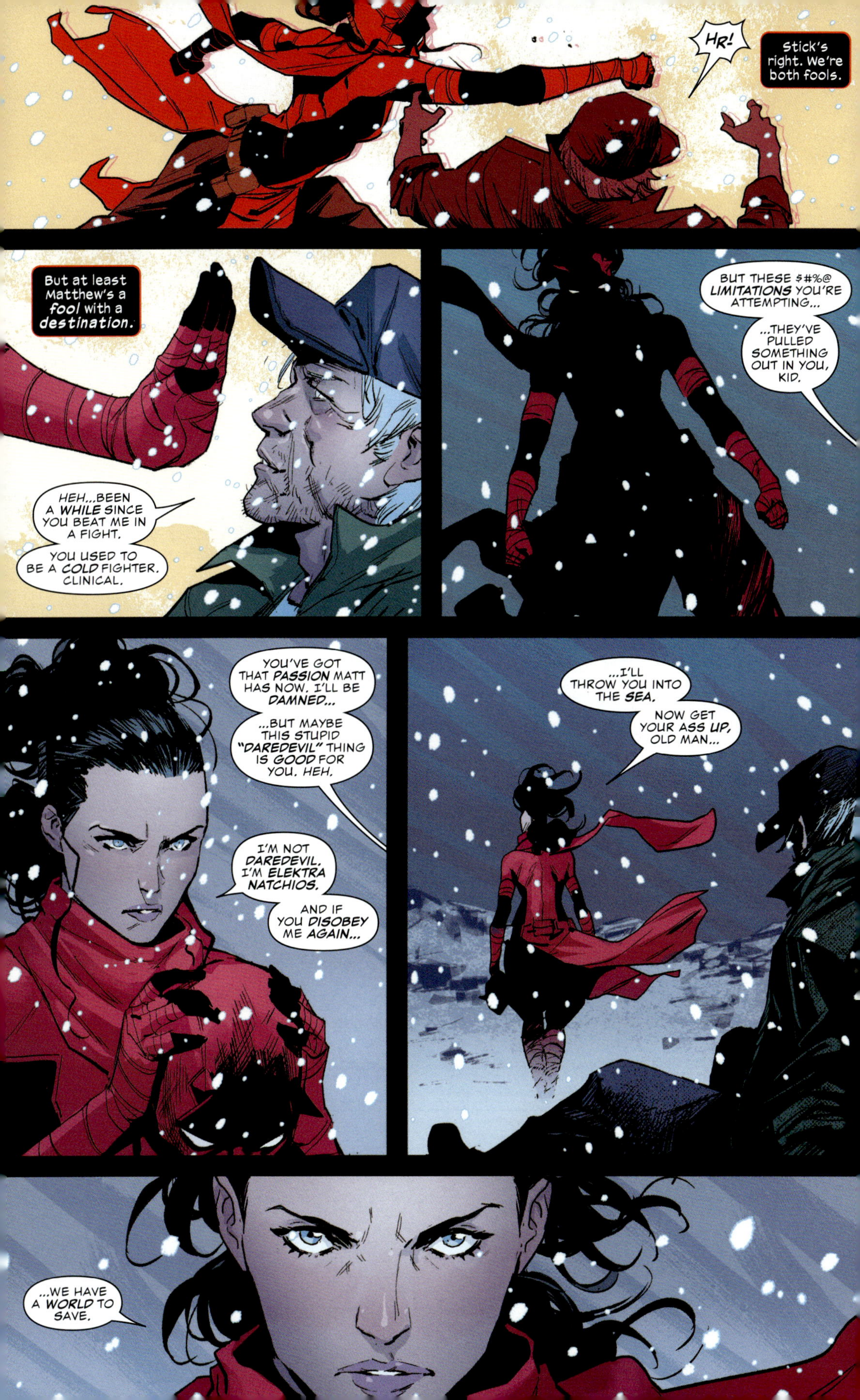
HR!
Stick's right. We're both fools.
But at least Matthew's a fool with a destination.
HEH...BEEN A WHILE SINCE YOU BEAT ME IN A FIGHT.
YOU USED TO BE A COLD FIGHTER. CLINICAL.
BUT THESE $#%@ LIMITATIONS YOU'RE ATTEMPTING...
...THEY'VE PULLED SOMETHING OUT IN YOU, KID.
YOU'VE GOT THAT PASSION MATT HAS NOW. I'LL BE DAMNED...
...BUT MAYBE THIS STUPID "DAREDEVIL" THING IS GOOD FOR YOU. HEH.
I'M NOT DAREDEVIL. I'M ELEKTRA NATCHIOS.
AND IF YOU DISOBEY ME AGAIN...
...I'LL THROW YOU INTO THE SEA.
NOW GET YOUR ASS UP, OLD MAN...
...WE HAVE A WORLD TO SAVE.

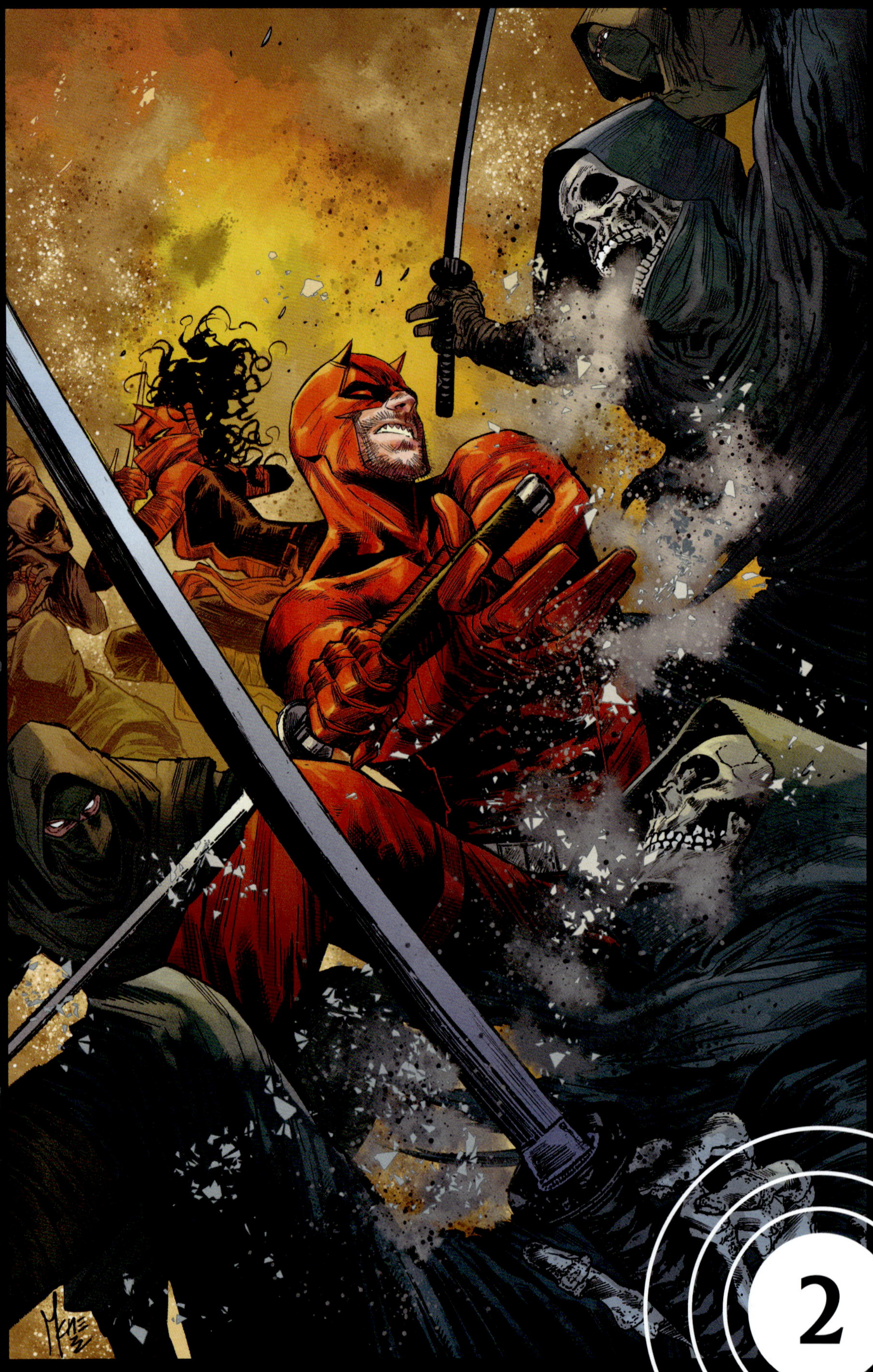
2

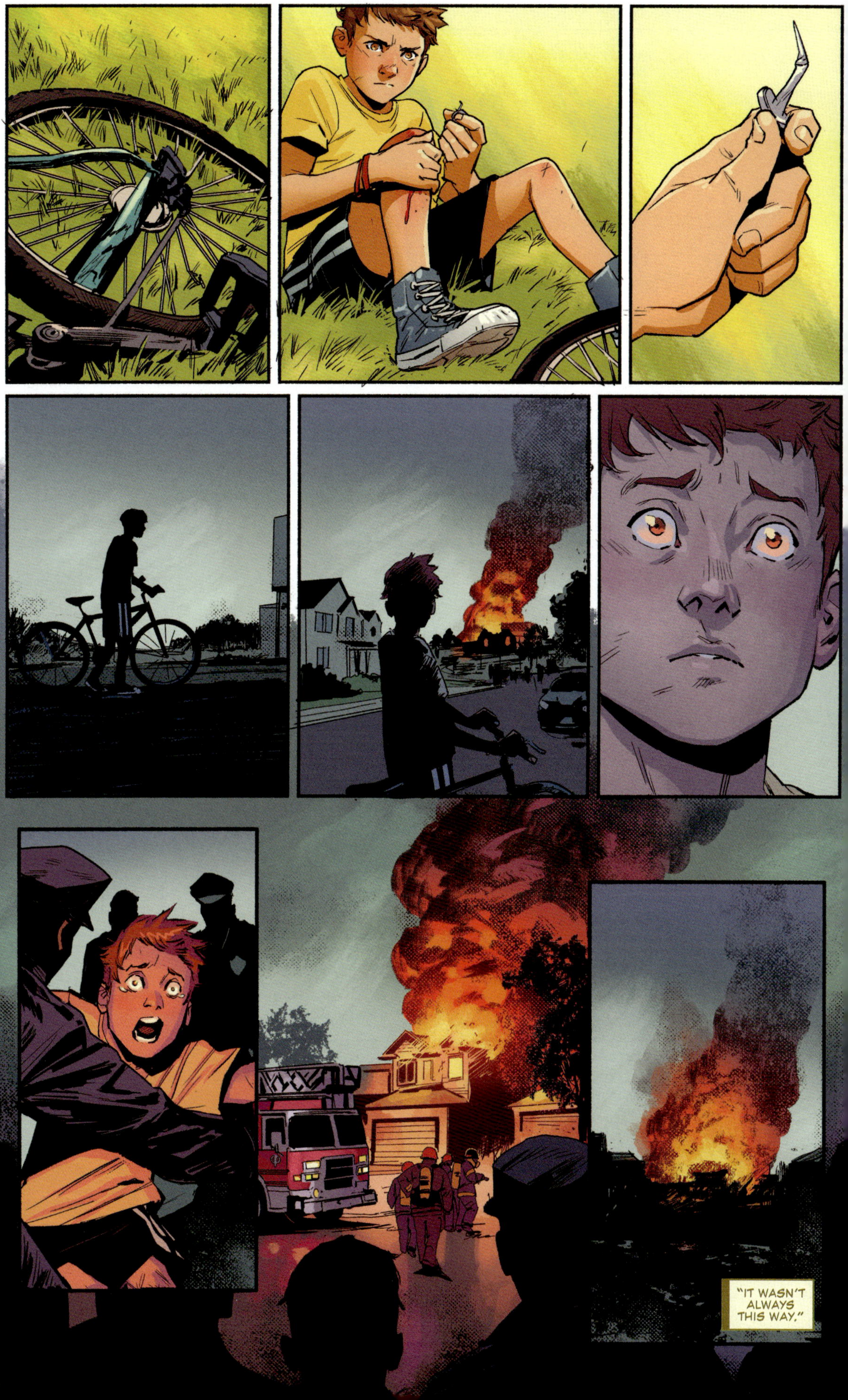
"IT WASN'T ALWAYS THIS WAY."

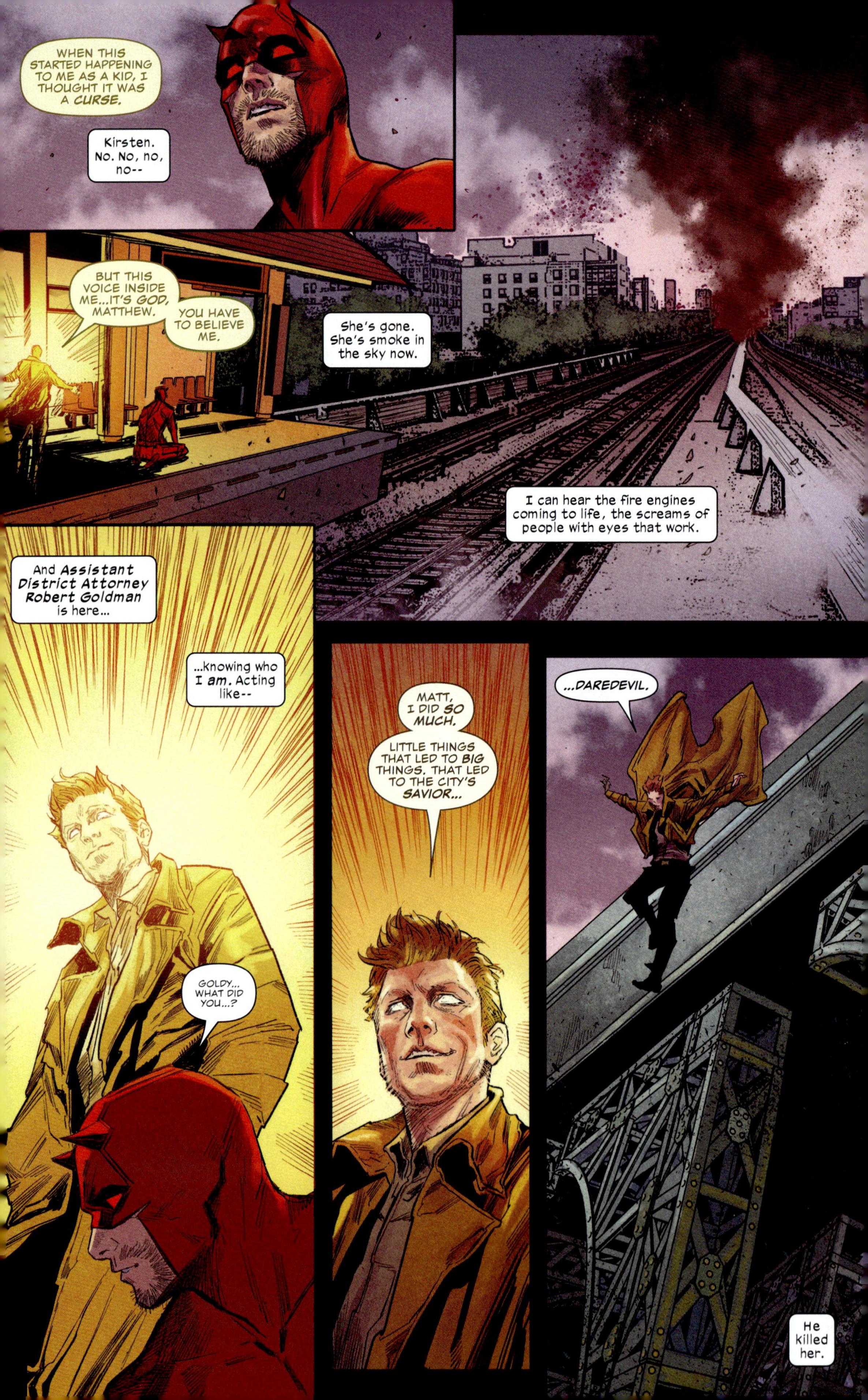

WHEN THIS STARTED HAPPENING TO ME AS A KID, I THOUGHT IT WAS A CURSE.
Kirsten. No. No, no, no--
BUT THIS VOICE INSIDE ME...IT'S GOD, MATTHEW.
YOU HAVE TO BELIEVE ME.
She's gone. She's smoke in the sky now.
I can hear the fire engines coming to life, the screams of people with eyes that work.
And Assistant District Attorney Robert Goldman is here...
...knowing who I am. Acting like--
GOLDY... WHAT DID YOU...?
MATT, I DID SO MUCH.
LITTLE THINGS THAT LED TO BIG THINGS. THAT LED TO THE CITY'S SAVIOR...
...DAREDEVIL.
He killed her.

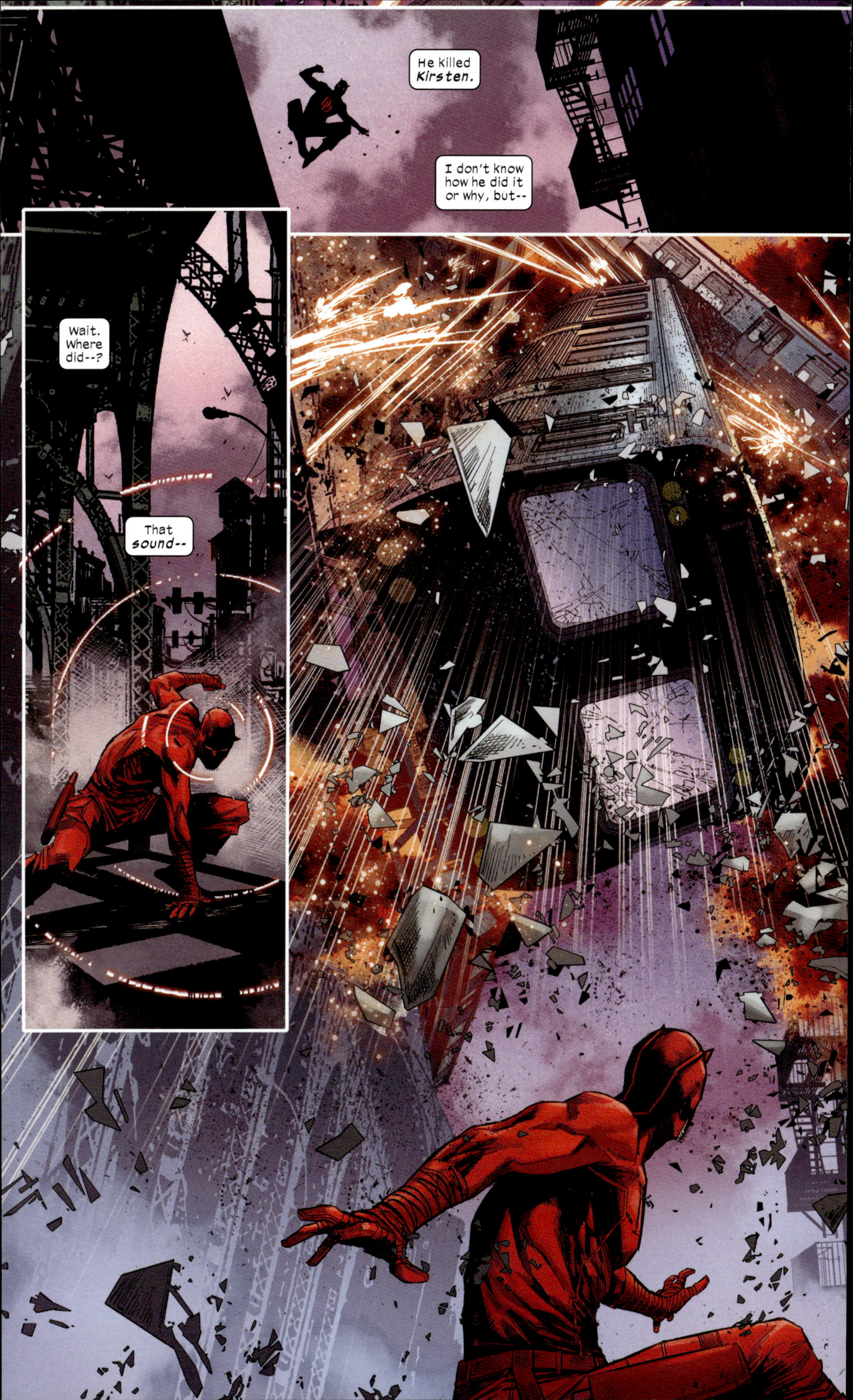
He killed Kirsten.
I don't know how he did it or why, but--
Wait. Where did--?
That sound--

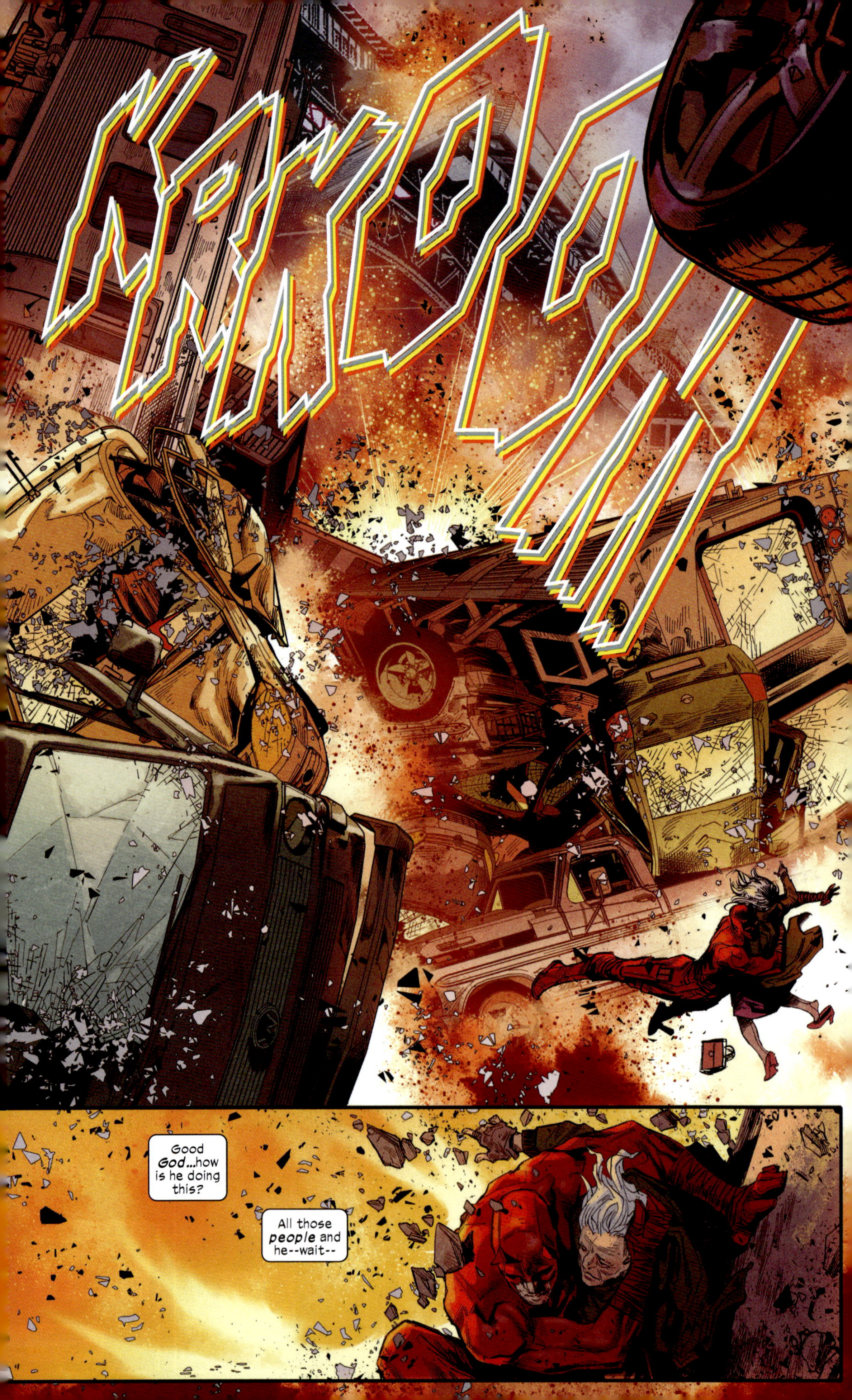
Good *God*...how is he doing this?
All those *people* and he--wait--

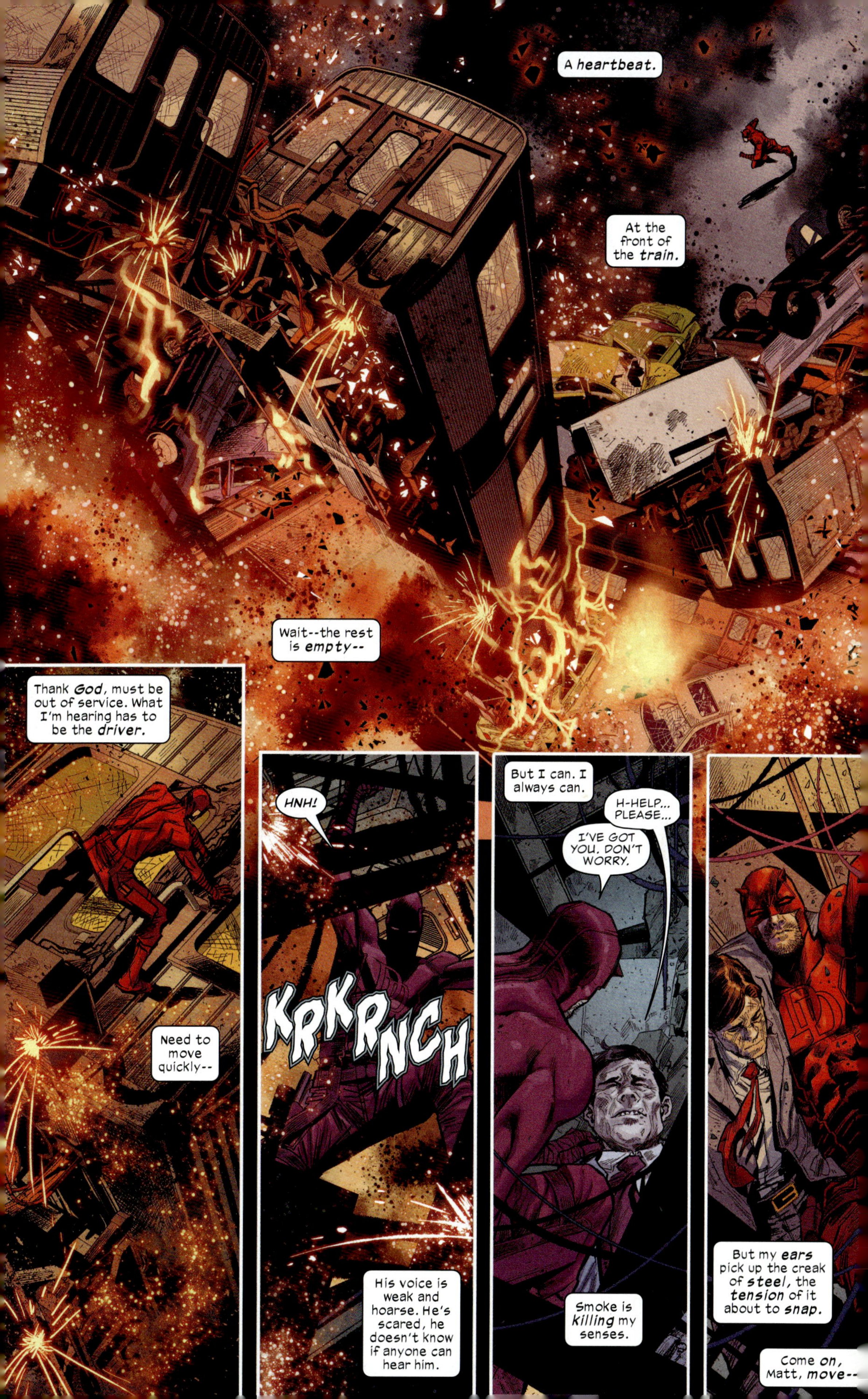
A heartbeat.
At the front of the train.
Wait--the rest is empty--
Thank God, must be out of service. What I'm hearing has to be the driver.
Need to move quickly--
HNH!
KRKRNCH
His voice is weak and hoarse. He's scared, he doesn't know if anyone can hear him.
But I can. I always can.
H-HELP... PLEASE...
I'VE GOT YOU. DON'T WORRY.
Smoke is killing my senses.
But my ears pick up the creak of steel, the tension of it about to snap.
Come on, Matt, move--

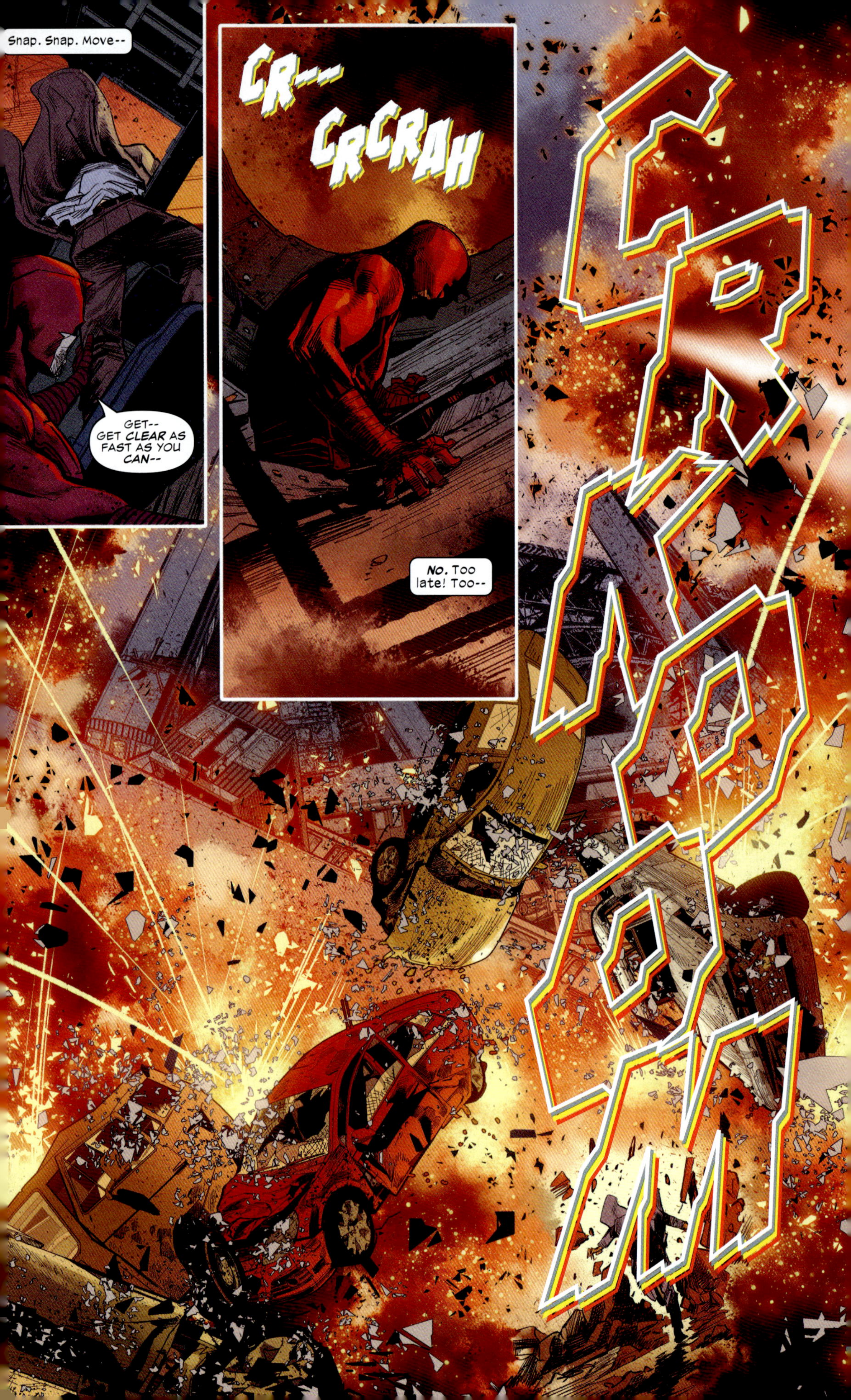

Snap. Snap. Move--
GET-- GET CLEAR AS FAST AS YOU CAN--
CR-- CRCRAH
NO. Too late! Too--

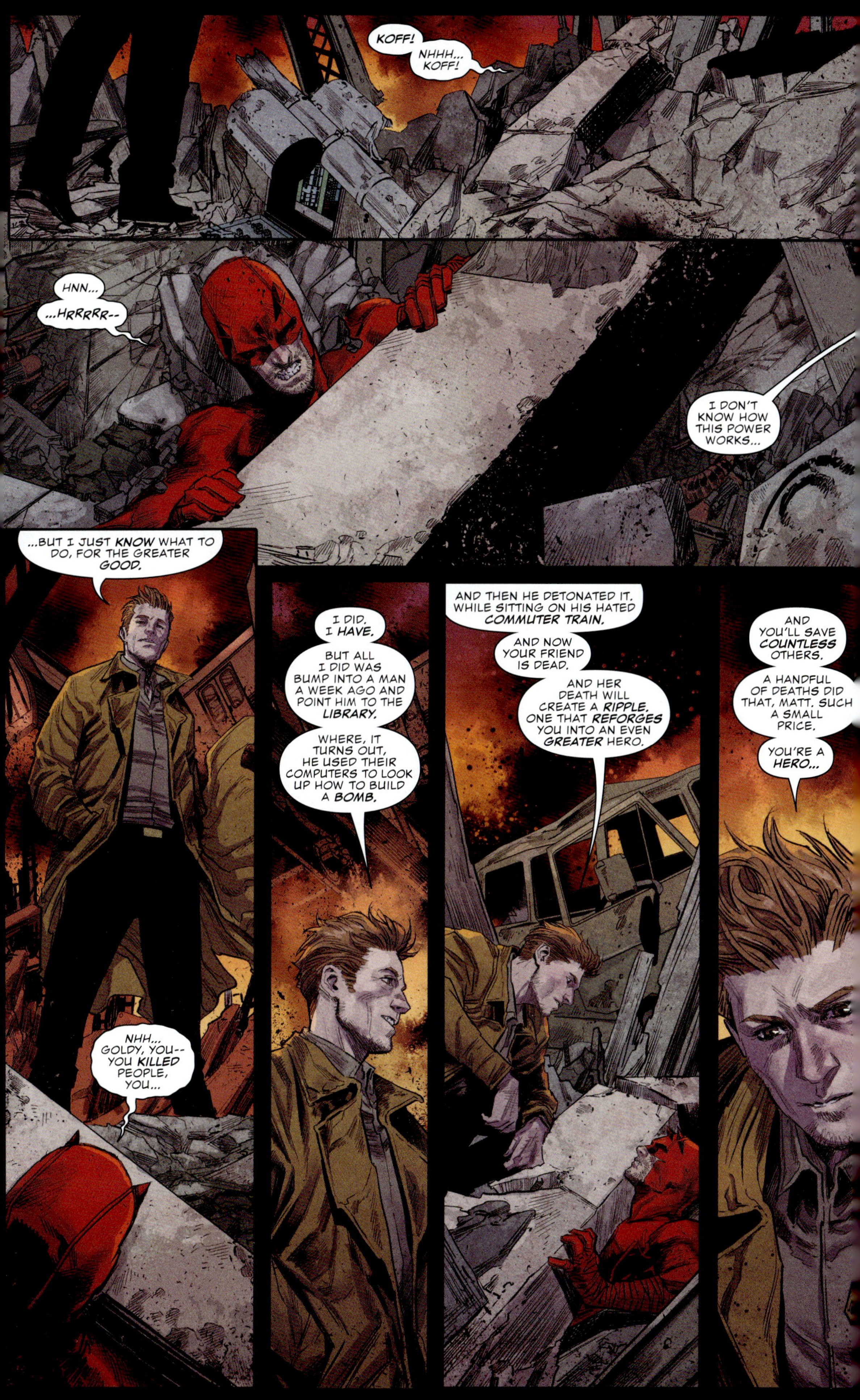
KOFF!
NHHH... KOFF!
HNN...
...HRRRRR--
I DON'T KNOW HOW THIS POWER WORKS...
...BUT I JUST KNOW WHAT TO DO, FOR THE GREATER GOOD.
NHH... GOLDY, YOU-- YOU KILLED PEOPLE, YOU...
I DID. I HAVE.
BUT ALL I DID WAS BUMP INTO A MAN A WEEK AGO AND POINT HIM TO THE LIBRARY.
WHERE, IT TURNS OUT, HE USED THEIR COMPUTERS TO LOOK UP HOW TO BUILD A BOMB.
AND THEN HE DETONATED IT. WHILE SITTING ON HIS HATED COMMUTER TRAIN.
AND NOW YOUR FRIEND IS DEAD.
AND HER DEATH WILL CREATE A RIPPLE. ONE THAT REFORGES YOU INTO AN EVEN GREATER HERO.
AND YOU'LL SAVE COUNTLESS OTHERS.
A HANDFUL OF DEATHS DID THAT, MATT. SUCH A SMALL PRICE.
YOU'RE A HERO...

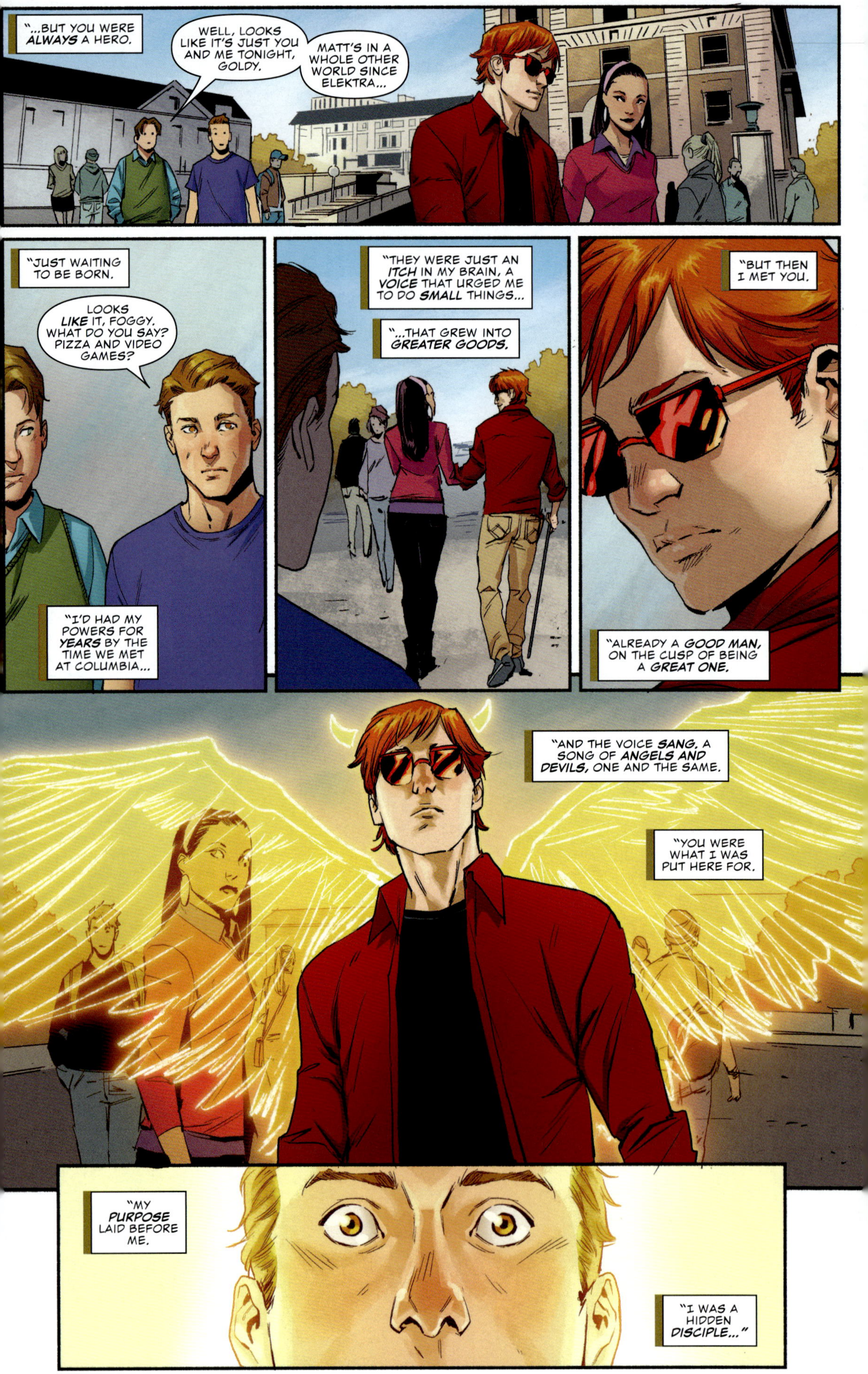
"...BUT YOU WERE ALWAYS A HERO.
WELL, LOOKS LIKE IT'S JUST YOU AND ME TONIGHT, GOLDY.
MATT'S IN A WHOLE OTHER WORLD SINCE ELEKTRA...
"JUST WAITING TO BE BORN.
LOOKS LIKE IT, FOGGY. WHAT DO YOU SAY? PIZZA AND VIDEO GAMES?
"I'D HAD MY POWERS FOR YEARS BY THE TIME WE MET AT COLUMBIA...
"THEY WERE JUST AN ITCH IN MY BRAIN, A VOICE THAT URGED ME TO DO SMALL THINGS...
"...THAT GREW INTO GREATER GOODS.
"BUT THEN I MET YOU.
"ALREADY A GOOD MAN, ON THE CUSP OF BEING A GREAT ONE.
"AND THE VOICE SANG, A SONG OF ANGELS AND DEVILS, ONE AND THE SAME.
"YOU WERE WHAT I WAS PUT HERE FOR.
"MY PURPOSE LAID BEFORE ME.
"I WAS A HIDDEN DISCIPLE..."

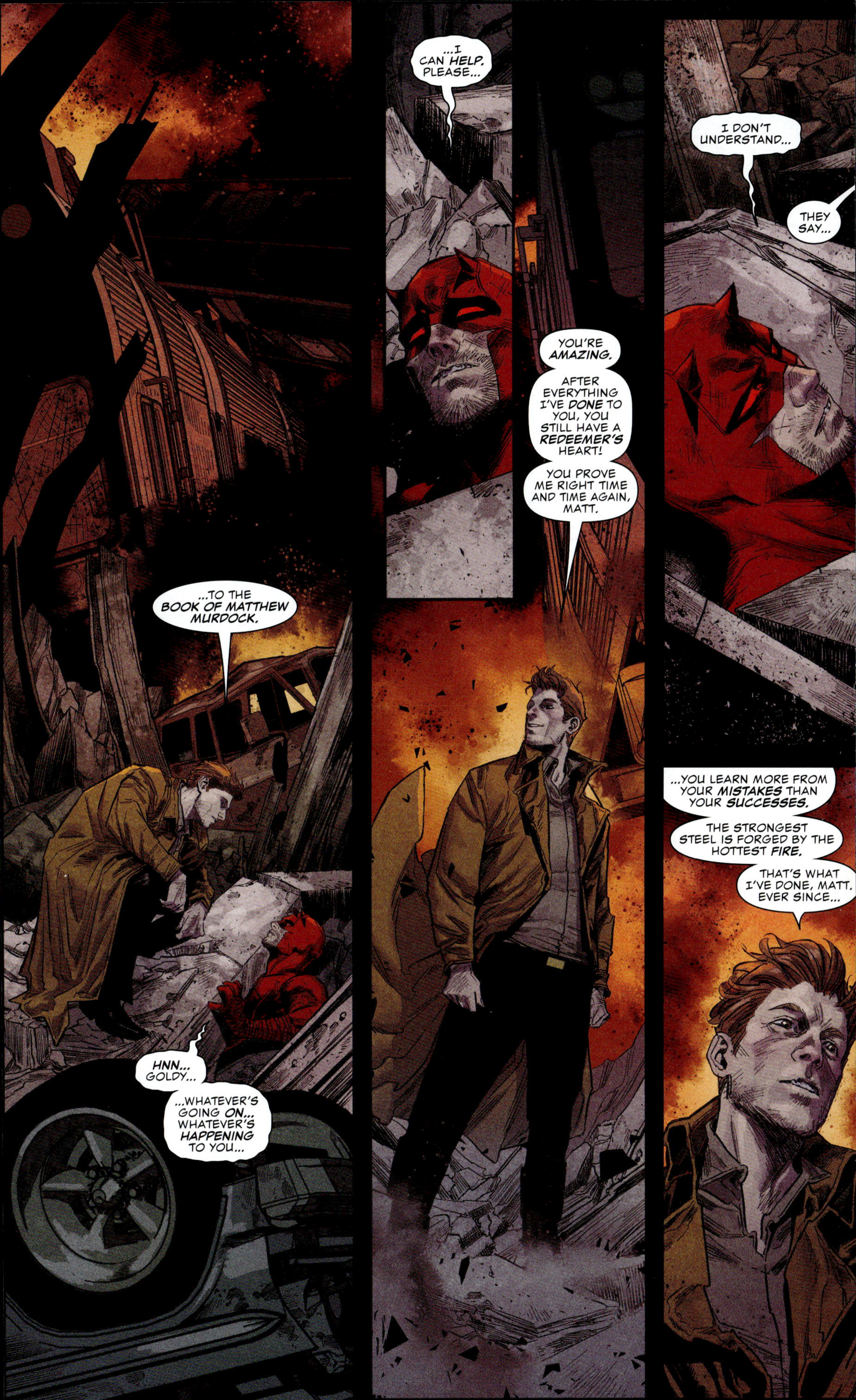
...TO THE BOOK OF MATTHEW MURDOCK.
HNN... GOLDY...
...WHATEVER'S GOING ON... WHATEVER'S HAPPENING TO YOU...
...I CAN HELP. PLEASE...
YOU'RE AMAZING.
AFTER EVERYTHING I'VE DONE TO YOU, YOU STILL HAVE A REDEEMER'S HEART!
YOU PROVE ME RIGHT TIME AND TIME AGAIN, MATT.
I DON'T UNDERSTAND...
THEY SAY...
...YOU LEARN MORE FROM YOUR MISTAKES THAN YOUR SUCCESSES.
THE STRONGEST STEEL IS FORGED BY THE HOTTEST FIRE.
THAT'S WHAT I'VE DONE, MATT. EVER SINCE...

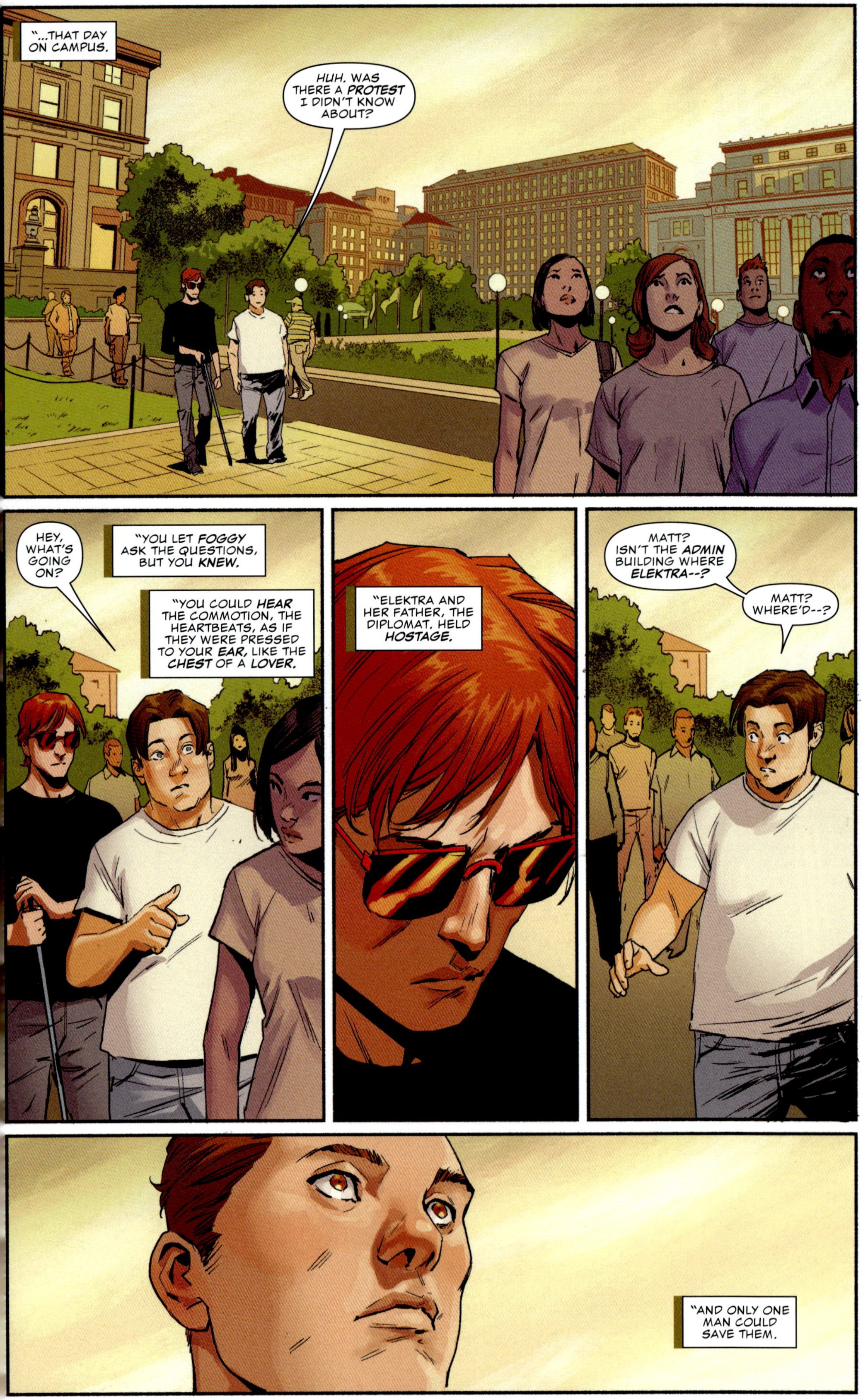
"...THAT DAY ON CAMPUS.
HUH. WAS THERE A PROTEST I DIDN'T KNOW ABOUT?
HEY, WHAT'S GOING ON?
"YOU LET FOGGY ASK THE QUESTIONS, BUT YOU KNEW.
"YOU COULD HEAR THE COMMOTION, THE HEARTBEATS, AS IF THEY WERE PRESSED TO YOUR EAR, LIKE THE CHEST OF A LOVER.
"ELEKTRA AND HER FATHER, THE DIPLOMAT, HELD HOSTAGE.
MATT? ISN'T THE ADMIN BUILDING WHERE ELEKTRA--?
MATT? WHERE'D--?
"AND ONLY ONE MAN COULD SAVE THEM.

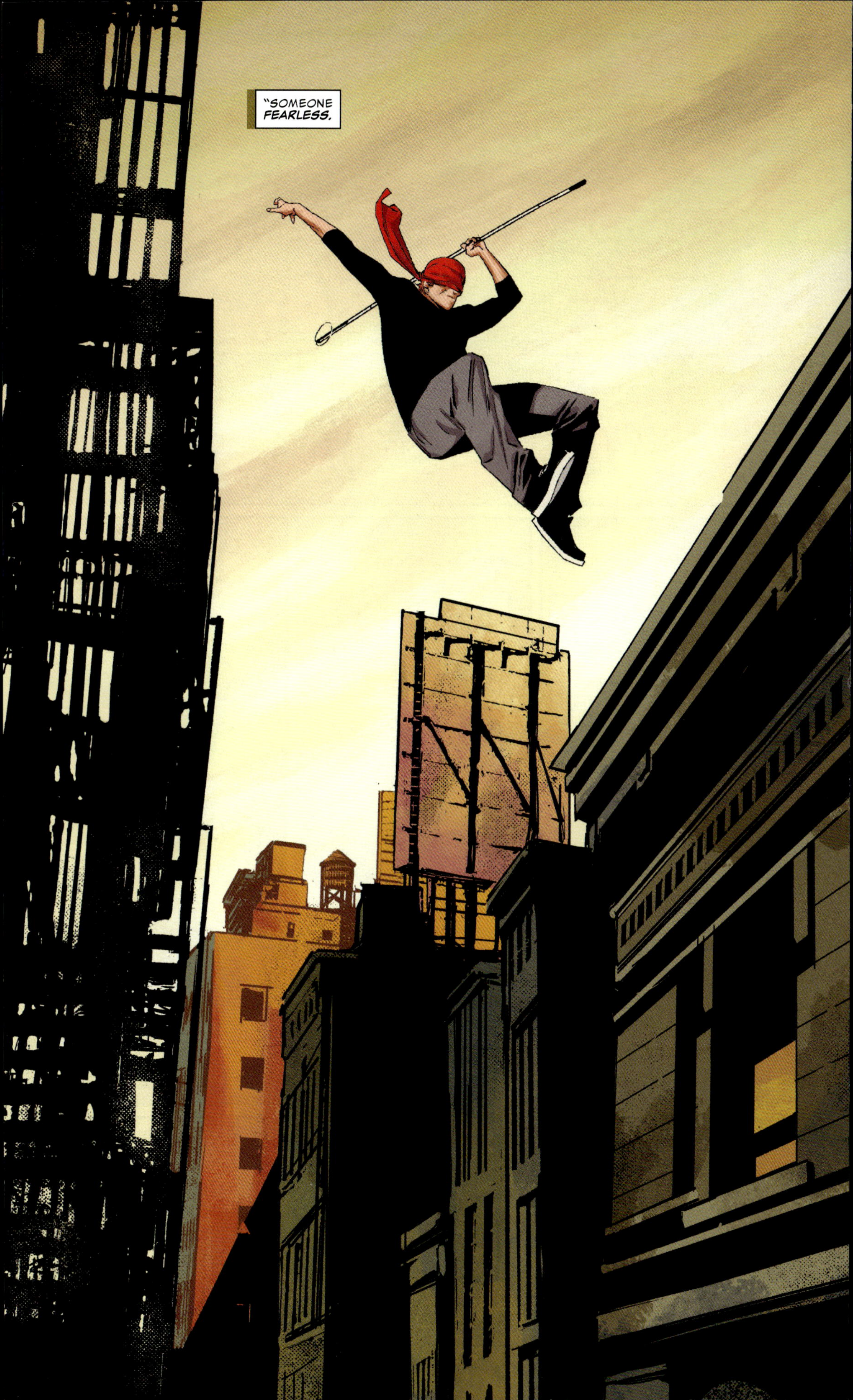
"SOMEONE FEARLESS.

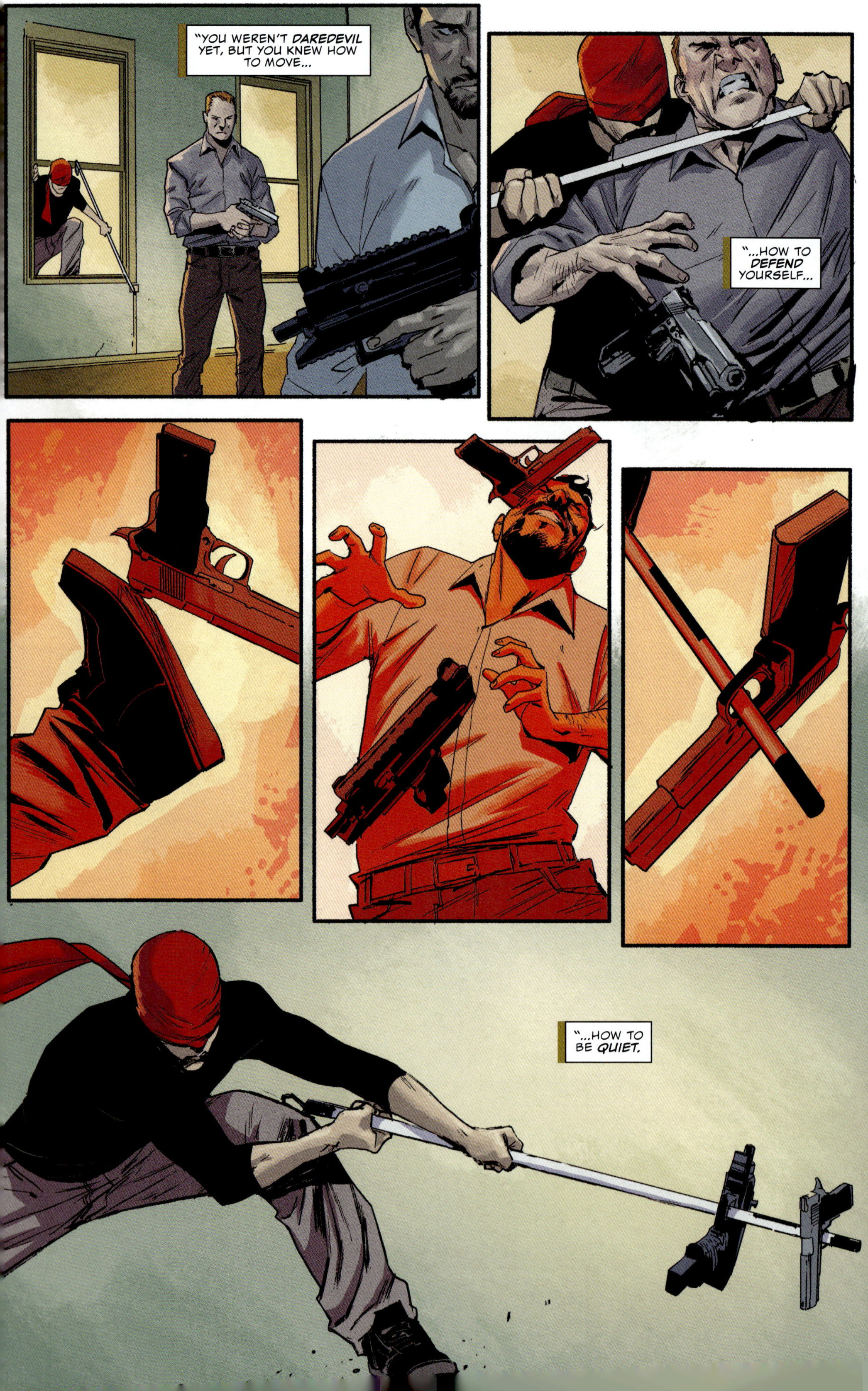
"YOU WEREN'T DAREDEVIL YET, BUT YOU KNEW HOW TO MOVE...
"...HOW TO DEFEND YOURSELF...
"...HOW TO BE QUIET.

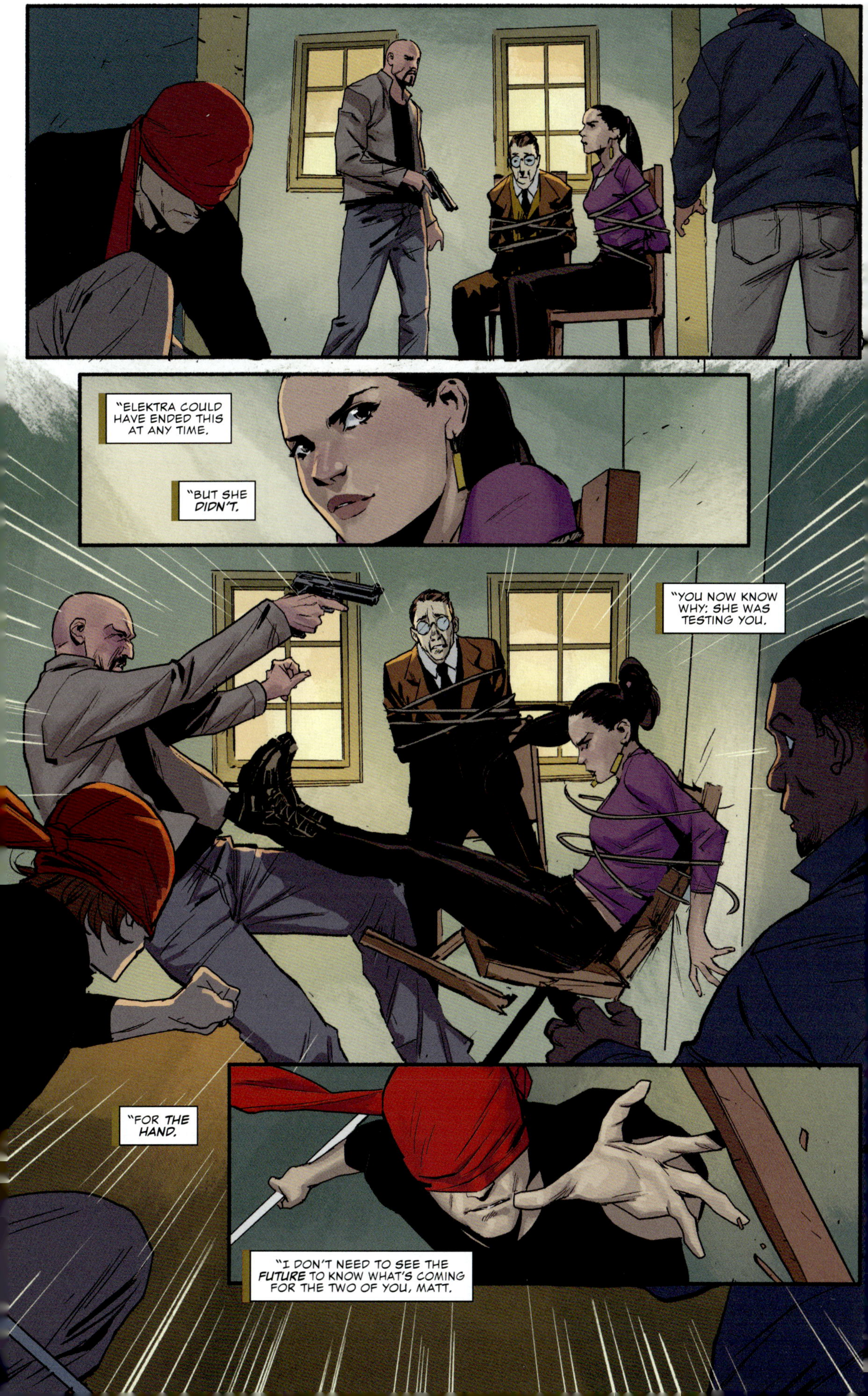
"ELEKTRA COULD HAVE ENDED THIS AT ANY TIME.
"BUT SHE DIDN'T.
"YOU NOW KNOW WHY: SHE WAS TESTING YOU.
"FOR THE HAND.
"I DON'T NEED TO SEE THE FUTURE TO KNOW WHAT'S COMING FOR THE TWO OF YOU, MATT.

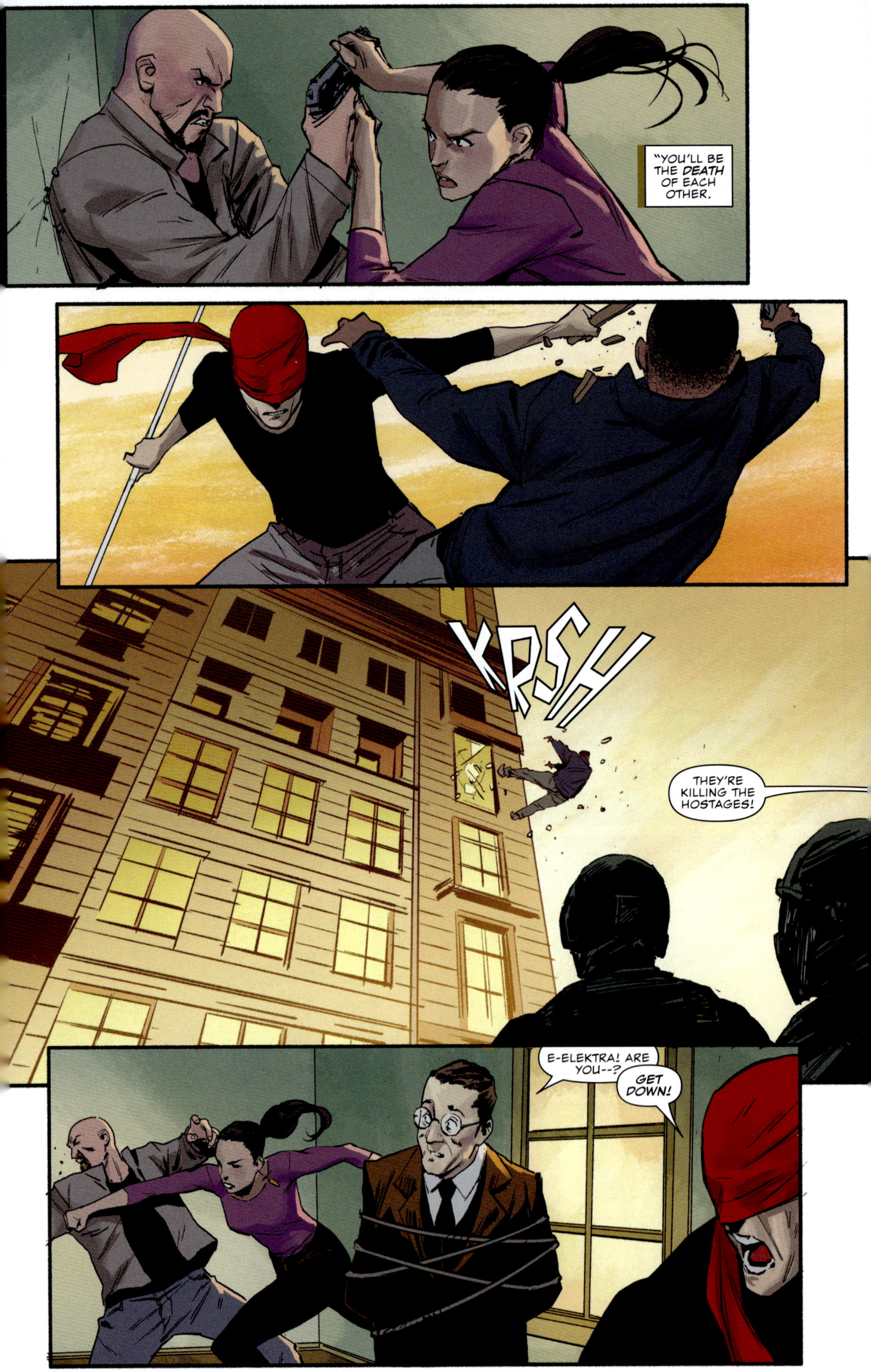
"YOU'LL BE THE DEATH OF EACH OTHER.
KRSH
THEY'RE KILLING THE HOSTAGES!
E-ELEKTRA! ARE YOU--?
GET DOWN!

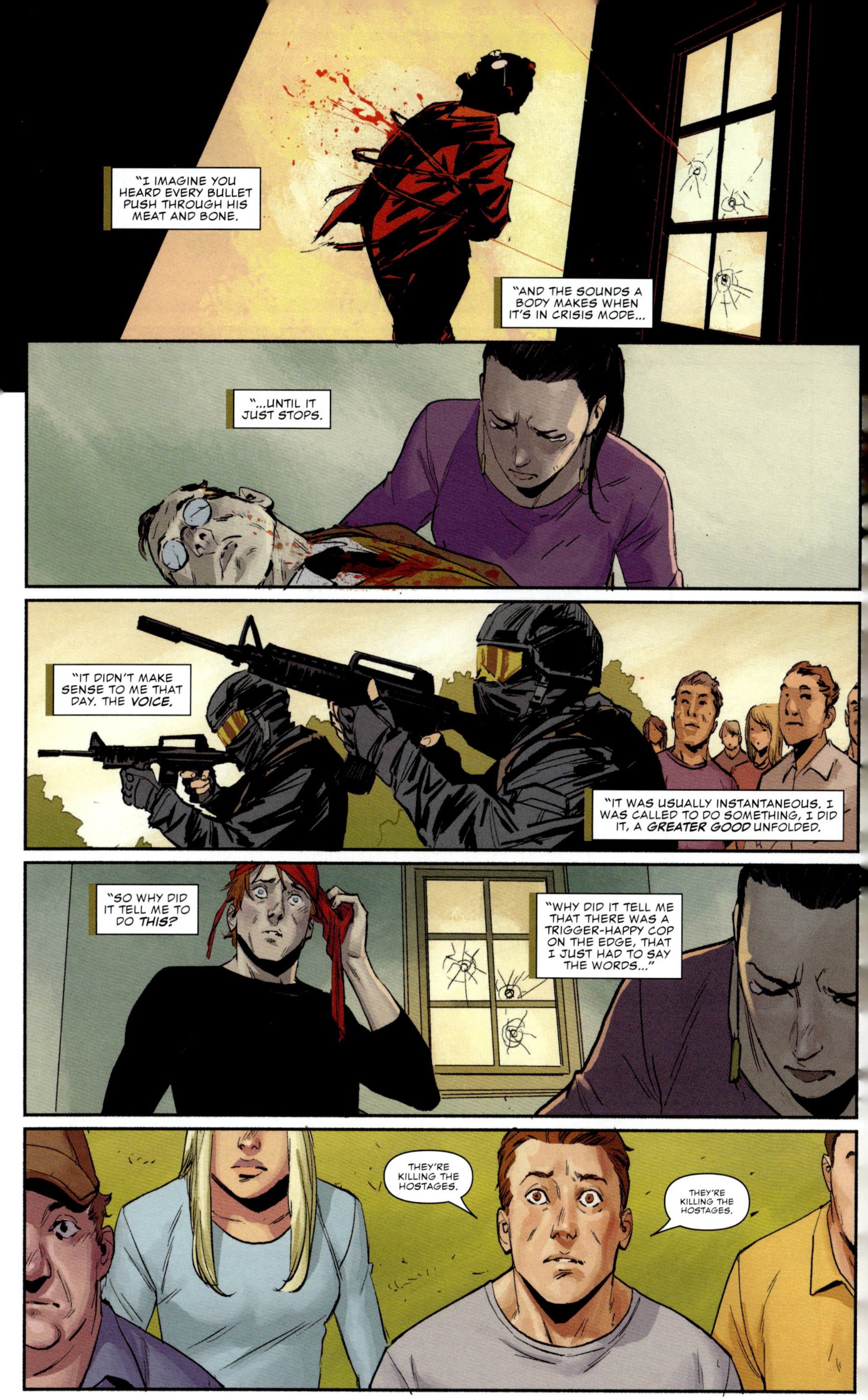
"I IMAGINE YOU HEARD EVERY BULLET PUSH THROUGH HIS MEAT AND BONE.
"AND THE SOUNDS A BODY MAKES WHEN IT'S IN CRISIS MODE...
"...UNTIL IT JUST STOPS.
"IT DIDN'T MAKE SENSE TO ME THAT DAY. THE *VOICE*.
"IT WAS USUALLY INSTANTANEOUS. I WAS CALLED TO DO SOMETHING, I DID IT, A *GREATER GOOD* UNFOLDED.
"SO WHY DID IT TELL ME TO DO *THIS?*
"WHY DID IT TELL ME THAT THERE WAS A TRIGGER-HAPPY COP ON THE EDGE, THAT I JUST HAD TO SAY THE WORDS..."
THEY'RE KILLING THE HOSTAGES.
THEY'RE KILLING THE HOSTAGES.

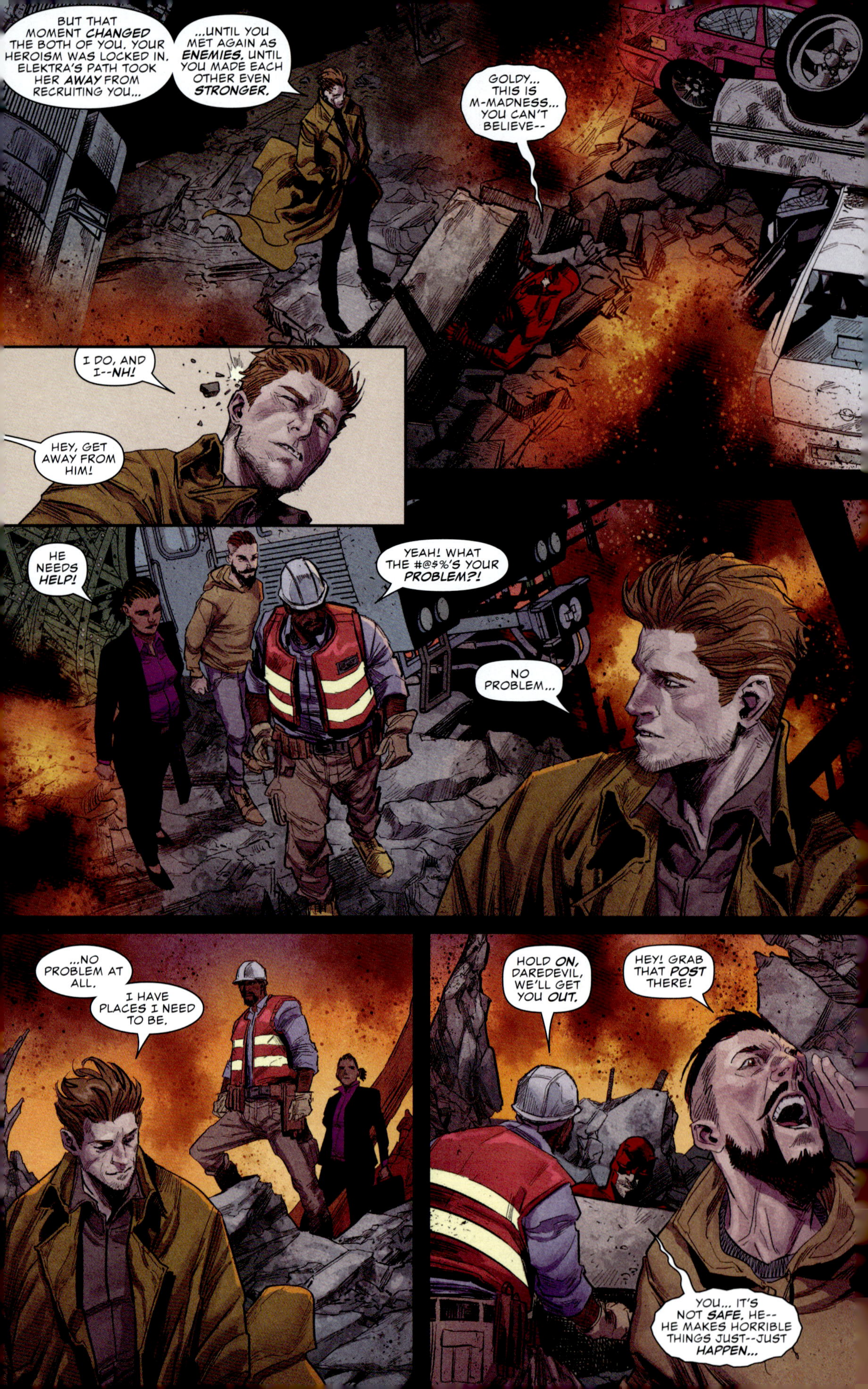
BUT THAT MOMENT CHANGED THE BOTH OF YOU. YOUR HEROISM WAS LOCKED IN. ELEKTRA'S PATH TOOK HER AWAY FROM RECRUITING YOU...
...UNTIL YOU MET AGAIN AS ENEMIES. UNTIL YOU MADE EACH OTHER EVEN STRONGER.
GOLDY... THIS IS M-MADNESS... YOU CAN'T BELIEVE--
I DO, AND I--NH!
HEY, GET AWAY FROM HIM!
HE NEEDS HELP!
YEAH! WHAT THE #@$%'S YOUR PROBLEM?!
NO PROBLEM...
...NO PROBLEM AT ALL.
I HAVE PLACES I NEED TO BE.
HOLD ON, DAREDEVIL, WE'LL GET YOU OUT.
HEY! GRAB THAT POST THERE!
YOU... IT'S NOT SAFE. HE-- HE MAKES HORRIBLE THINGS JUST--JUST HAPPEN...

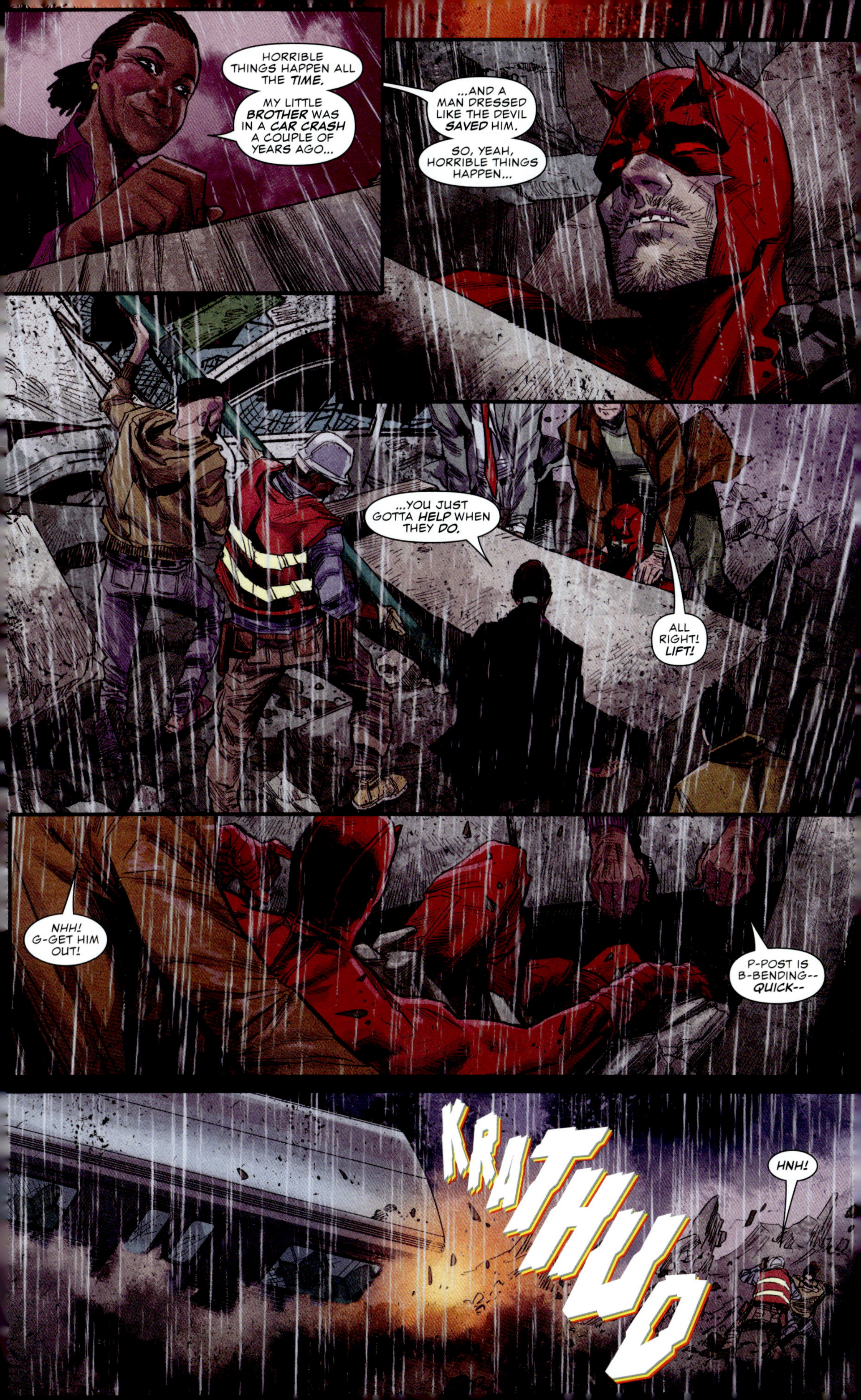
HORRIBLE THINGS HAPPEN ALL THE TIME.
MY LITTLE BROTHER WAS IN A CAR CRASH A COUPLE OF YEARS AGO...
...AND A MAN DRESSED LIKE THE DEVIL SAVED HIM.
SO, YEAH, HORRIBLE THINGS HAPPEN...
...YOU JUST GOTTA HELP WHEN THEY DO.
ALL RIGHT! LIFT!
NHH! G-GET HIM OUT!
P-POST IS B-BENDING-- QUICK--
KRATHUD
HNH!

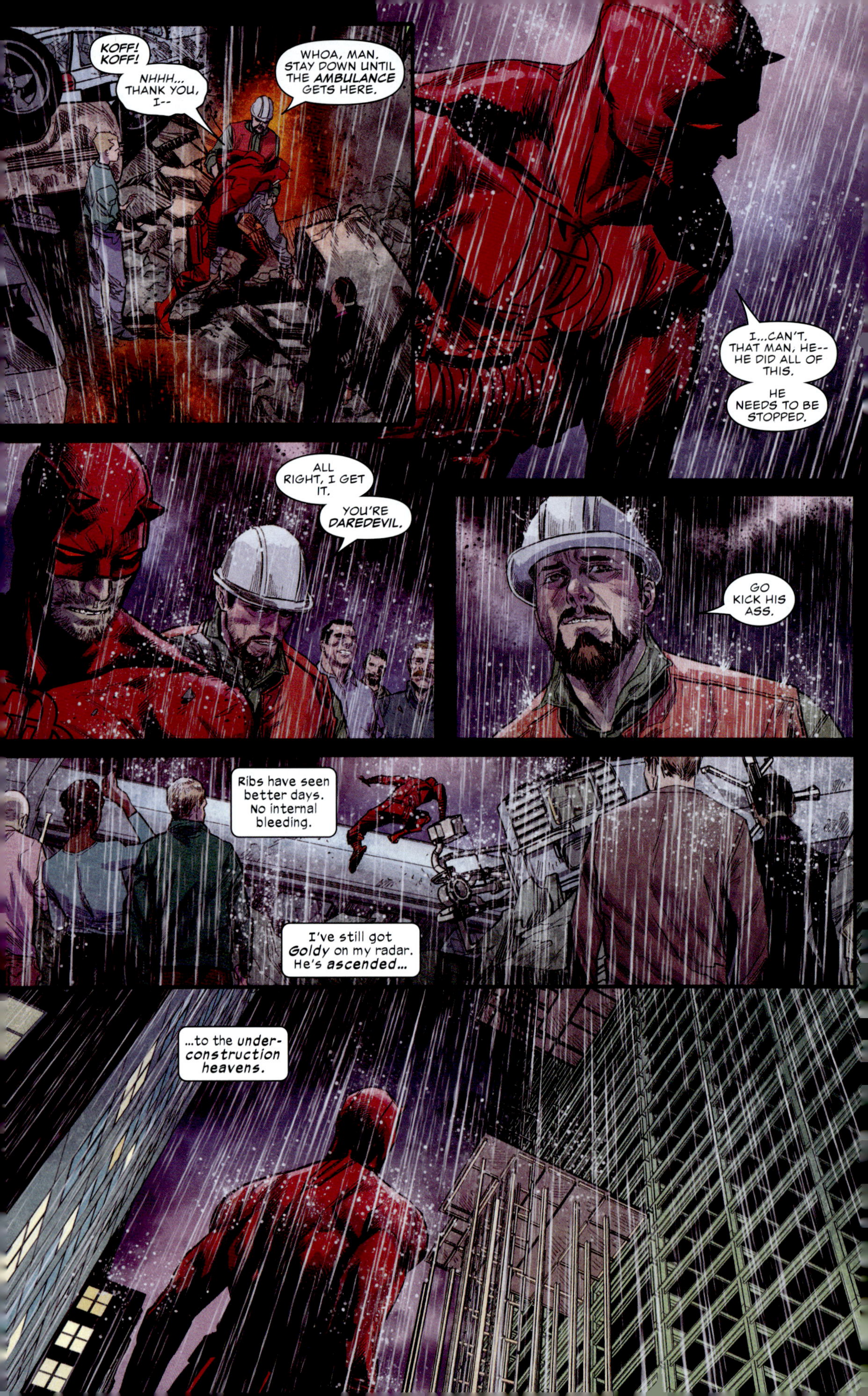
KOFF! KOFF!
NHHH... THANK YOU, I--
WHOA, MAN. STAY DOWN UNTIL THE AMBULANCE GETS HERE.
I...CAN'T. THAT MAN, HE-- HE DID ALL OF THIS.
HE NEEDS TO BE STOPPED.
ALL RIGHT, I GET IT.
YOU'RE DAREDEVIL.
GO KICK HIS ASS.
Ribs have seen better days. No internal bleeding.
I've still got Goldy on my radar. He's ascended...
...to the under-construction heavens.

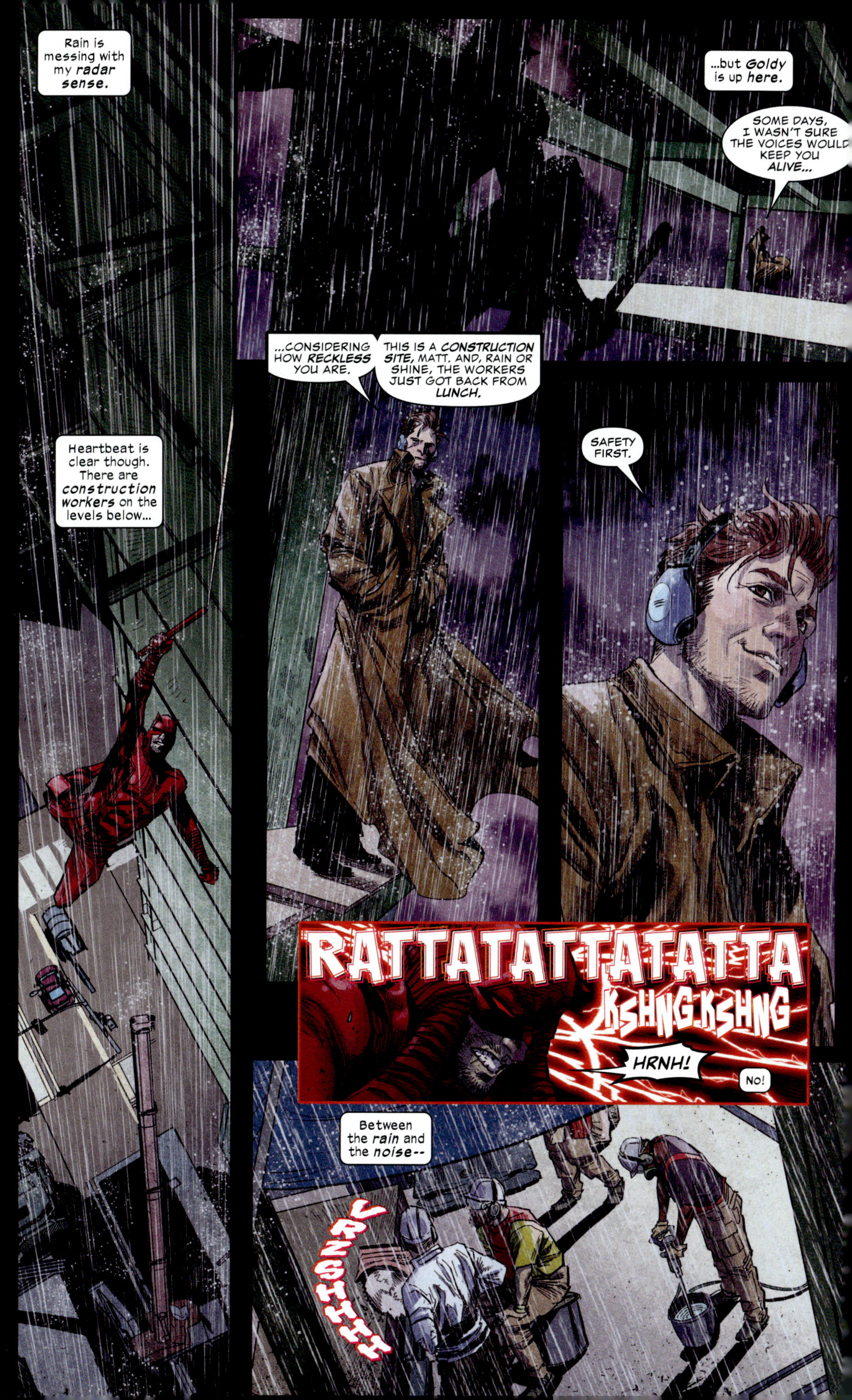
Rain is messing with my radar sense.
...but Goldy is up here.
SOME DAYS, I WASN'T SURE THE VOICES WOULD KEEP YOU ALIVE...
...CONSIDERING HOW RECKLESS YOU ARE.
THIS IS A CONSTRUCTION SITE, MATT. AND, RAIN OR SHINE, THE WORKERS JUST GOT BACK FROM LUNCH.
Heartbeat is clear though. There are construction workers on the levels below...
SAFETY FIRST.
RATTATATTATATTA
KSHNG KSHNG
HRNH!
NO!
Between the rain and the noise--
VRZSHHHH

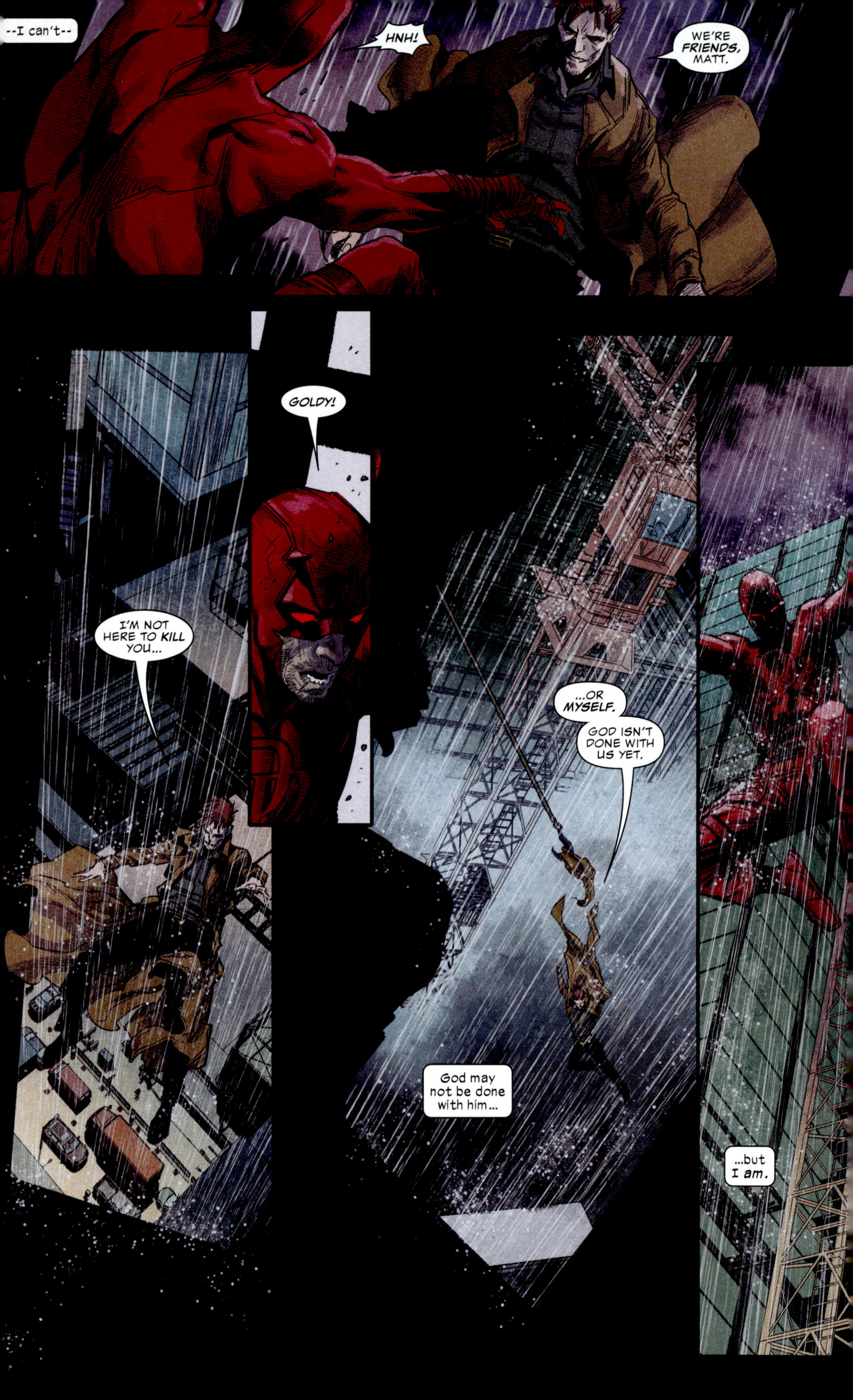
--I can't--
HNH!
WE'RE FRIENDS, MATT.
GOLDY!
I'M NOT HERE TO KILL YOU...
...OR MYSELF.
GOD ISN'T DONE WITH US YET.
God may not be done with him...
...but I am.

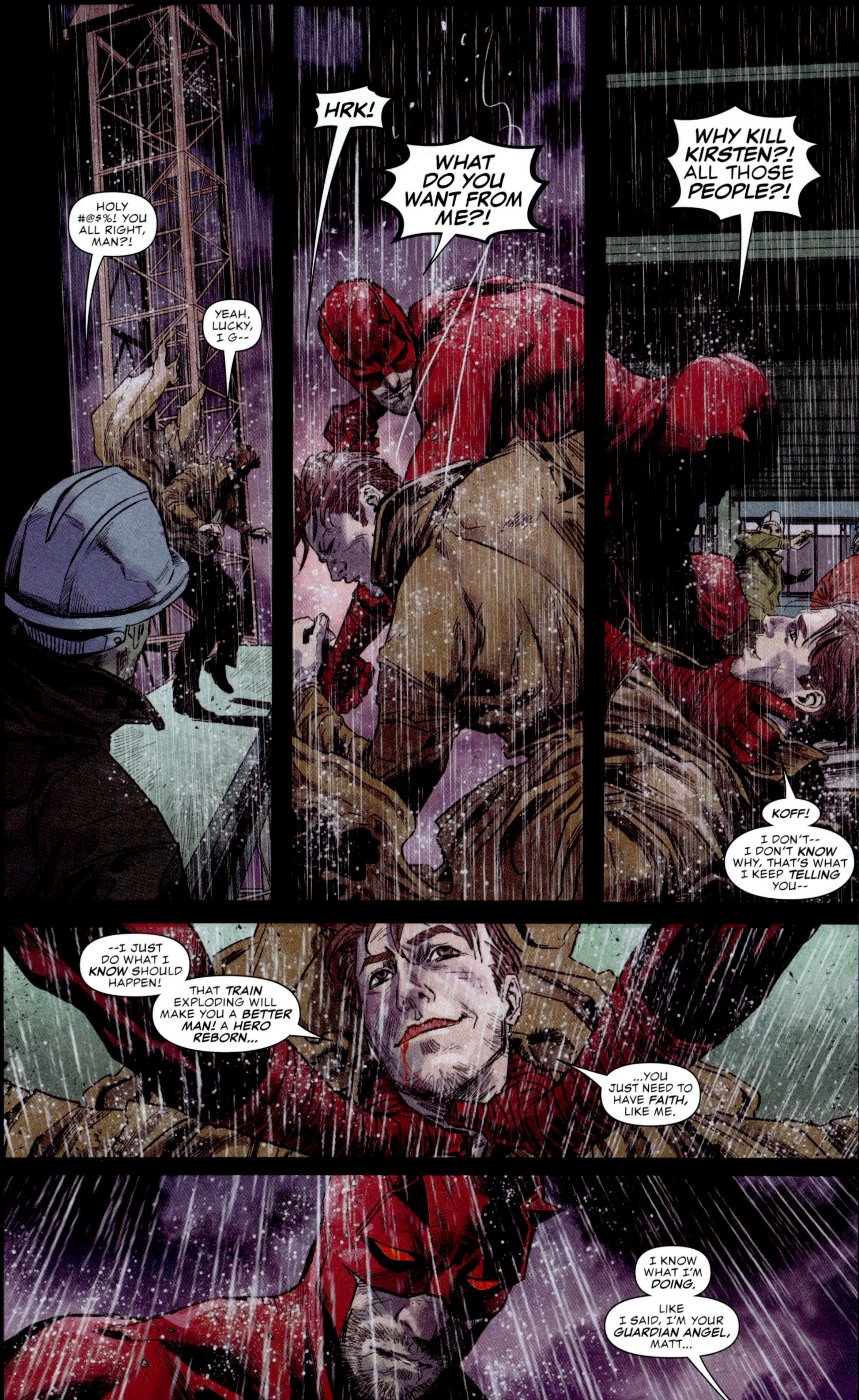
HOLY #@$%! YOU ALL RIGHT, MAN?!
YEAH, LUCKY, I G--
HRK!
WHAT DO YOU WANT FROM ME?!
WHY KILL KIRSTEN?! ALL THOSE PEOPLE?!
KOFF!
I DON'T-- I DON'T KNOW WHY, THAT'S WHAT I KEEP TELLING YOU--
--I JUST DO WHAT I KNOW SHOULD HAPPEN!
THAT TRAIN EXPLODING WILL MAKE YOU A BETTER MAN! A HERO REBORN...
...YOU JUST NEED TO HAVE FAITH, LIKE ME.
I KNOW WHAT I'M DOING.
LIKE I SAID, I'M YOUR GUARDIAN ANGEL, MATT...

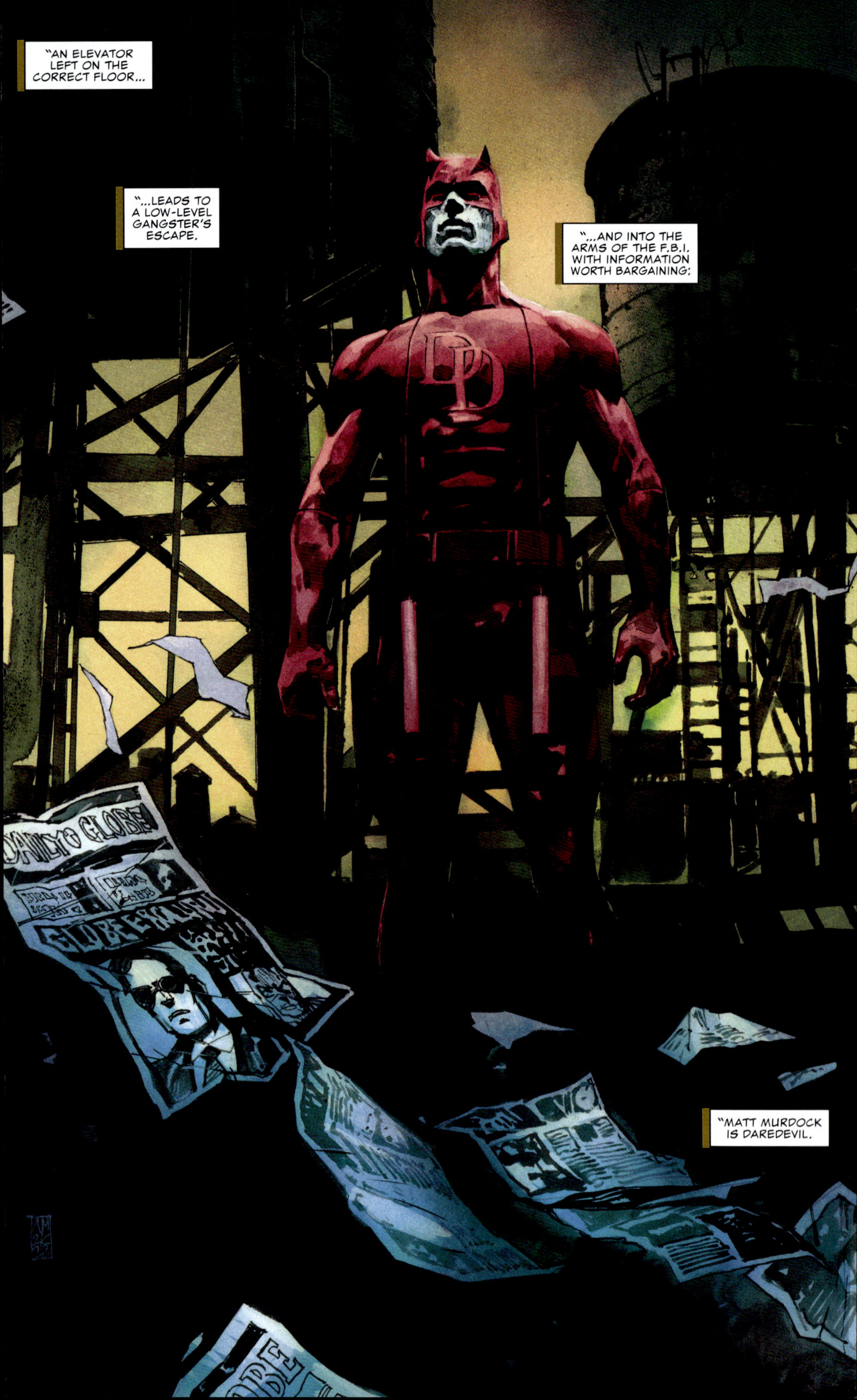
"AN ELEVATOR LEFT ON THE CORRECT FLOOR...
"...LEADS TO A LOW-LEVEL GANGSTER'S ESCAPE.
"...AND INTO THE ARMS OF THE F.B.I. WITH INFORMATION WORTH BARGAINING:
"MATT MURDOCK IS DAREDEVIL.

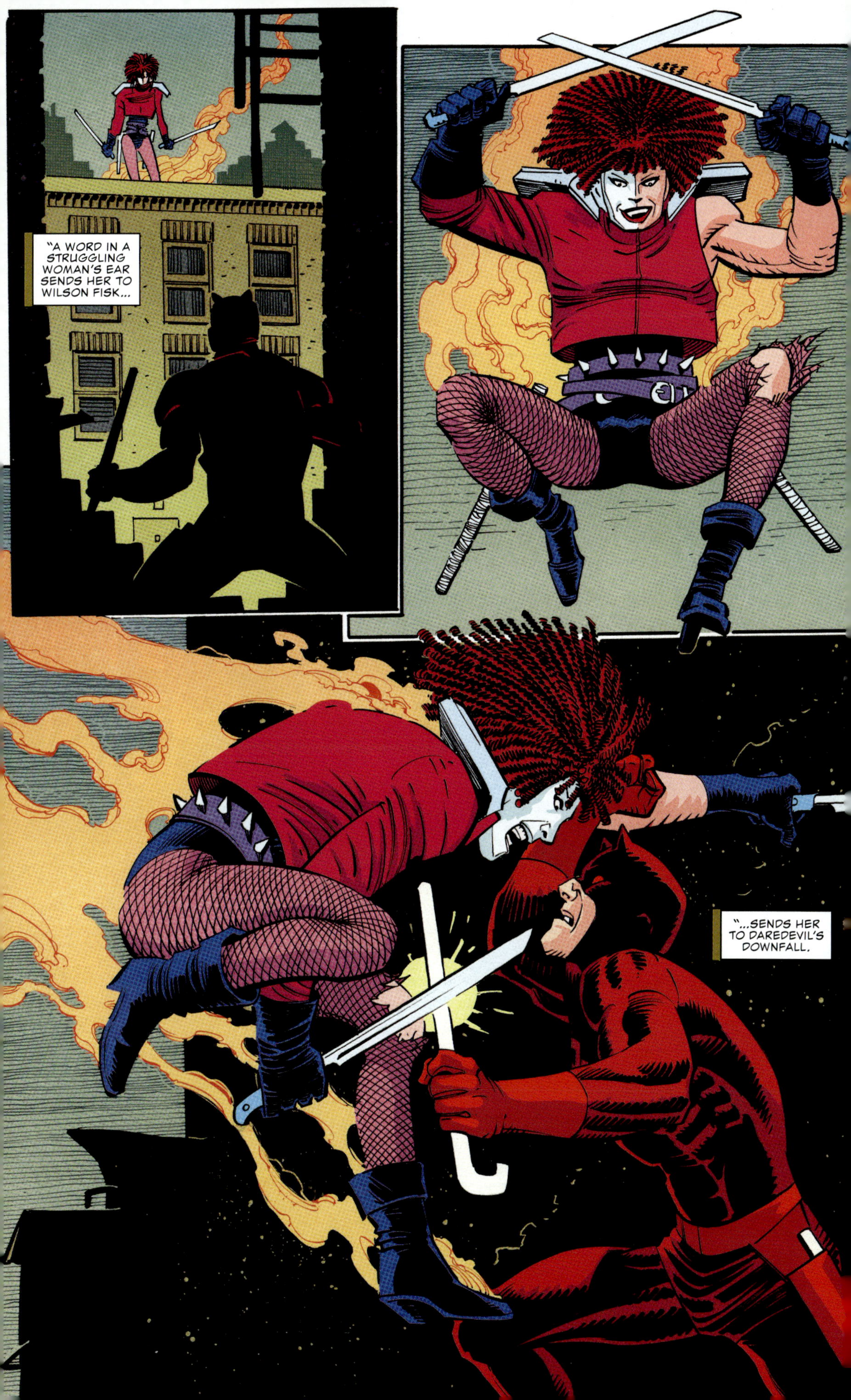
"A WORD IN A STRUGGLING WOMAN'S EAR SENDS HER TO WILSON FISK...
"...SENDS HER TO DAREDEVIL'S DOWNFALL.

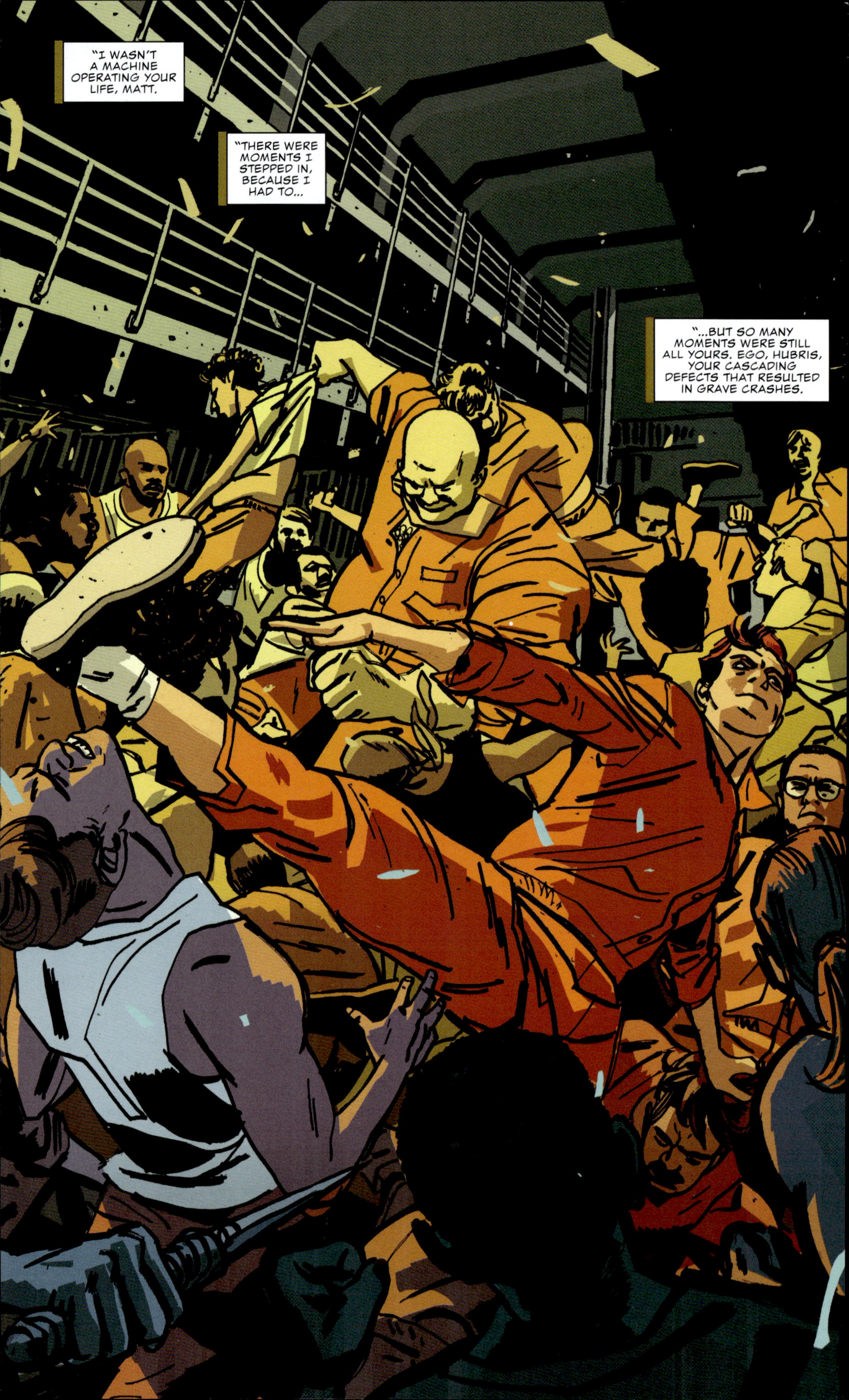
"I WASN'T A MACHINE OPERATING YOUR LIFE, MATT.
"THERE WERE MOMENTS I STEPPED IN, BECAUSE I HAD TO...
"...BUT SO MANY MOMENTS WERE STILL ALL YOURS. EGO, HUBRIS, YOUR CASCADING DEFECTS THAT RESULTED IN GRAVE CRASHES.

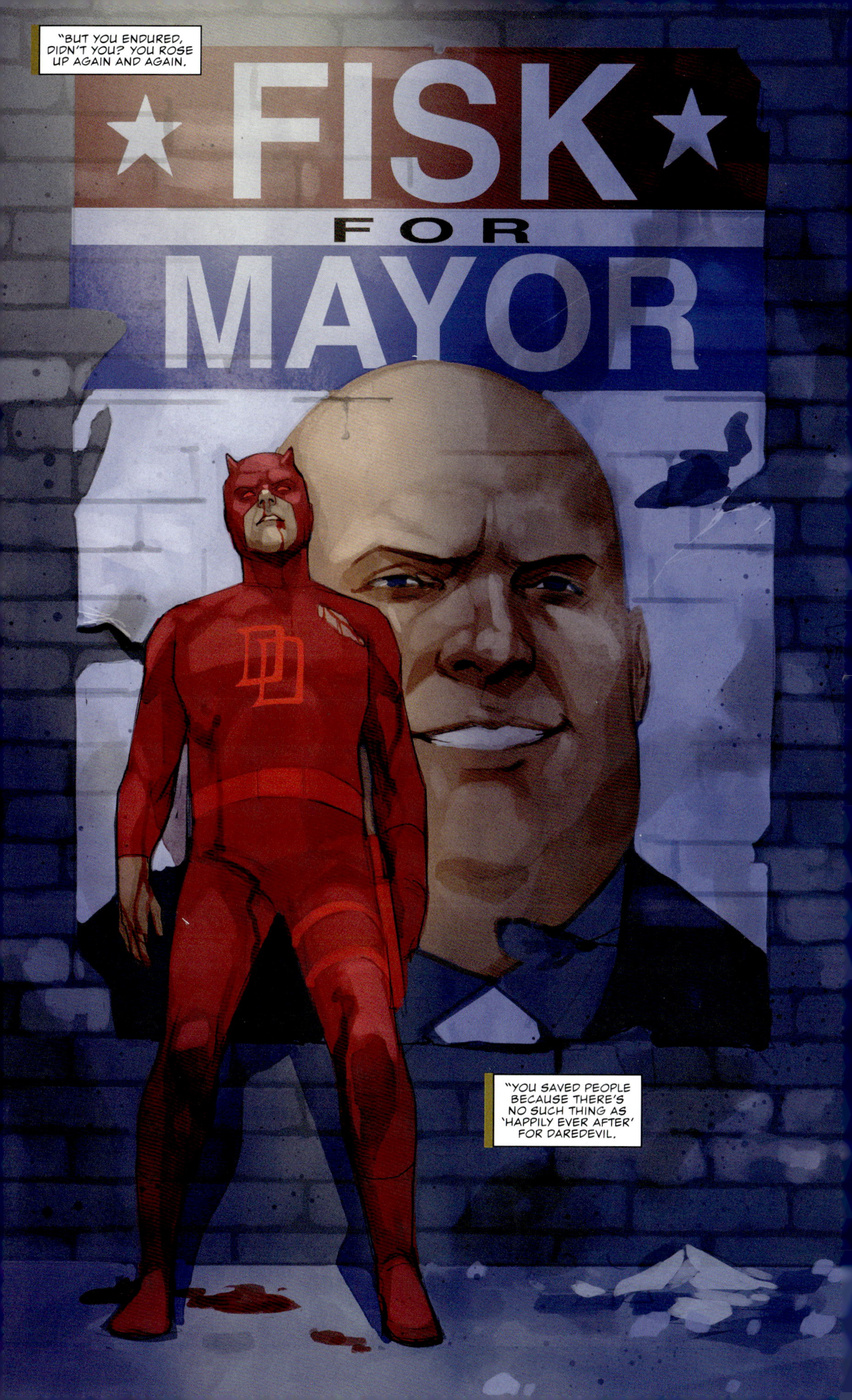
"BUT YOU ENDURED, DIDN'T YOU? YOU ROSE UP AGAIN AND AGAIN.
FISK FOR MAYOR
"YOU SAVED PEOPLE BECAUSE THERE'S NO SUCH THING AS 'HAPPILY EVER AFTER' FOR DAREDEVIL.

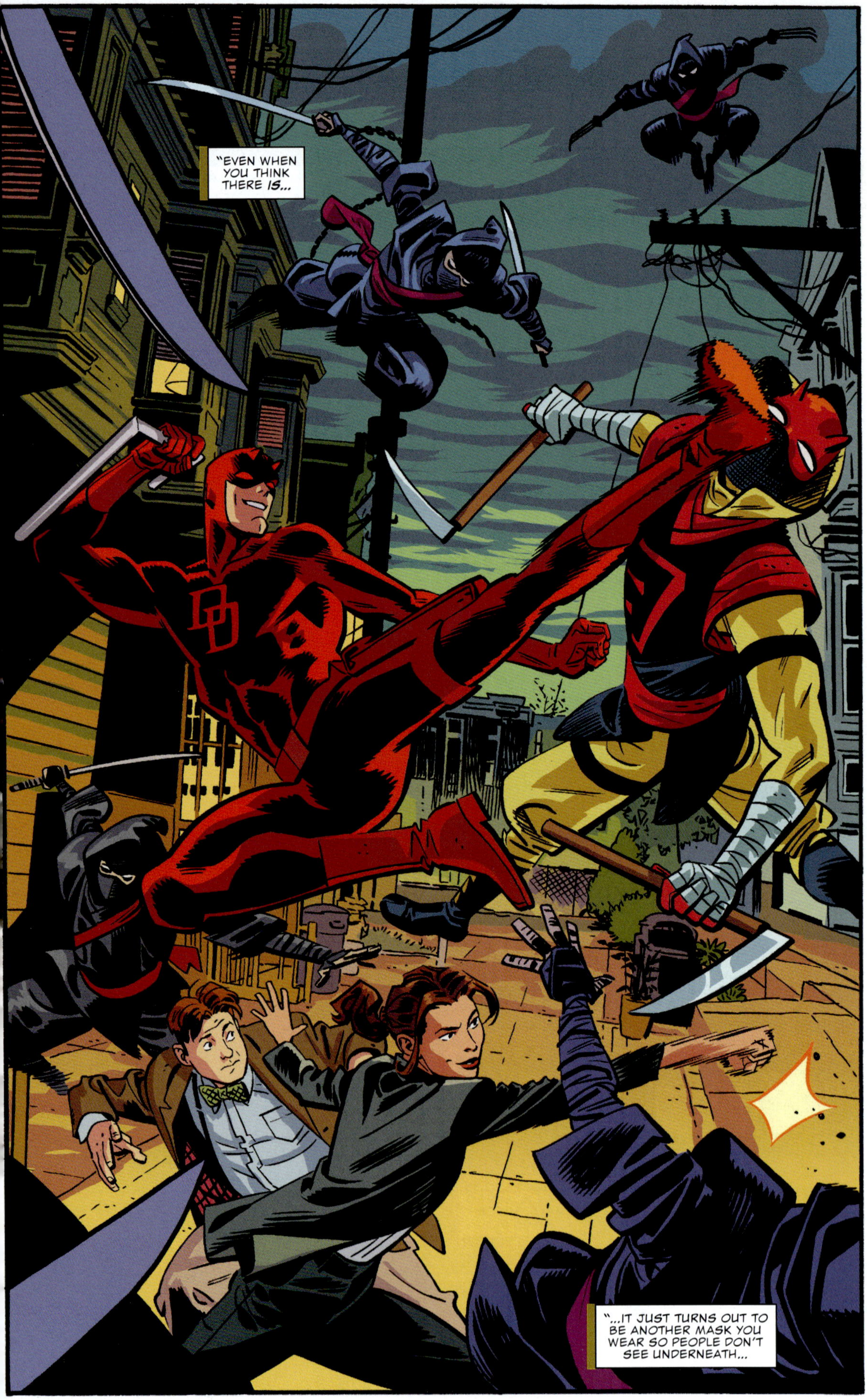
"EVEN WHEN YOU THINK THERE IS...
"...IT JUST TURNS OUT TO BE ANOTHER MASK YOU WEAR SO PEOPLE DON'T SEE UNDERNEATH...

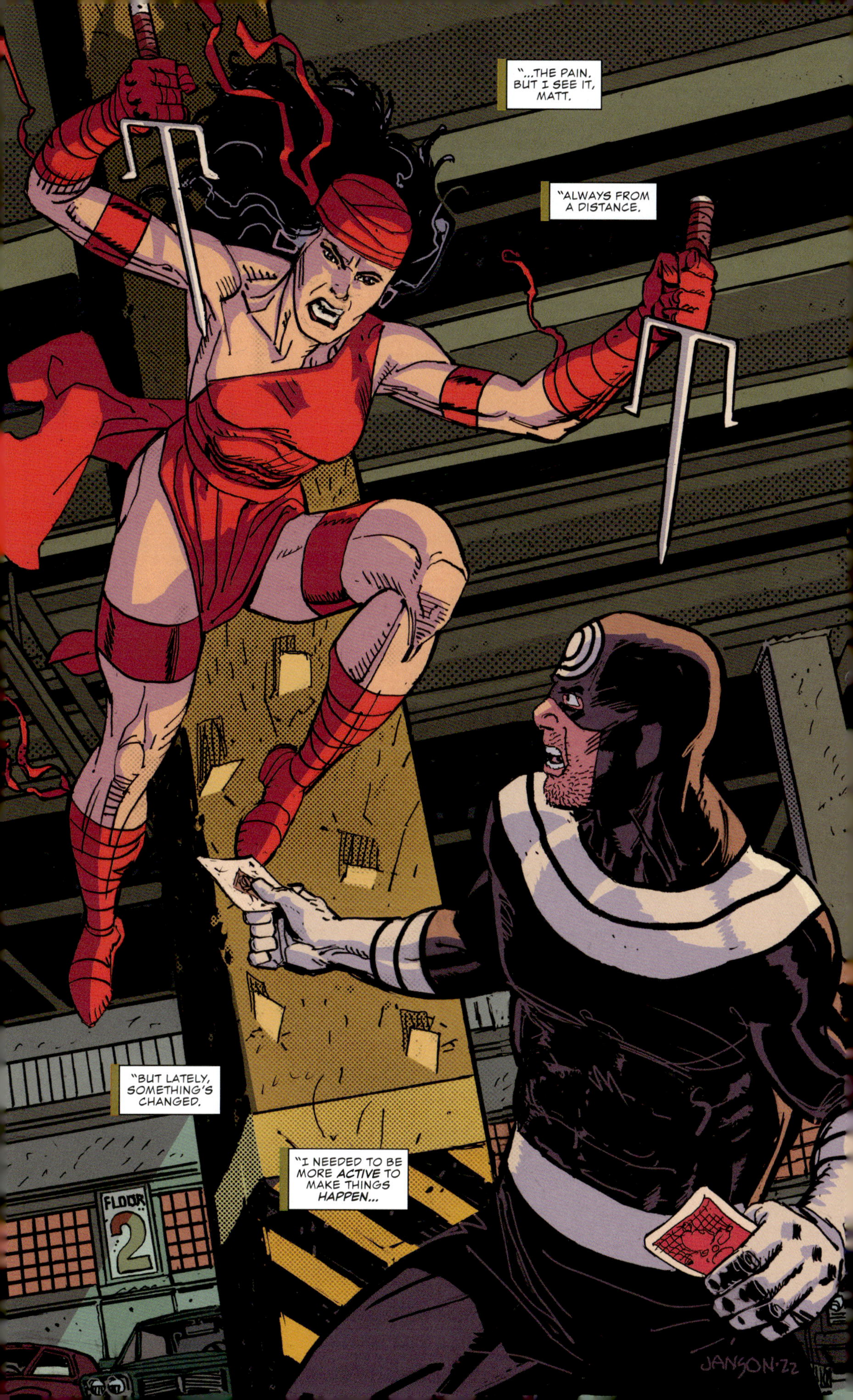
"...THE PAIN. BUT I SEE IT, MATT.
"ALWAYS FROM A DISTANCE.
"BUT LATELY, SOMETHING'S CHANGED.
"I NEEDED TO BE MORE *ACTIVE* TO MAKE THINGS *HAPPEN*...
FLOOR 2
JANSON·22

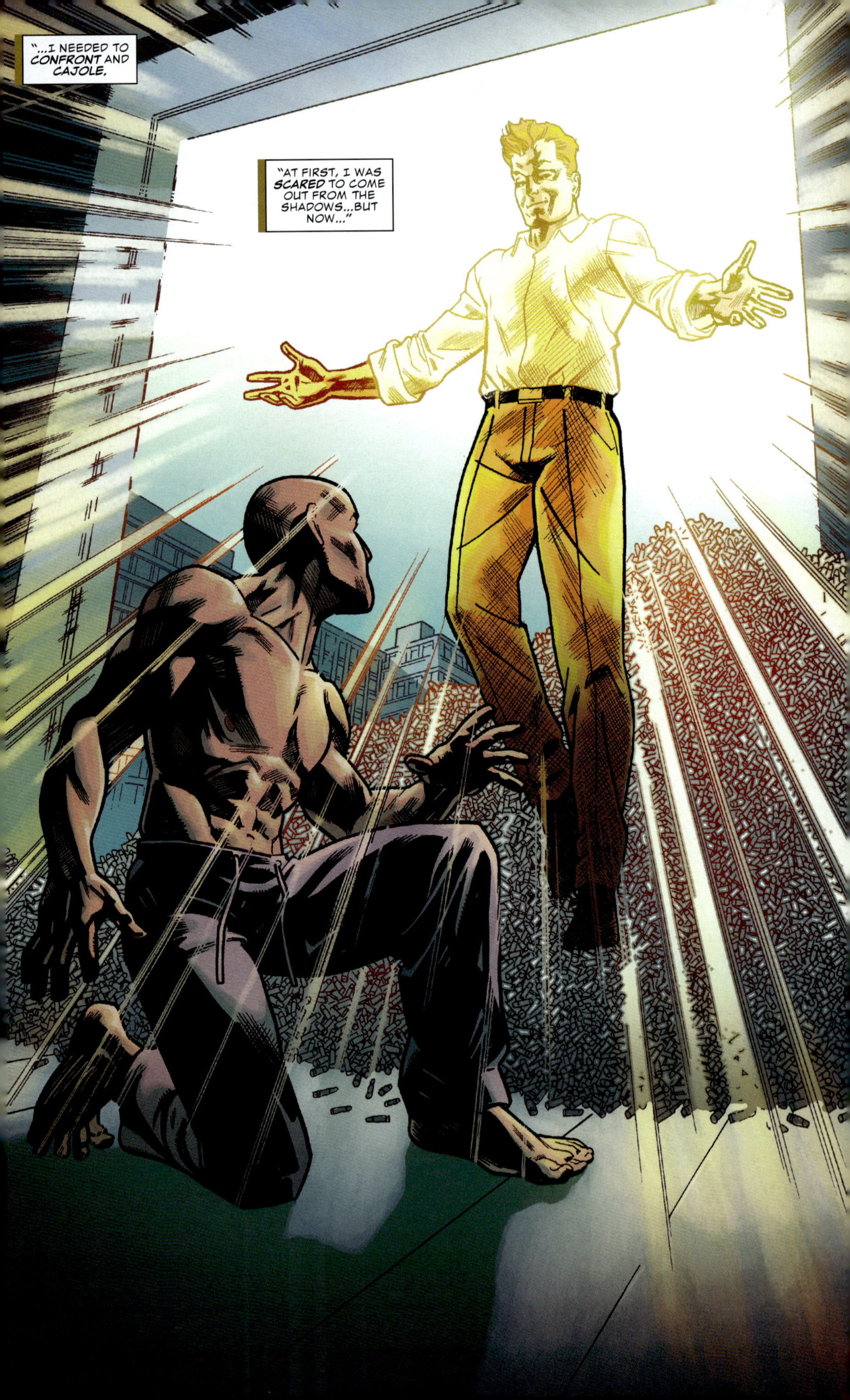
"...I NEEDED TO CONFRONT AND CAJOLE.
"AT FIRST, I WAS SCARED TO COME OUT FROM THE SHADOWS...BUT NOW..."

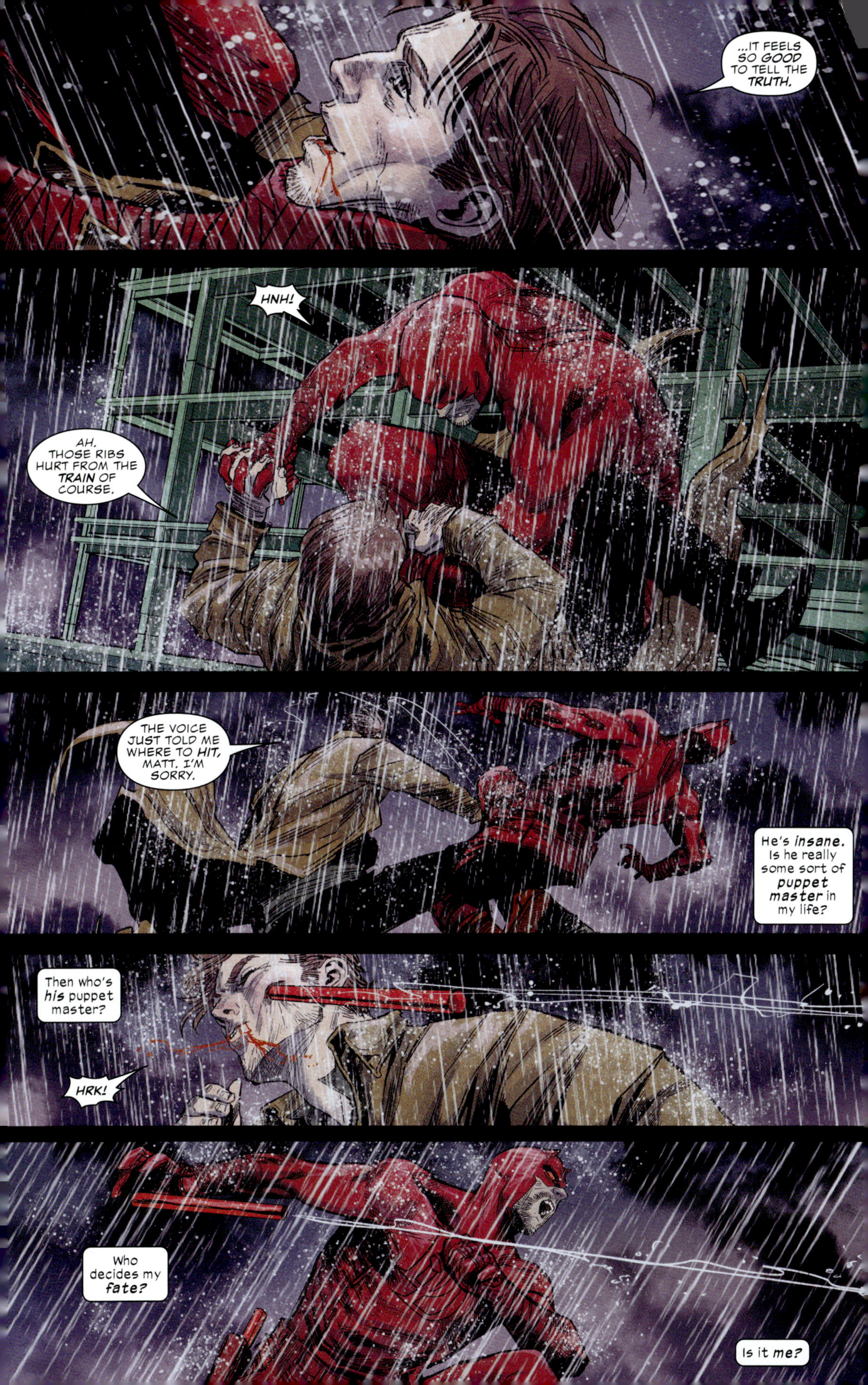
...IT FEELS SO GOOD TO TELL THE TRUTH.
HNH!
AH. THOSE RIBS HURT FROM THE TRAIN OF COURSE.
THE VOICE JUST TOLD ME WHERE TO HIT, MATT. I'M SORRY.
He's insane. Is he really some sort of puppet master in my life?
Then who's his puppet master?
HRK!
Who decides my fate?
Is it me?

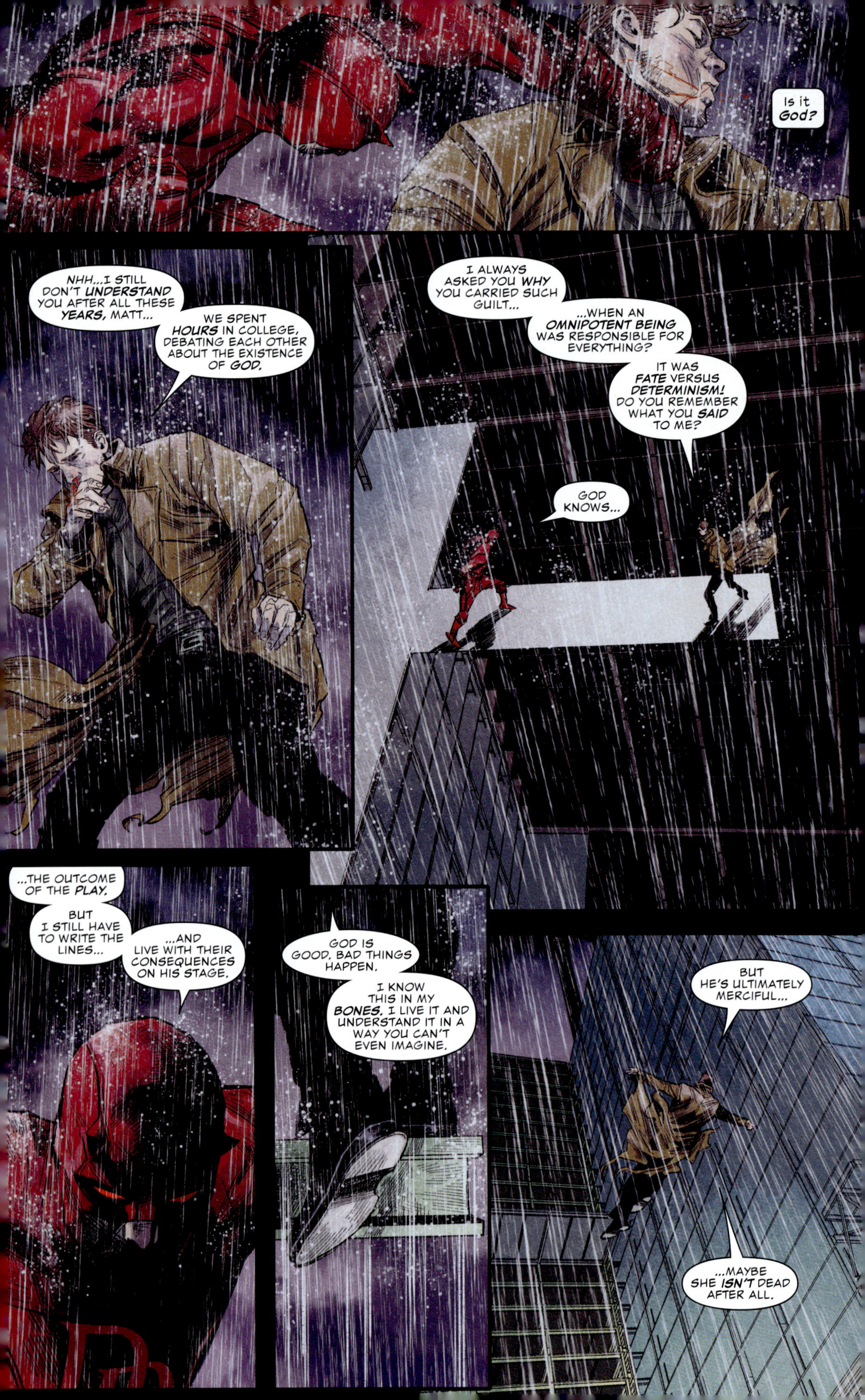

Is it God?
NHH...I STILL DON'T UNDERSTAND YOU AFTER ALL THESE YEARS, MATT...
WE SPENT HOURS IN COLLEGE, DEBATING EACH OTHER ABOUT THE EXISTENCE OF GOD.
I ALWAYS ASKED YOU WHY YOU CARRIED SUCH GUILT...
...WHEN AN OMNIPOTENT BEING WAS RESPONSIBLE FOR EVERYTHING?
IT WAS FATE VERSUS DETERMINISM! DO YOU REMEMBER WHAT YOU SAID TO ME?
GOD KNOWS...
...THE OUTCOME OF THE PLAY.
BUT I STILL HAVE TO WRITE THE LINES...
...AND LIVE WITH THEIR CONSEQUENCES ON HIS STAGE.
GOD IS GOOD. BAD THINGS HAPPEN.
I KNOW THIS IN MY BONES. I LIVE IT AND UNDERSTAND IT IN A WAY YOU CAN'T EVEN IMAGINE.
BUT HE'S ULTIMATELY MERCIFUL...
...MAYBE SHE ISN'T DEAD AFTER ALL.

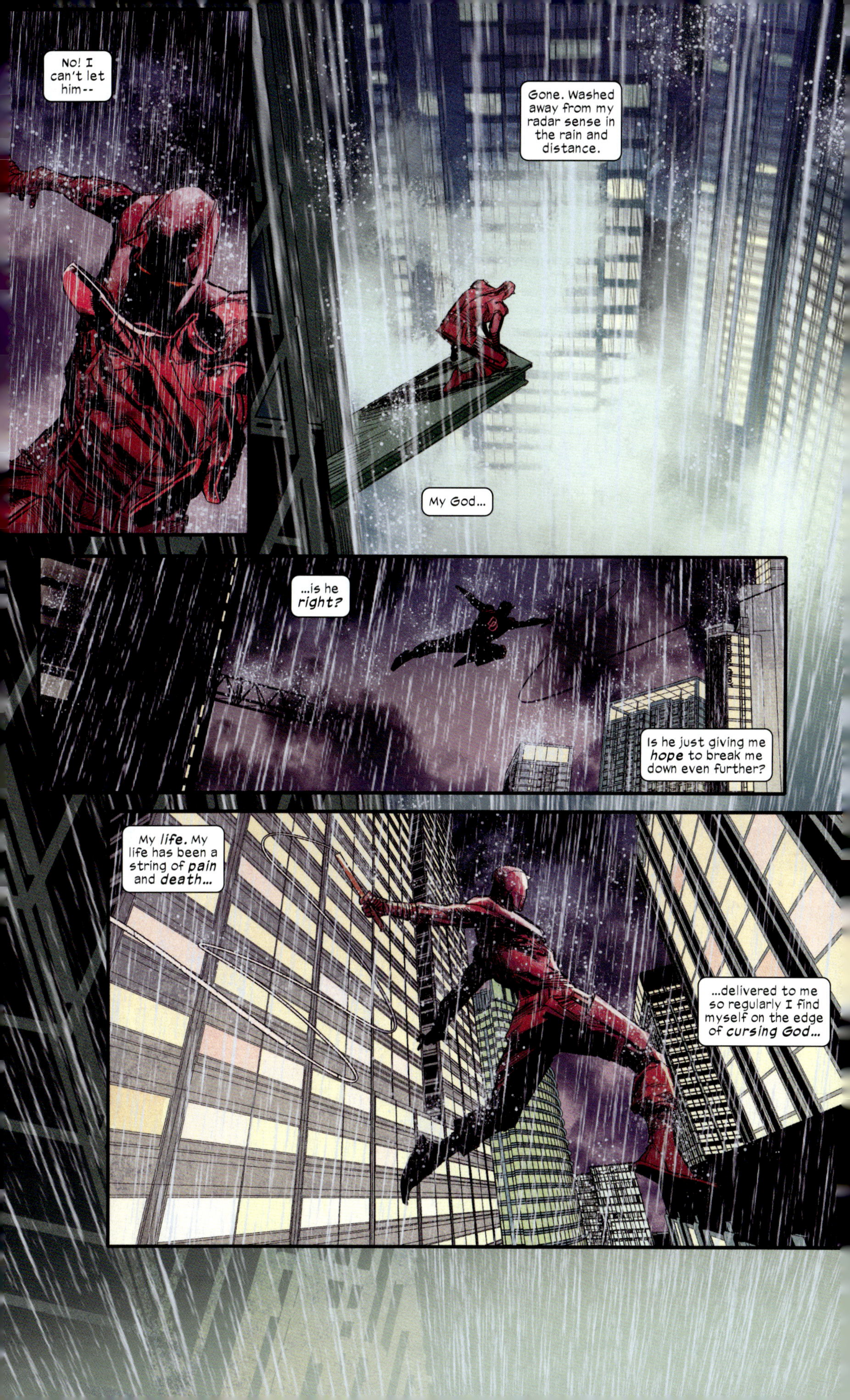
No! I can't let him--
Gone. Washed away from my radar sense in the rain and distance.
My God...
...is he *right?*
Is he just giving me *hope* to break me down even further?
My *life.* My life has been a string of *pain* and *death*...
...delivered to me so regularly I find myself on the edge of *cursing God*...

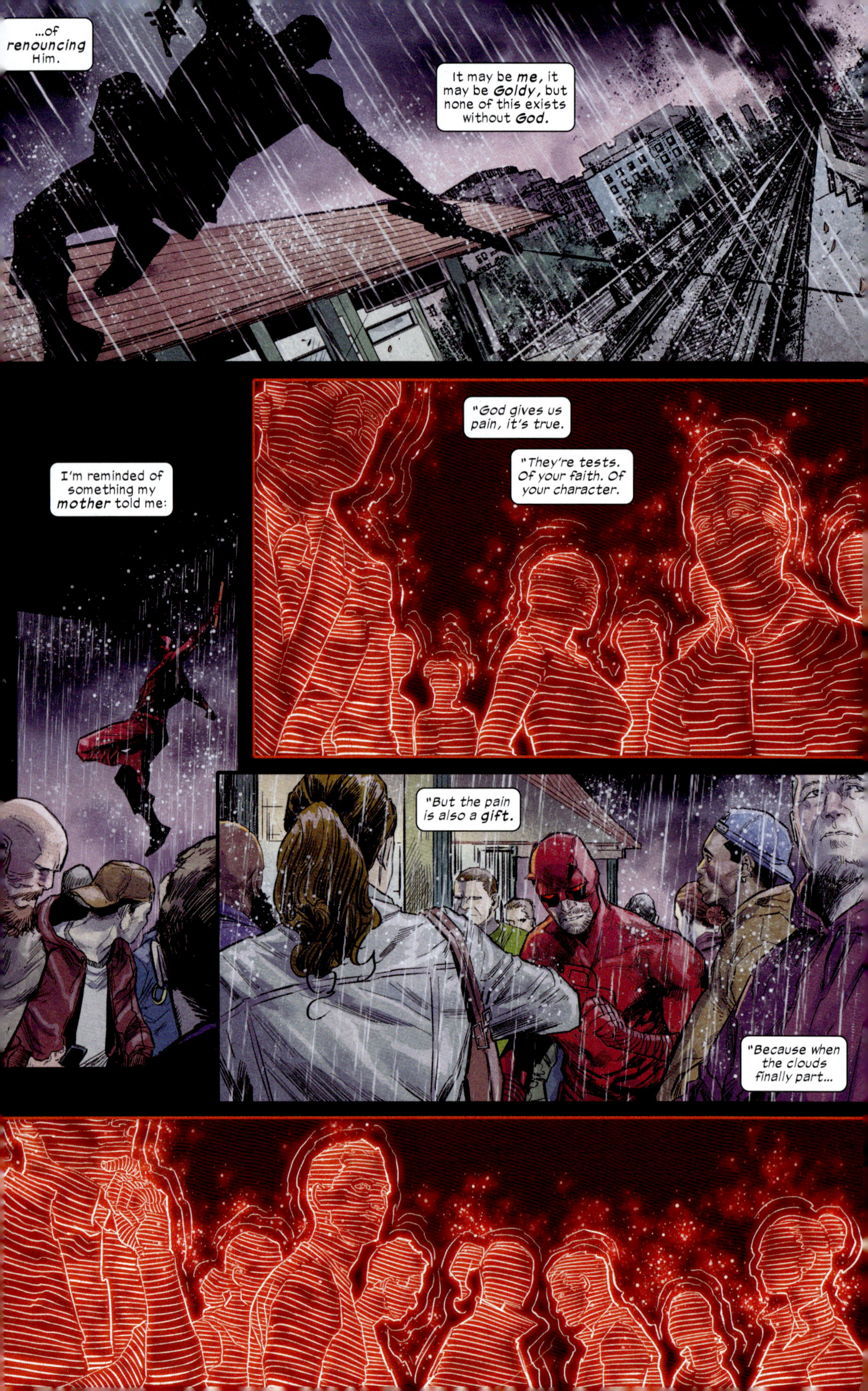

...of renouncing Him.
It may be me, it may be Goldy, but none of this exists without God.
I'm reminded of something my mother told me:
"God gives us pain, it's true.
"They're tests. Of your faith. Of your character.
"But the pain is also a gift.
"Because when the clouds finally part...

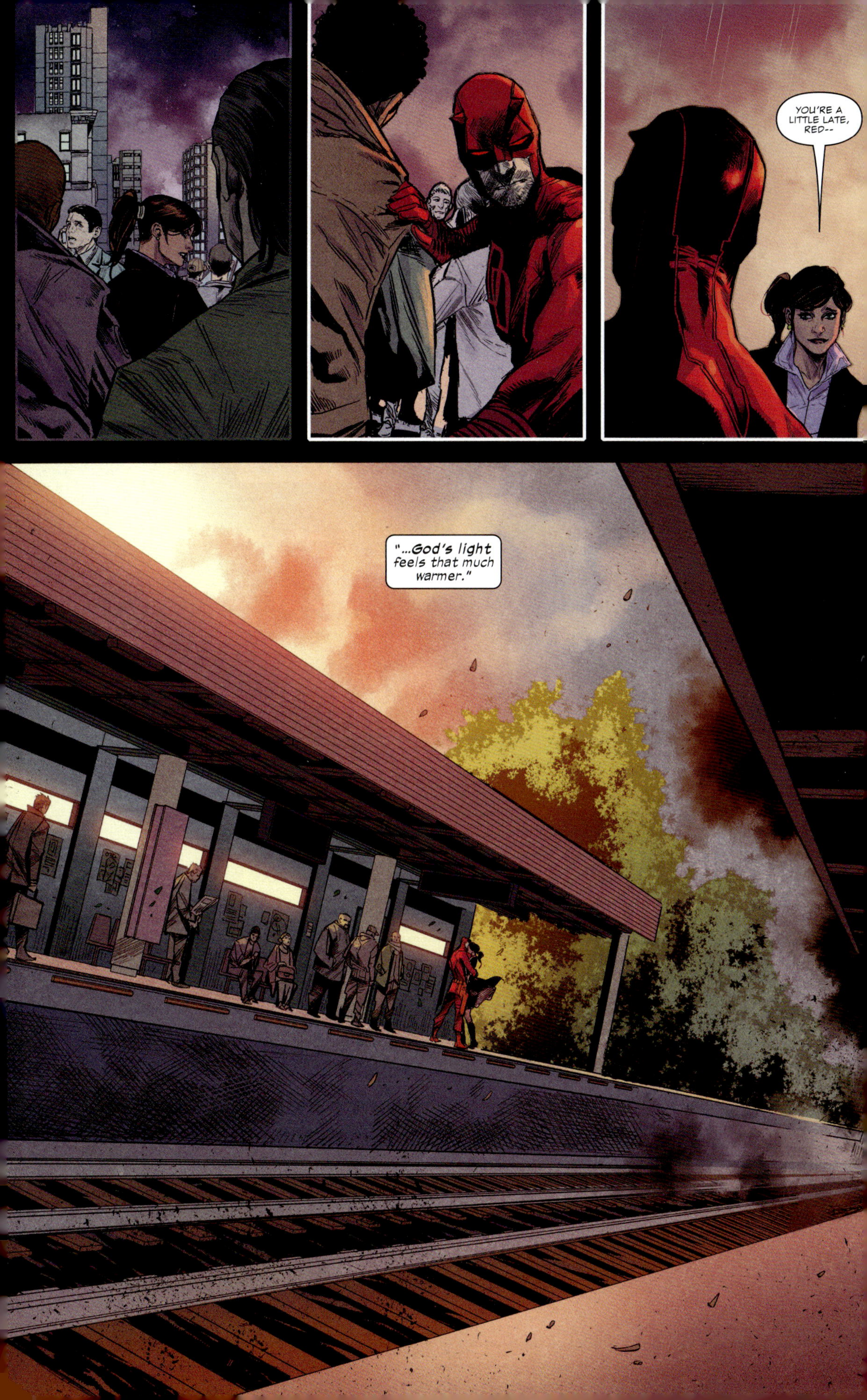
YOU'RE A LITTLE LATE, RED--
"...God's light feels that much warmer."

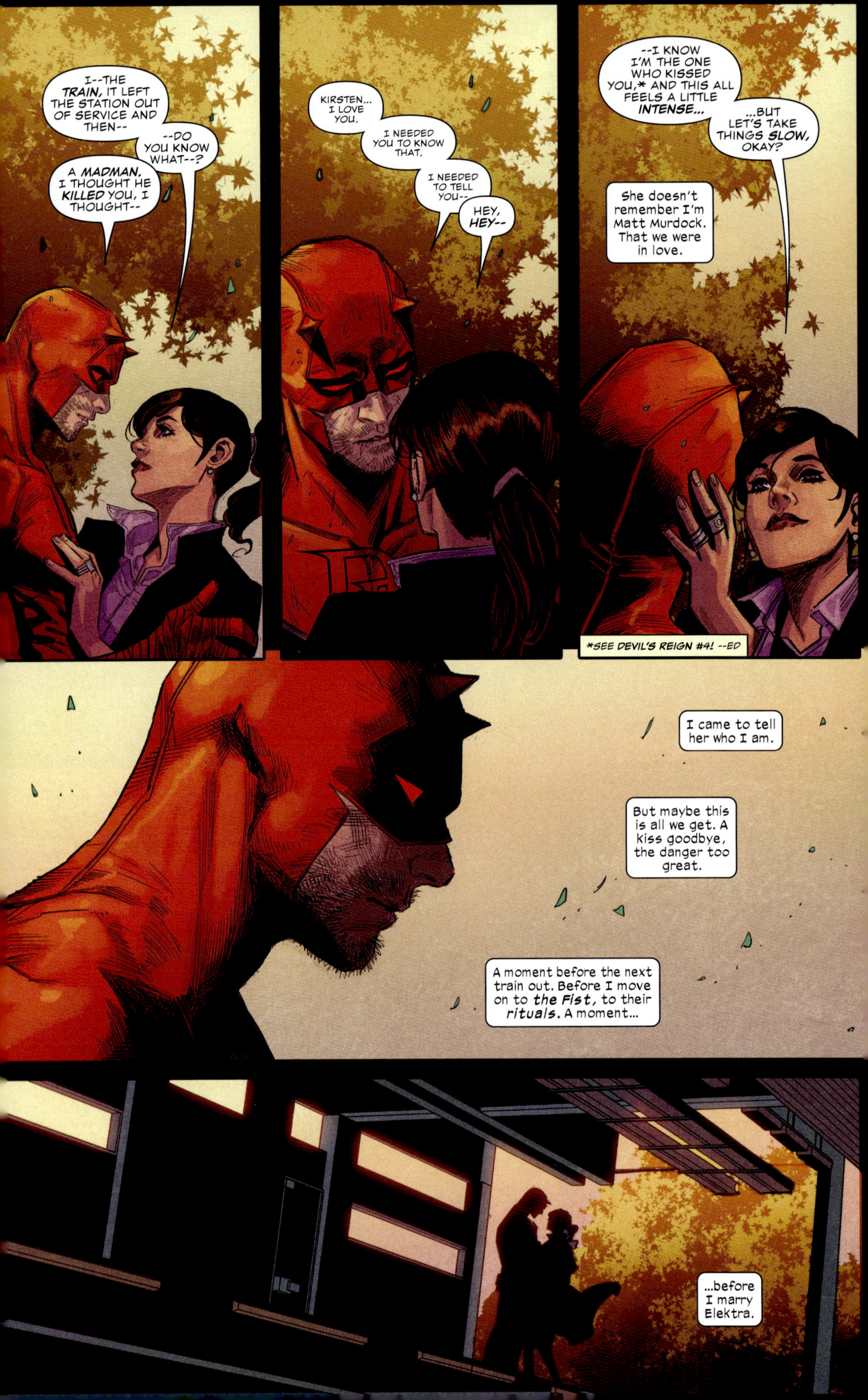
I--THE TRAIN, IT LEFT THE STATION OUT OF SERVICE AND THEN--
--DO YOU KNOW WHAT--?
A MADMAN, I THOUGHT HE KILLED YOU, I THOUGHT--
KIRSTEN... I LOVE YOU.
I NEEDED YOU TO KNOW THAT.
I NEEDED TO TELL YOU--
HEY, HEY--
--I KNOW I'M THE ONE WHO KISSED YOU,* AND THIS ALL FEELS A LITTLE INTENSE...
...BUT LET'S TAKE THINGS SLOW, OKAY?
She doesn't remember I'm Matt Murdock. That we were in love.
*SEE DEVIL'S REIGN #4! --ED
I came to tell her who I am.
But maybe this is all we get. A kiss goodbye, the danger too great.
A moment before the next train out. Before I move on to the Fist, to their rituals. A moment...
...before I marry Elektra.

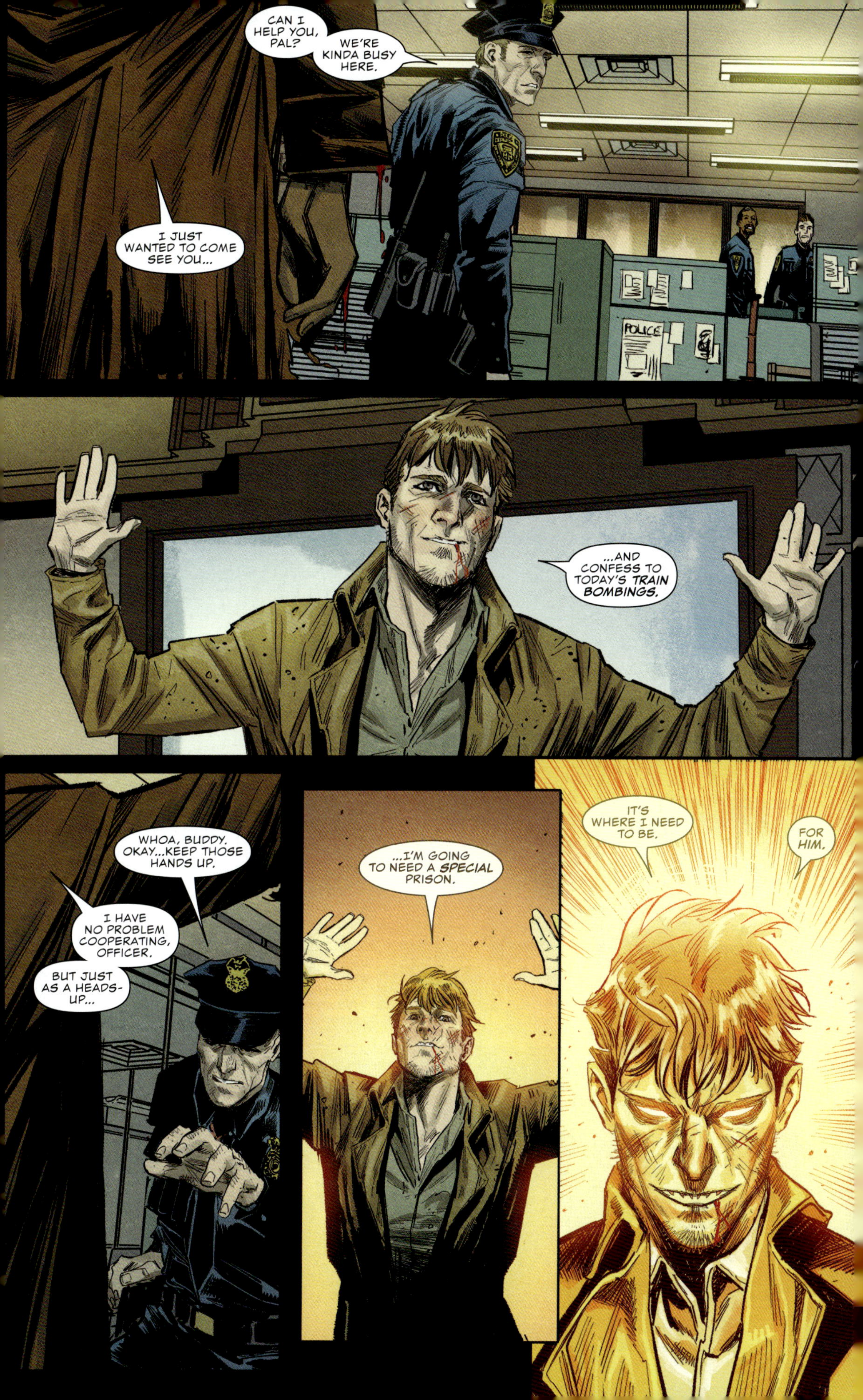
CAN I HELP YOU, PAL?
WE'RE KINDA BUSY HERE.
I JUST WANTED TO COME SEE YOU...
...AND CONFESS TO TODAY'S **TRAIN BOMBINGS.**
WHOA, BUDDY. OKAY...KEEP THOSE HANDS UP.
I HAVE NO PROBLEM COOPERATING, OFFICER.
BUT JUST AS A HEADS-UP...
...I'M GOING TO NEED A **SPECIAL** PRISON.
IT'S WHERE I NEED TO BE.
FOR **HIM.**

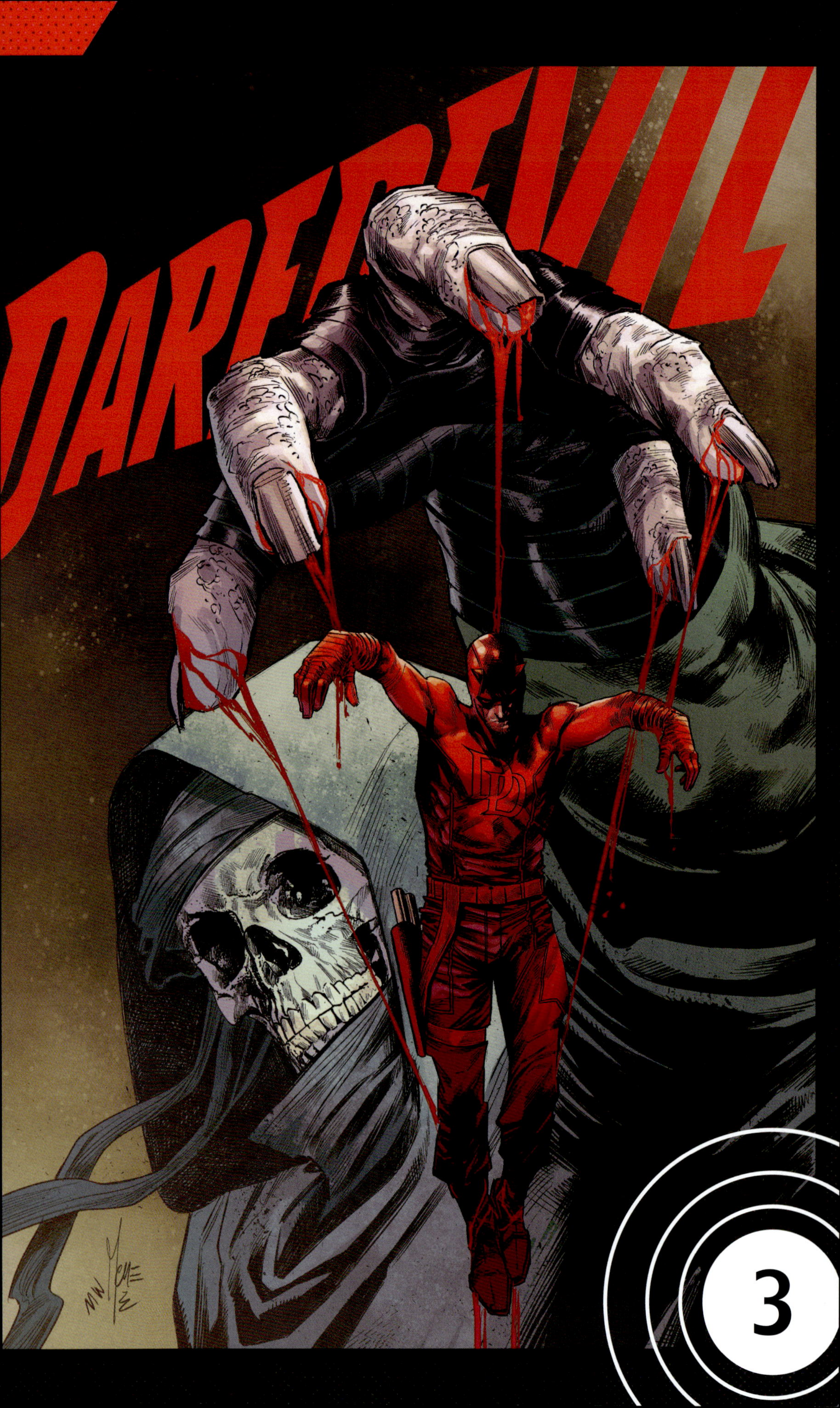
3

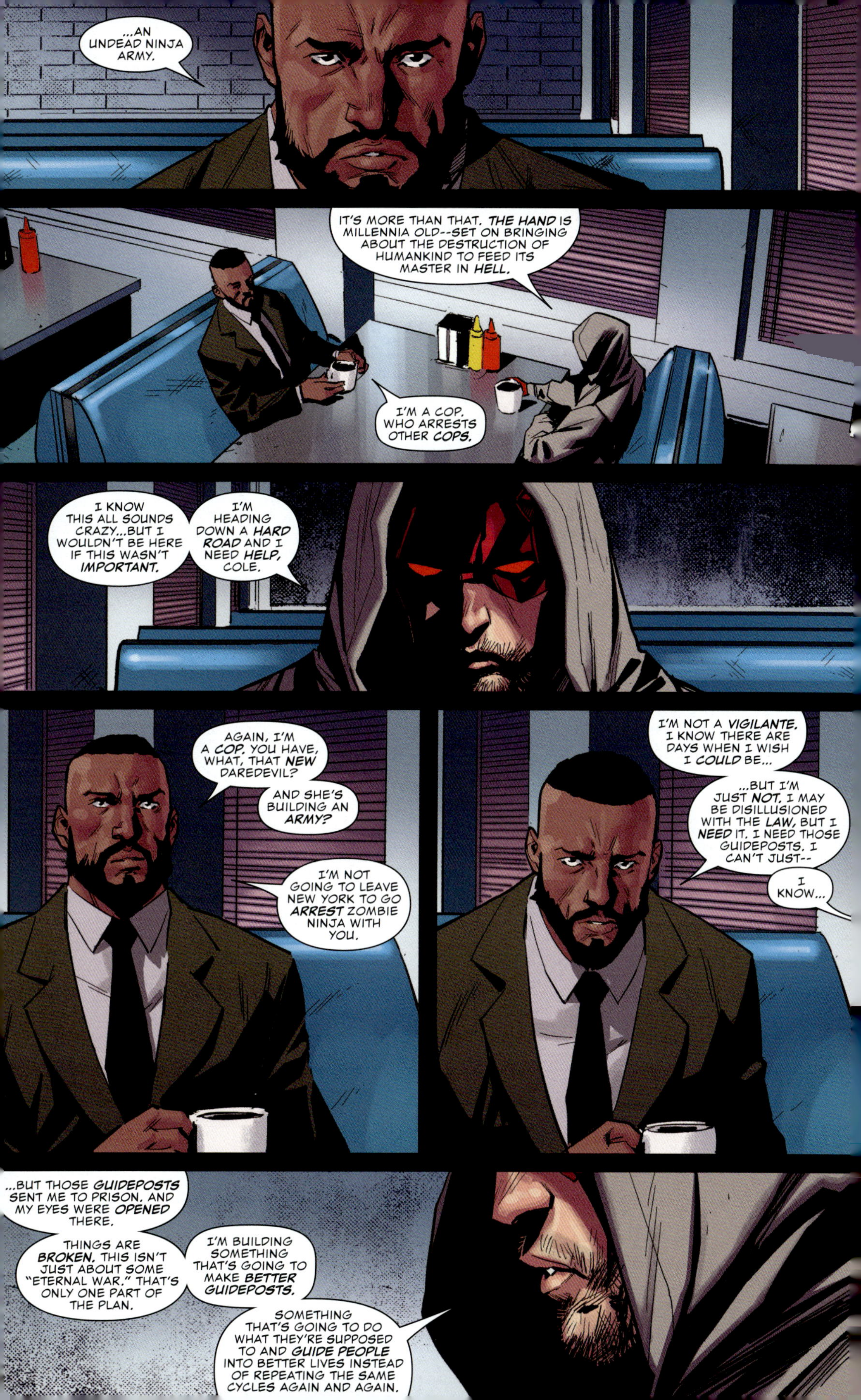
...AN UNDEAD NINJA ARMY.
IT'S MORE THAN THAT. THE HAND IS MILLENNIA OLD--SET ON BRINGING ABOUT THE DESTRUCTION OF HUMANKIND TO FEED ITS MASTER IN HELL.
I'M A COP. WHO ARRESTS OTHER COPS.
I KNOW THIS ALL SOUNDS CRAZY...BUT I WOULDN'T BE HERE IF THIS WASN'T IMPORTANT.
I'M HEADING DOWN A HARD ROAD AND I NEED HELP, COLE.
AGAIN, I'M A COP. YOU HAVE, WHAT, THAT NEW DAREDEVIL?
AND SHE'S BUILDING AN ARMY?
I'M NOT GOING TO LEAVE NEW YORK TO GO ARREST ZOMBIE NINJA WITH YOU.
I'M NOT A VIGILANTE. I KNOW THERE ARE DAYS WHEN I WISH I COULD BE...
...BUT I'M JUST NOT. I MAY BE DISILLUSIONED WITH THE LAW, BUT I NEED IT. I NEED THOSE GUIDEPOSTS. I CAN'T JUST--
I KNOW...
...BUT THOSE GUIDEPOSTS SENT ME TO PRISON. AND MY EYES WERE OPENED THERE.
THINGS ARE BROKEN. THIS ISN'T JUST ABOUT SOME "ETERNAL WAR." THAT'S ONLY ONE PART OF THE PLAN.
I'M BUILDING SOMETHING THAT'S GOING TO MAKE BETTER GUIDEPOSTS.
SOMETHING THAT'S GOING TO DO WHAT THEY'RE SUPPOSED TO AND GUIDE PEOPLE INTO BETTER LIVES INSTEAD OF REPEATING THE SAME CYCLES AGAIN AND AGAIN.

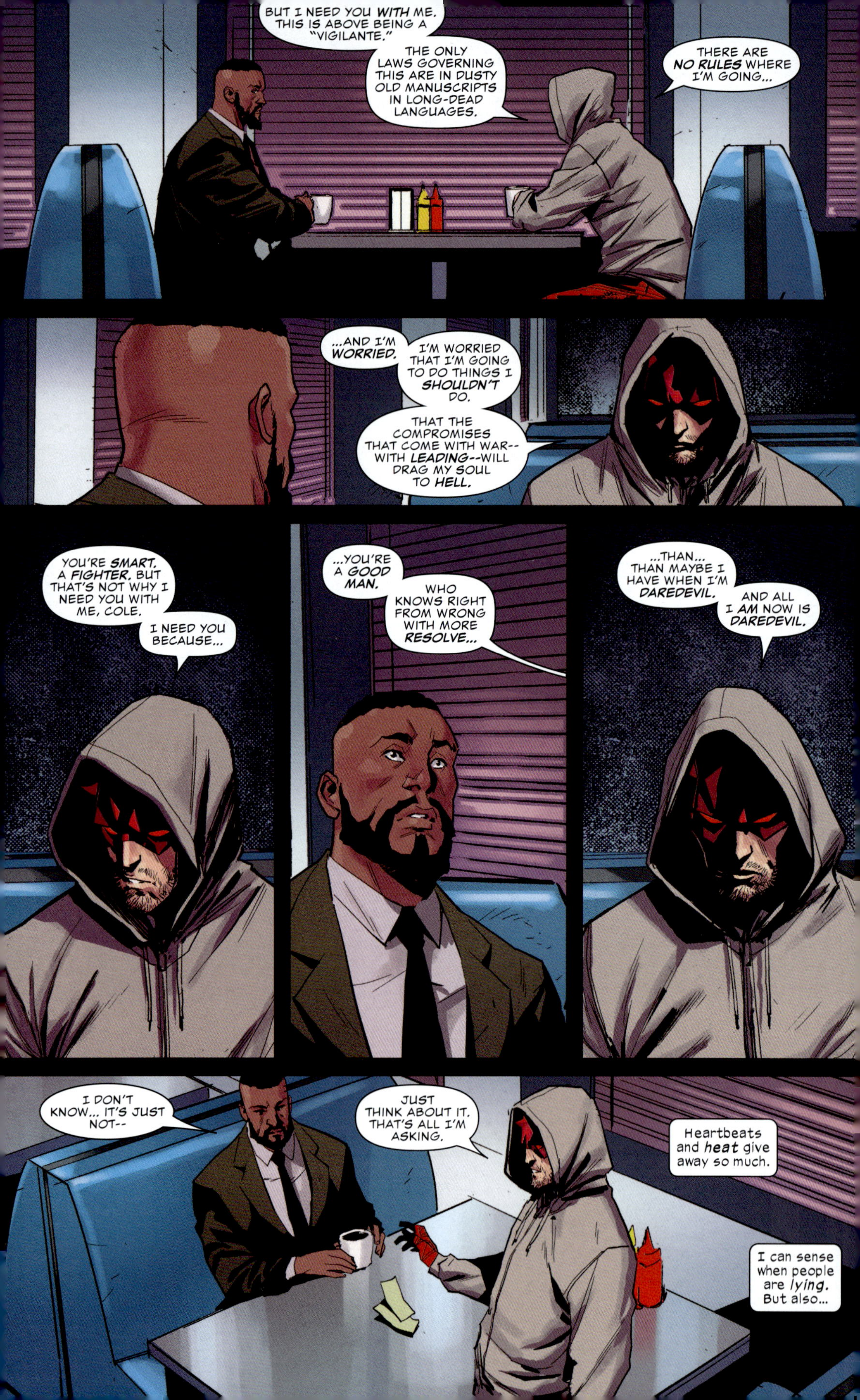

BUT I NEED YOU WITH ME. THIS IS ABOVE BEING A "VIGILANTE."
THE ONLY LAWS GOVERNING THIS ARE IN DUSTY OLD MANUSCRIPTS IN LONG-DEAD LANGUAGES.
THERE ARE NO RULES WHERE I'M GOING...
...AND I'M WORRIED.
I'M WORRIED THAT I'M GOING TO DO THINGS I SHOULDN'T DO.
THAT THE COMPROMISES THAT COME WITH WAR--WITH LEADING--WILL DRAG MY SOUL TO HELL.
YOU'RE SMART. A FIGHTER. BUT THAT'S NOT WHY I NEED YOU WITH ME, COLE.
I NEED YOU BECAUSE...
...YOU'RE A GOOD MAN.
WHO KNOWS RIGHT FROM WRONG WITH MORE RESOLVE...
...THAN... THAN MAYBE I HAVE WHEN I'M DAREDEVIL.
AND ALL I AM NOW IS DAREDEVIL.
I DON'T KNOW... IT'S JUST NOT--
JUST THINK ABOUT IT. THAT'S ALL I'M ASKING.
Heartbeats and heat give away so much.
I can sense when people are lying. But also...

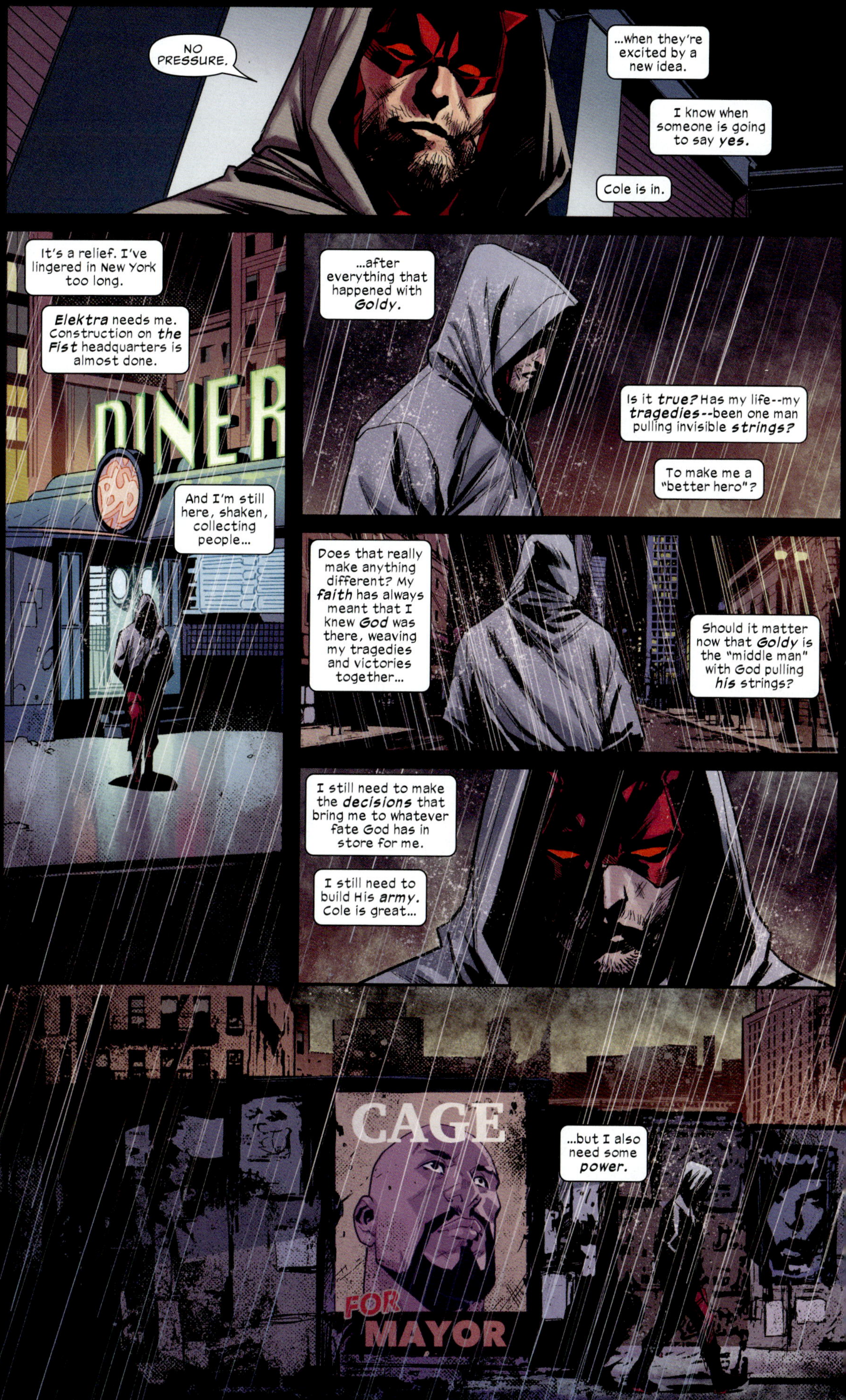
NO PRESSURE.
...when they're excited by a new idea.
I know when someone is going to say yes.
Cole is in.
It's a relief. I've lingered in New York too long.
Elektra needs me. Construction on the Fist headquarters is almost done.
DINER
And I'm still here, shaken, collecting people...
...after everything that happened with Goldy.
Is it true? Has my life--my tragedies--been one man pulling invisible strings?
To make me a "better hero"?
Does that really make anything different? My faith has always meant that I knew God was there, weaving my tragedies and victories together...
Should it matter now that Goldy is the "middle man" with God pulling his strings?
I still need to make the decisions that bring me to whatever fate God has in store for me.
I still need to build His army. Cole is great...
CAGE
FOR MAYOR
...but I also need some power.

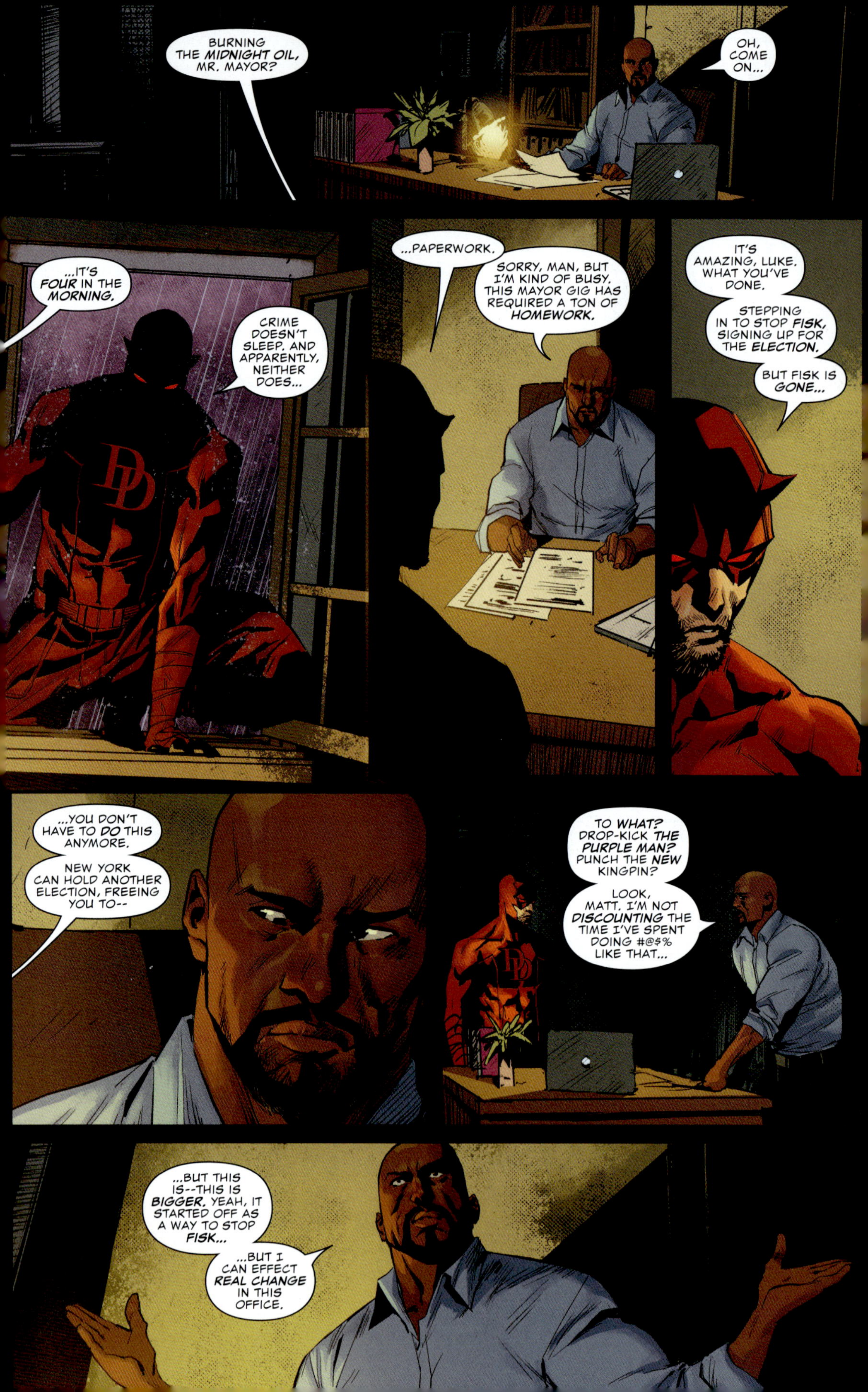
BURNING THE MIDNIGHT OIL, MR. MAYOR?
OH, COME ON...
...IT'S FOUR IN THE MORNING.
CRIME DOESN'T SLEEP. AND APPARENTLY, NEITHER DOES...
...PAPERWORK.
SORRY, MAN, BUT I'M KIND OF BUSY. THIS MAYOR GIG HAS REQUIRED A TON OF HOMEWORK.
IT'S AMAZING, LUKE. WHAT YOU'VE DONE.
STEPPING IN TO STOP FISK, SIGNING UP FOR THE ELECTION.
BUT FISK IS GONE...
...YOU DON'T HAVE TO DO THIS ANYMORE.
NEW YORK CAN HOLD ANOTHER ELECTION, FREEING YOU TO--
TO WHAT? DROP-KICK THE PURPLE MAN? PUNCH THE NEW KINGPIN?
LOOK, MATT. I'M NOT DISCOUNTING THE TIME I'VE SPENT DOING #@$% LIKE THAT...
...BUT THIS IS--THIS IS BIGGER. YEAH, IT STARTED OFF AS A WAY TO STOP FISK...
...BUT I CAN EFFECT REAL CHANGE IN THIS OFFICE.

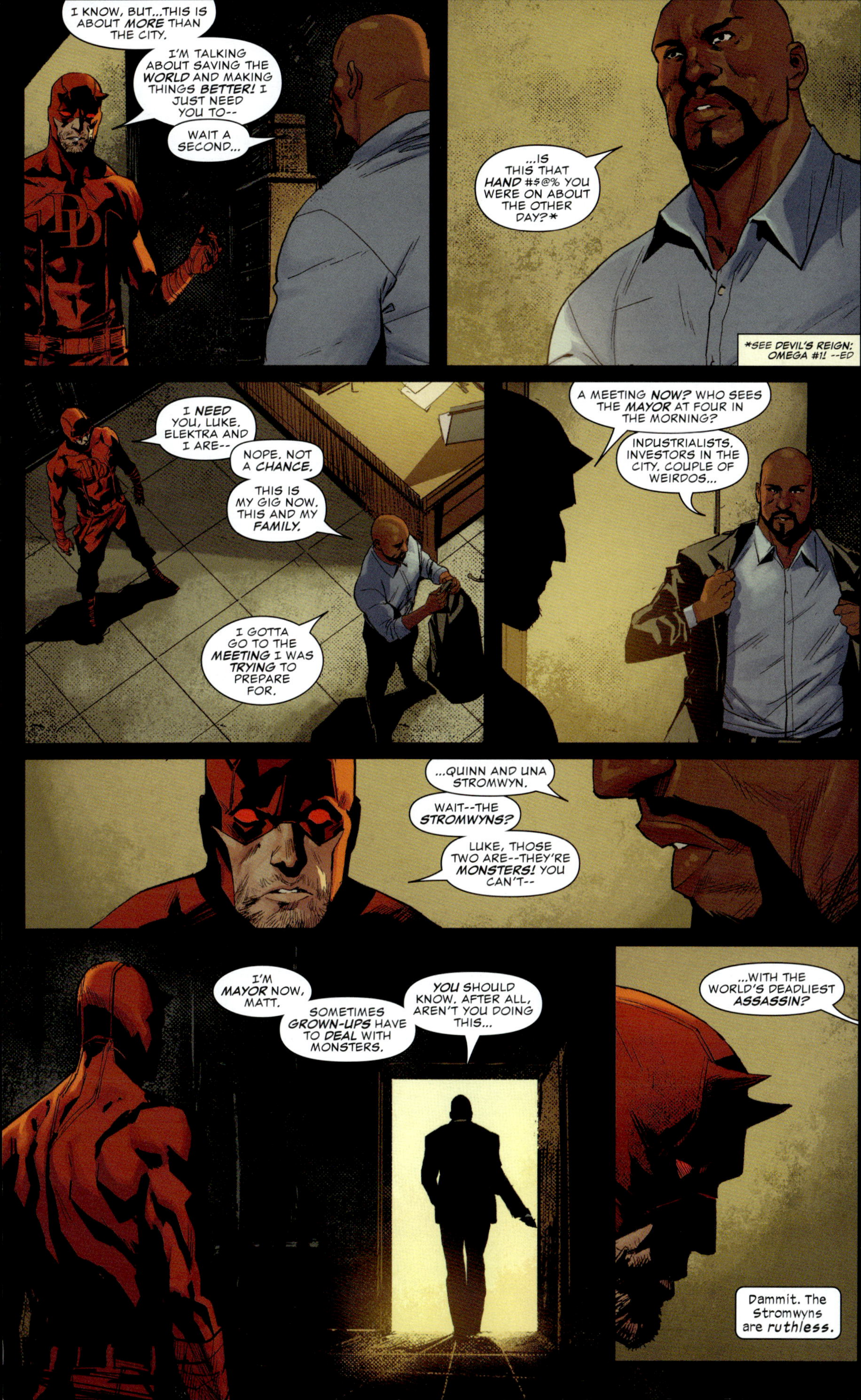
I KNOW, BUT...THIS IS ABOUT MORE THAN THE CITY.
I'M TALKING ABOUT SAVING THE WORLD AND MAKING THINGS BETTER! I JUST NEED YOU TO--
WAIT A SECOND...
...IS THIS THAT HAND #$@% YOU WERE ON ABOUT THE OTHER DAY?*
*SEE DEVIL'S REIGN: OMEGA #1! --ED
I NEED YOU, LUKE. ELEKTRA AND I ARE--
NOPE. NOT A CHANCE.
THIS IS MY GIG NOW. THIS AND MY FAMILY.
I GOTTA GO TO THE MEETING I WAS TRYING TO PREPARE FOR.
A MEETING NOW? WHO SEES THE MAYOR AT FOUR IN THE MORNING?
INDUSTRIALISTS. INVESTORS IN THE CITY. COUPLE OF WEIRDOS...
...QUINN AND UNA STROMWYN.
WAIT--THE STROMWYNS?
LUKE, THOSE TWO ARE--THEY'RE MONSTERS! YOU CAN'T--
I'M MAYOR NOW, MATT.
SOMETIMES GROWN-UPS HAVE TO DEAL WITH MONSTERS.
YOU SHOULD KNOW. AFTER ALL, AREN'T YOU DOING THIS...
...WITH THE WORLD'S DEADLIEST ASSASSIN?
Dammit. The Stromwyns are ruthless.

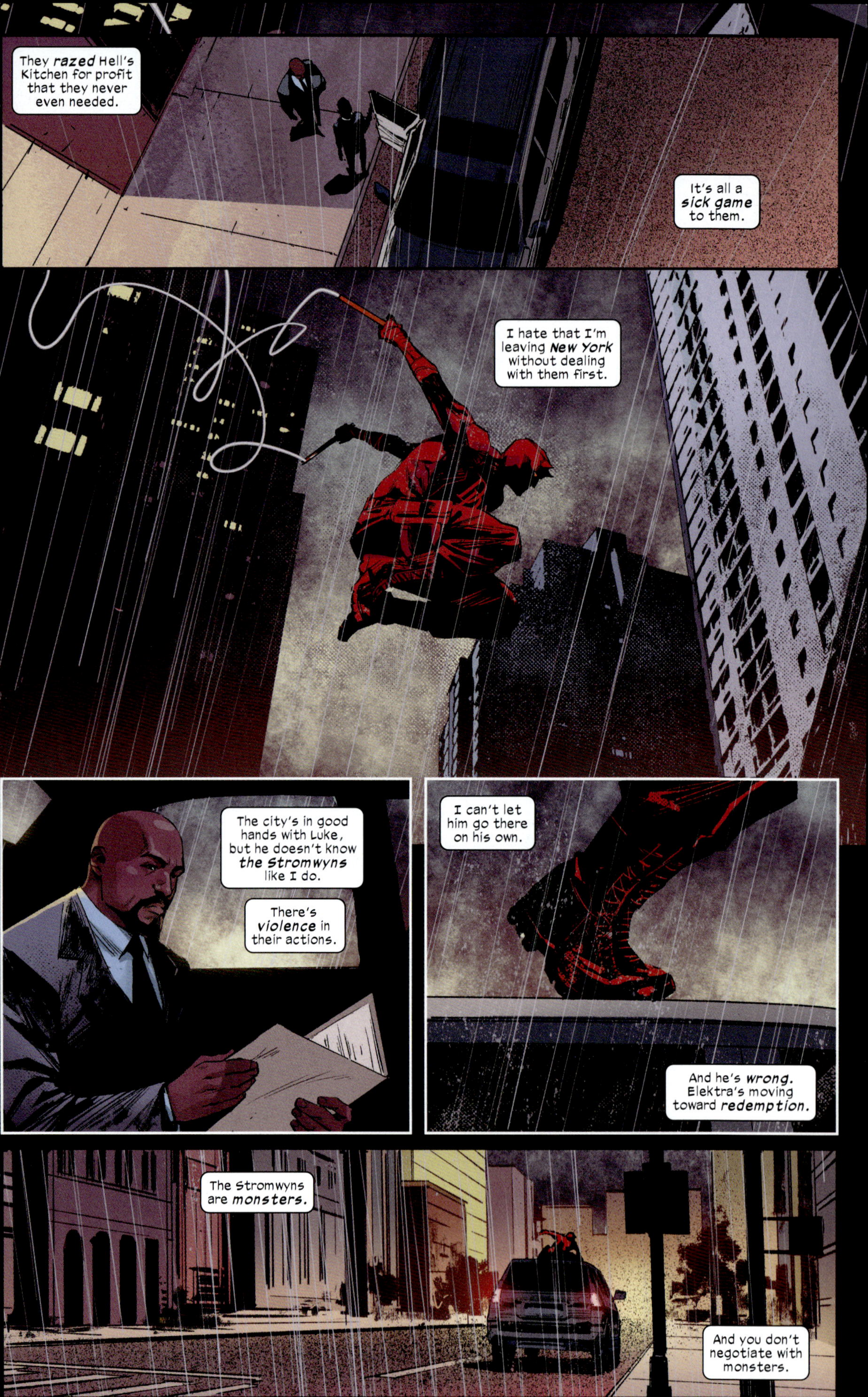
They razed Hell's Kitchen for profit that they never even needed.
It's all a sick game to them.
I hate that I'm leaving New York without dealing with them first.
The city's in good hands with Luke, but he doesn't know the Stromwyns like I do.
There's violence in their actions.
I can't let him go there on his own.
And he's wrong. Elektra's moving toward redemption.
The Stromwyns are monsters.
And you don't negotiate with monsters.

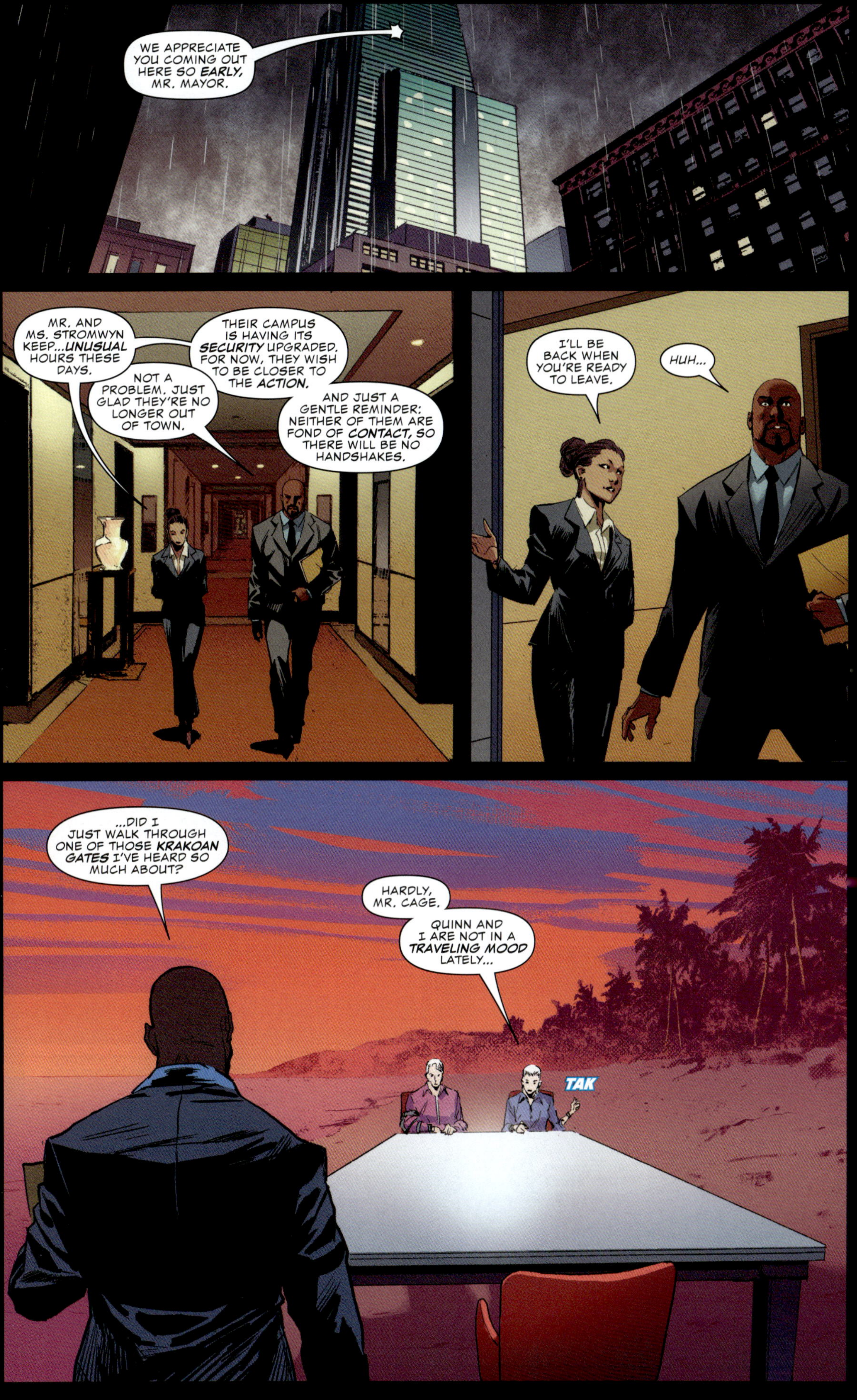
WE APPRECIATE YOU COMING OUT HERE SO EARLY, MR. MAYOR.
MR. AND MS. STROMWYN KEEP...UNUSUAL HOURS THESE DAYS.
THEIR CAMPUS IS HAVING ITS SECURITY UPGRADED. FOR NOW, THEY WISH TO BE CLOSER TO THE ACTION.
NOT A PROBLEM. JUST GLAD THEY'RE NO LONGER OUT OF TOWN.
AND JUST A GENTLE REMINDER: NEITHER OF THEM ARE FOND OF CONTACT, SO THERE WILL BE NO HANDSHAKES.
I'LL BE BACK WHEN YOU'RE READY TO LEAVE.
HUH...
...DID I JUST WALK THROUGH ONE OF THOSE KRAKOAN GATES I'VE HEARD SO MUCH ABOUT?
HARDLY, MR. CAGE.
QUINN AND I ARE NOT IN A TRAVELING MOOD LATELY...
TAK

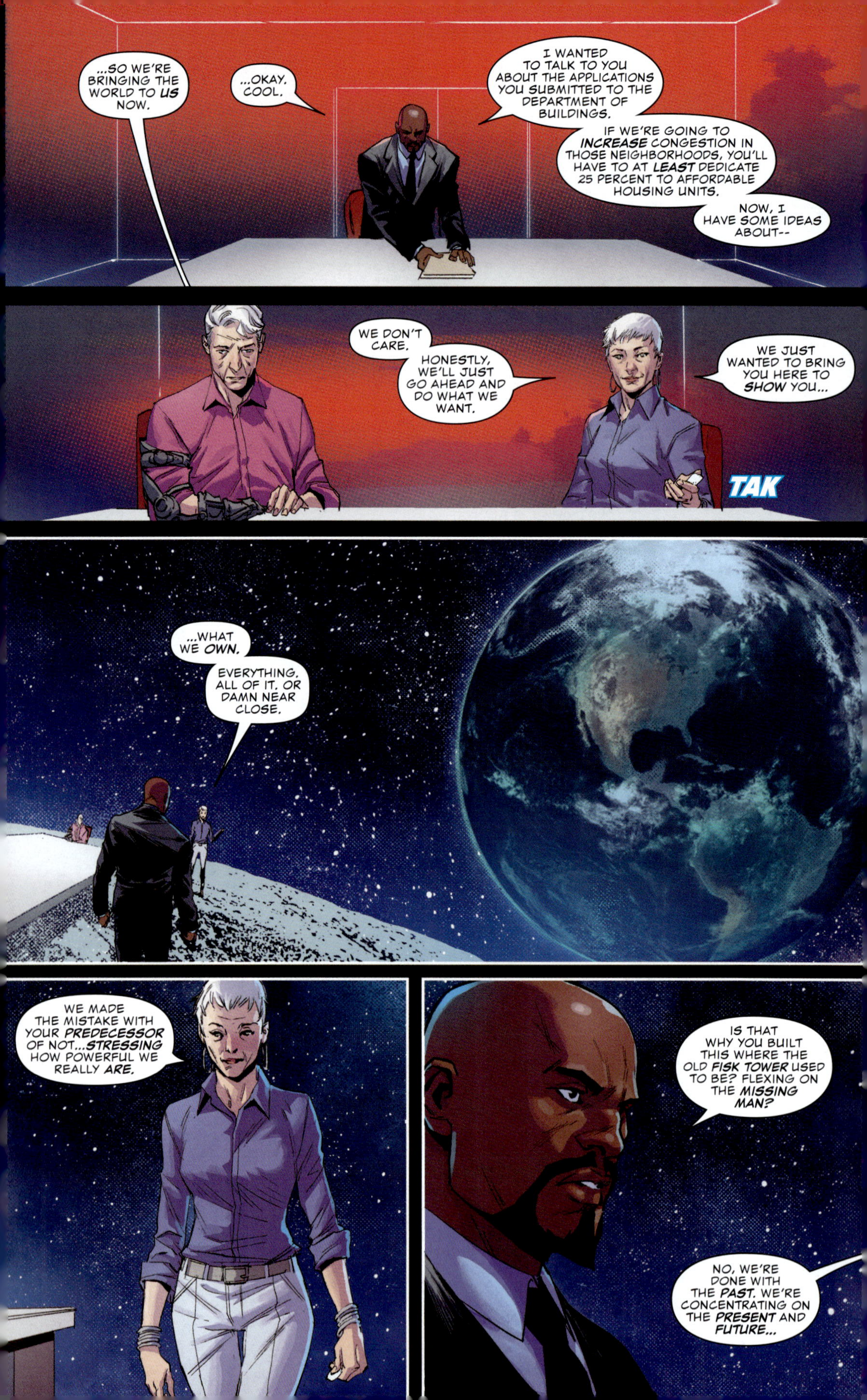
...SO WE'RE BRINGING THE WORLD TO US NOW.
...OKAY. COOL.
I WANTED TO TALK TO YOU ABOUT THE APPLICATIONS YOU SUBMITTED TO THE DEPARTMENT OF BUILDINGS.
IF WE'RE GOING TO INCREASE CONGESTION IN THOSE NEIGHBORHOODS, YOU'LL HAVE TO AT LEAST DEDICATE 25 PERCENT TO AFFORDABLE HOUSING UNITS.
NOW, I HAVE SOME IDEAS ABOUT--
WE DON'T CARE.
HONESTLY, WE'LL JUST GO AHEAD AND DO WHAT WE WANT.
WE JUST WANTED TO BRING YOU HERE TO SHOW YOU...
TAK
...WHAT WE OWN.
EVERYTHING. ALL OF IT. OR DAMN NEAR CLOSE.
WE MADE THE MISTAKE WITH YOUR PREDECESSOR OF NOT...STRESSING HOW POWERFUL WE REALLY ARE.
IS THAT WHY YOU BUILT THIS WHERE THE OLD FISK TOWER USED TO BE? FLEXING ON THE MISSING MAN?
NO, WE'RE DONE WITH THE PAST. WE'RE CONCENTRATING ON THE PRESENT AND FUTURE...

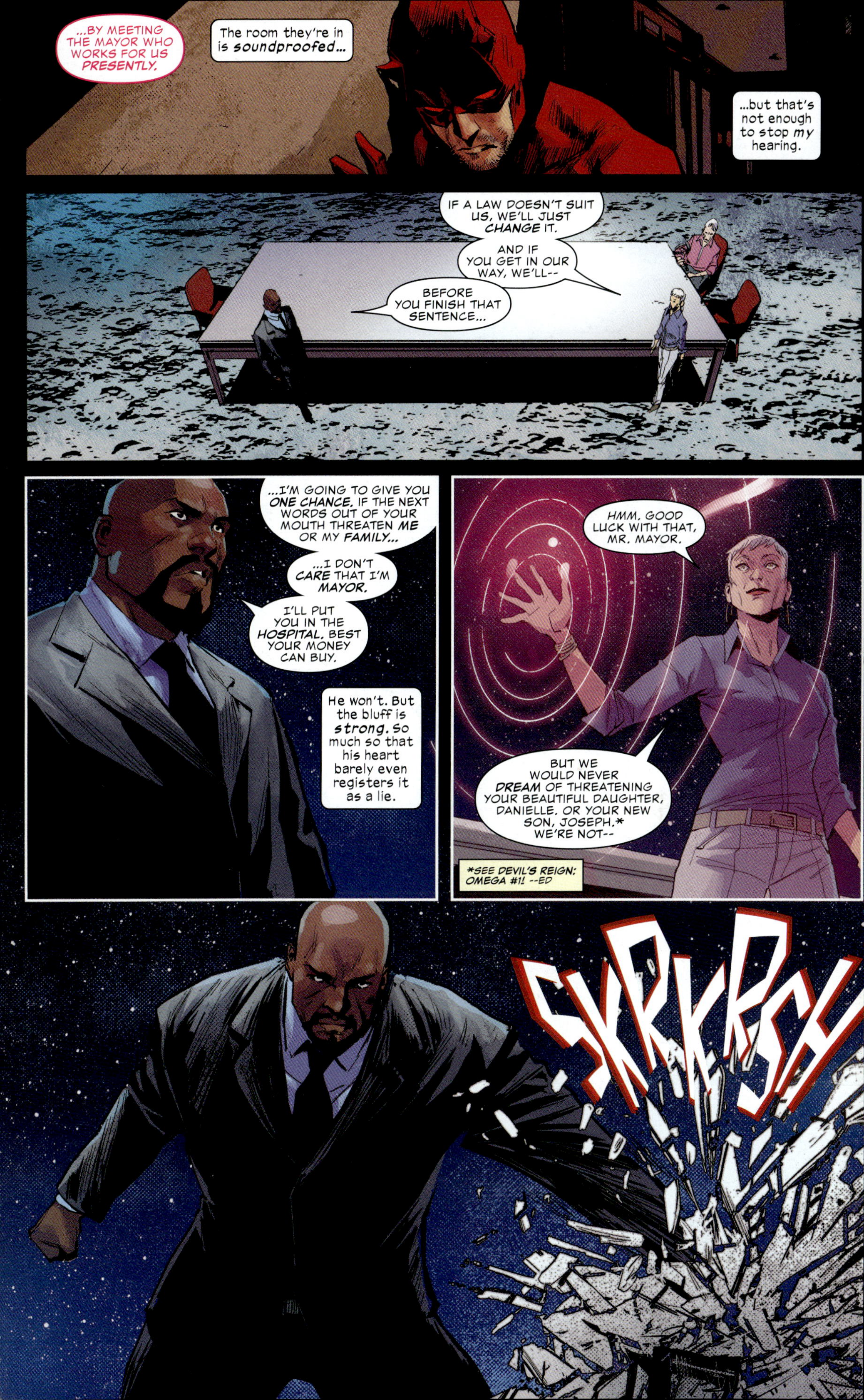
...BY MEETING THE MAYOR WHO WORKS FOR US PRESENTLY.
The room they're in is soundproofed...
...but that's not enough to stop my hearing.
IF A LAW DOESN'T SUIT US, WE'LL JUST CHANGE IT.
AND IF YOU GET IN OUR WAY, WE'LL--
BEFORE YOU FINISH THAT SENTENCE...
...I'M GOING TO GIVE YOU ONE CHANCE. IF THE NEXT WORDS OUT OF YOUR MOUTH THREATEN ME OR MY FAMILY...
...I DON'T CARE THAT I'M MAYOR.
I'LL PUT YOU IN THE HOSPITAL. BEST YOUR MONEY CAN BUY.
He won't. But the bluff is strong. So much so that his heart barely even registers it as a lie.
HMM. GOOD LUCK WITH THAT, MR. MAYOR.
BUT WE WOULD NEVER DREAM OF THREATENING YOUR BEAUTIFUL DAUGHTER, DANIELLE, OR YOUR NEW SON, JOSEPH.* WE'RE NOT--
*SEE DEVIL'S REIGN: OMEGA #1! --ED
SKRKRSH

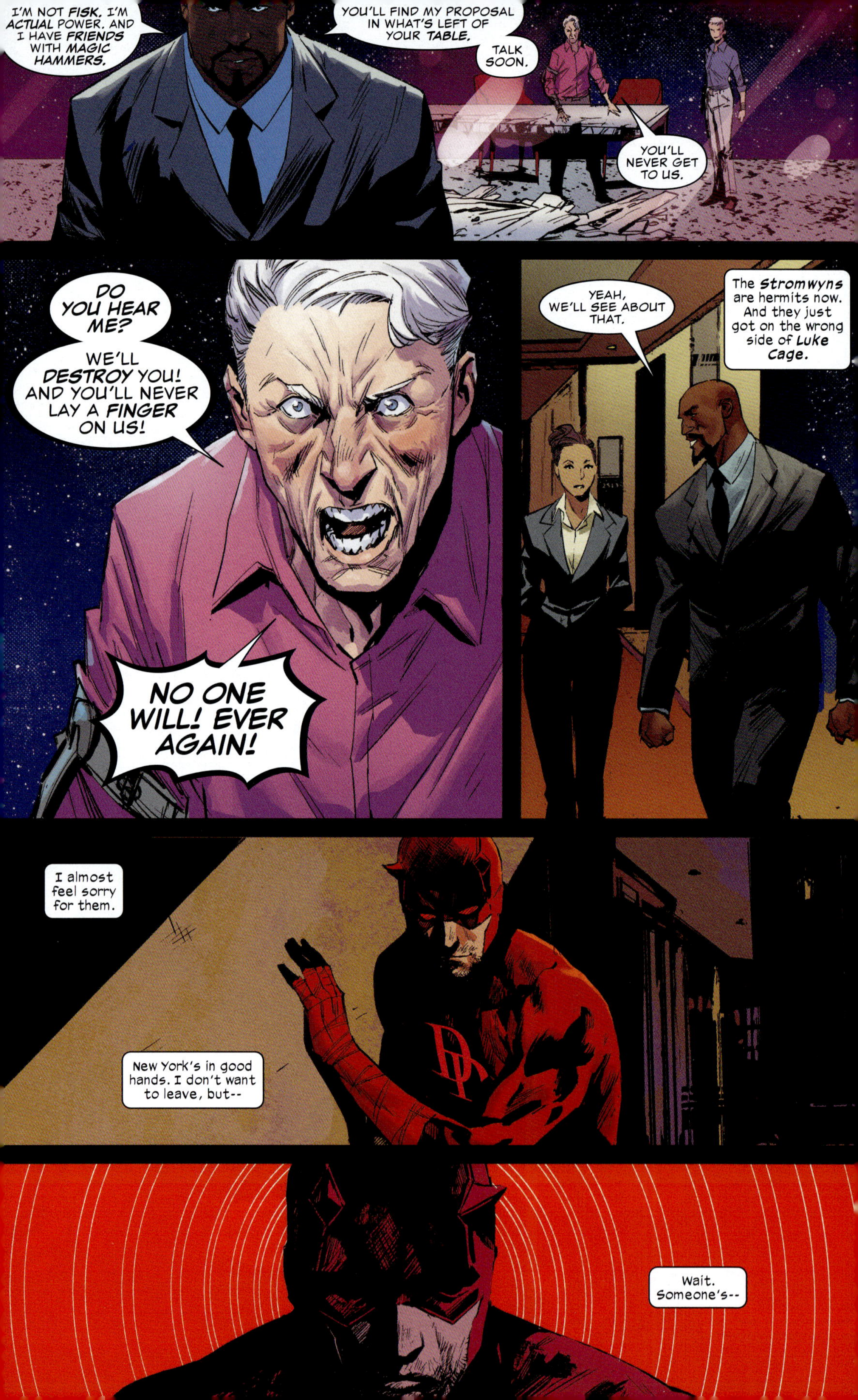

I'M NOT FISK. I'M ACTUAL POWER. AND I HAVE FRIENDS WITH MAGIC HAMMERS.
YOU'LL FIND MY PROPOSAL IN WHAT'S LEFT OF YOUR TABLE.
TALK SOON.
YOU'LL NEVER GET TO US.
DO YOU HEAR ME?
WE'LL DESTROY YOU! AND YOU'LL NEVER LAY A FINGER ON US!
NO ONE WILL! EVER AGAIN!
YEAH, WE'LL SEE ABOUT THAT.
The Stromwyns are hermits now. And they just got on the wrong side of Luke Cage.
I almost feel sorry for them.
New York's in good hands. I don't want to leave, but--
Wait. Someone's--

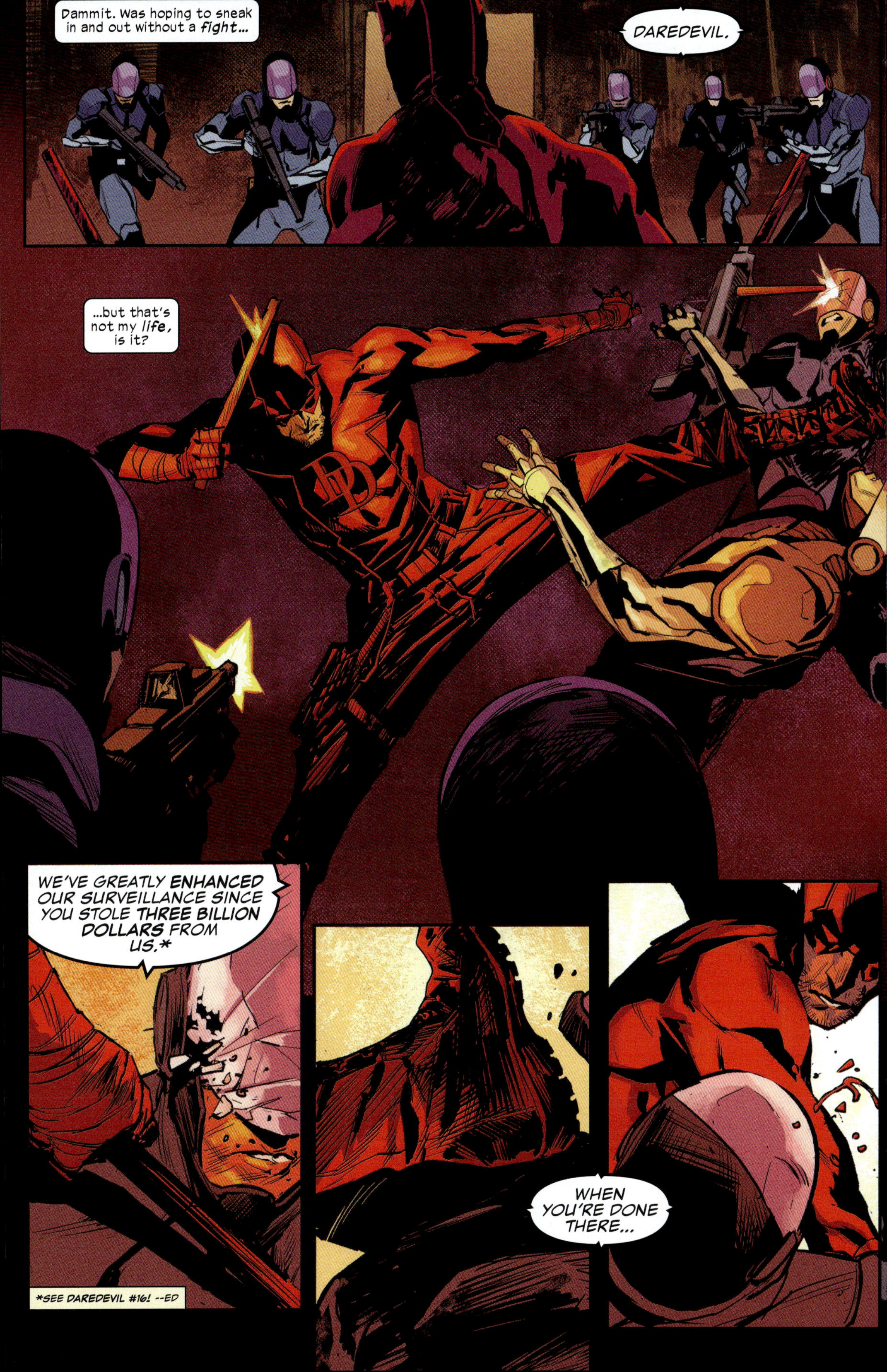

Dammit. Was hoping to sneak in and out without a *fight*...
DAREDEVIL.
...but that's not my *life*, is it?
WE'VE GREATLY **ENHANCED** OUR SURVEILLANCE SINCE YOU STOLE **THREE BILLION DOLLARS** FROM US.*
*SEE DAREDEVIL #16! --ED
WHEN YOU'RE DONE THERE...

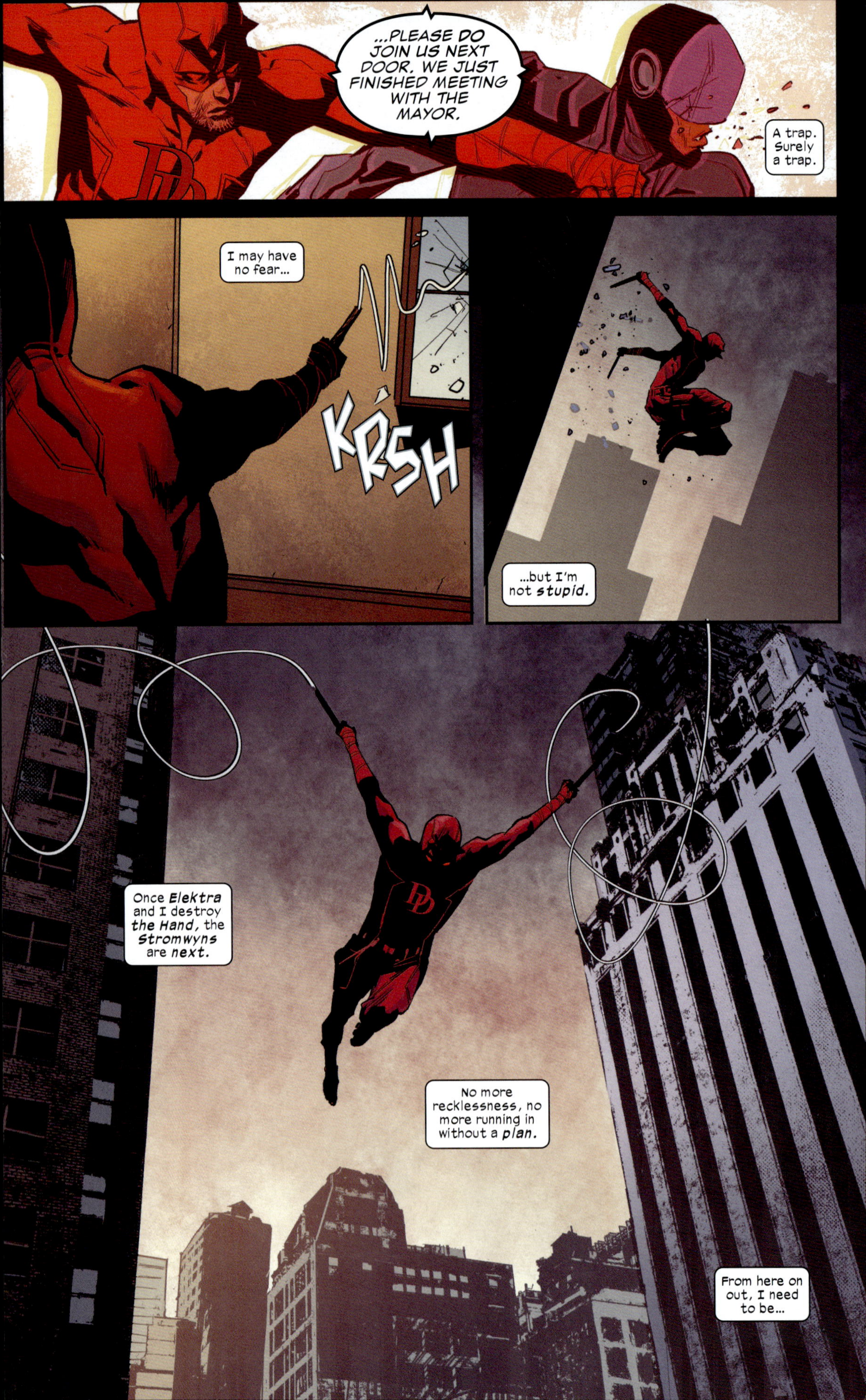
...PLEASE DO JOIN US NEXT DOOR. WE JUST FINISHED MEETING WITH THE MAYOR.
A trap. Surely a trap.
I may have no fear...
KRSH
...but I'm not *stupid*.
Once **Elektra** and I destroy **the Hand**, the **Stromwyns** are **next**.
No more recklessness, no more running in without a *plan*.
From here on out, I need to be...

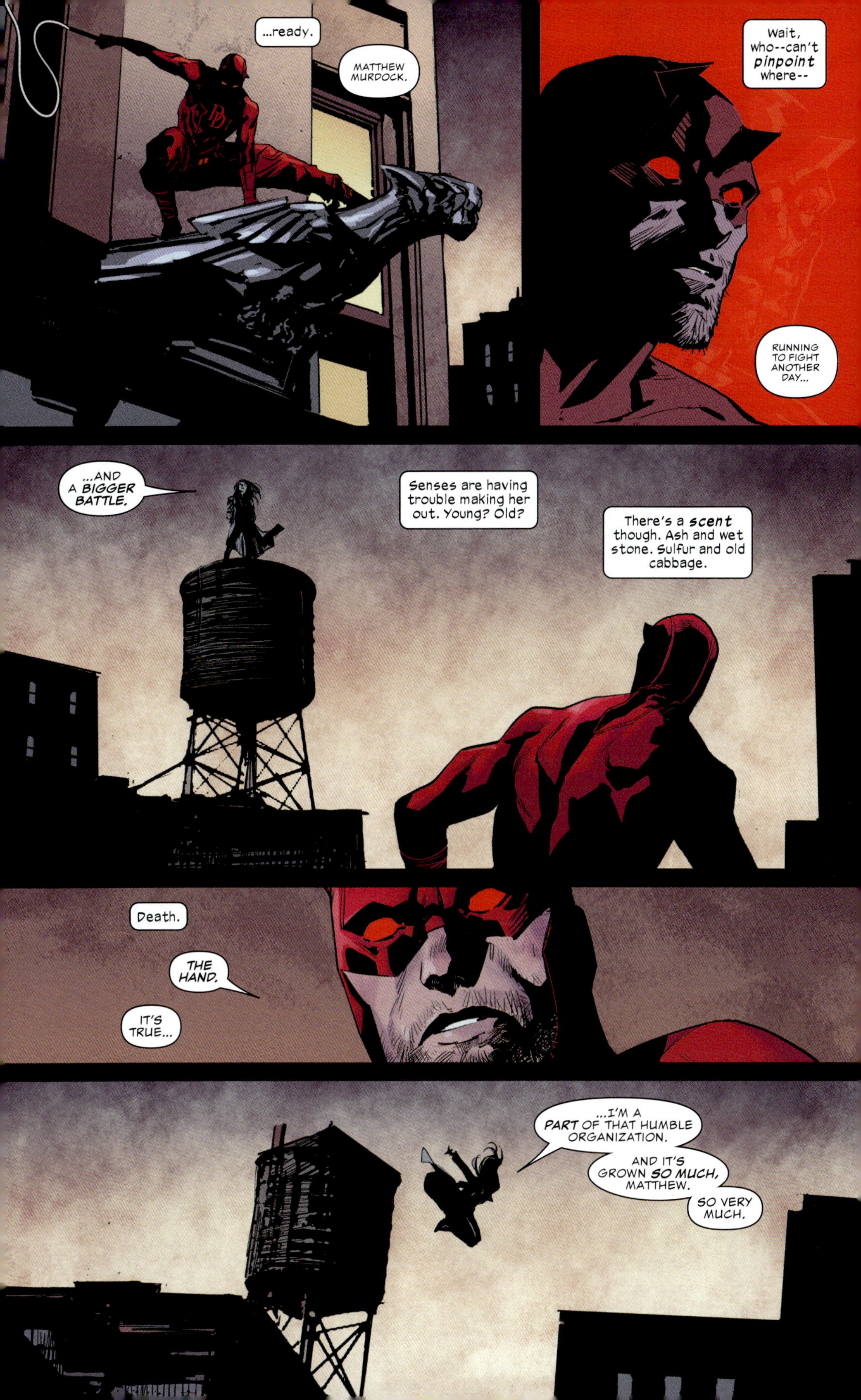

...ready.
MATTHEW MURDOCK.
Wait, who--can't *pinpoint* where--
RUNNING TO FIGHT ANOTHER DAY...
...AND A ***BIGGER BATTLE.***
Senses are having trouble making her out. Young? Old?
There's a ***scent*** though. Ash and wet stone. Sulfur and old cabbage.
Death.
THE HAND.
IT'S TRUE...
...I'M A ***PART*** OF THAT HUMBLE ORGANIZATION.
AND IT'S GROWN ***SO MUCH,*** MATTHEW.
SO VERY MUCH.

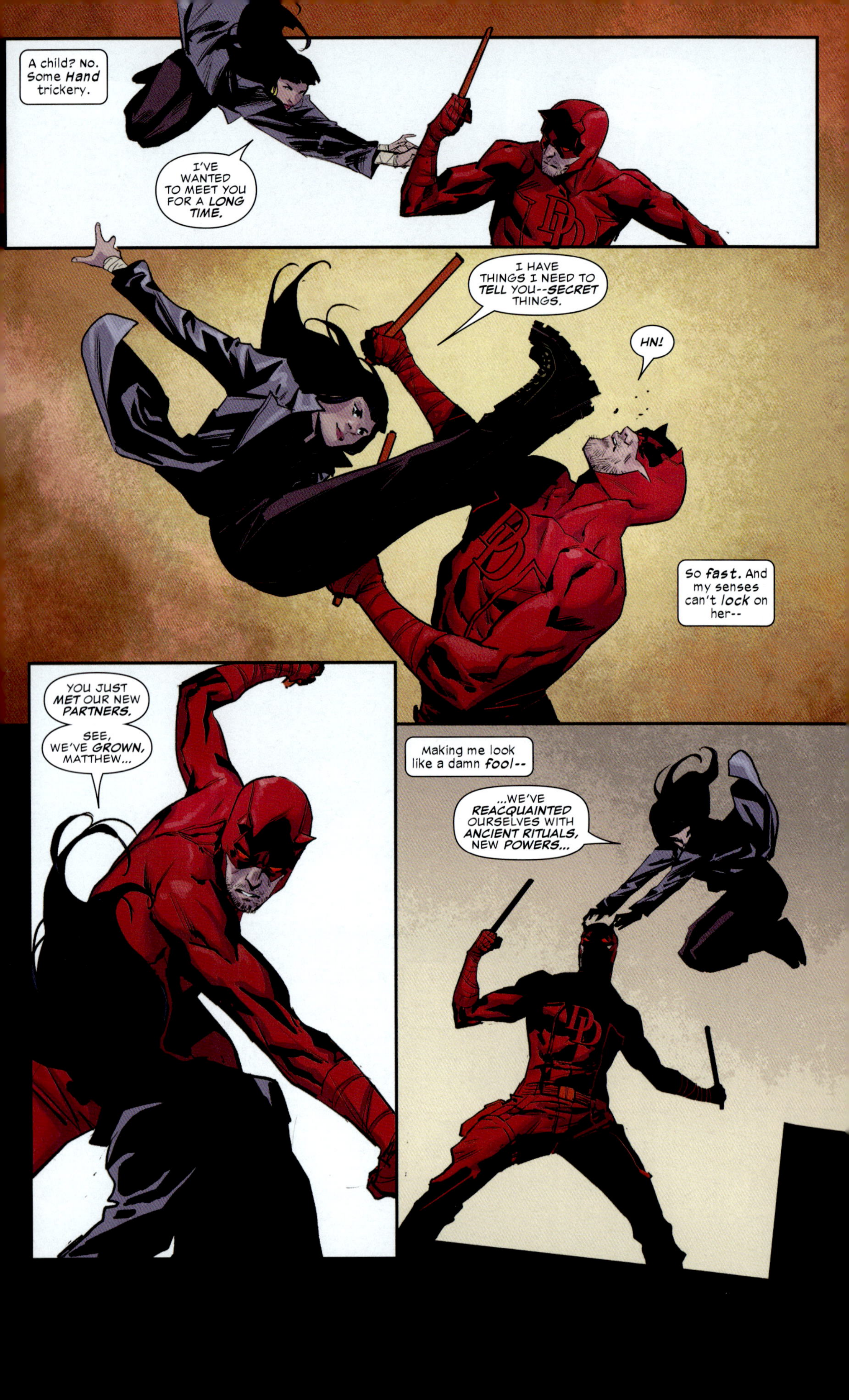
A child? No. Some Hand trickery.
I'VE WANTED TO MEET YOU FOR A LONG TIME.
I HAVE THINGS I NEED TO TELL YOU--SECRET THINGS.
HN!
So fast. And my senses can't lock on her--
YOU JUST MET OUR NEW PARTNERS.
SEE, WE'VE GROWN, MATTHEW...
Making me look like a damn fool--
...WE'VE REACQUAINTED OURSELVES WITH ANCIENT RITUALS, NEW POWERS...

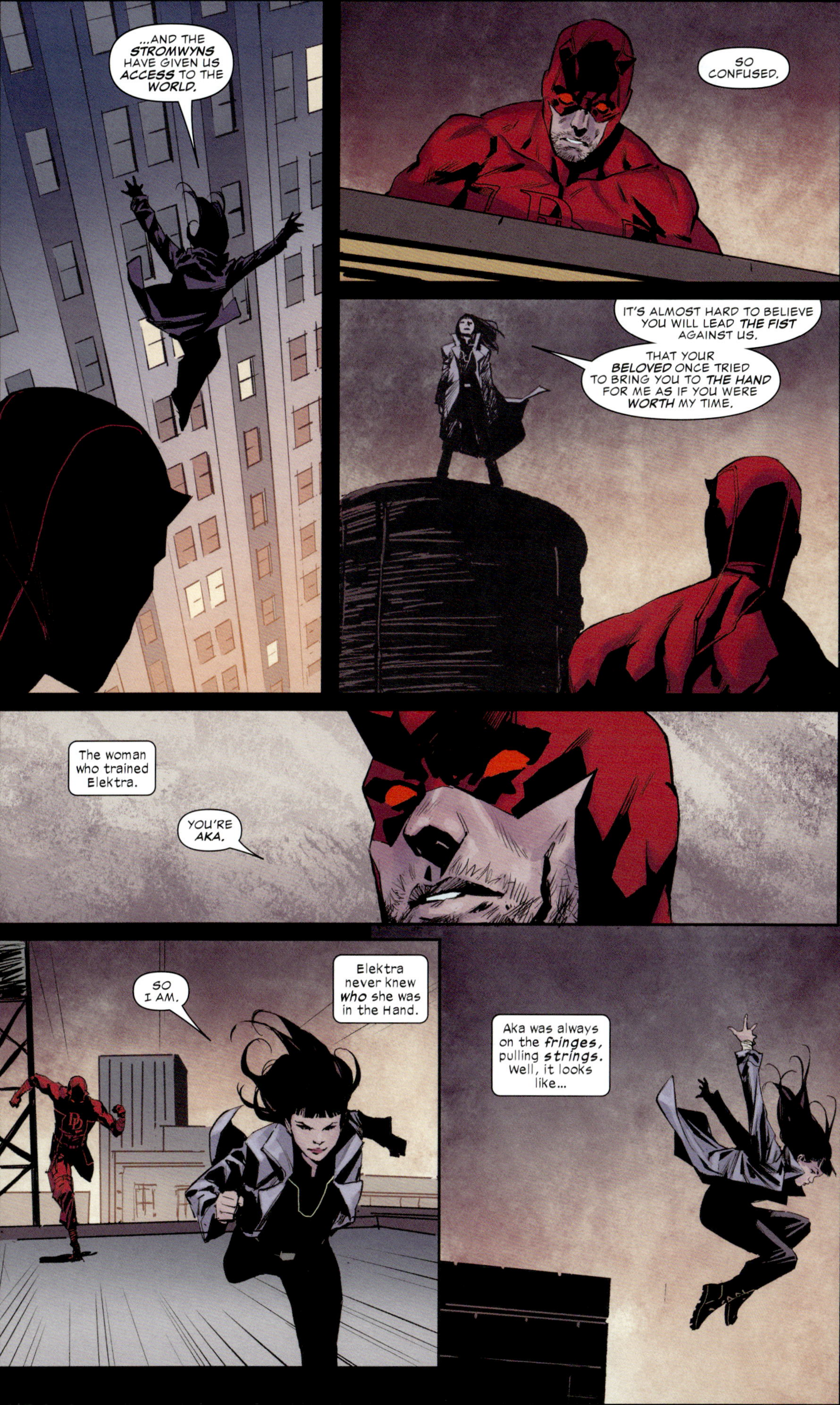

...AND THE STROMWYNS HAVE GIVEN US ACCESS TO THE WORLD.
SO CONFUSED.
IT'S ALMOST HARD TO BELIEVE YOU WILL LEAD THE FIST AGAINST US.
THAT YOUR BELOVED ONCE TRIED TO BRING YOU TO THE HAND FOR ME AS IF YOU WERE WORTH MY TIME.
The woman who trained Elektra.
YOU'RE AKA.
SO I AM.
Elektra never knew who she was in the Hand.
Aka was always on the fringes, pulling strings. Well, it looks like...

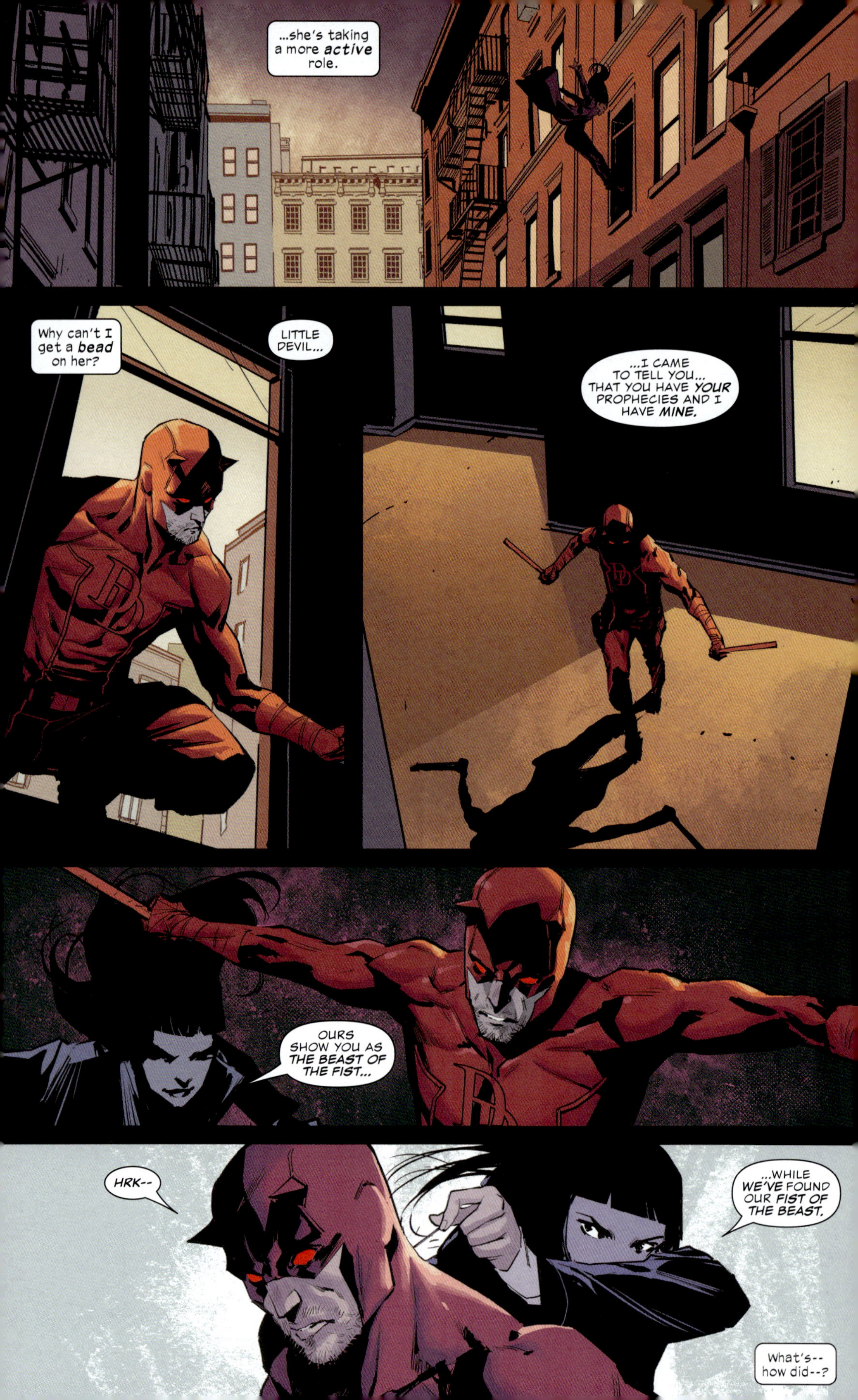
...she's taking a more *active* role.
Why can't I get a *bead* on her?
LITTLE DEVIL...
...I CAME TO TELL YOU... THAT YOU HAVE *YOUR* PROPHECIES AND I HAVE *MINE*.
OURS SHOW YOU AS *THE BEAST OF THE FIST*...
HRK--
...WHILE *WE'VE* FOUND OUR *FIST OF THE BEAST*.
What's-- how did--?

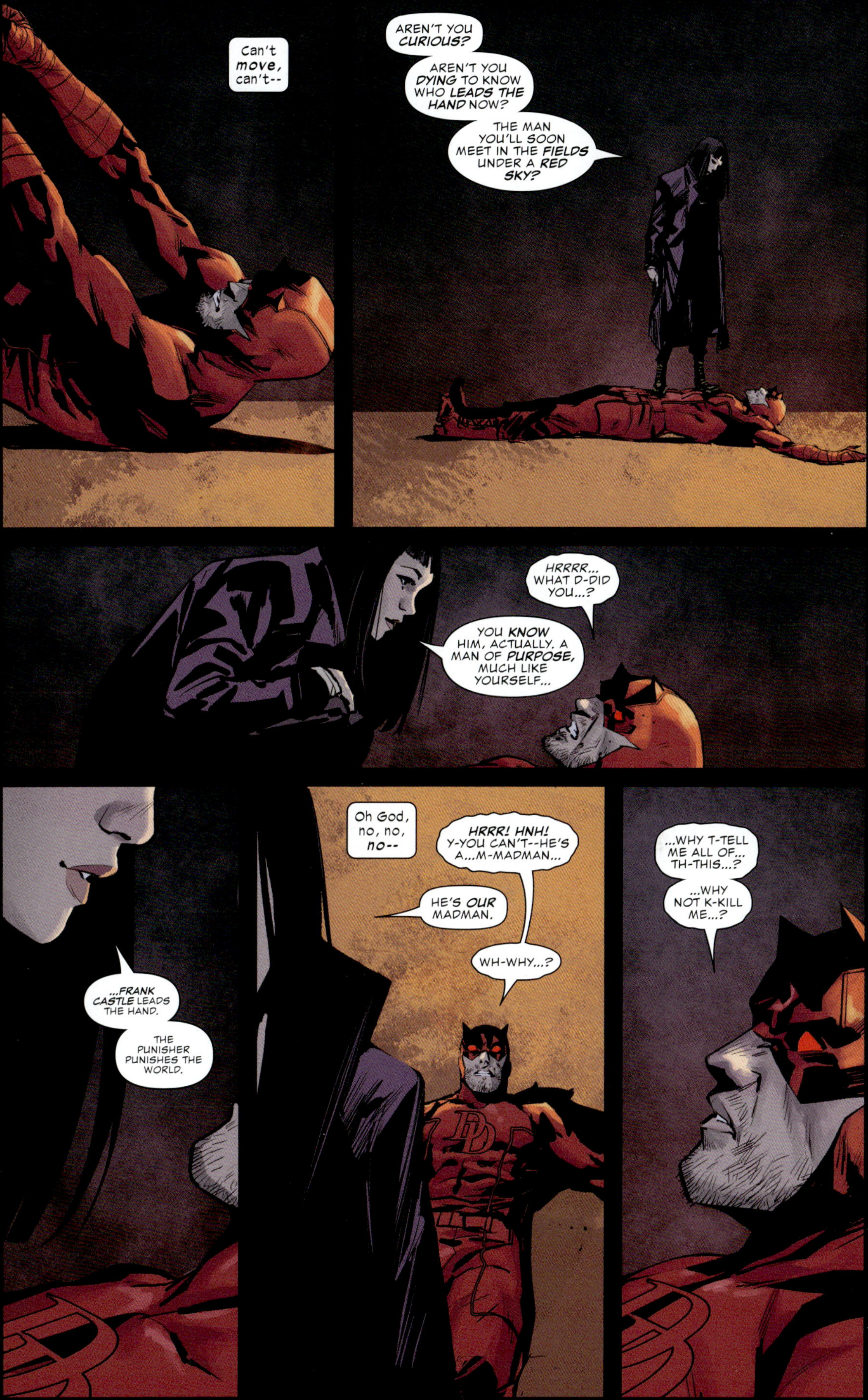
Can't move, can't--
AREN'T YOU CURIOUS?
AREN'T YOU DYING TO KNOW WHO LEADS THE HAND NOW?
THE MAN YOU'LL SOON MEET IN THE FIELDS UNDER A RED SKY?
HRRRR... WHAT D-DID YOU...?
YOU KNOW HIM, ACTUALLY. A MAN OF PURPOSE, MUCH LIKE YOURSELF...
...FRANK CASTLE LEADS THE HAND.
THE PUNISHER PUNISHES THE WORLD.
Oh God, no, no, no--
HRRR! HNH! Y-YOU CAN'T--HE'S A...M-MADMAN...
HE'S OUR MADMAN.
WH-WHY...?
...WHY T-TELL ME ALL OF... TH-THIS...?
...WHY NOT K-KILL ME...?

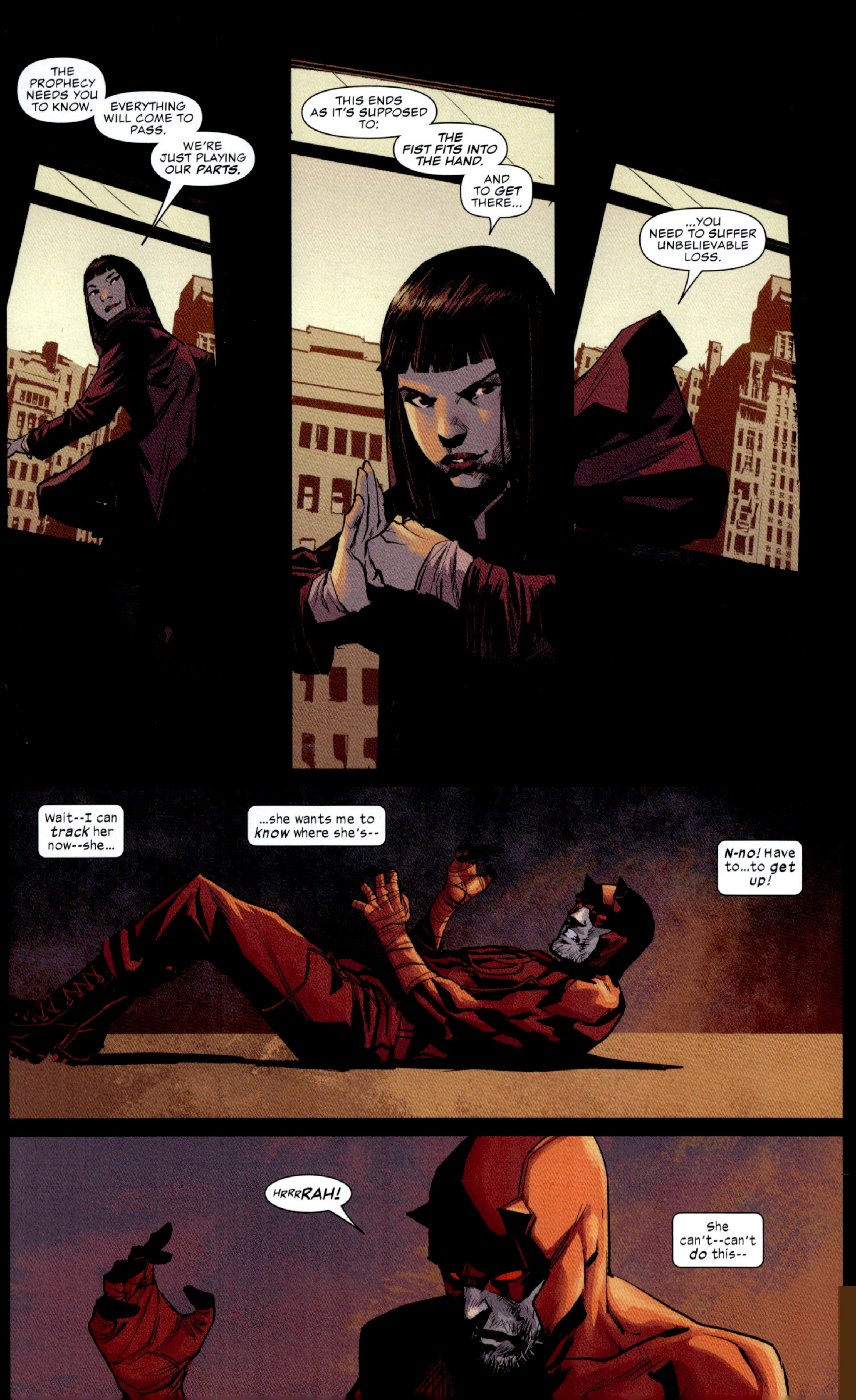
THE PROPHECY NEEDS YOU TO KNOW.
EVERYTHING WILL COME TO PASS.
WE'RE JUST PLAYING OUR PARTS.
THIS ENDS AS IT'S SUPPOSED TO:
THE FIST FITS INTO THE HAND.
AND TO GET THERE...
...YOU NEED TO SUFFER UNBELIEVABLE LOSS.
Wait--I can track her now--she...
...she wants me to know where she's--
N-no! Have to...to get up!
HRRRRAH!
She can't--can't do this--

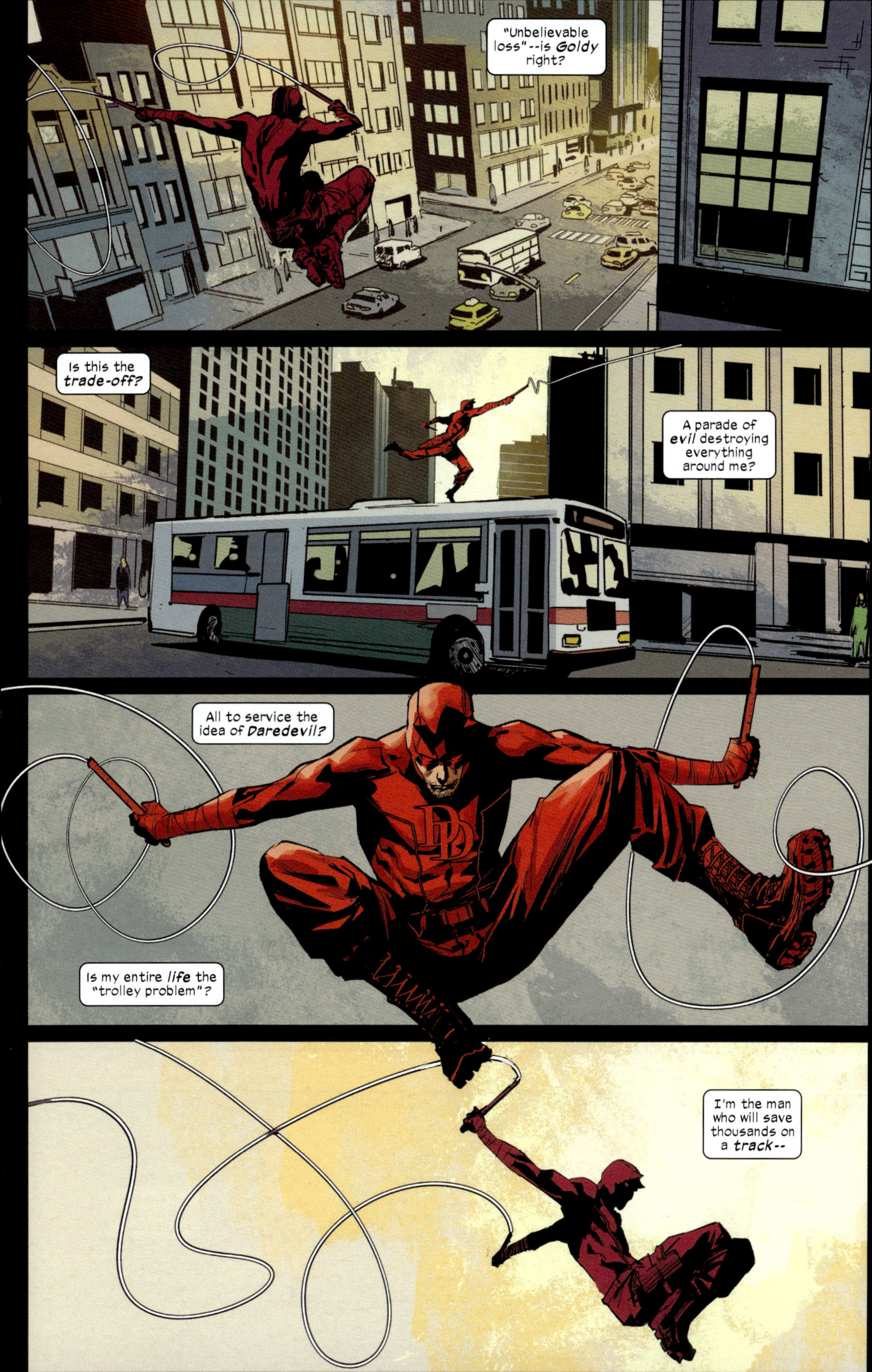
"Unbelievable loss"--is *Goldy* right?
Is this the *trade-off?*
A parade of *evil* destroying everything around me?
All to service the idea of *Daredevil?*
Is my entire *life* the "trolley problem"?
I'm the man who will save thousands on a *track*--

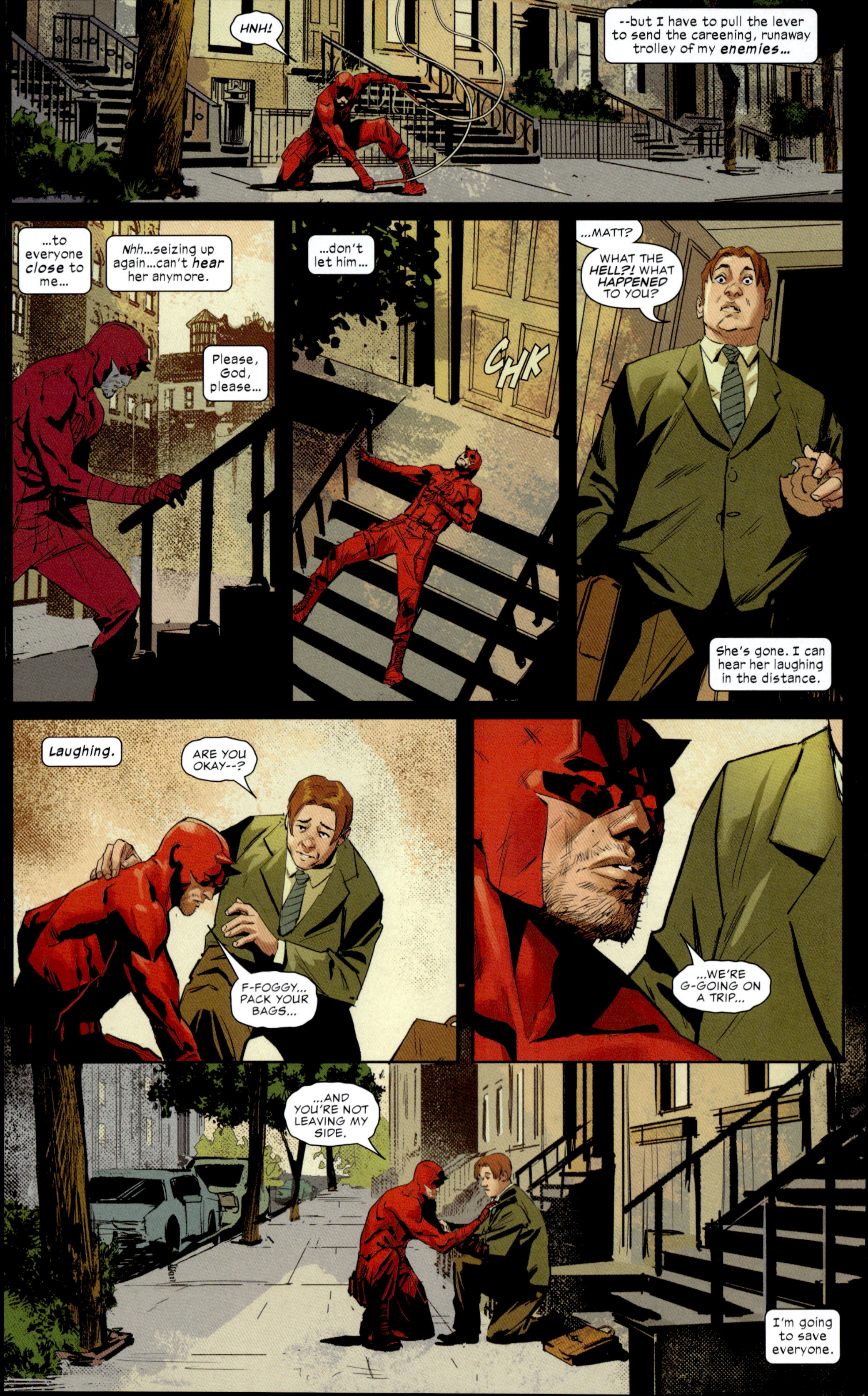
HNH!
--but I have to pull the lever to send the careening, runaway trolley of my enemies...
...to everyone close to me...
Nhh...seizing up again...can't hear her anymore.
Please, God, please...
...don't let him...
CHK
...MATT?
WHAT THE HELL?! WHAT HAPPENED TO YOU?
She's gone. I can hear her laughing in the distance.
Laughing.
ARE YOU OKAY--?
F-FOGGY... PACK YOUR BAGS...
...WE'RE G-GOING ON A TRIP...
...AND YOU'RE NOT LEAVING MY SIDE.
I'm going to save everyone.

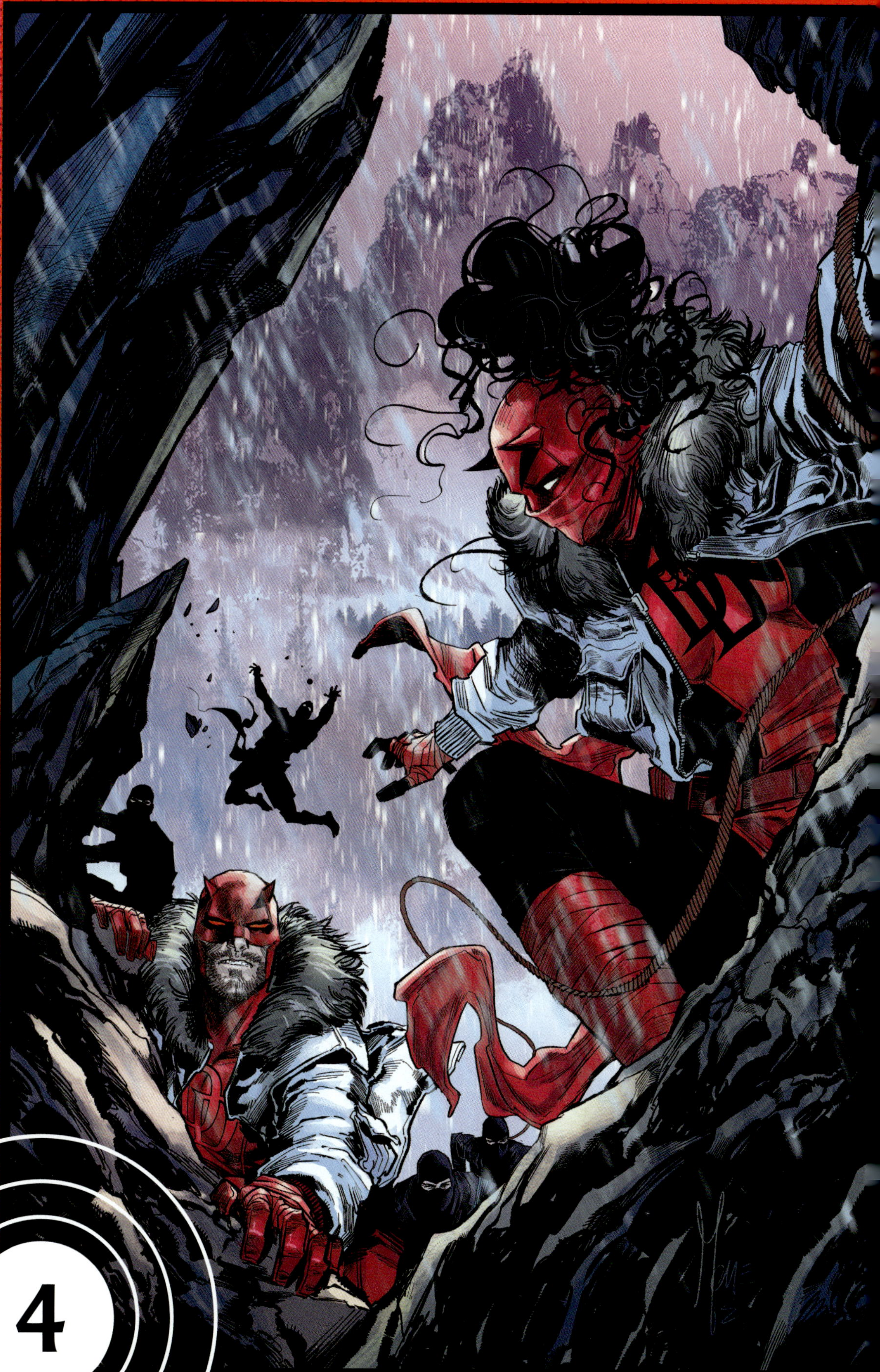

4

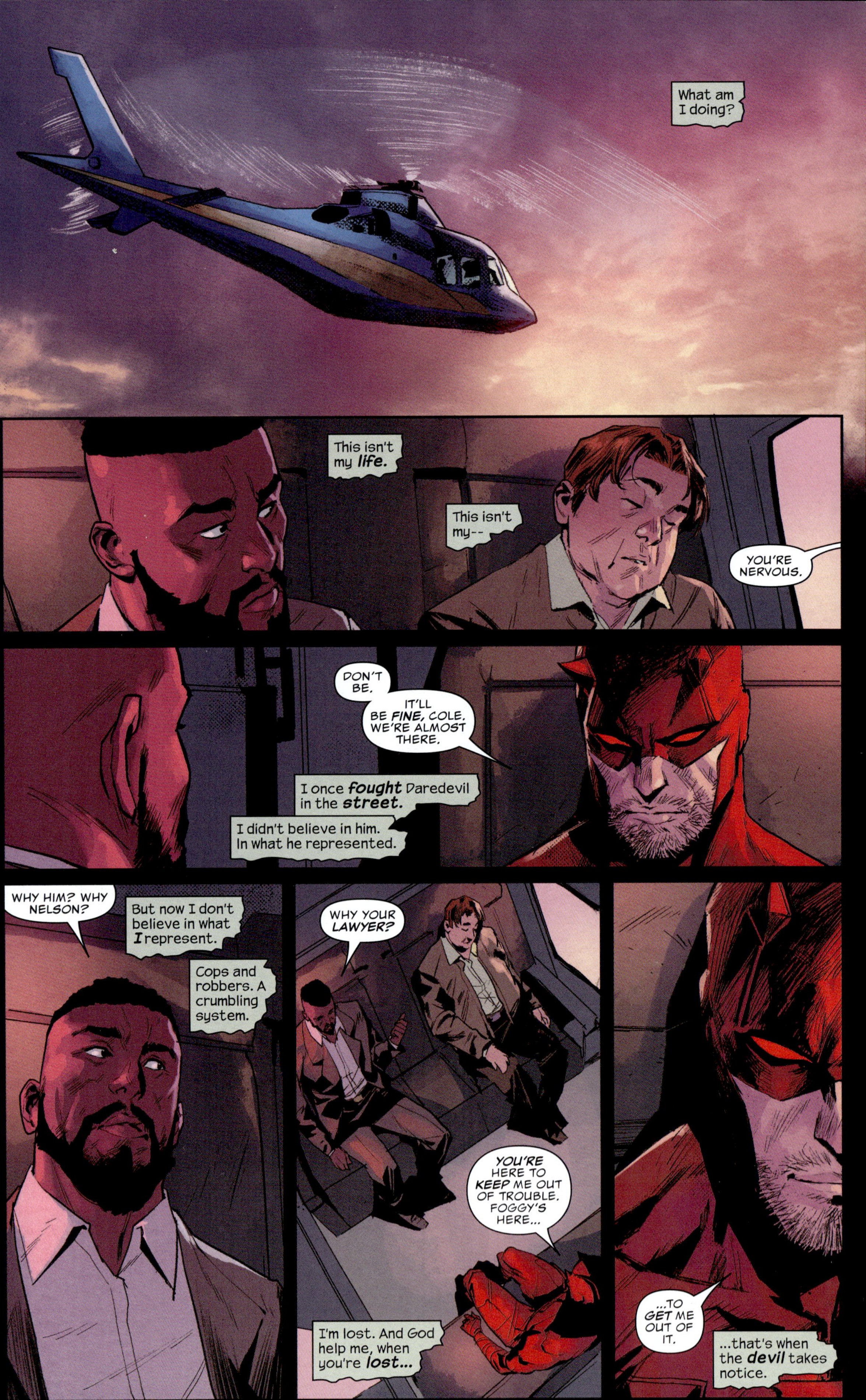
What am I doing?
This isn't my life.
This isn't my--
YOU'RE NERVOUS.
DON'T BE.
IT'LL BE FINE, COLE. WE'RE ALMOST THERE.
I once fought Daredevil in the street.
I didn't believe in him. In what he represented.
WHY HIM? WHY NELSON?
But now I don't believe in what I represent.
Cops and robbers. A crumbling system.
WHY YOUR LAWYER?
YOU'RE HERE TO KEEP ME OUT OF TROUBLE. FOGGY'S HERE...
I'm lost. And God help me, when you're lost...
...TO GET ME OUT OF IT.
...that's when the devil takes notice.

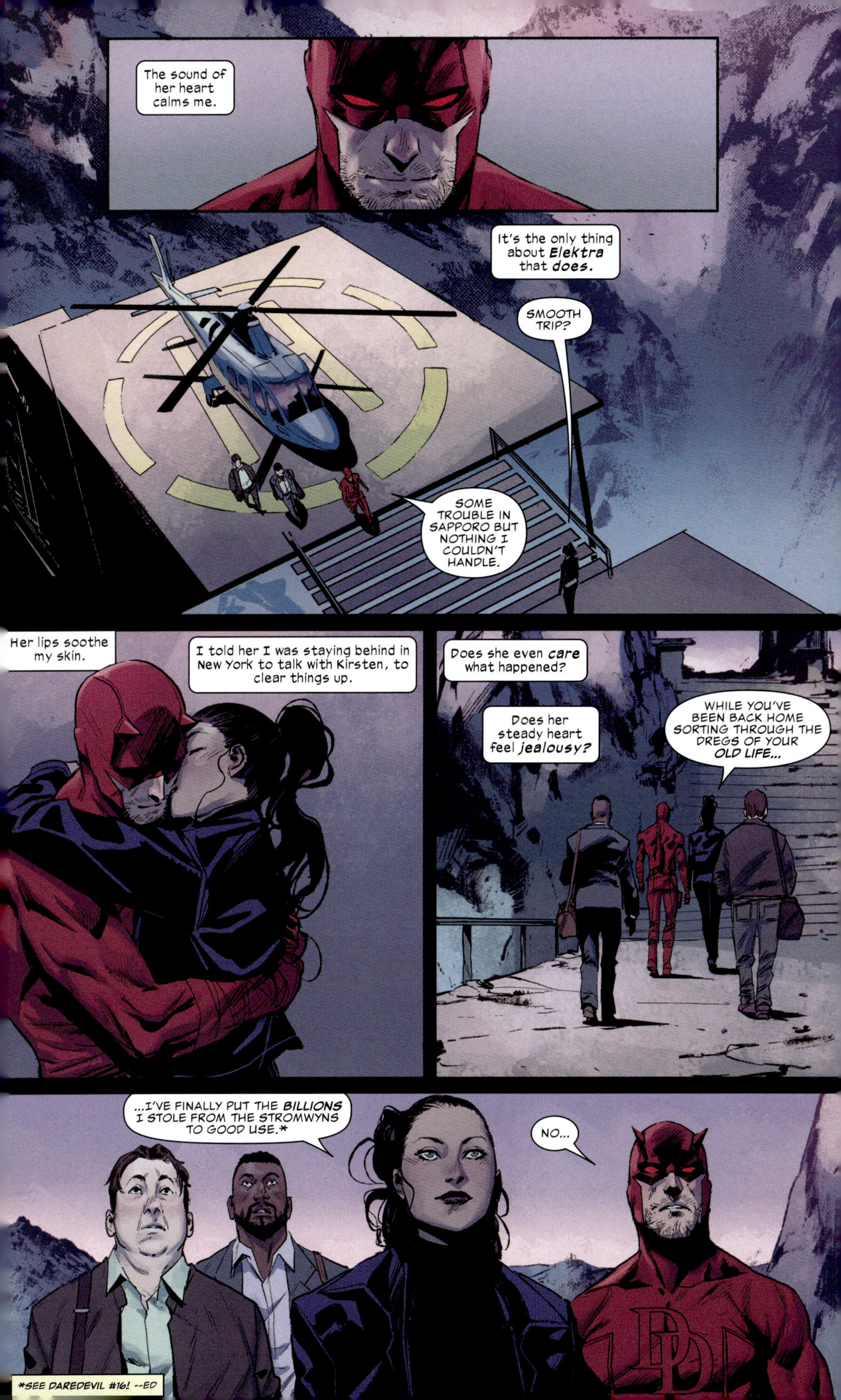

The sound of her heart calms me.
It's the only thing about Elektra that does.
SMOOTH TRIP?
SOME TROUBLE IN SAPPORO BUT NOTHING I COULDN'T HANDLE.
Her lips soothe my skin.
I told her I was staying behind in New York to talk with Kirsten, to clear things up.
Does she even care what happened?
Does her steady heart feel jealousy?
WHILE YOU'VE BEEN BACK HOME SORTING THROUGH THE DREGS OF YOUR OLD LIFE...
...I'VE FINALLY PUT THE BILLIONS I STOLE FROM THE STROMWYNS TO GOOD USE.*
NO...
*SEE DAREDEVIL #16! --ED

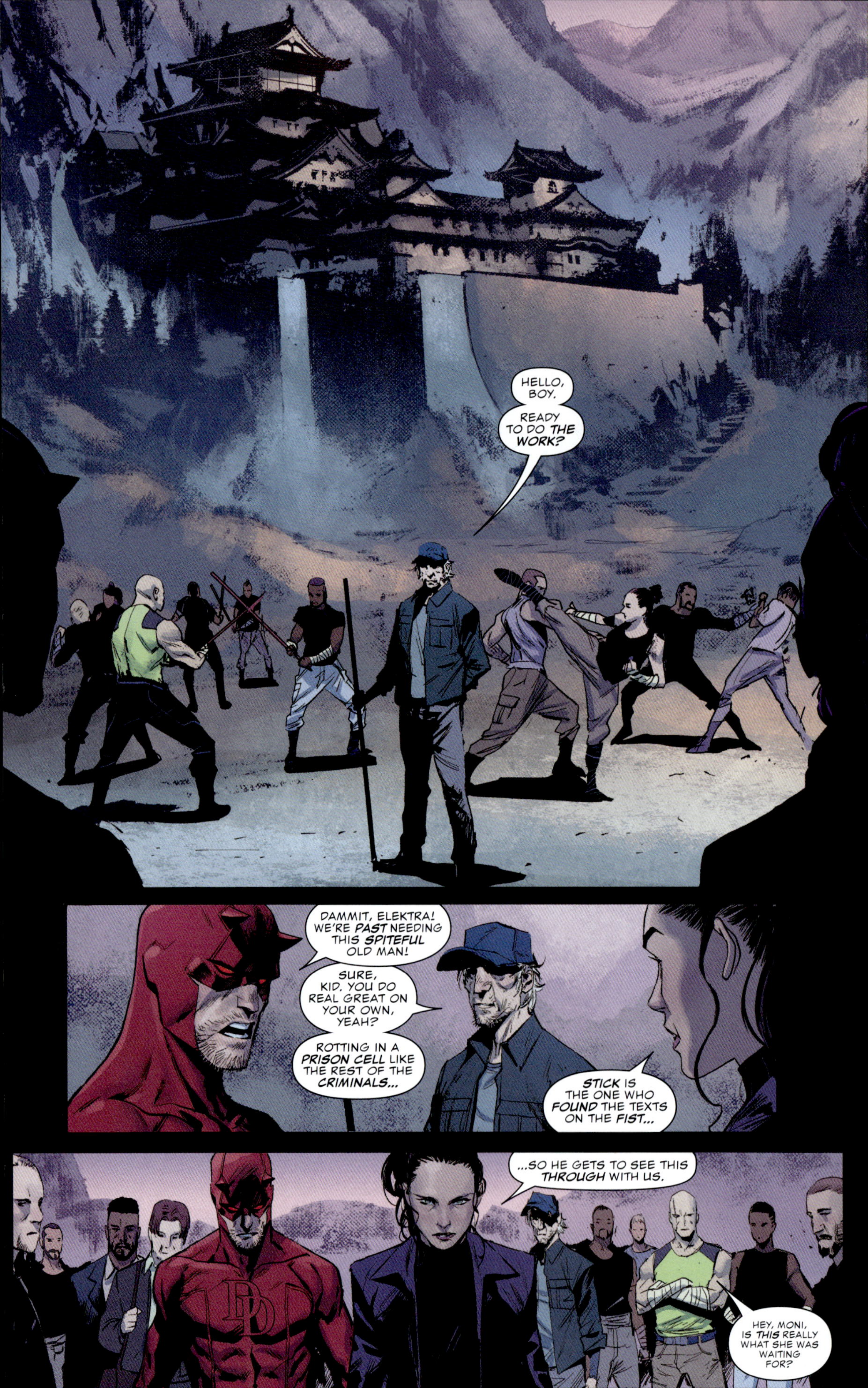
HELLO, BOY. READY TO DO THE WORK?
DAMMIT, ELEKTRA! WE'RE PAST NEEDING THIS SPITEFUL OLD MAN!
SURE, KID, YOU DO REAL GREAT ON YOUR OWN, YEAH?
ROTTING IN A PRISON CELL LIKE THE REST OF THE CRIMINALS...
STICK IS THE ONE WHO FOUND THE TEXTS ON THE FIST...
...SO HE GETS TO SEE THIS THROUGH WITH US.
HEY, MONI, IS THIS REALLY WHAT SHE WAS WAITING FOR?

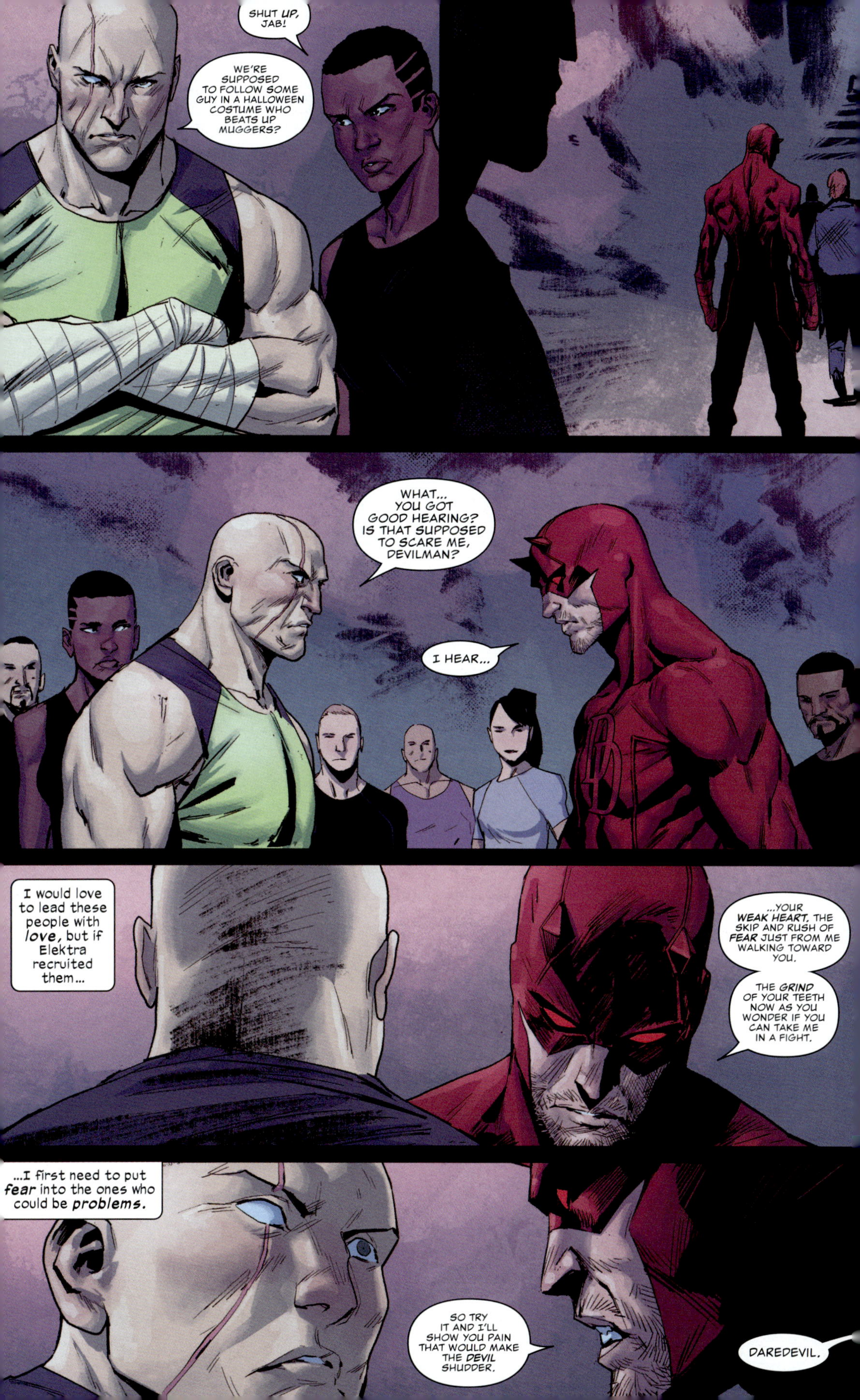
SHUT UP, JAB!
WE'RE SUPPOSED TO FOLLOW SOME GUY IN A HALLOWEEN COSTUME WHO BEATS UP MUGGERS?
WHAT... YOU GOT GOOD HEARING? IS THAT SUPPOSED TO SCARE ME, DEVILMAN?
I HEAR...
I would love to lead these people with *love*, but if Elektra recruited them...
...YOUR *WEAK HEART*. THE SKIP AND RUSH OF *FEAR* JUST FROM ME WALKING TOWARD YOU.
THE *GRIND* OF YOUR TEETH NOW AS YOU WONDER IF YOU CAN TAKE ME IN A FIGHT.
...I first need to put *fear* into the ones who could be *problems*.
SO TRY IT AND I'LL SHOW YOU PAIN THAT WOULD MAKE THE *DEVIL* SHUDDER.
DAREDEVIL.

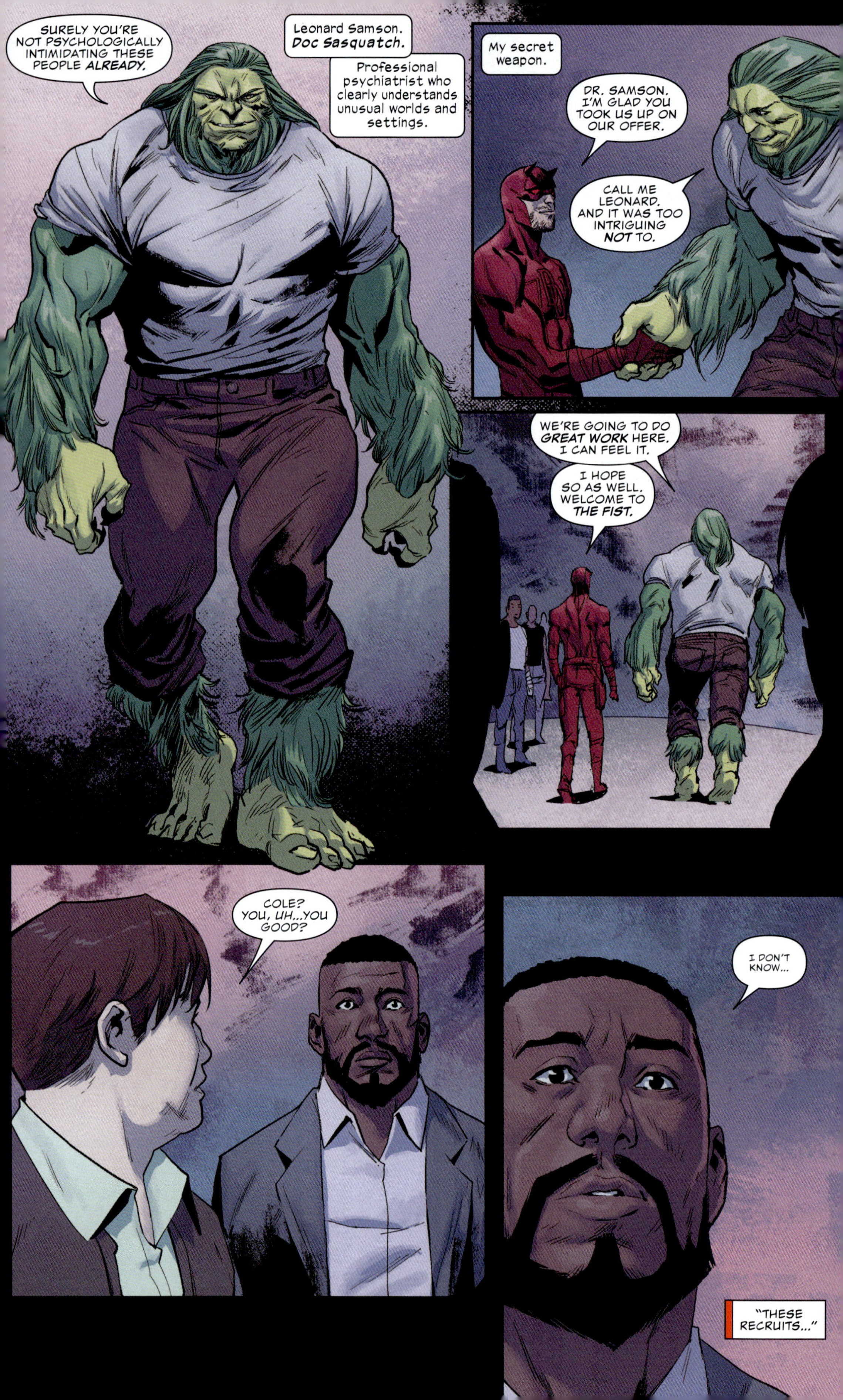
SURELY YOU'RE NOT PSYCHOLOGICALLY INTIMIDATING THESE PEOPLE ALREADY.
Leonard Samson. Doc Sasquatch.
Professional psychiatrist who clearly understands unusual worlds and settings.
My secret weapon.
DR. SAMSON. I'M GLAD YOU TOOK US UP ON OUR OFFER.
CALL ME LEONARD. AND IT WAS TOO INTRIGUING NOT TO.
WE'RE GOING TO DO GREAT WORK HERE. I CAN FEEL IT.
I HOPE SO AS WELL. WELCOME TO THE FIST.
COLE? YOU, UH...YOU GOOD?
I DON'T KNOW...
"THESE RECRUITS..."

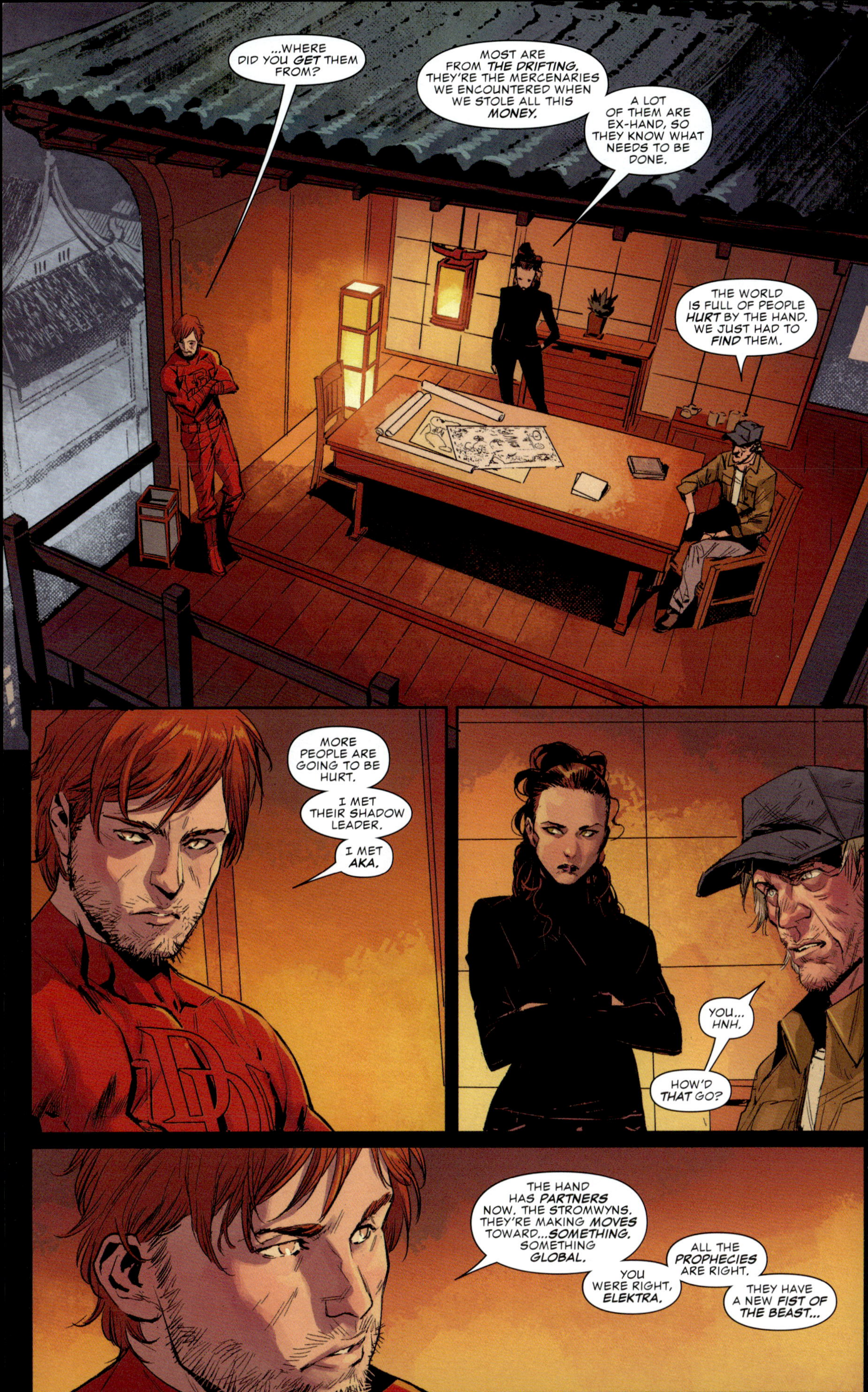
...WHERE DID YOU GET THEM FROM?
MOST ARE FROM THE DRIFTING. THEY'RE THE MERCENARIES WE ENCOUNTERED WHEN WE STOLE ALL THIS MONEY.
A LOT OF THEM ARE EX-HAND, SO THEY KNOW WHAT NEEDS TO BE DONE.
THE WORLD IS FULL OF PEOPLE HURT BY THE HAND. WE JUST HAD TO FIND THEM.
MORE PEOPLE ARE GOING TO BE HURT.
I MET THEIR SHADOW LEADER.
I MET AKA.
YOU... HNH.
HOW'D THAT GO?
THE HAND HAS PARTNERS NOW. THE STROMWYNS. THEY'RE MAKING MOVES TOWARD...SOMETHING. SOMETHING GLOBAL.
YOU WERE RIGHT, ELEKTRA.
ALL THE PROPHECIES ARE RIGHT.
THEY HAVE A NEW FIST OF THE BEAST...

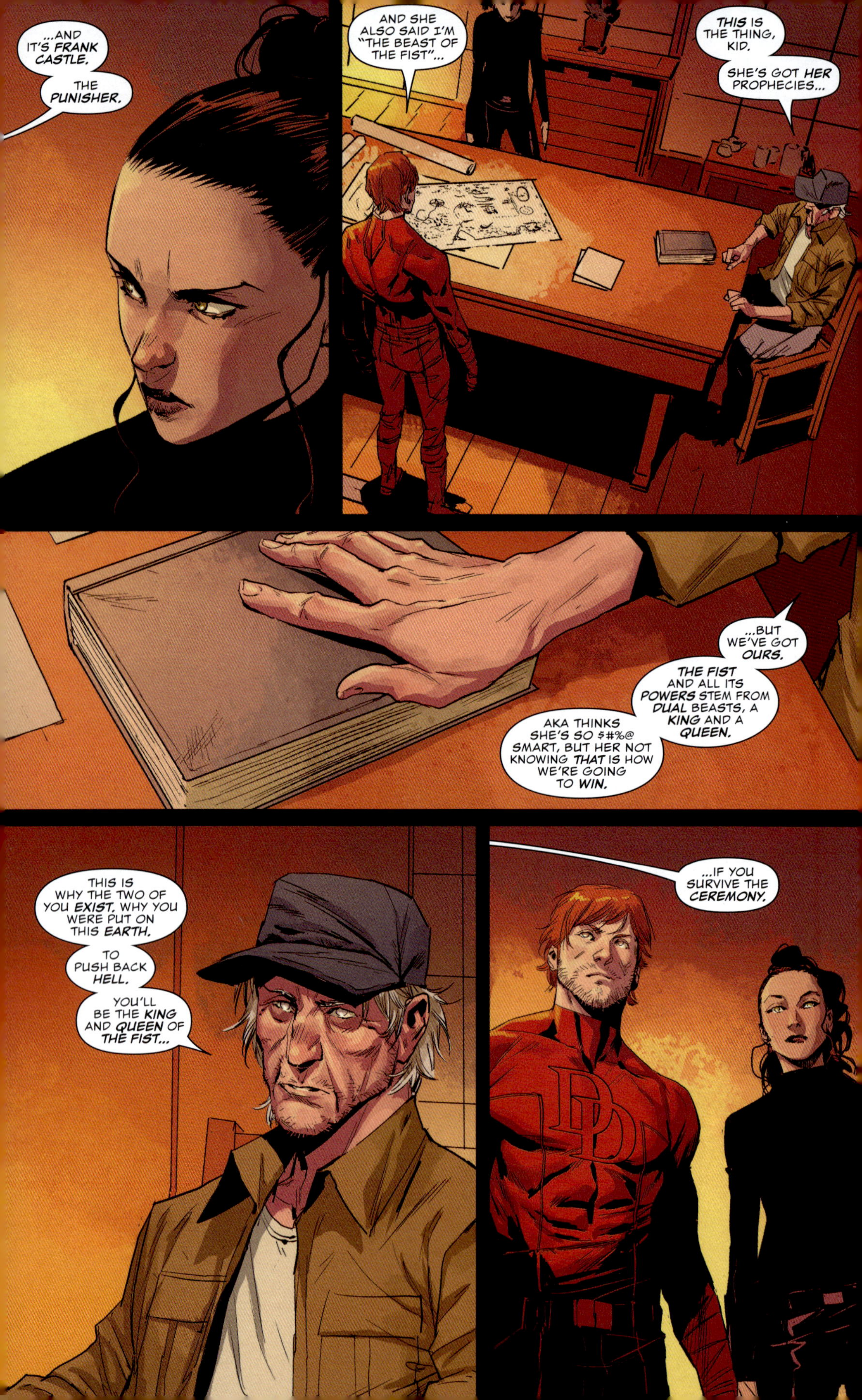
...AND IT'S FRANK CASTLE.
THE PUNISHER.
AND SHE ALSO SAID I'M "THE BEAST OF THE FIST"...
THIS IS THE THING, KID.
SHE'S GOT HER PROPHECIES...
...BUT WE'VE GOT OURS.
THE FIST AND ALL ITS POWERS STEM FROM DUAL BEASTS, A KING AND A QUEEN.
AKA THINKS SHE'S SO $#%@ SMART, BUT HER NOT KNOWING THAT IS HOW WE'RE GOING TO WIN.
THIS IS WHY THE TWO OF YOU EXIST. WHY YOU WERE PUT ON THIS EARTH.
TO PUSH BACK HELL.
YOU'LL BE THE KING AND QUEEN OF THE FIST...
...IF YOU SURVIVE THE CEREMONY.

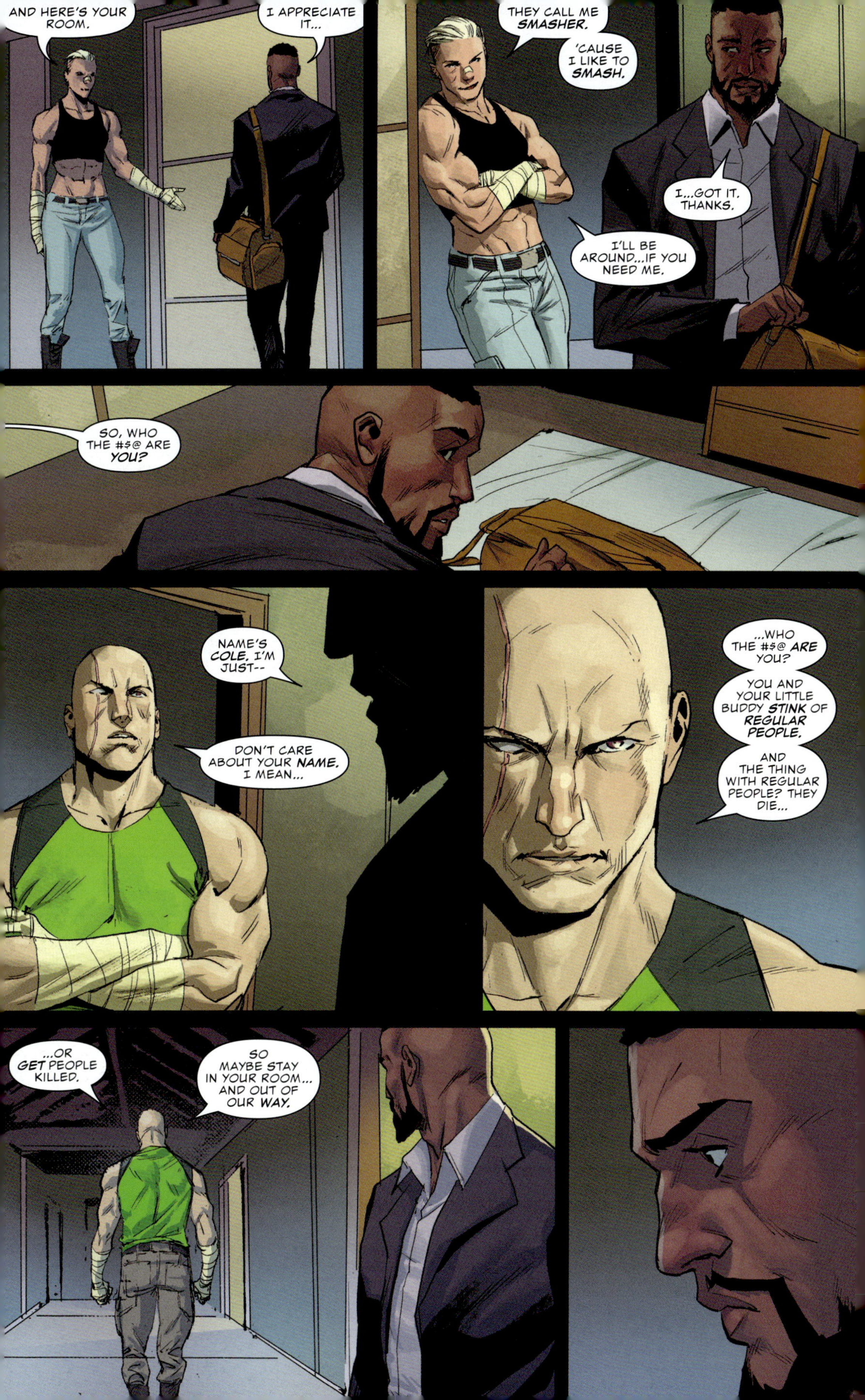

AND HERE'S YOUR ROOM.
I APPRECIATE IT...
THEY CALL ME SMASHER.
'CAUSE I LIKE TO SMASH.
I...GOT IT. THANKS.
I'LL BE AROUND...IF YOU NEED ME.
SO, WHO THE #$@ ARE YOU?
NAME'S COLE. I'M JUST--
DON'T CARE ABOUT YOUR NAME. I MEAN...
...WHO THE #$@ ARE YOU?
YOU AND YOUR LITTLE BUDDY STINK OF REGULAR PEOPLE.
AND THE THING WITH REGULAR PEOPLE? THEY DIE...
...OR GET PEOPLE KILLED.
SO MAYBE STAY IN YOUR ROOM... AND OUT OF OUR WAY.

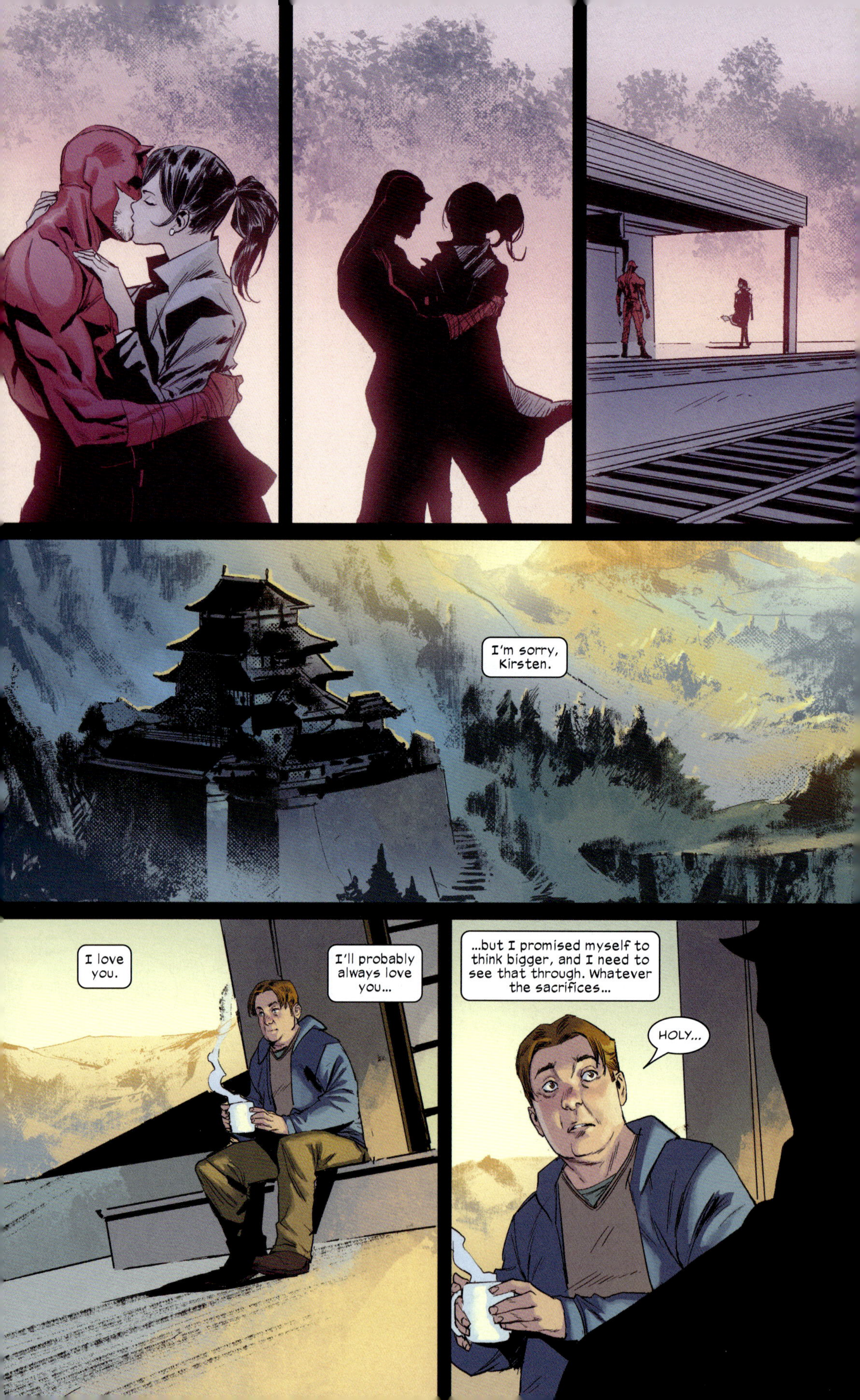
I'm sorry, Kirsten.
I love you.
I'll probably always love you...
...but I promised myself to think bigger, and I need to see that through. Whatever the sacrifices...
HOLY...

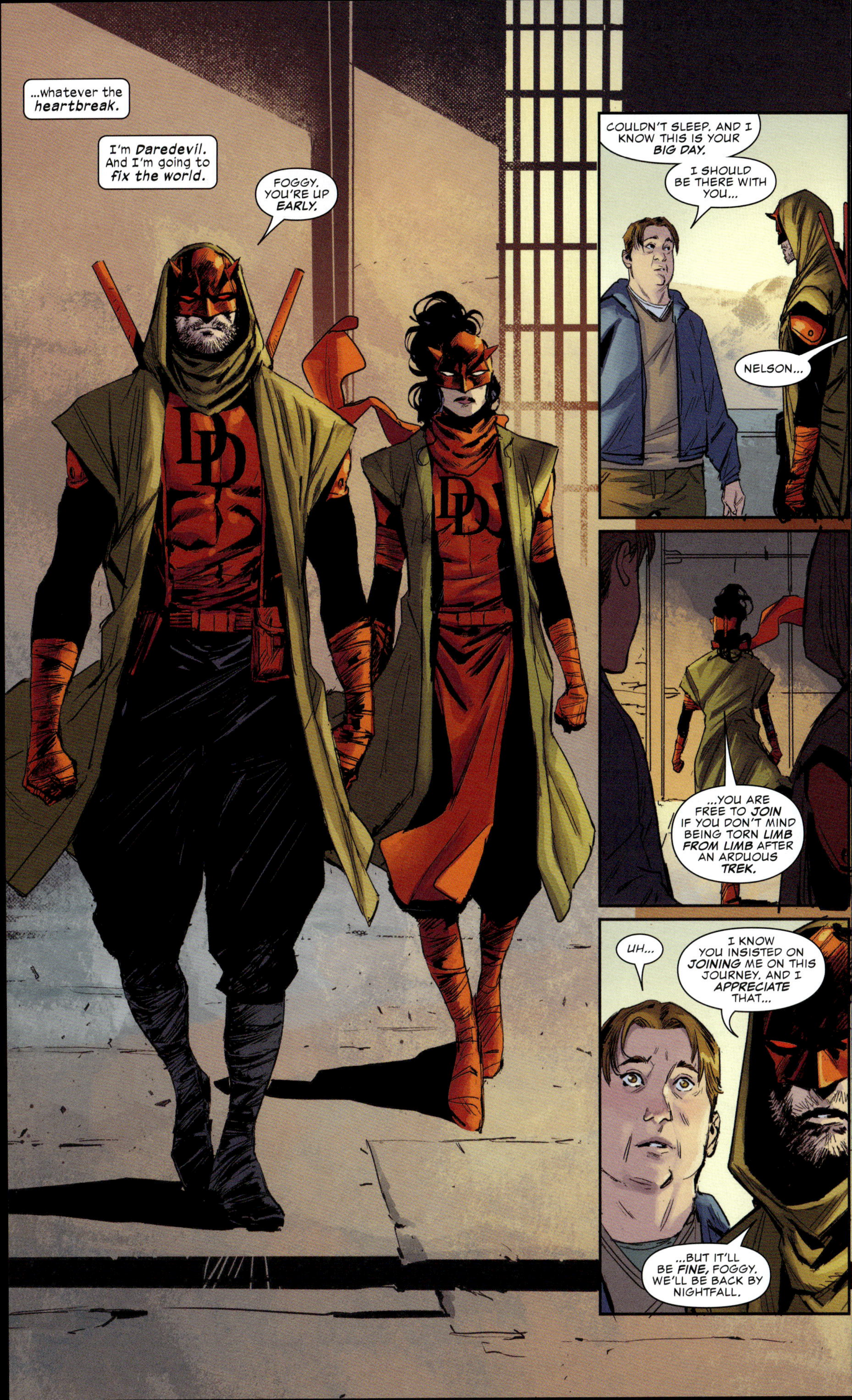
...whatever the *heartbreak.*
I'm *Daredevil.* And I'm going to *fix the world.*
FOGGY. YOU'RE UP *EARLY.*
COULDN'T SLEEP. AND I KNOW THIS IS YOUR *BIG DAY.*
I SHOULD BE THERE WITH YOU...
NELSON...
...YOU ARE FREE TO *JOIN* IF YOU DON'T MIND BEING TORN *LIMB FROM LIMB* AFTER AN ARDUOUS *TREK.*
UH...
I KNOW YOU INSISTED ON *JOINING* ME ON THIS JOURNEY, AND I *APPRECIATE* THAT...
...BUT IT'LL BE *FINE,* FOGGY. WE'LL BE BACK BY NIGHTFALL.

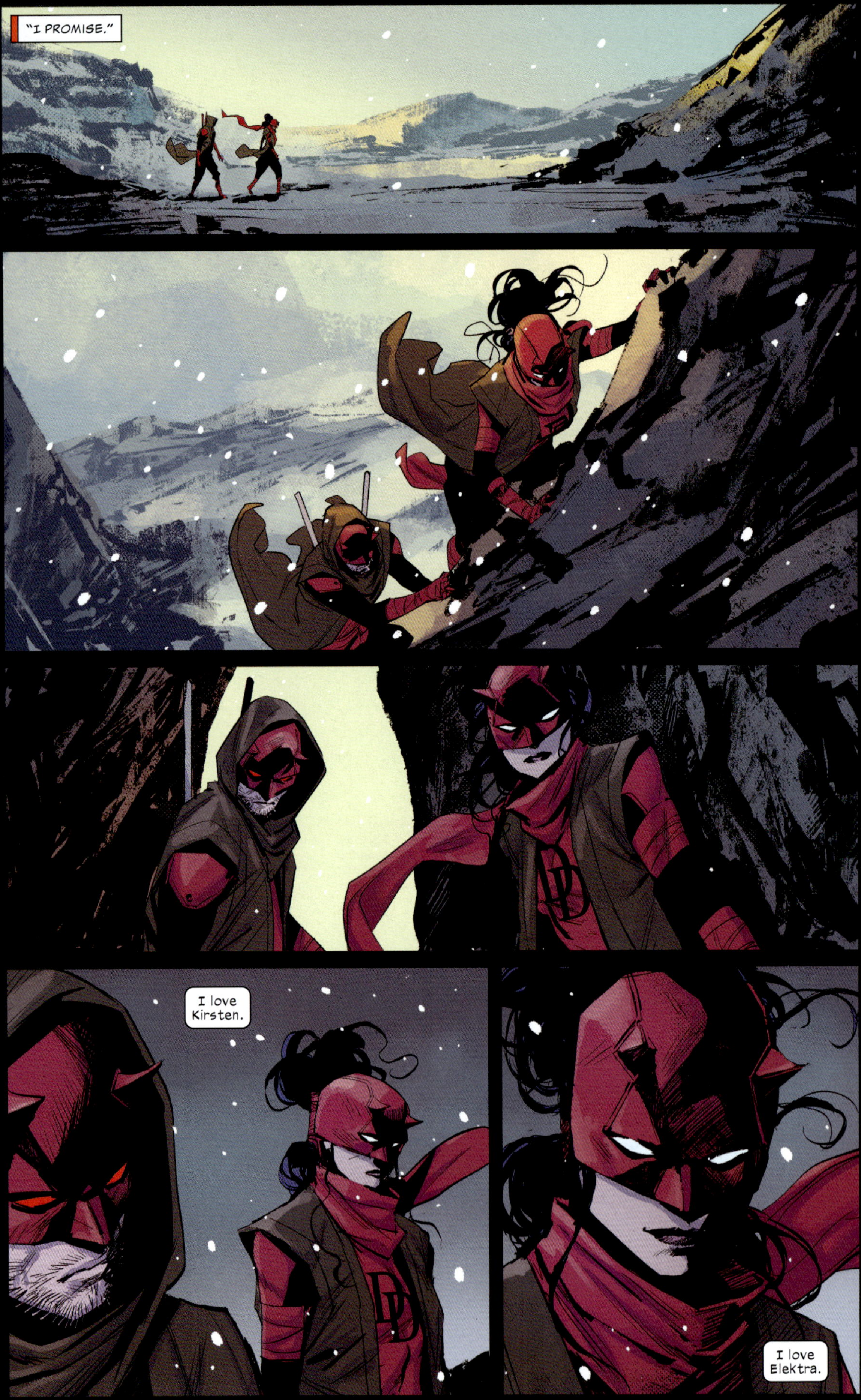
"I PROMISE."
I love Kirsten.
I love Elektra.

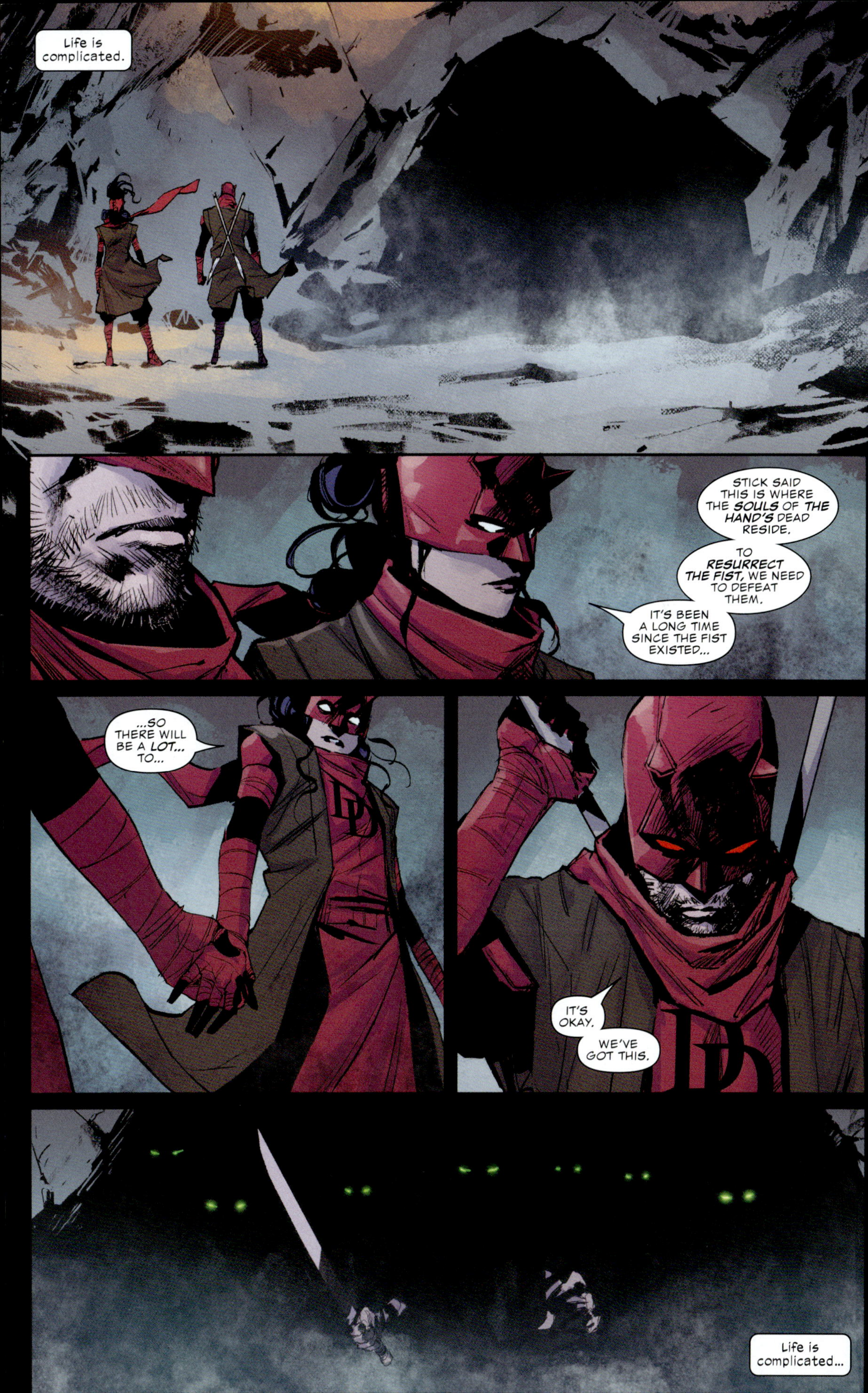
Life is complicated.
STICK SAID THIS IS WHERE THE SOULS OF THE HAND'S DEAD RESIDE.
TO RESURRECT THE FIST, WE NEED TO DEFEAT THEM.
IT'S BEEN A LONG TIME SINCE THE FIST EXISTED...
...SO THERE WILL BE A LOT... TO...
IT'S OKAY.
WE'VE GOT THIS.
Life is complicated...

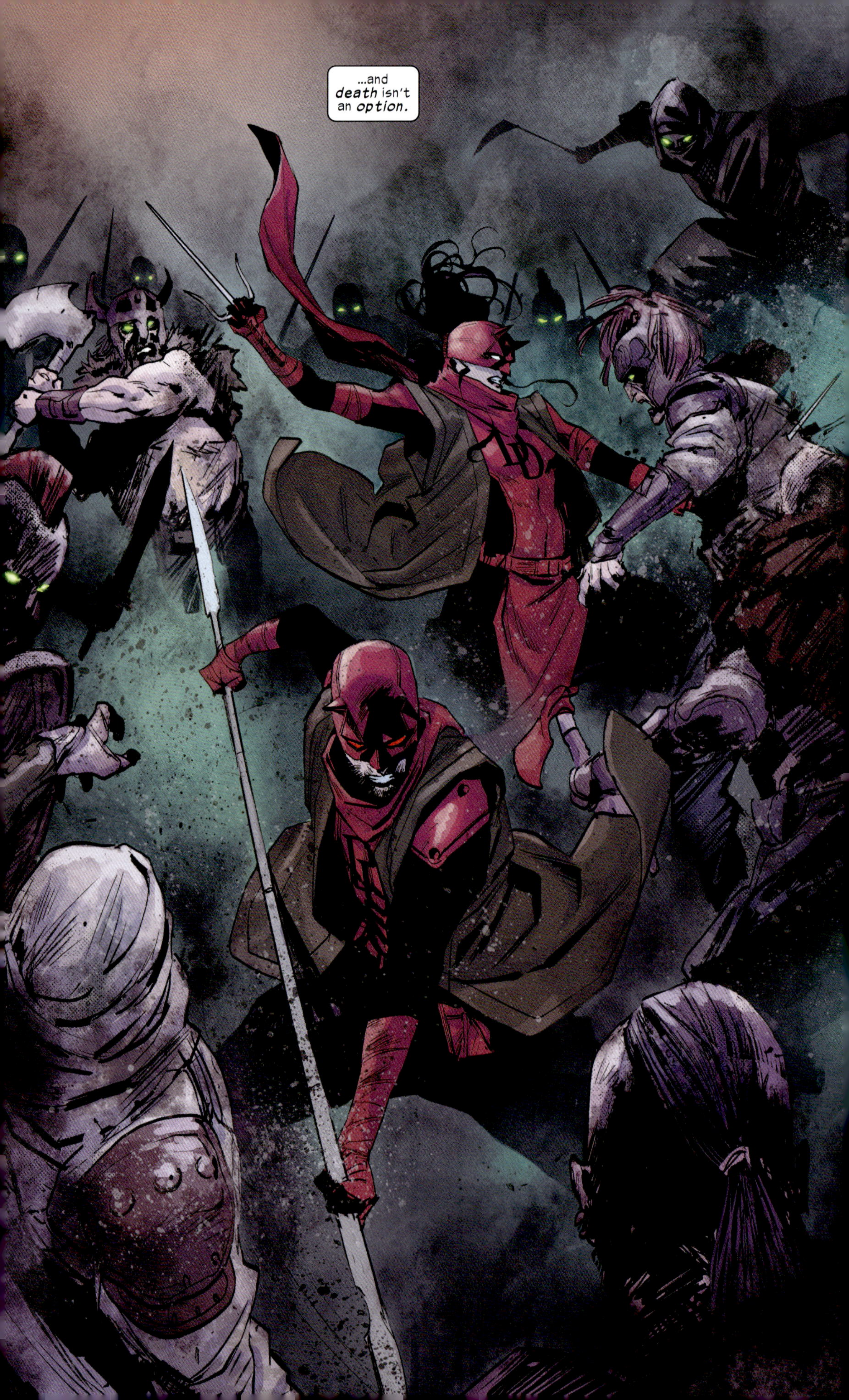
...and *death* isn't an *option.*

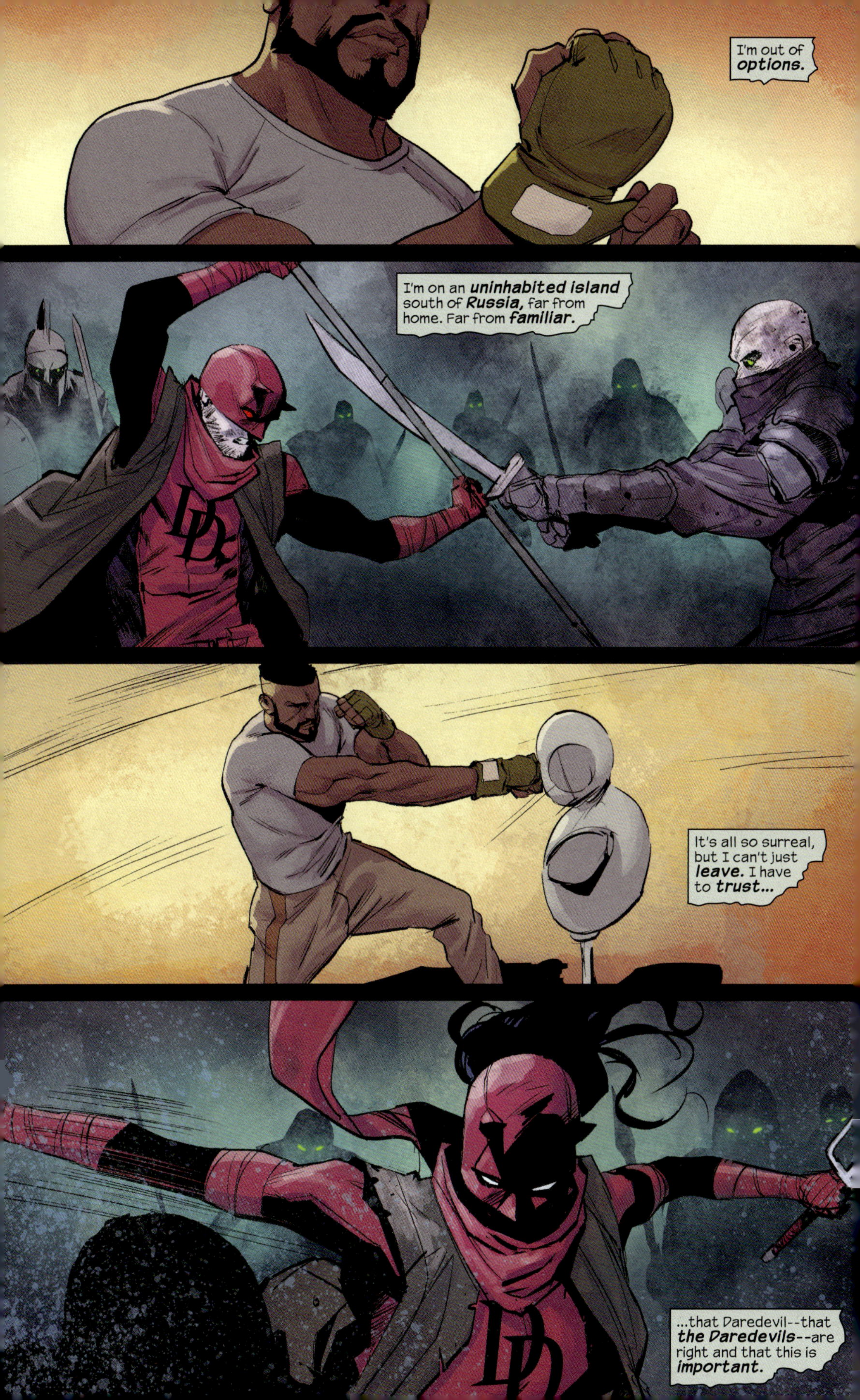
I'm out of options.
I'm on an uninhabited island south of Russia, far from home. Far from familiar.
It's all so surreal, but I can't just leave. I have to trust...
...that Daredevil--that the Daredevils--are right and that this is important.

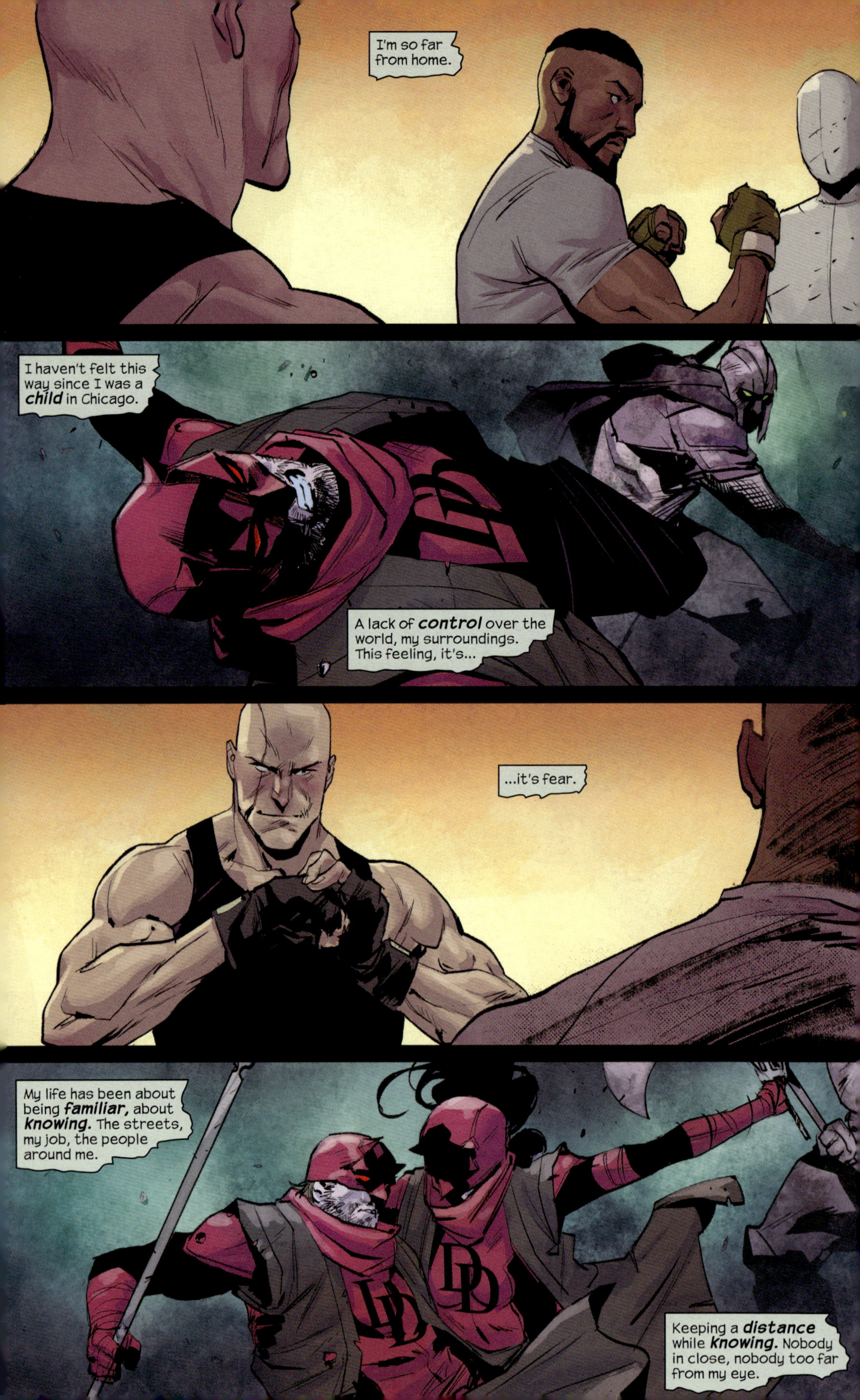

I'm so far from home.
I haven't felt this way since I was a **child** in Chicago.
A lack of **control** over the world, my surroundings. This feeling, it's...
...it's fear.
My life has been about being **familiar,** about **knowing.** The streets, my job, the people around me.
Keeping a **distance** while **knowing.** Nobody in close, nobody too far from my eye.

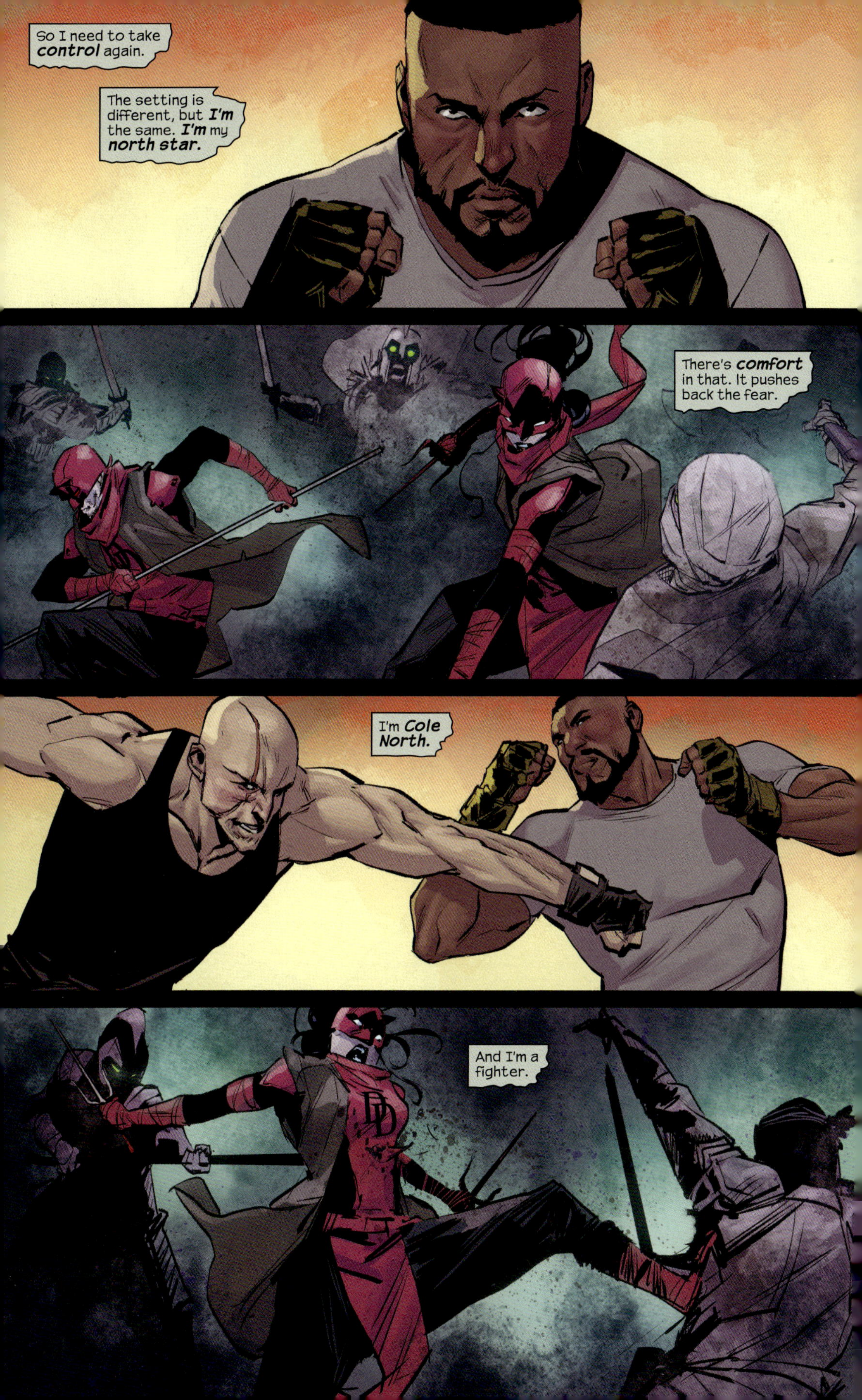
So I need to take **control** again.
The setting is different, but ***I'm*** the same. ***I'm*** my ***north star.***
There's ***comfort*** in that. It pushes back the fear.
I'm ***Cole North.***
And I'm a fighter.

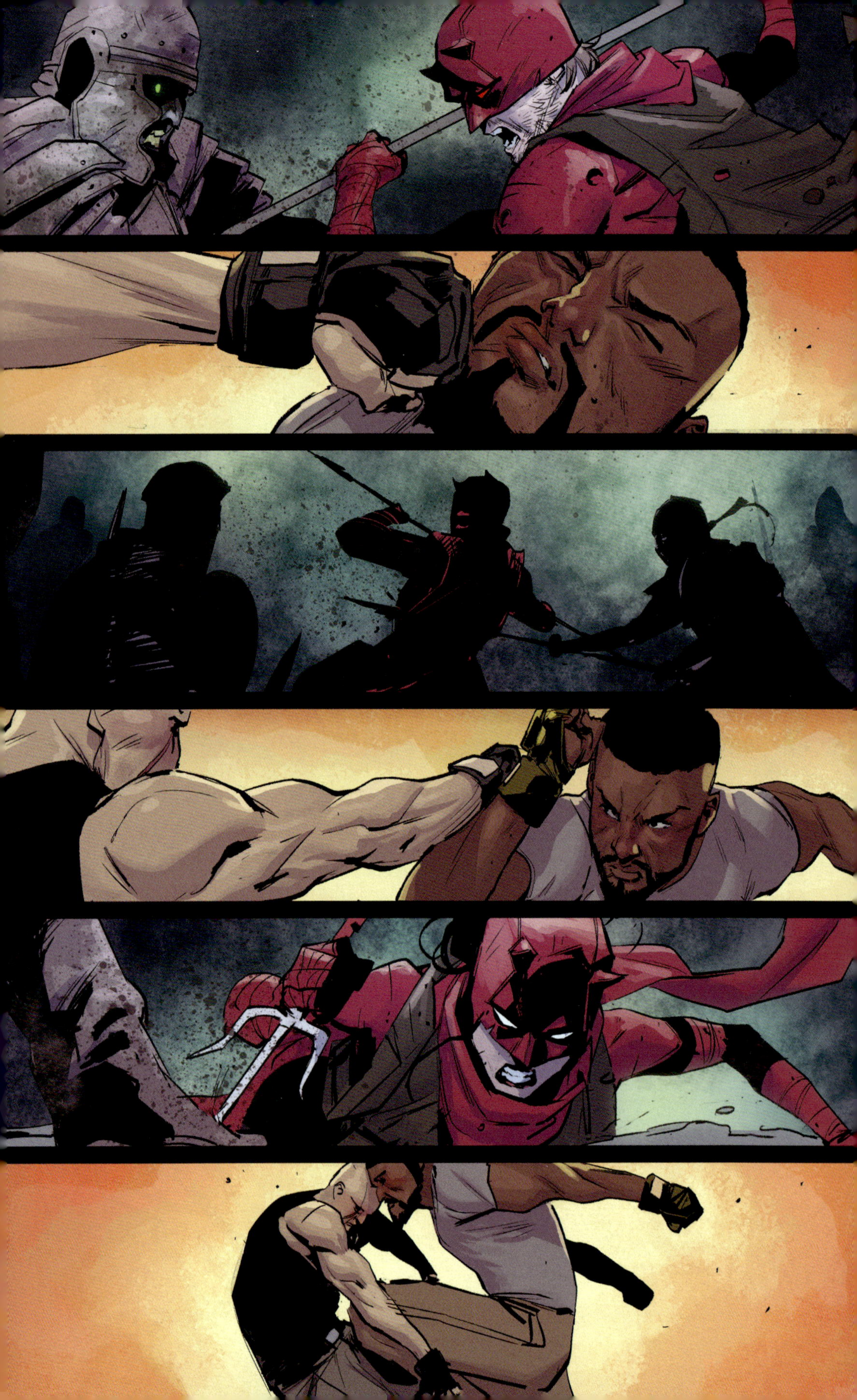

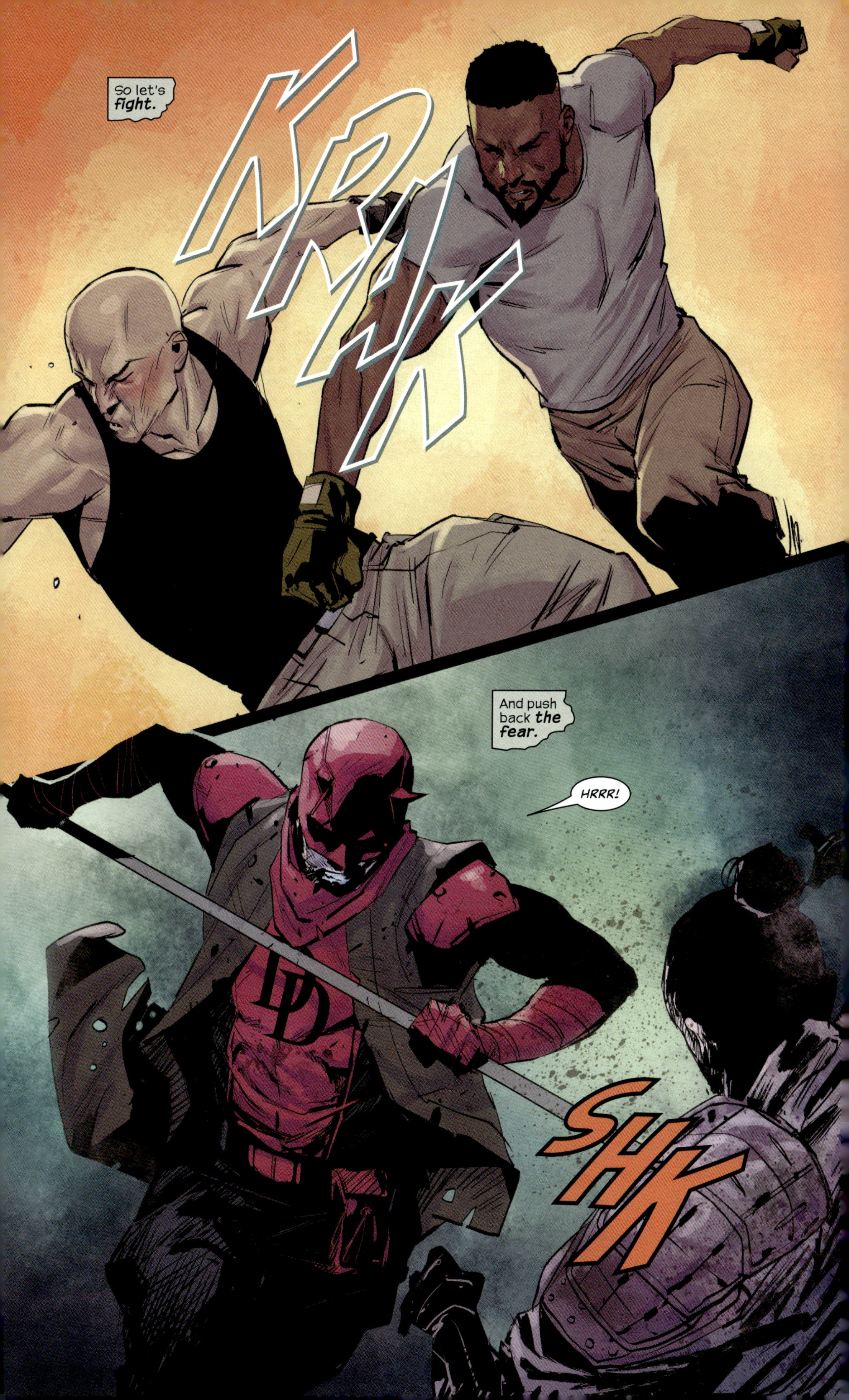

So let's *fight.*
And push back *the fear.*
HRRR!
SHK

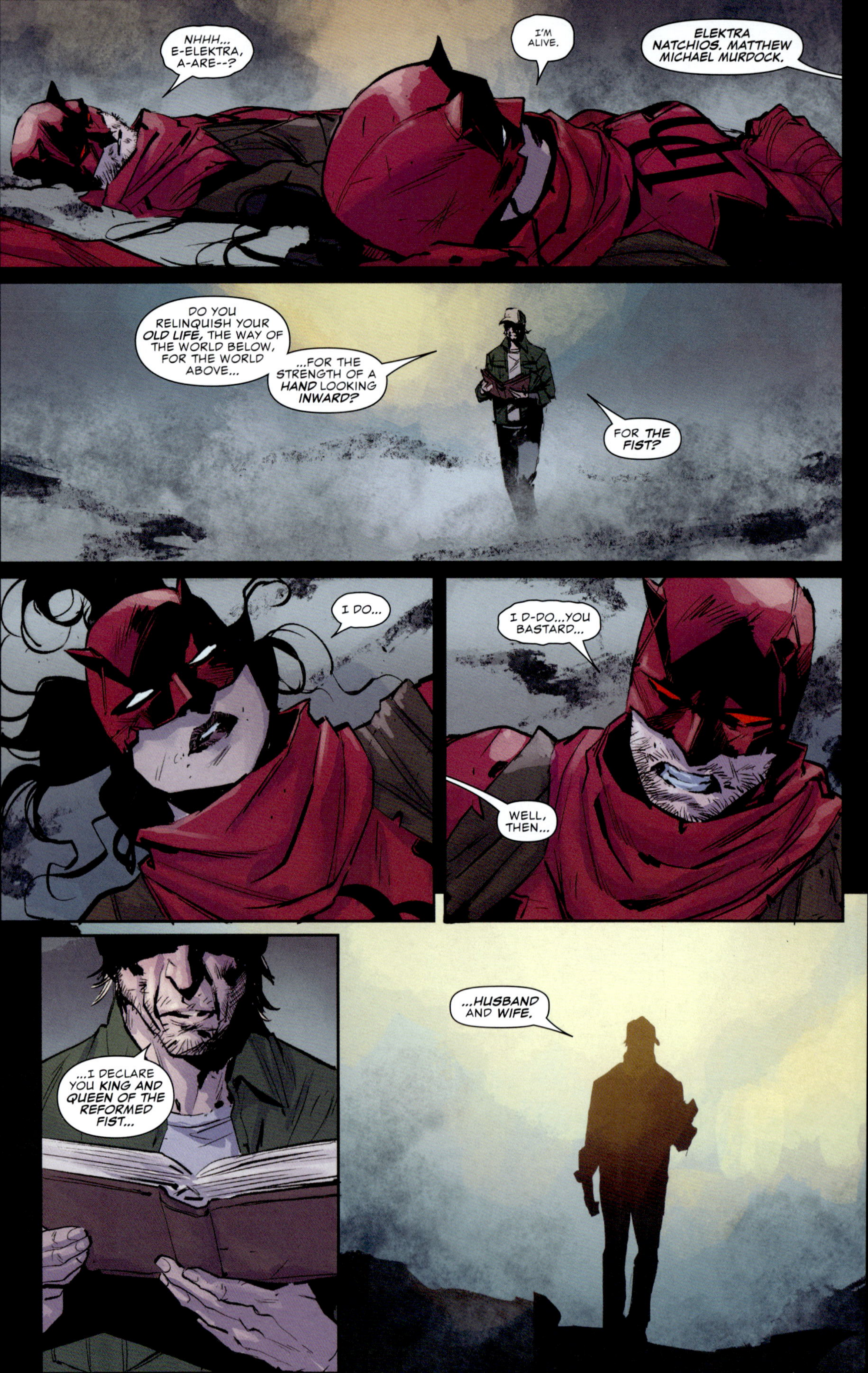
NHHH... E-ELEKTRA, A-ARE--?
I'M ALIVE.
ELEKTRA NATCHIOS. MATTHEW MICHAEL MURDOCK.
DO YOU RELINQUISH YOUR OLD LIFE, THE WAY OF THE WORLD BELOW, FOR THE WORLD ABOVE...
...FOR THE STRENGTH OF A HAND LOOKING INWARD?
FOR THE FIST?
I DO...
I D-DO...YOU BASTARD...
WELL, THEN...
...I DECLARE YOU KING AND QUEEN OF THE REFORMED FIST...
...HUSBAND AND WIFE.

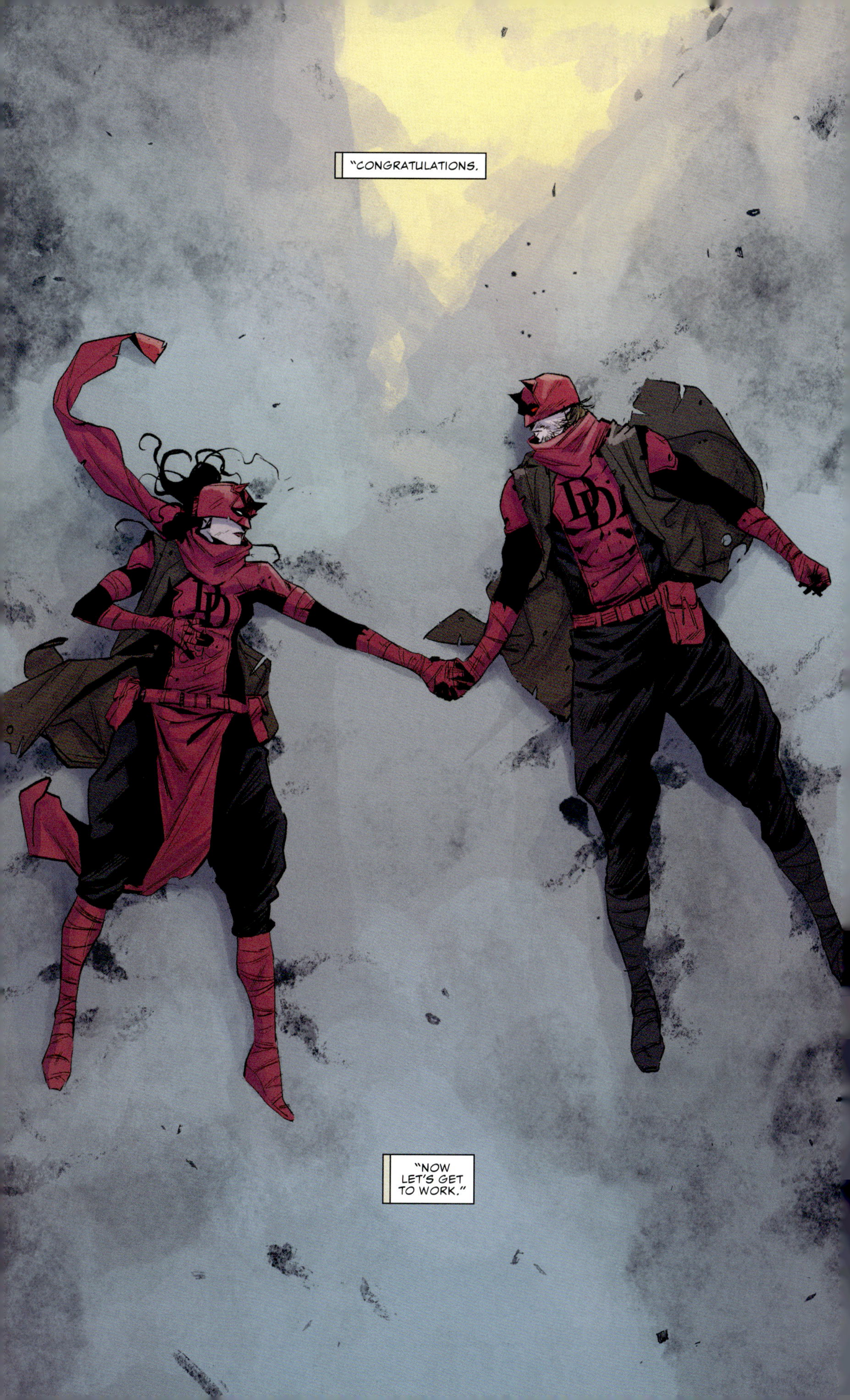
"CONGRATULATIONS.
"NOW LET'S GET TO WORK."

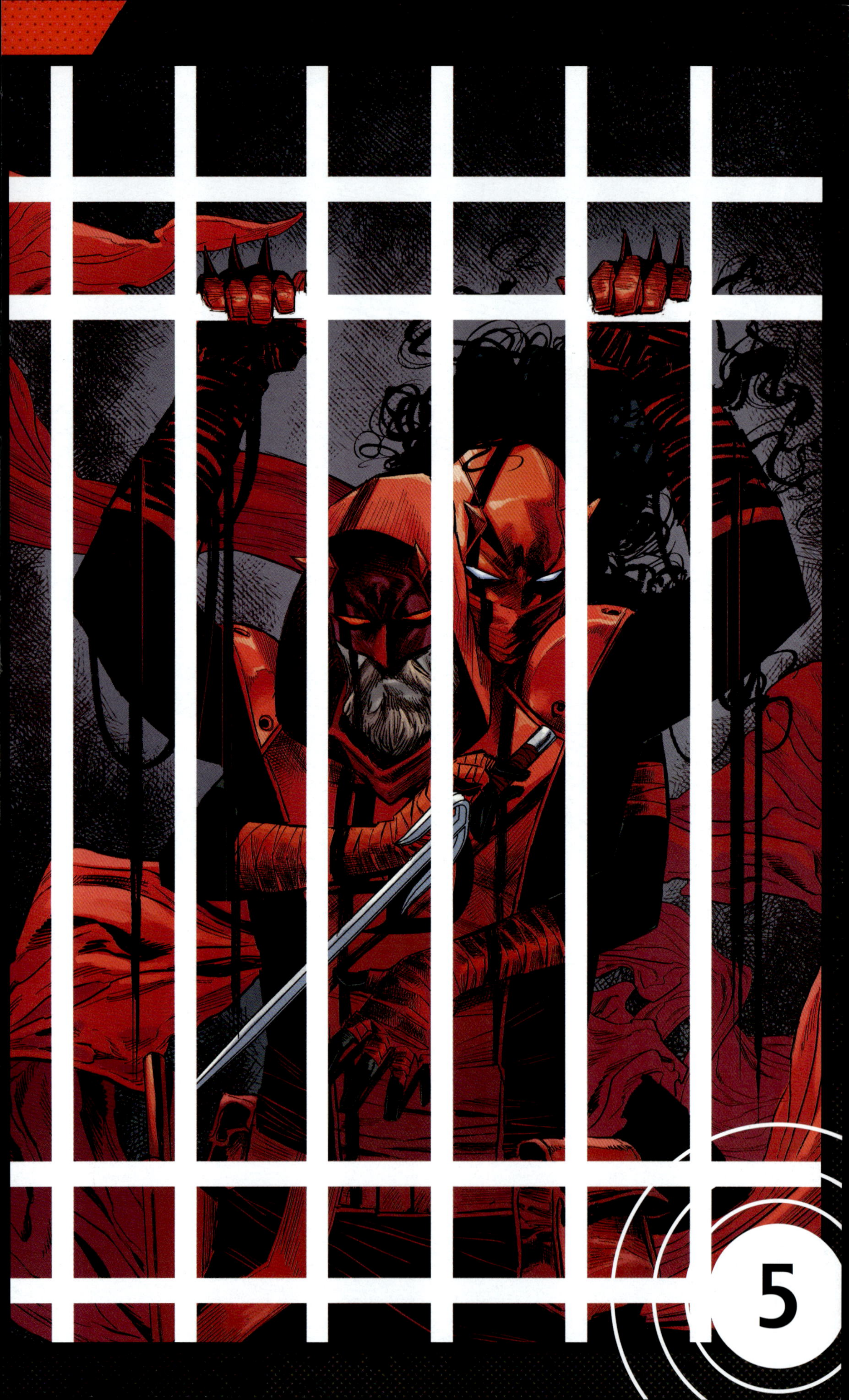

5

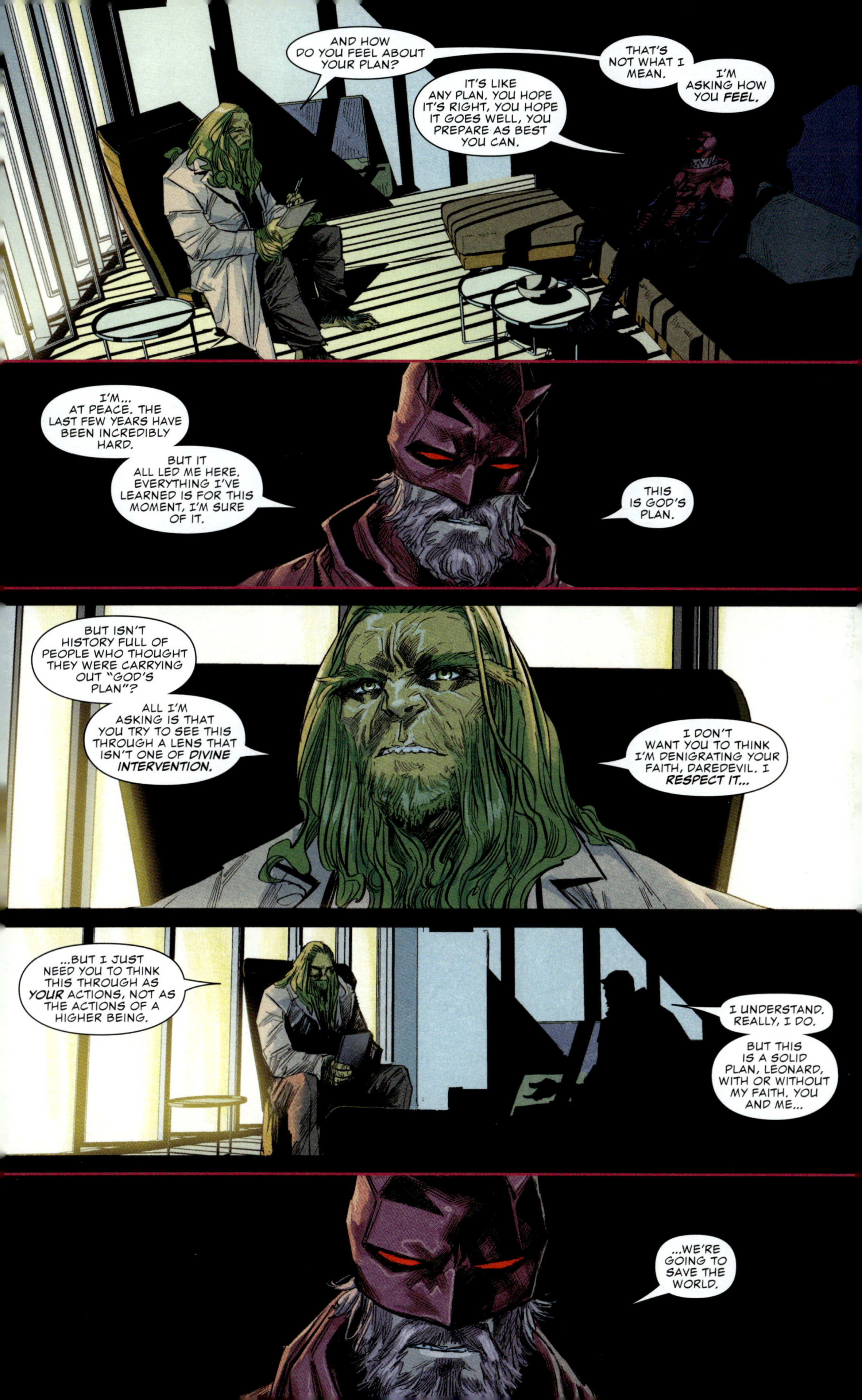
AND HOW DO YOU FEEL ABOUT YOUR PLAN?
IT'S LIKE ANY PLAN. YOU HOPE IT'S RIGHT, YOU HOPE IT GOES WELL, YOU PREPARE AS BEST YOU CAN.
THAT'S NOT WHAT I MEAN.
I'M ASKING HOW YOU *FEEL.*
I'M... AT PEACE. THE LAST FEW YEARS HAVE BEEN INCREDIBLY HARD.
BUT IT ALL LED ME HERE. EVERYTHING I'VE LEARNED IS FOR THIS MOMENT, I'M SURE OF IT.
THIS IS GOD'S PLAN.
BUT ISN'T HISTORY FULL OF PEOPLE WHO THOUGHT THEY WERE CARRYING OUT "GOD'S PLAN"?
ALL I'M ASKING IS THAT YOU TRY TO SEE THIS THROUGH A LENS THAT ISN'T ONE OF *DIVINE INTERVENTION.*
I DON'T WANT YOU TO THINK I'M DENIGRATING YOUR FAITH, DAREDEVIL. I *RESPECT IT...*
...BUT I JUST NEED YOU TO THINK THIS THROUGH AS *YOUR* ACTIONS, NOT AS THE ACTIONS OF A HIGHER BEING.
I UNDERSTAND. REALLY, I DO.
BUT THIS IS A SOLID PLAN, LEONARD, WITH OR WITHOUT MY FAITH. YOU AND ME...
...WE'RE GOING TO SAVE THE WORLD.

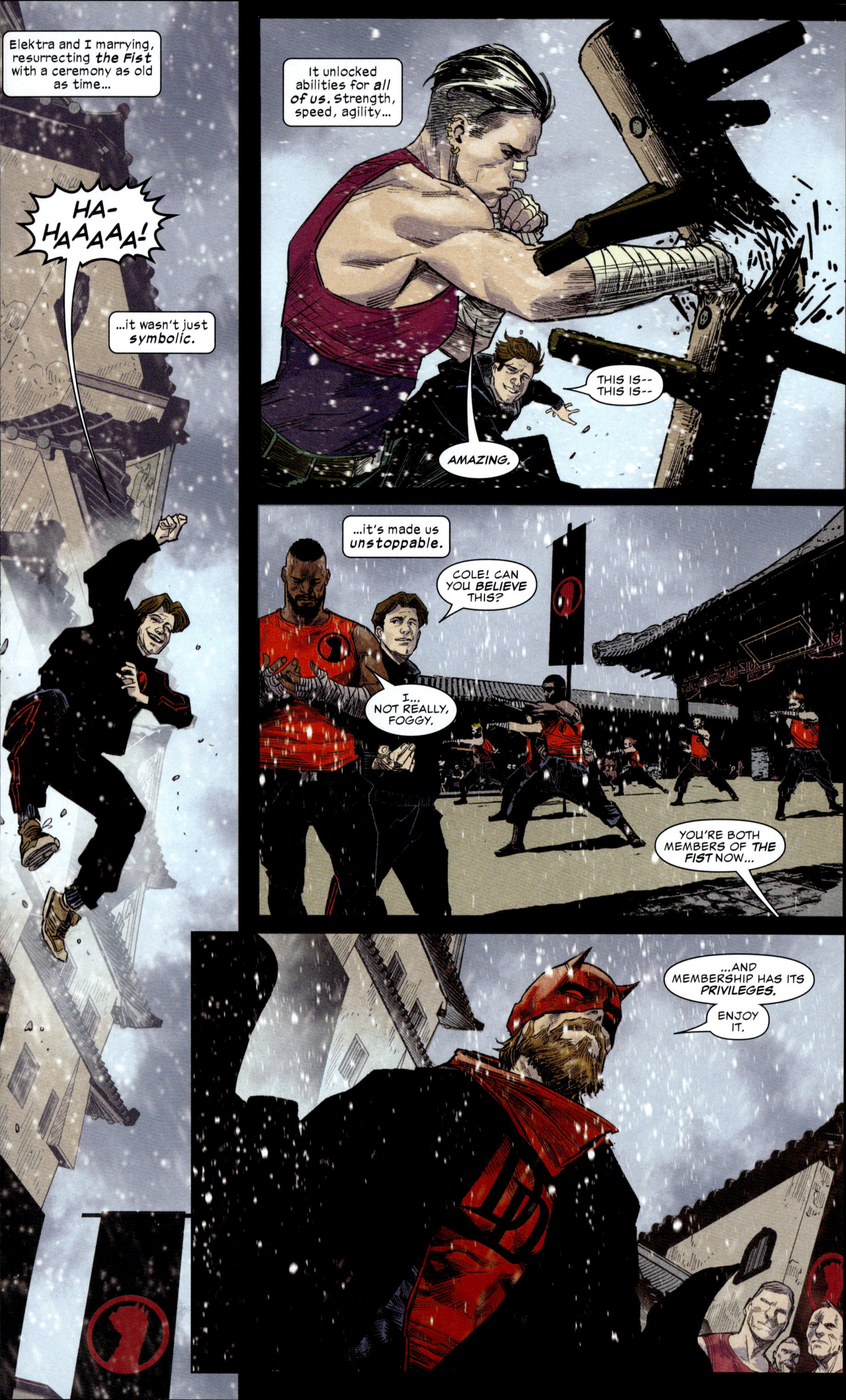

Elektra and I marrying, resurrecting *the Fist* with a ceremony as old as time...
HA-HAAAAA!
...it wasn't just *symbolic.*
It unlocked abilities for *all of us.* Strength, speed, agility...
THIS IS-- THIS IS--
AMAZING.
...it's made us *unstoppable.*
COLE! CAN YOU *BELIEVE* THIS?
I... NOT REALLY, FOGGY.
YOU'RE BOTH MEMBERS OF *THE FIST* NOW...
...AND MEMBERSHIP HAS ITS *PRIVILEGES.*
ENJOY IT.

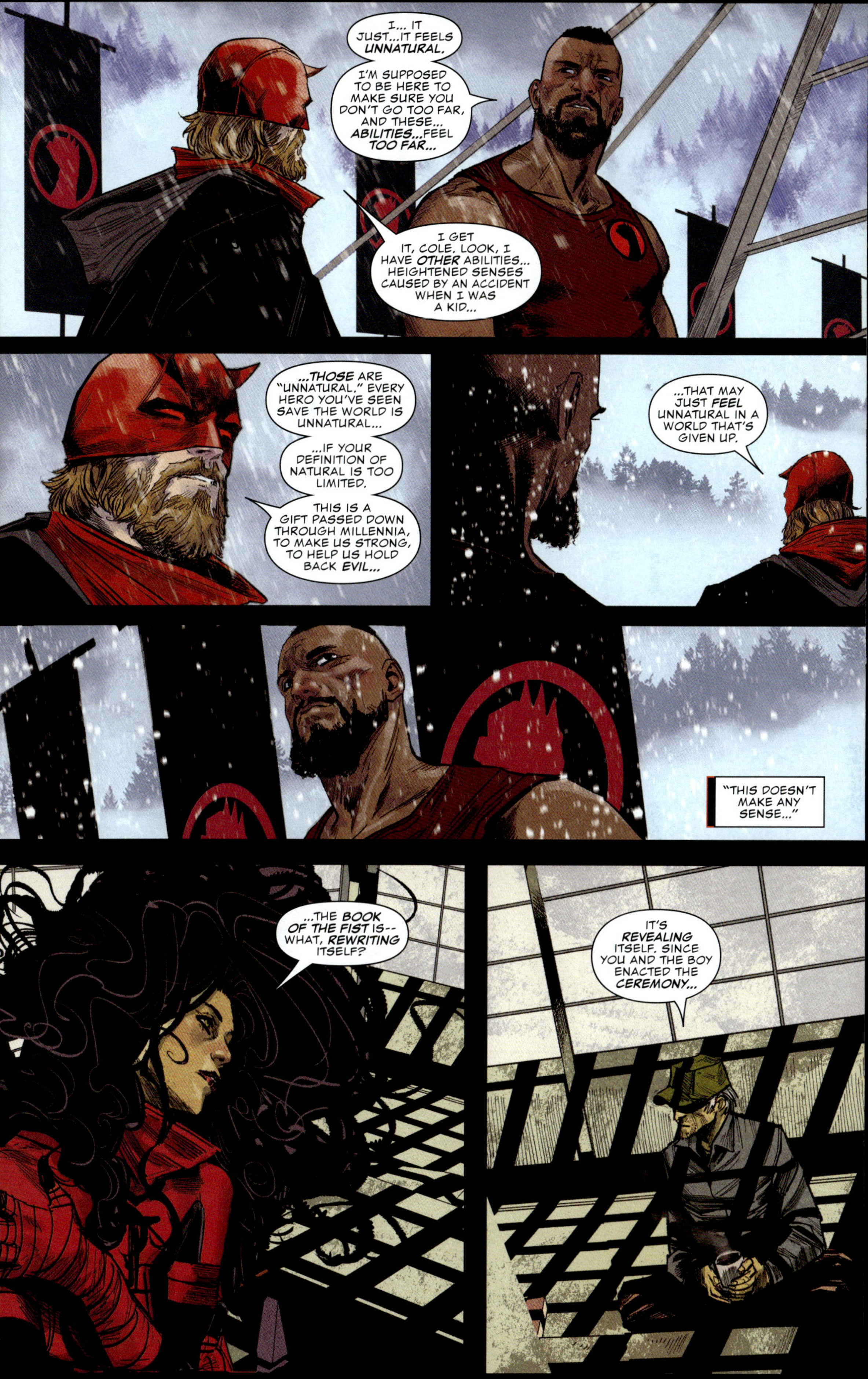
I... IT JUST...IT FEELS UNNATURAL.
I'M SUPPOSED TO BE HERE TO MAKE SURE YOU DON'T GO TOO FAR, AND THESE... ABILITIES...FEEL TOO FAR...
I GET IT, COLE. LOOK, I HAVE OTHER ABILITIES... HEIGHTENED SENSES CAUSED BY AN ACCIDENT WHEN I WAS A KID...
...THOSE ARE "UNNATURAL." EVERY HERO YOU'VE SEEN SAVE THE WORLD IS UNNATURAL...
...IF YOUR DEFINITION OF NATURAL IS TOO LIMITED.
THIS IS A GIFT PASSED DOWN THROUGH MILLENNIA, TO MAKE US STRONG, TO HELP US HOLD BACK EVIL...
...THAT MAY JUST FEEL UNNATURAL IN A WORLD THAT'S GIVEN UP.
"THIS DOESN'T MAKE ANY SENSE..."
...THE BOOK OF THE FIST IS-- WHAT, REWRITING ITSELF?
IT'S REVEALING ITSELF. SINCE YOU AND THE BOY ENACTED THE CEREMONY...

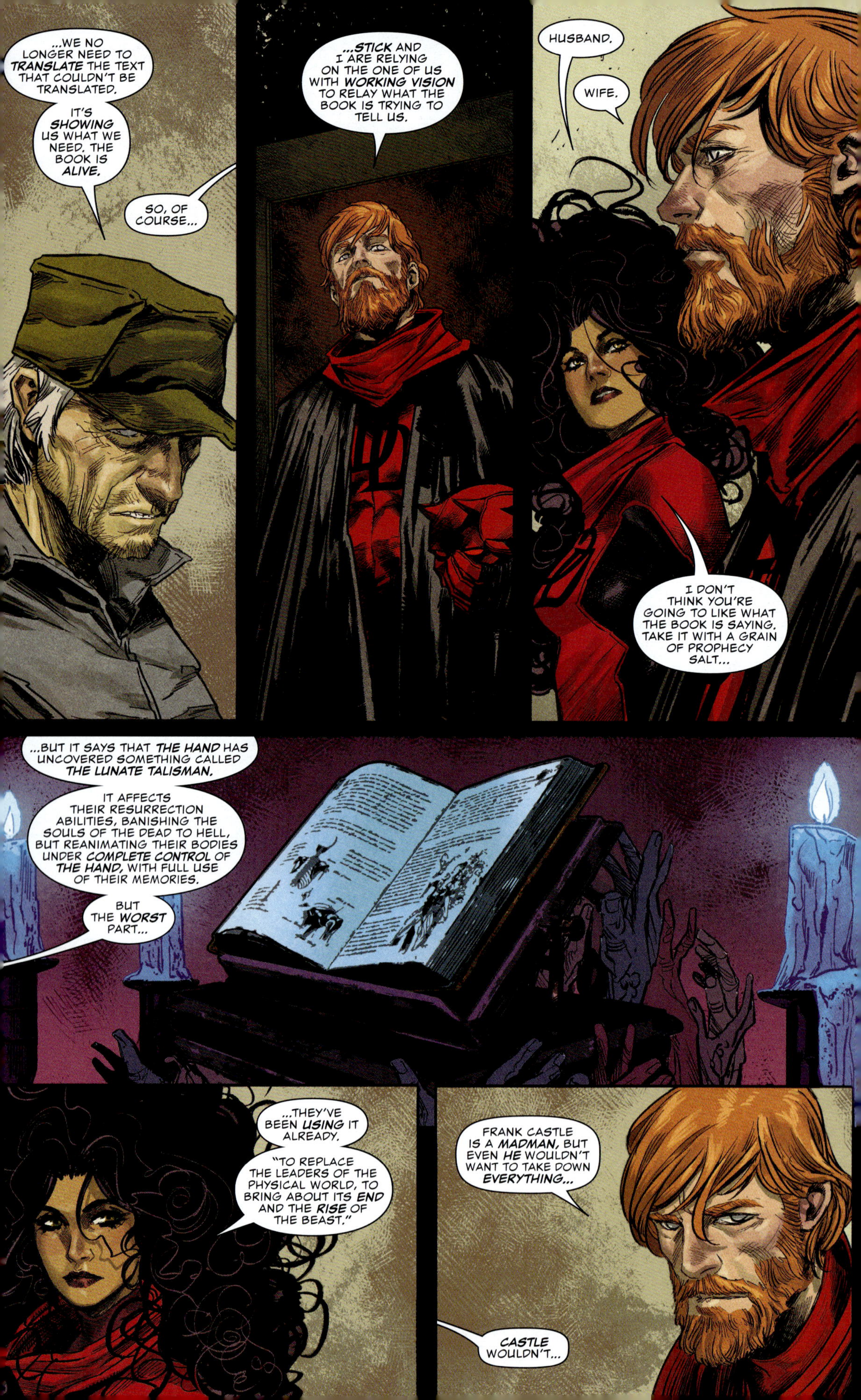

...WE NO LONGER NEED TO TRANSLATE THE TEXT THAT COULDN'T BE TRANSLATED.
IT'S SHOWING US WHAT WE NEED. THE BOOK IS ALIVE.
SO, OF COURSE...
...STICK AND I ARE RELYING ON THE ONE OF US WITH WORKING VISION TO RELAY WHAT THE BOOK IS TRYING TO TELL US.
HUSBAND.
WIFE.
I DON'T THINK YOU'RE GOING TO LIKE WHAT THE BOOK IS SAYING. TAKE IT WITH A GRAIN OF PROPHECY SALT...
...BUT IT SAYS THAT THE HAND HAS UNCOVERED SOMETHING CALLED THE LUNATE TALISMAN.
IT AFFECTS THEIR RESURRECTION ABILITIES, BANISHING THE SOULS OF THE DEAD TO HELL, BUT REANIMATING THEIR BODIES UNDER COMPLETE CONTROL OF THE HAND, WITH FULL USE OF THEIR MEMORIES.
BUT THE WORST PART...
...THEY'VE BEEN USING IT ALREADY.
"TO REPLACE THE LEADERS OF THE PHYSICAL WORLD, TO BRING ABOUT ITS END AND THE RISE OF THE BEAST."
FRANK CASTLE IS A MADMAN, BUT EVEN HE WOULDN'T WANT TO TAKE DOWN EVERYTHING...
CASTLE WOULDN'T...

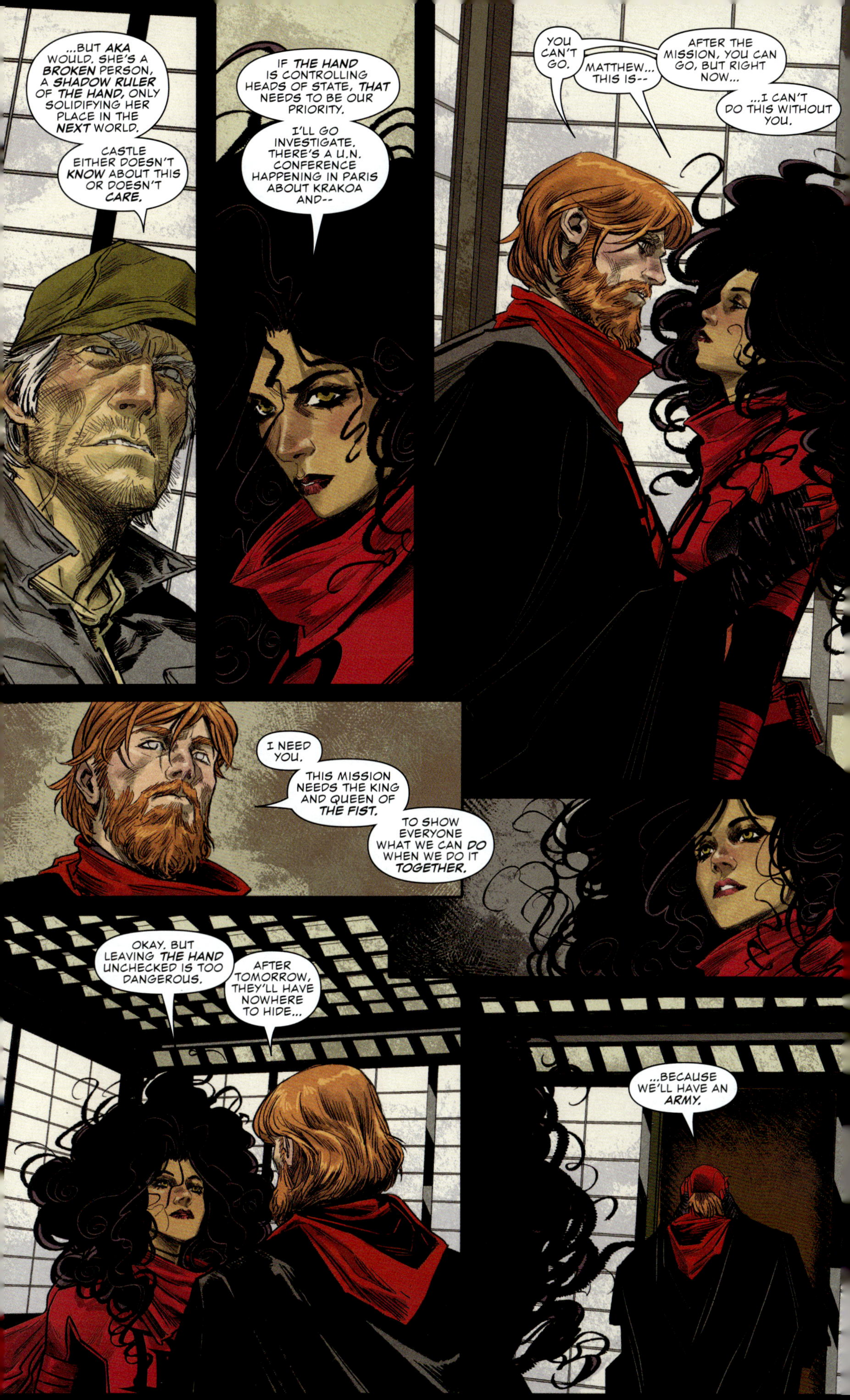
...BUT AKA WOULD. SHE'S A BROKEN PERSON, A SHADOW RULER OF THE HAND, ONLY SOLIDIFYING HER PLACE IN THE NEXT WORLD.
CASTLE EITHER DOESN'T KNOW ABOUT THIS OR DOESN'T CARE.
IF THE HAND IS CONTROLLING HEADS OF STATE, THAT NEEDS TO BE OUR PRIORITY.
I'LL GO INVESTIGATE. THERE'S A U.N. CONFERENCE HAPPENING IN PARIS ABOUT KRAKOA AND--
YOU CAN'T GO.
MATTHEW... THIS IS--
AFTER THE MISSION, YOU CAN GO, BUT RIGHT NOW...
...I CAN'T DO THIS WITHOUT YOU.
I NEED YOU.
THIS MISSION NEEDS THE KING AND QUEEN OF THE FIST.
TO SHOW EVERYONE WHAT WE CAN DO WHEN WE DO IT TOGETHER.
OKAY. BUT LEAVING THE HAND UNCHECKED IS TOO DANGEROUS.
AFTER TOMORROW, THEY'LL HAVE NOWHERE TO HIDE...
...BECAUSE WE'LL HAVE AN ARMY.

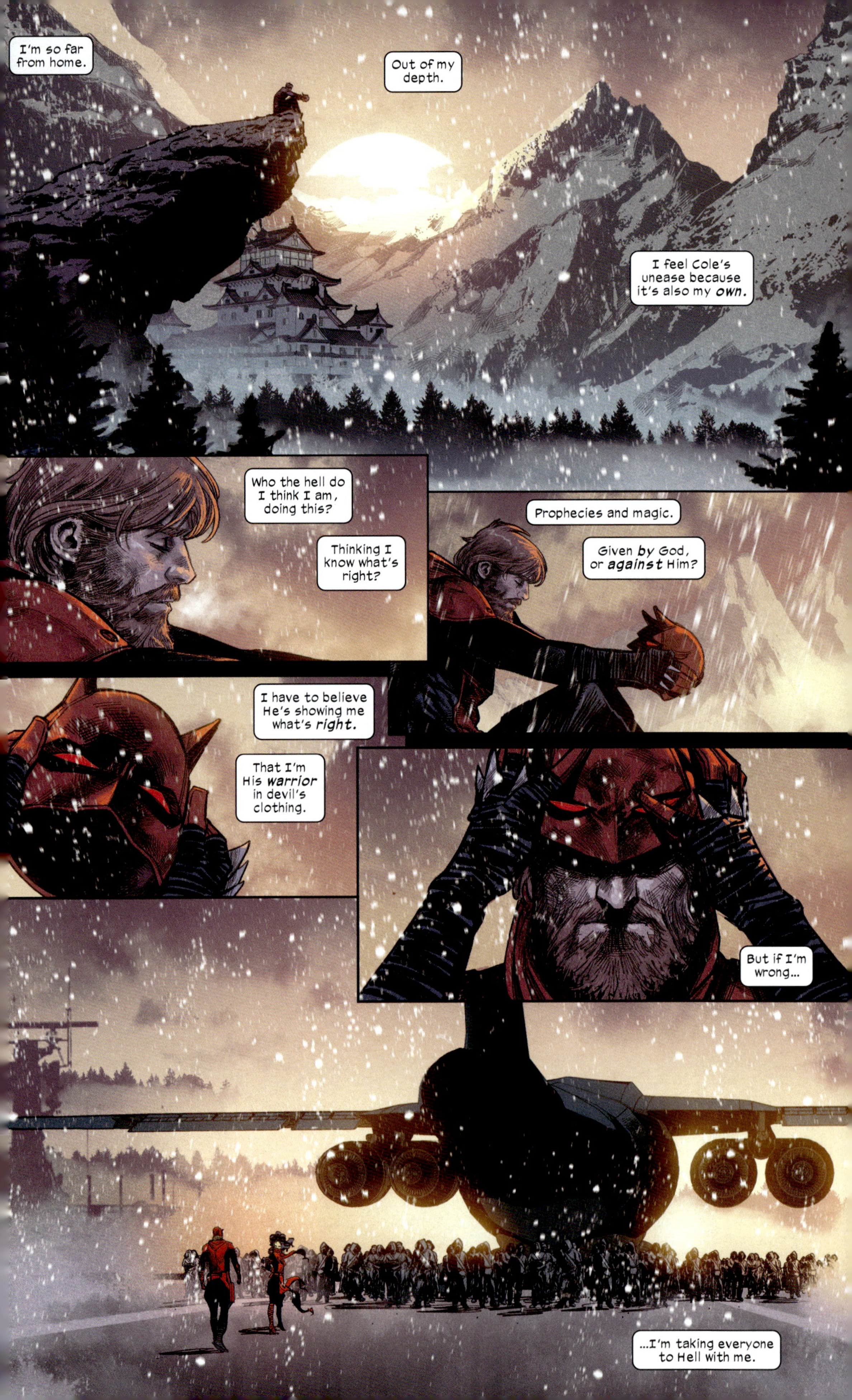
I'm so far from home.
Out of my depth.
I feel Cole's unease because it's also my *own.*
Who the hell do I think I am, doing this?
Thinking I know what's right?
Prophecies and magic.
Given *by* God, or *against* Him?
I have to believe He's showing me what's *right.*
That I'm His *warrior* in devil's clothing.
But if I'm wrong...
...I'm taking everyone to Hell with me.

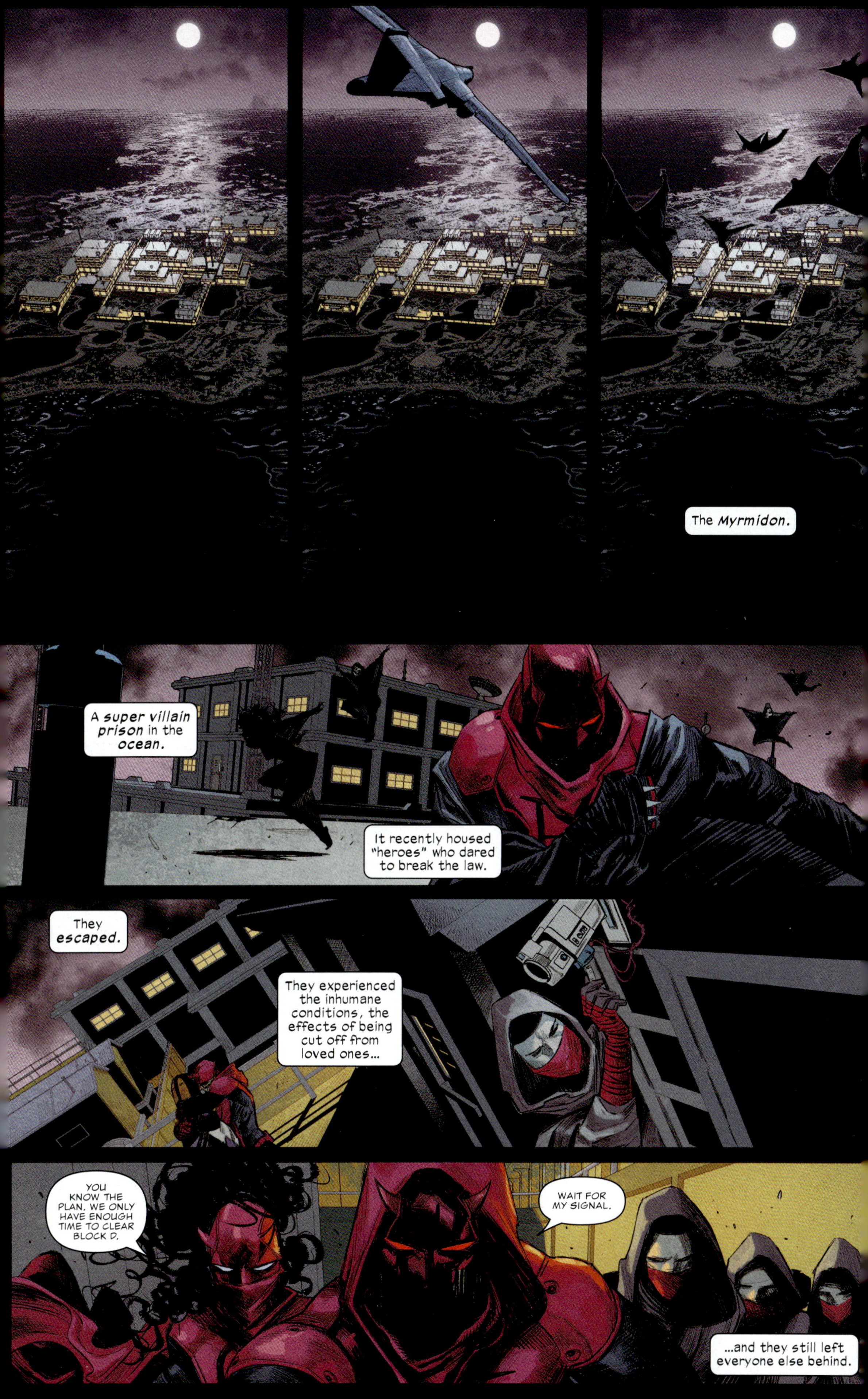
The *Myrmidon.*
A *super villain prison* in the *ocean.*
It recently housed "heroes" who dared to break the law.
They *escaped.*
They experienced the inhumane conditions, the effects of being cut off from loved ones...
YOU KNOW THE PLAN. WE ONLY HAVE ENOUGH TIME TO CLEAR BLOCK D.
WAIT FOR MY SIGNAL.
...and they still left everyone else behind.

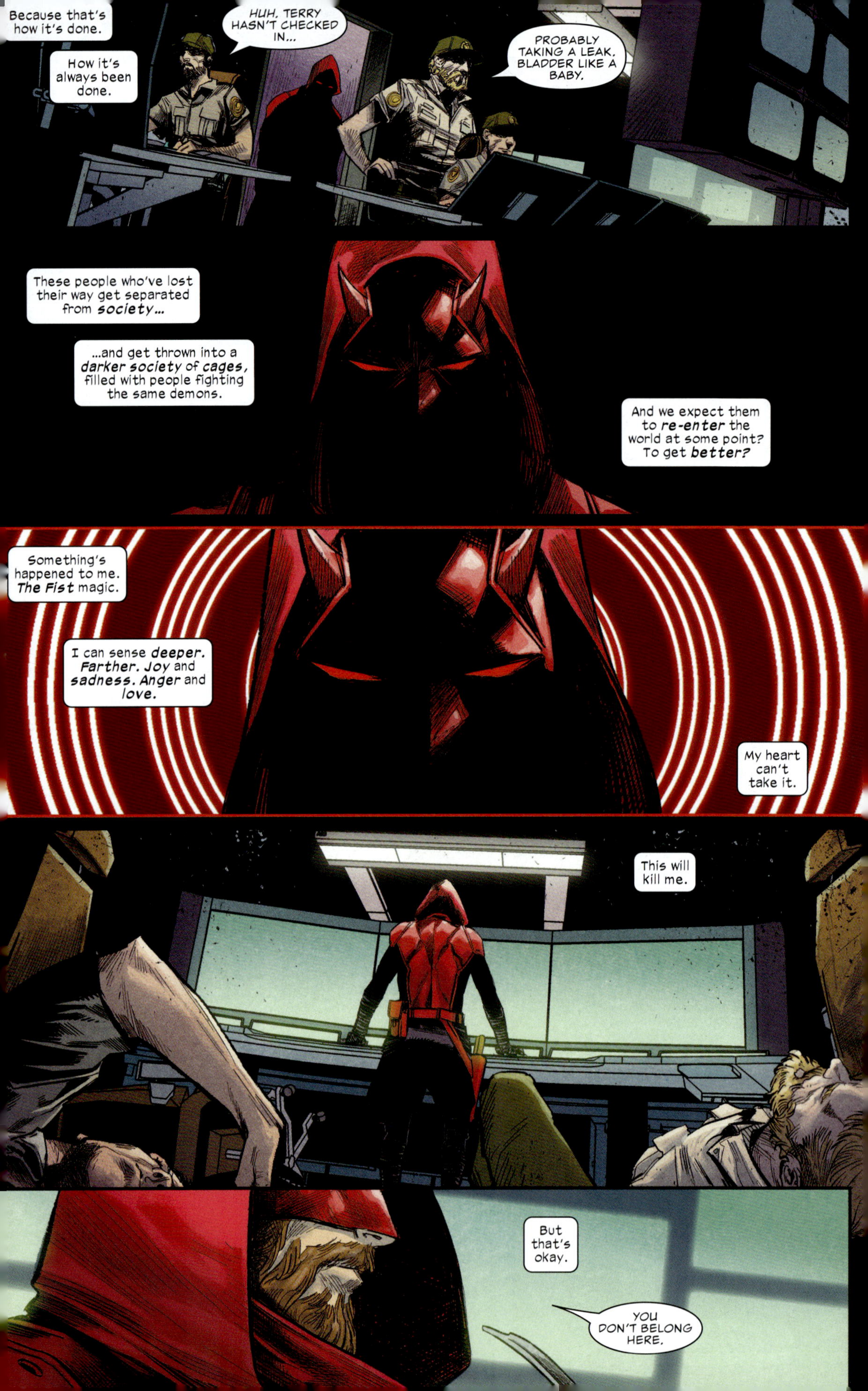
Because that's how it's done.
HUH. TERRY HASN'T CHECKED IN...
How it's always been done.
PROBABLY TAKING A LEAK. BLADDER LIKE A BABY.
These people who've lost their way get separated from *society*...
...and get thrown into a *darker society* of *cages*, filled with people fighting the same demons.
And we expect them to *re-enter* the world at some point? To get *better?*
Something's happened to me. *The Fist* magic.
I can sense *deeper. Farther. Joy* and *sadness. Anger* and *love.*
My heart can't take it.
This will kill me.
But that's okay.
YOU DON'T BELONG HERE.

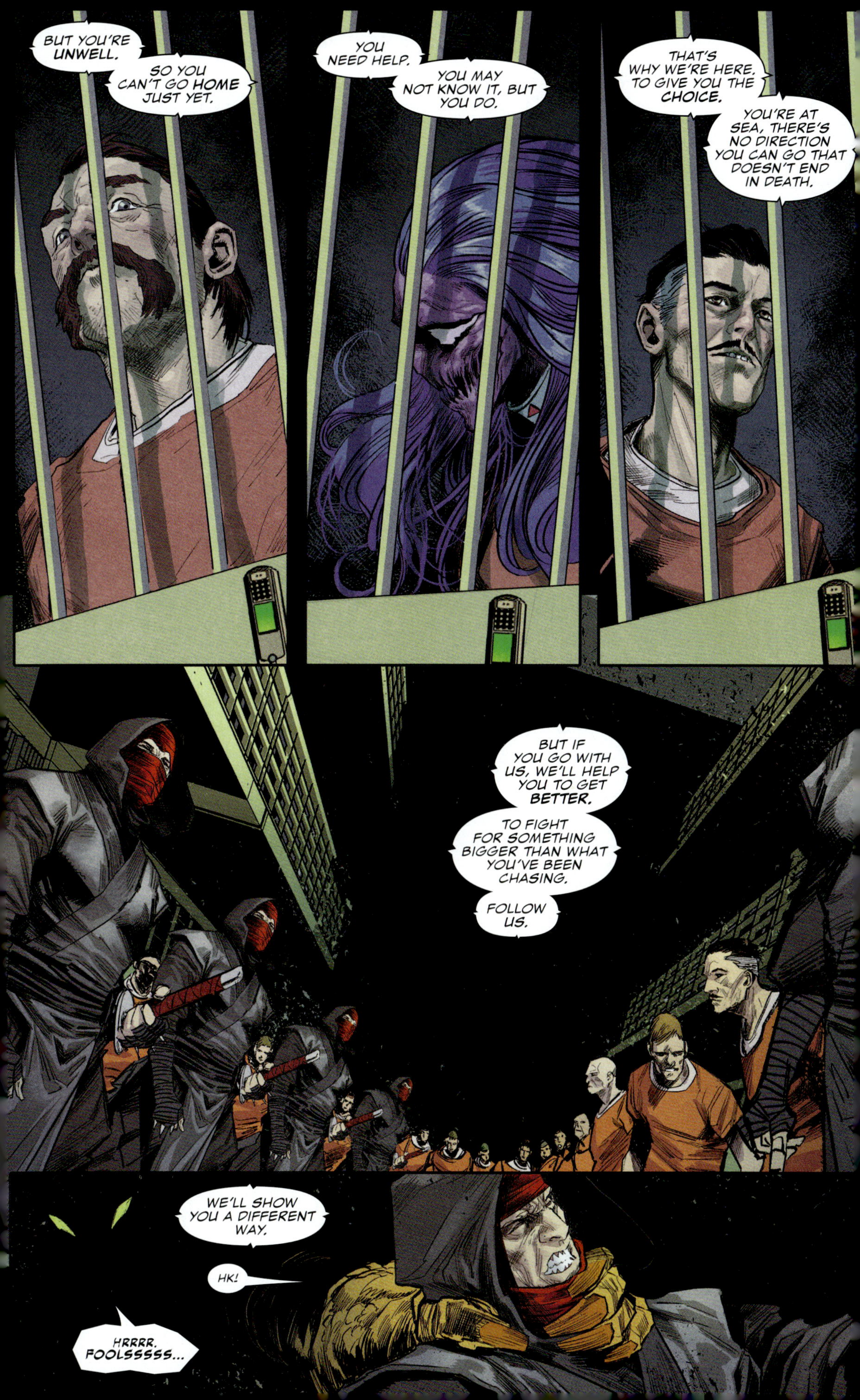
BUT YOU'RE UNWELL.
SO YOU CAN'T GO HOME JUST YET.
YOU NEED HELP.
YOU MAY NOT KNOW IT, BUT YOU DO.
THAT'S WHY WE'RE HERE. TO GIVE YOU THE CHOICE.
YOU'RE AT SEA. THERE'S NO DIRECTION YOU CAN GO THAT DOESN'T END IN DEATH.
BUT IF YOU GO WITH US, WE'LL HELP YOU TO GET BETTER.
TO FIGHT FOR SOMETHING BIGGER THAN WHAT YOU'VE BEEN CHASING.
FOLLOW US.
WE'LL SHOW YOU A DIFFERENT WAY.
HK!
HRRRR. FOOLSSSSS...

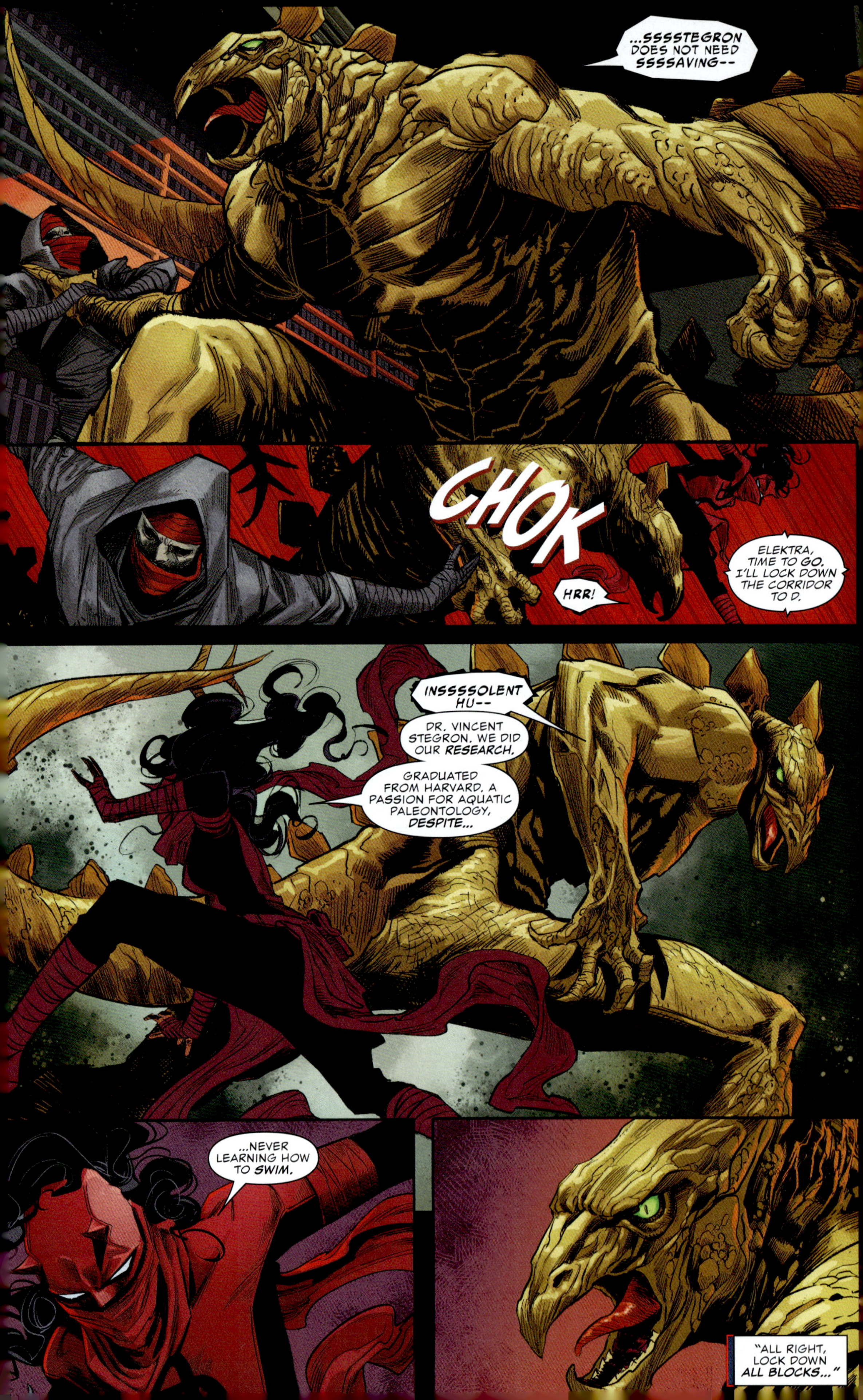
...SSSSTEGRON DOES NOT NEED SSSSAVING--
CHOK
HRR!
ELEKTRA, TIME TO GO. I'LL LOCK DOWN THE CORRIDOR TO D.
INSSSSOLENT HU--
DR. VINCENT STEGRON. WE DID OUR RESEARCH.
GRADUATED FROM HARVARD. A PASSION FOR AQUATIC PALEONTOLOGY, DESPITE...
...NEVER LEARNING HOW TO SWIM.
"ALL RIGHT, LOCK DOWN ALL BLOCKS..."

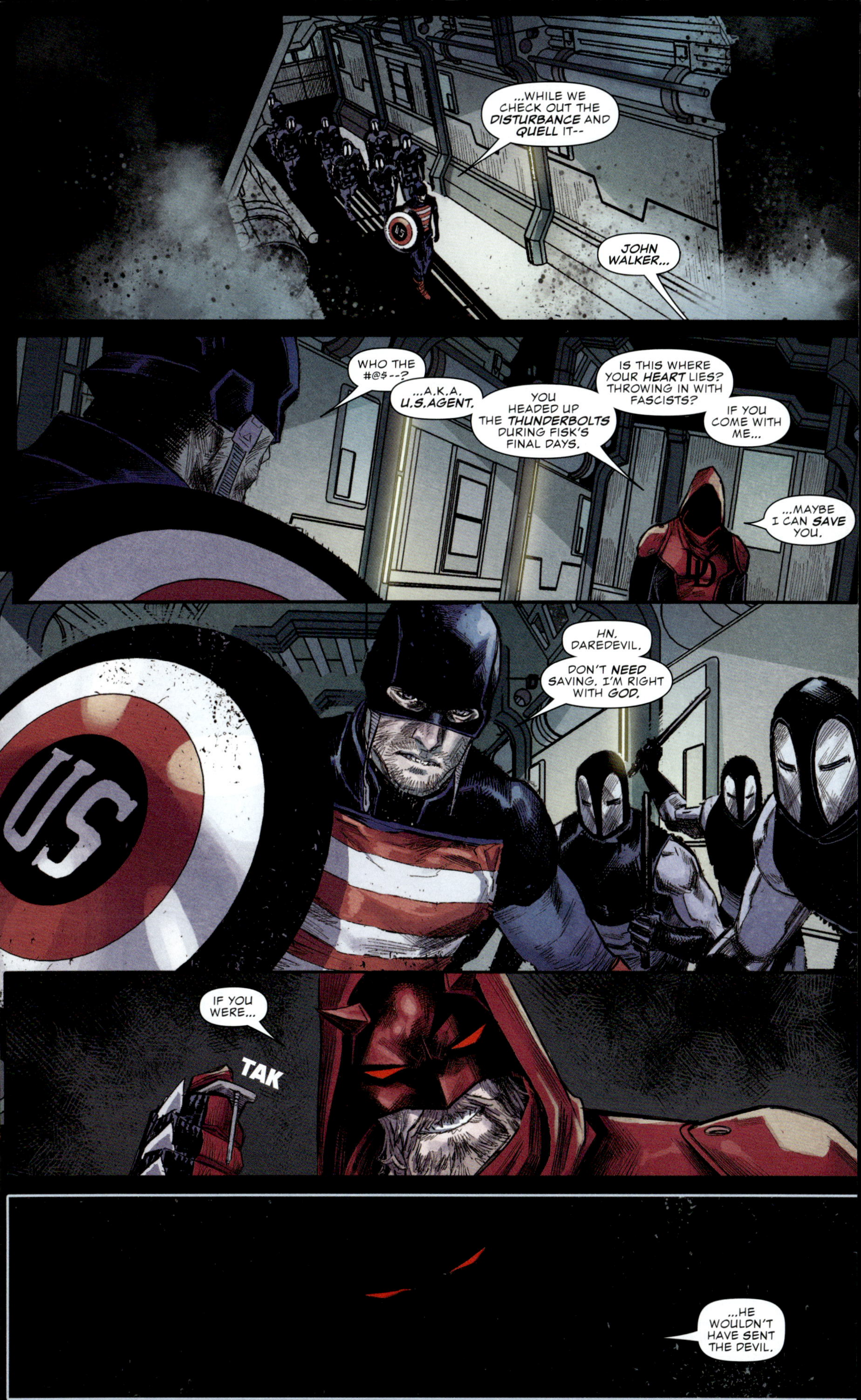
...WHILE WE CHECK OUT THE DISTURBANCE AND QUELL IT--
JOHN WALKER...
WHO THE #@$--?
...A.K.A. U.S.AGENT.
YOU HEADED UP THE THUNDERBOLTS DURING FISK'S FINAL DAYS.
IS THIS WHERE YOUR HEART LIES? THROWING IN WITH FASCISTS?
IF YOU COME WITH ME...
...MAYBE I CAN SAVE YOU.
HN. DAREDEVIL.
DON'T NEED SAVING. I'M RIGHT WITH GOD.
IF YOU WERE...
TAK
...HE WOULDN'T HAVE SENT THE DEVIL.

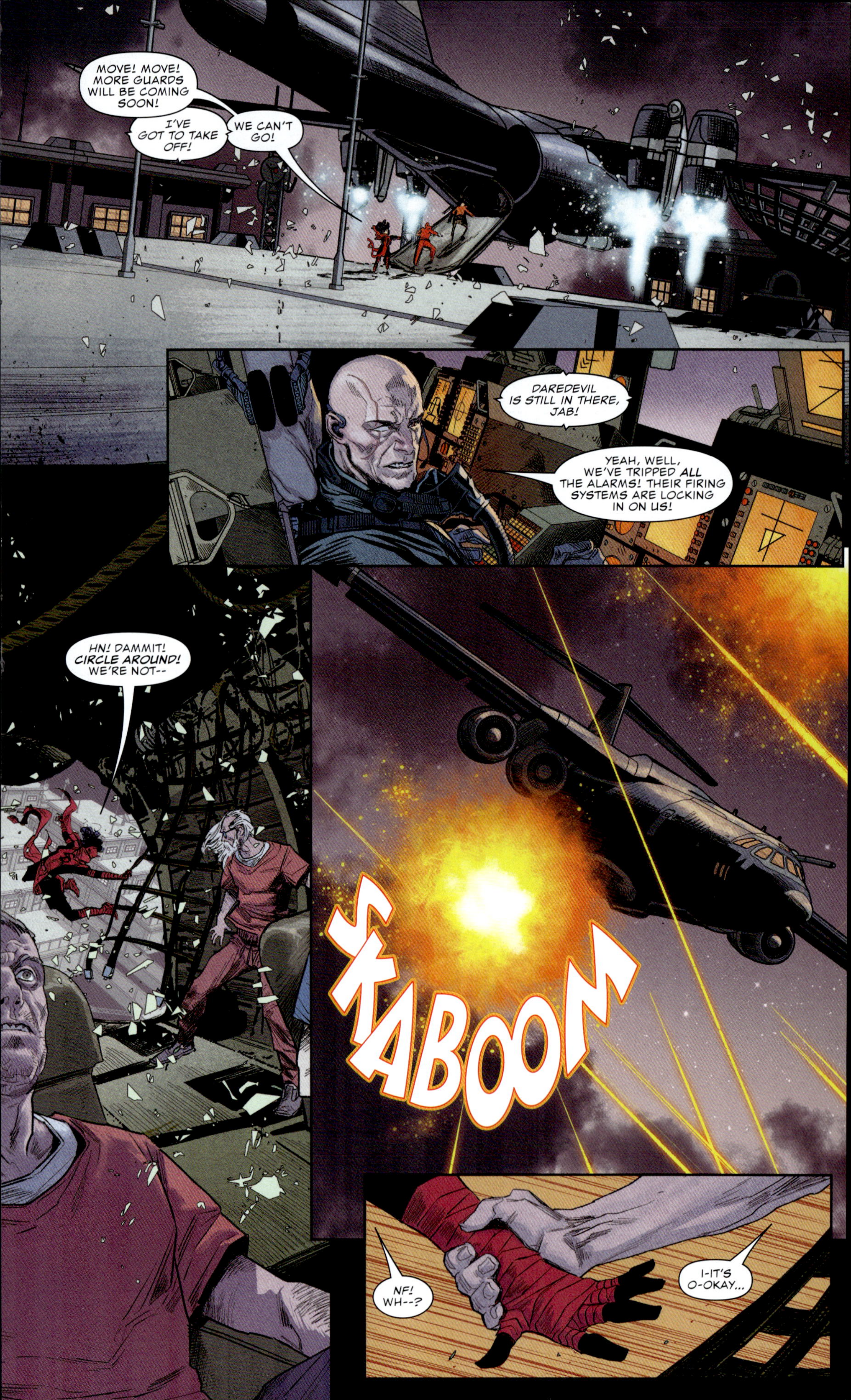
MOVE! MOVE! MORE GUARDS WILL BE COMING SOON!
I'VE GOT TO TAKE OFF!
WE CAN'T GO!
DAREDEVIL IS STILL IN THERE, JAB!
YEAH, WELL, WE'VE TRIPPED ALL THE ALARMS! THEIR FIRING SYSTEMS ARE LOCKING IN ON US!
HN! DAMMIT! CIRCLE AROUND! WE'RE NOT--
SKABOOM
NF! WH--?
I-IT'S O-OKAY...

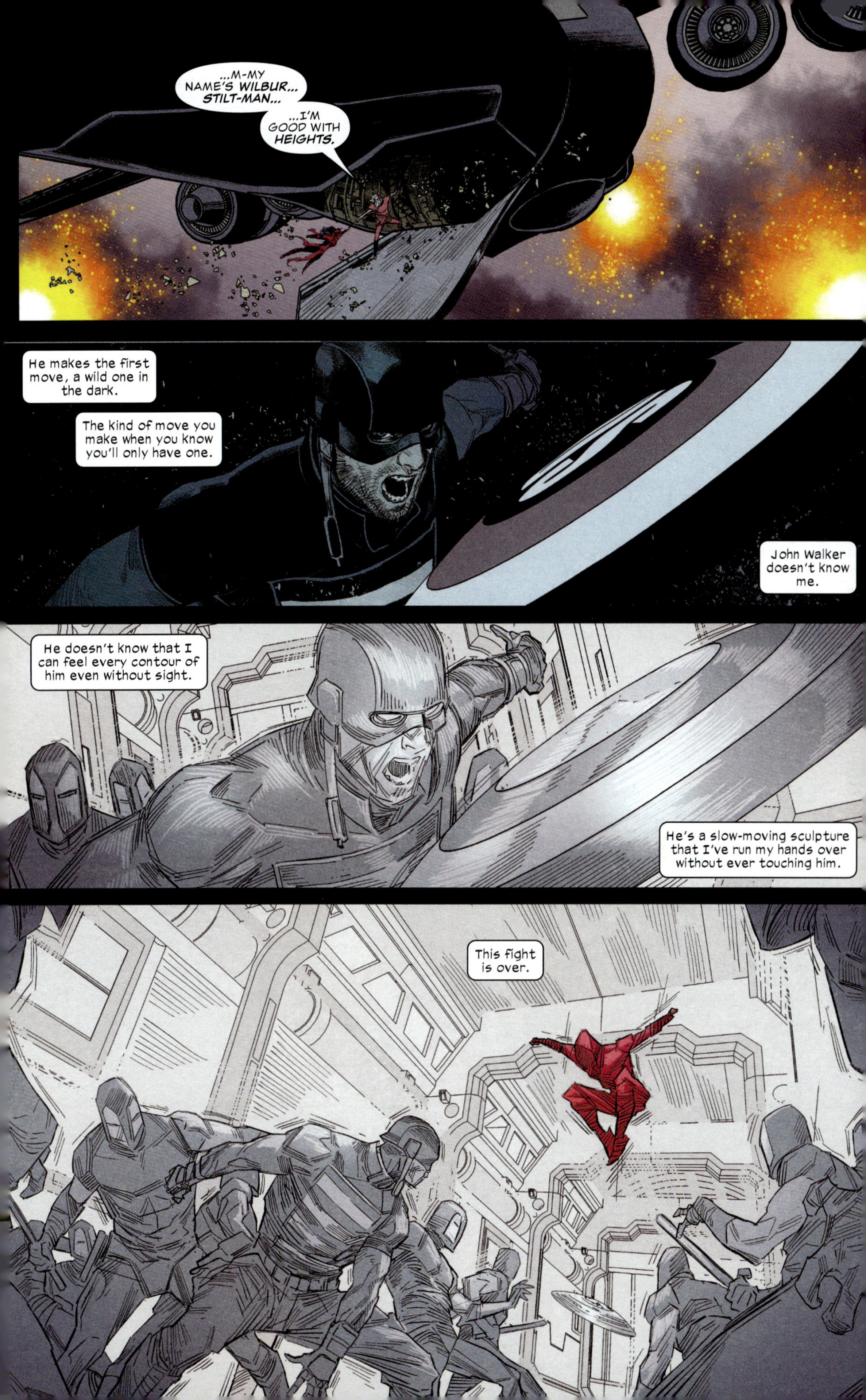
...M-MY NAME'S WILBUR... STILT-MAN...
...I'M GOOD WITH HEIGHTS.
He makes the first move, a wild one in the dark.
The kind of move you make when you know you'll only have one.
John Walker doesn't know me.
He doesn't know that I can feel every contour of him even without sight.
He's a slow-moving sculpture that I've run my hands over without ever touching him.
This fight is over.

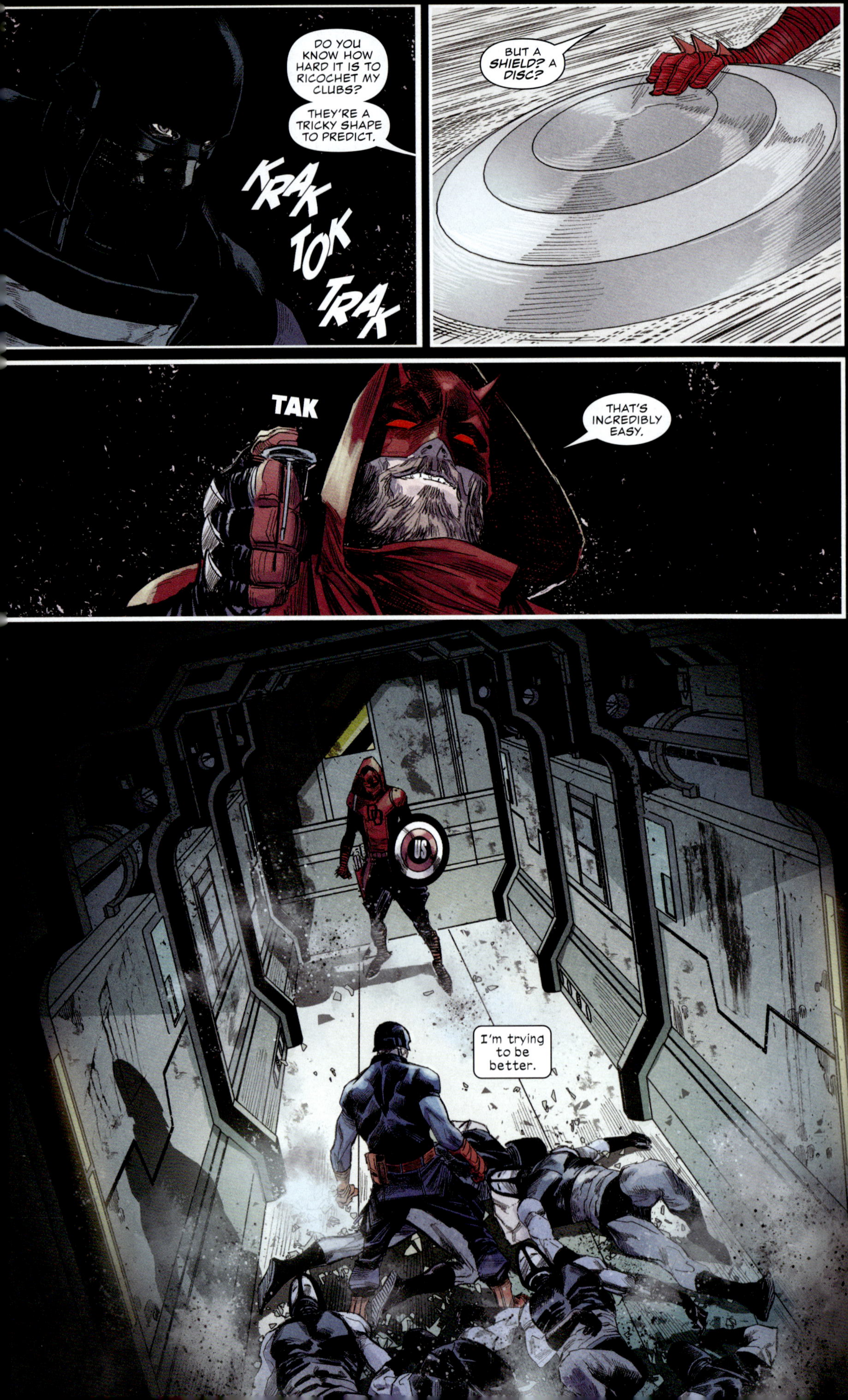

DO YOU KNOW HOW HARD IT IS TO RICOCHET MY CLUBS?
THEY'RE A TRICKY SHAPE TO PREDICT.
KRAK
TOK
TRAK
BUT A SHIELD? A DISC?
TAK
THAT'S INCREDIBLY EASY.
US
I'm trying to be better.

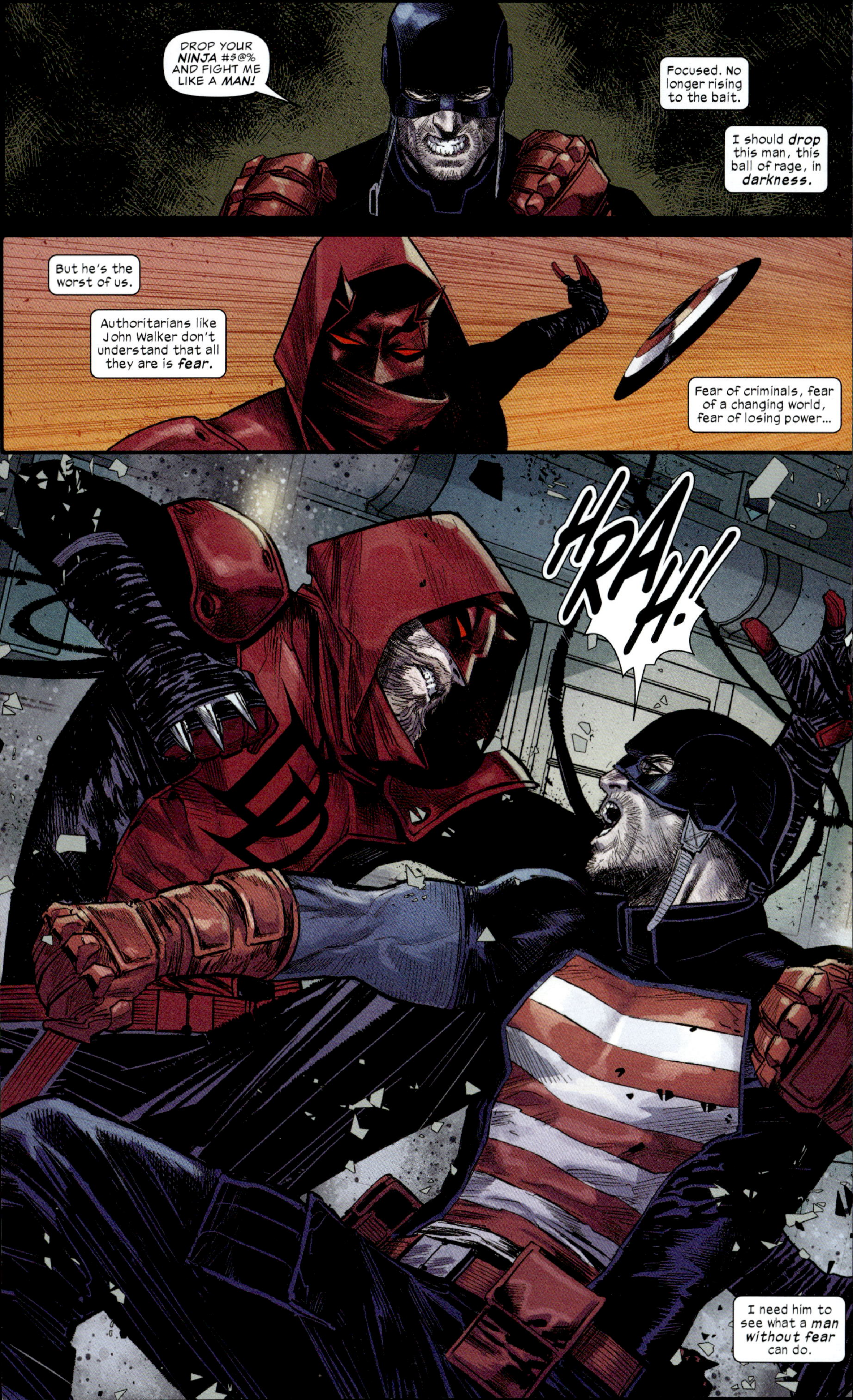

DROP YOUR NINJA #$@% AND FIGHT ME LIKE A MAN!
Focused. No longer rising to the bait.
I should drop this man, this ball of rage, in darkness.
But he's the worst of us.
Authoritarians like John Walker don't understand that all they are is fear.
Fear of criminals, fear of a changing world, fear of losing power...
HRAAH!
I need him to see what a man without fear can do.

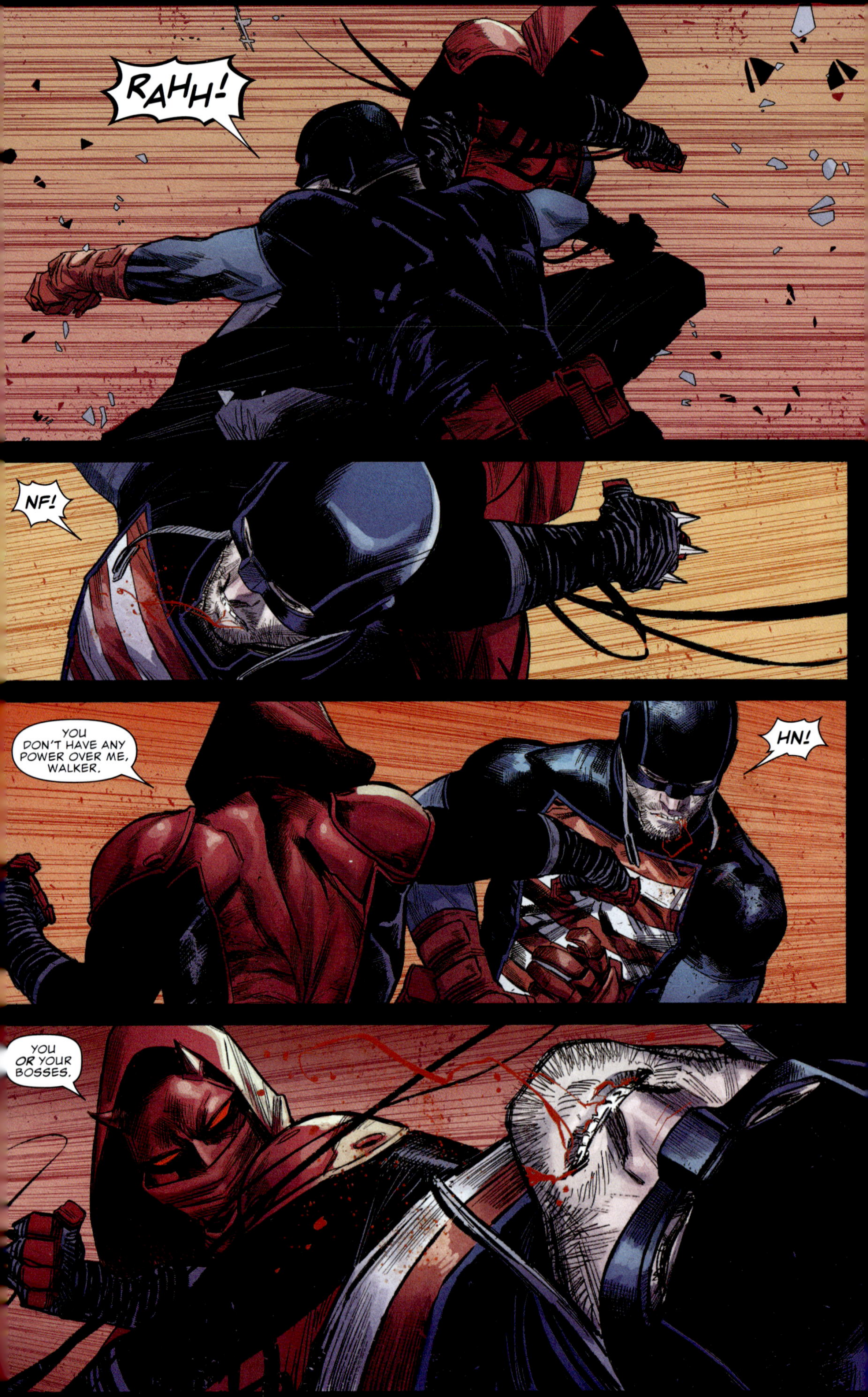
RAHH!
NF!
YOU DON'T HAVE ANY POWER OVER ME, WALKER.
HN!
YOU OR YOUR BOSSES.

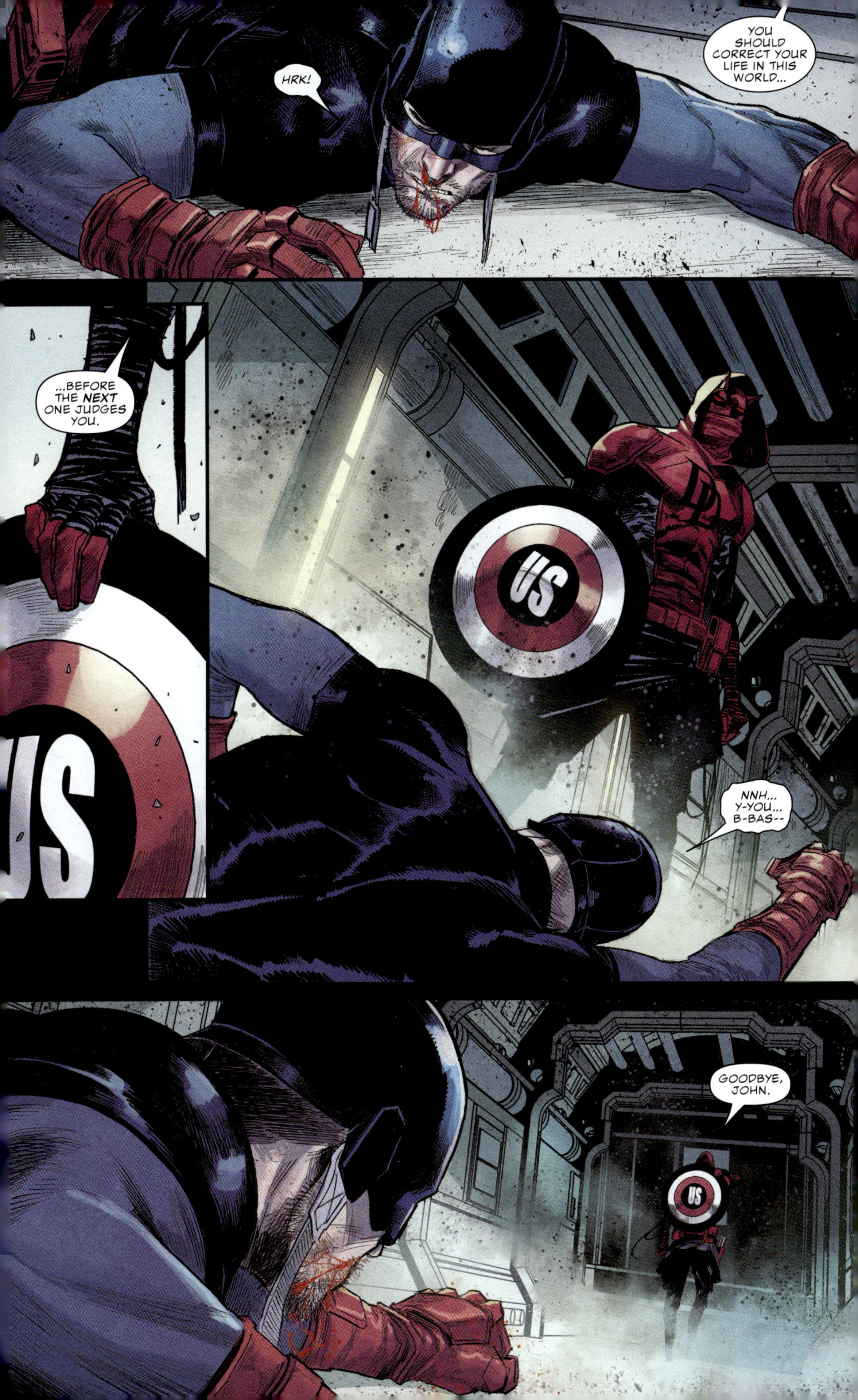
HRK!
YOU SHOULD CORRECT YOUR LIFE IN THIS WORLD...
...BEFORE THE NEXT ONE JUDGES YOU.
US
US
NNH... Y-YOU... B-BAS--
GOODBYE, JOHN.
US

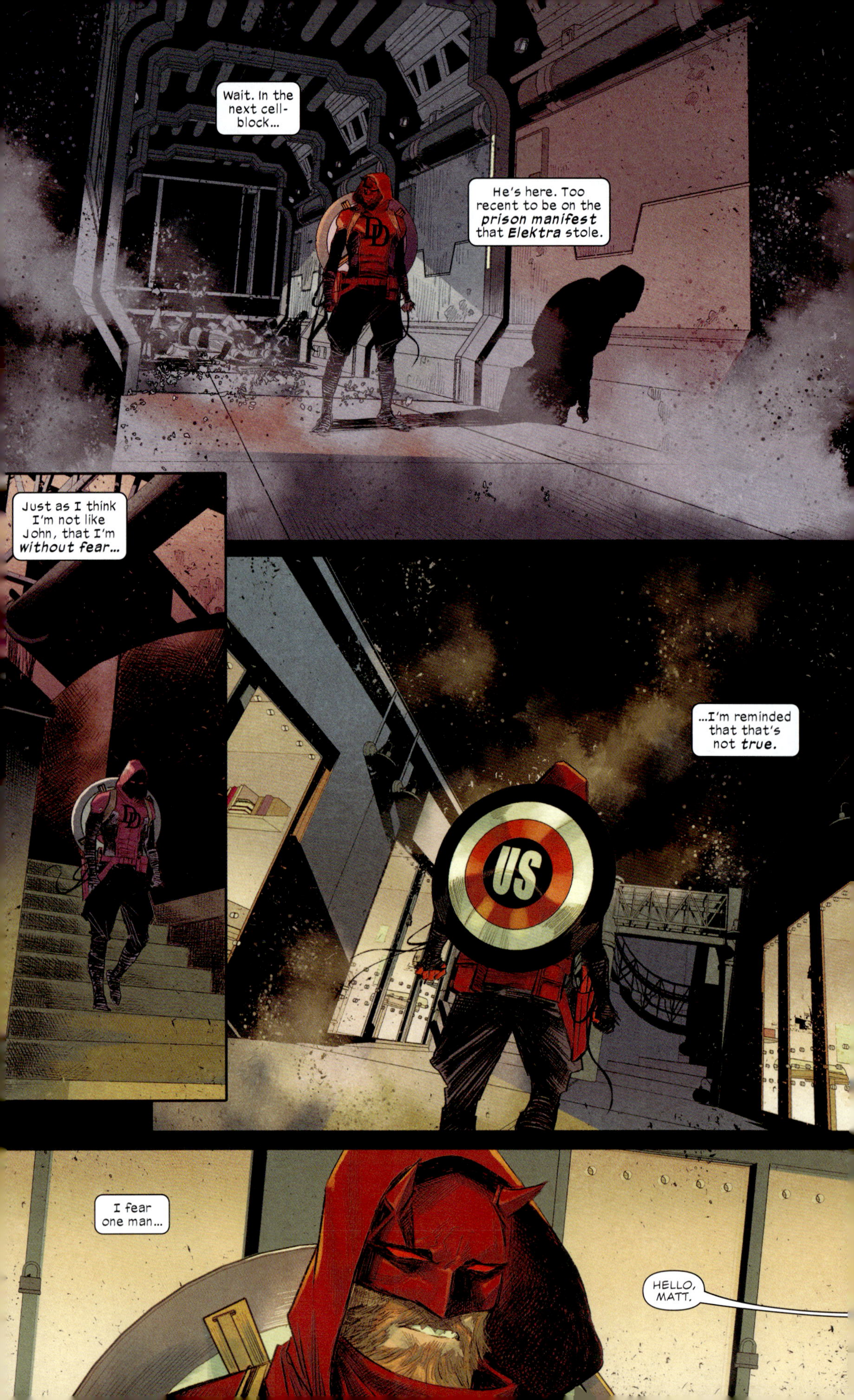
Wait. In the next cell-block...
He's here. Too recent to be on the *prison manifest* that *Elektra* stole.
Just as I think I'm not like John, that I'm *without fear...*
...I'm reminded that that's not *true.*
I fear one man...
HELLO, MATT.

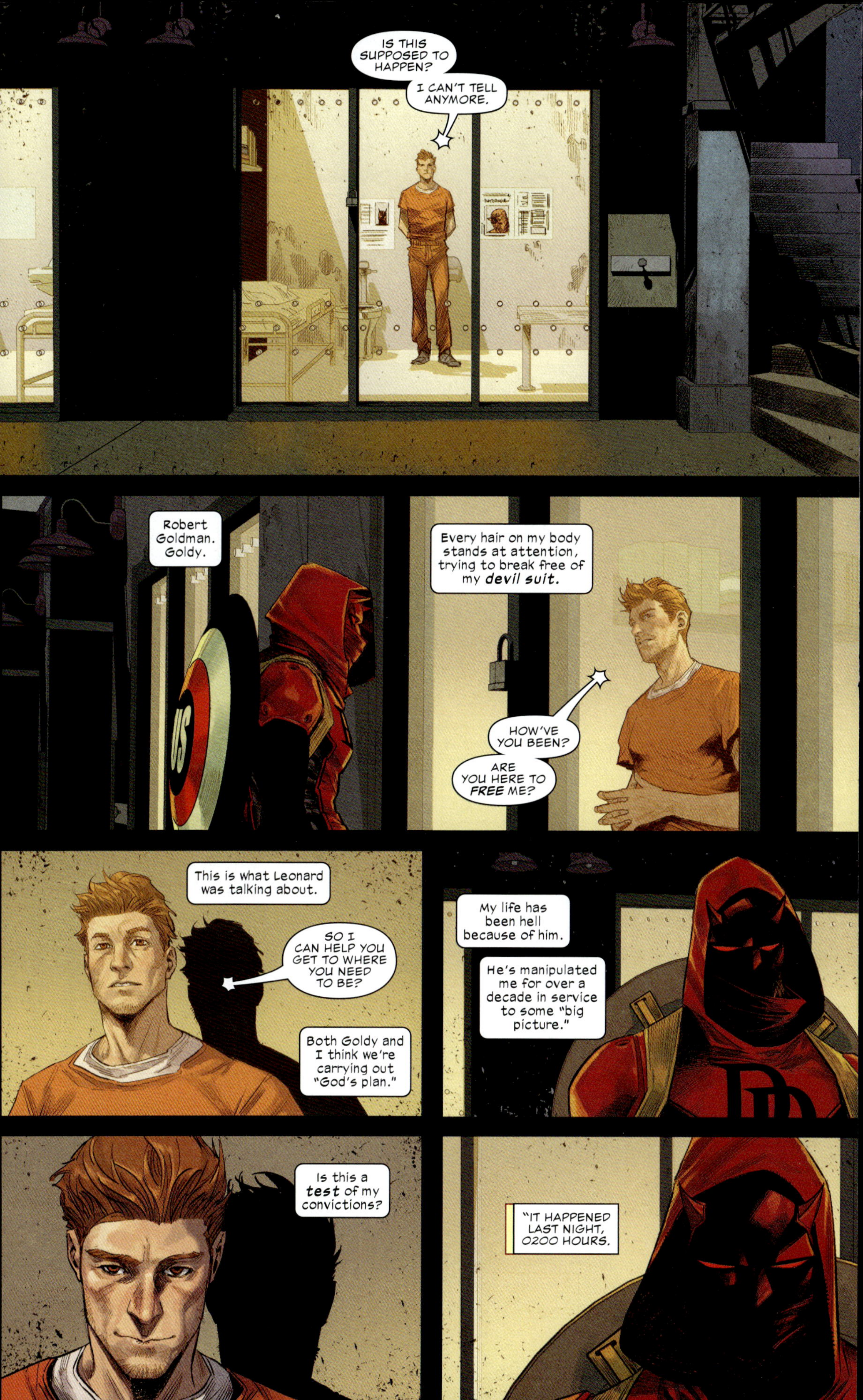
IS THIS SUPPOSED TO HAPPEN?
I CAN'T TELL ANYMORE.
Robert Goldman. Goldy.
Every hair on my body stands at attention, trying to break free of my *devil suit.*
HOW'VE YOU BEEN?
ARE YOU HERE TO *FREE* ME?
This is what Leonard was talking about.
SO I CAN HELP YOU GET TO WHERE YOU NEED TO BE?
Both Goldy and I think we're carrying out "God's plan."
My life has been hell because of him.
He's manipulated me for over a decade in service to some "big picture."
Is this a *test* of my convictions?
"IT HAPPENED LAST NIGHT, 0200 HOURS.

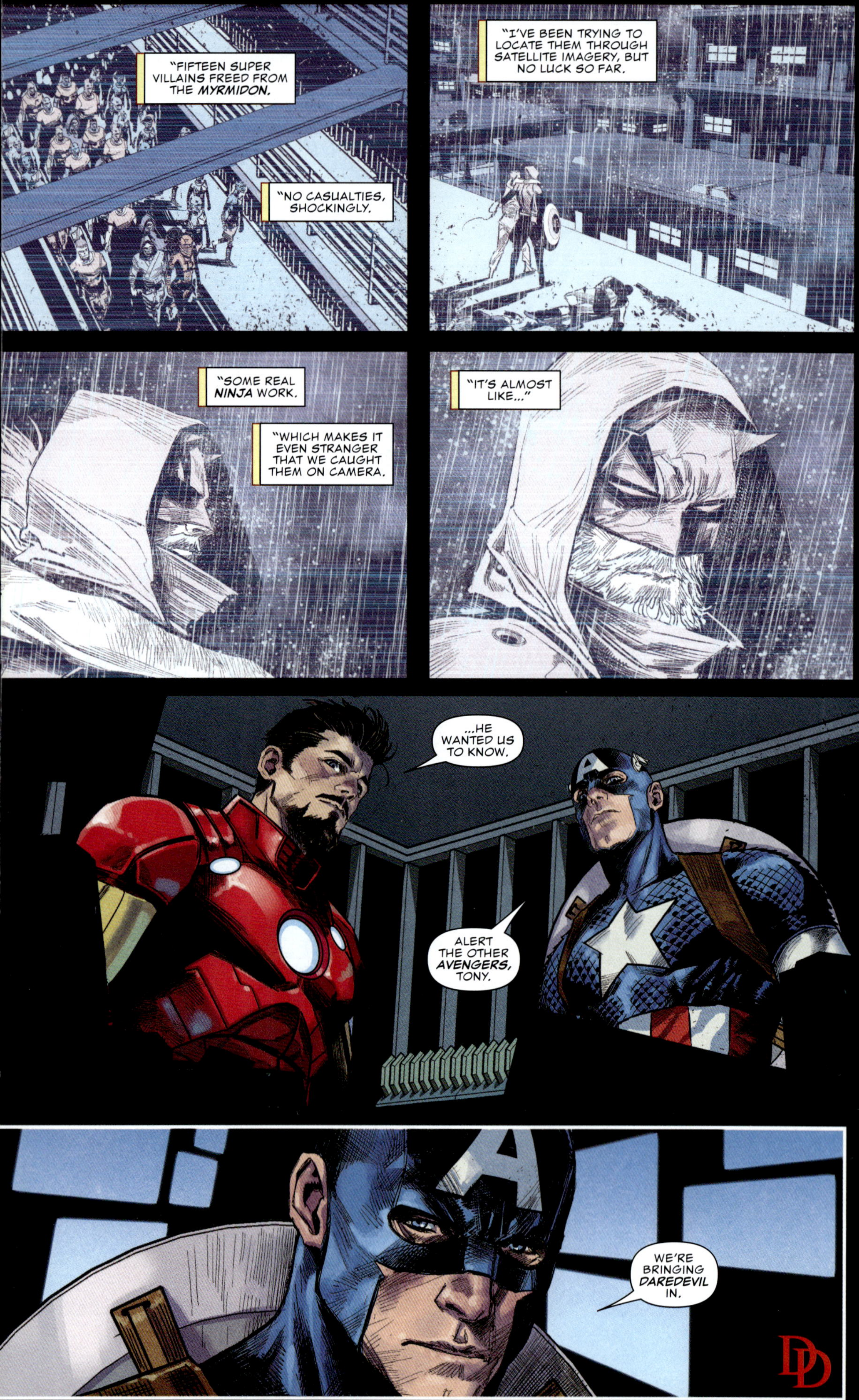
"FIFTEEN SUPER VILLAINS FREED FROM THE *MYRMIDON.*
"NO CASUALTIES, SHOCKINGLY.
"I'VE BEEN TRYING TO LOCATE THEM THROUGH SATELLITE IMAGERY, BUT NO LUCK SO FAR.
"SOME REAL *NINJA* WORK.
"WHICH MAKES IT EVEN STRANGER THAT WE CAUGHT THEM ON CAMERA.
"IT'S ALMOST LIKE..."
...HE WANTED US TO KNOW.
ALERT THE OTHER *AVENGERS,* TONY.
WE'RE BRINGING *DAREDEVIL* IN.

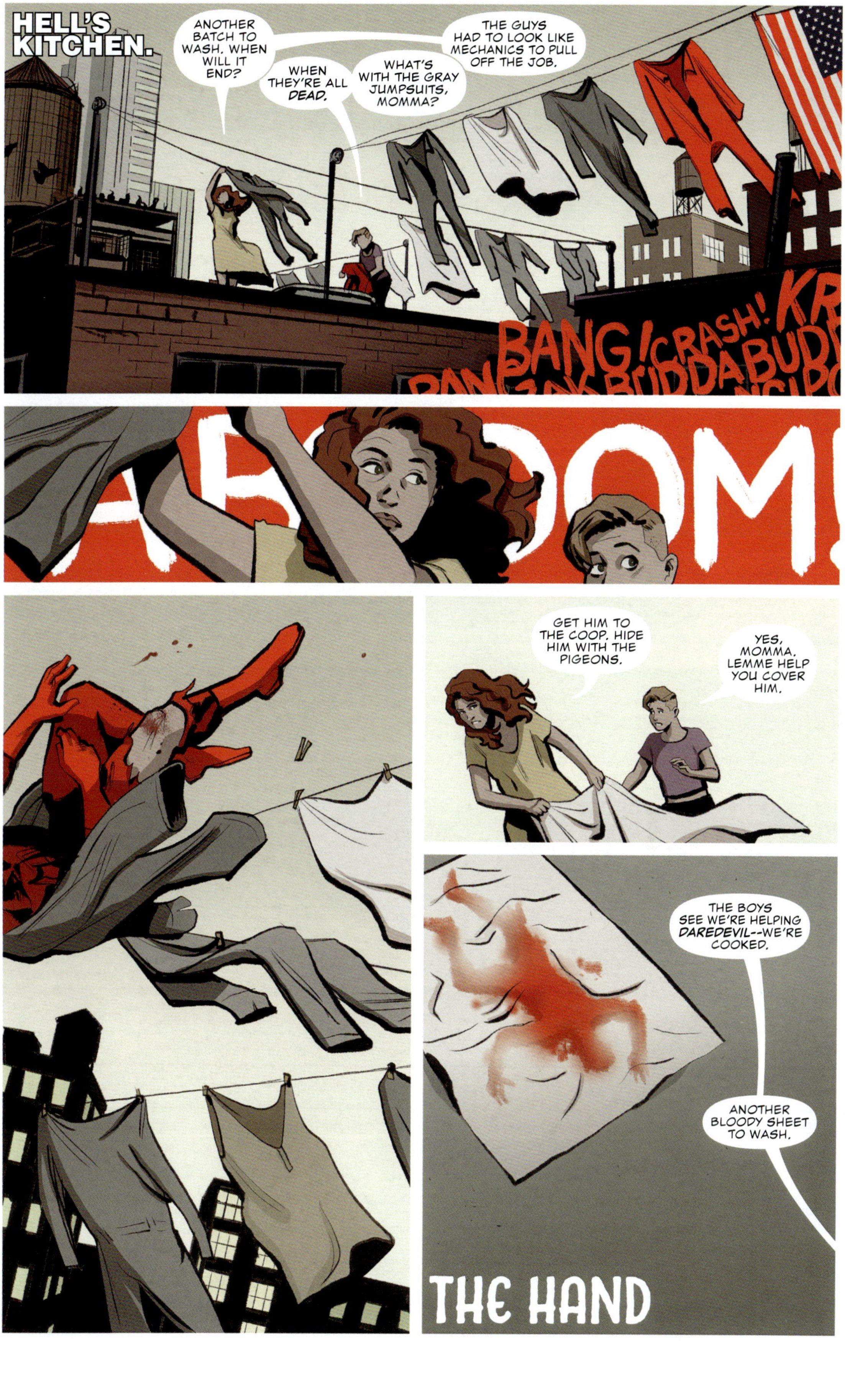
HELL'S KITCHEN.
ANOTHER BATCH TO WASH. WHEN WILL IT END?
THE GUYS HAD TO LOOK LIKE MECHANICS TO PULL OFF THE JOB.
WHAT'S WITH THE GRAY JUMPSUITS, MOMMA?
WHEN THEY'RE ALL *DEAD.*
BANG! CRASH!
GET HIM TO THE COOP. HIDE HIM WITH THE PIGEONS.
YES, MOMMA. LEMME HELP YOU COVER HIM.
THE BOYS SEE WE'RE HELPING *DAREDEVIL*--WE'RE COOKED.
ANOTHER BLOODY SHEET TO WASH.
THE HAND

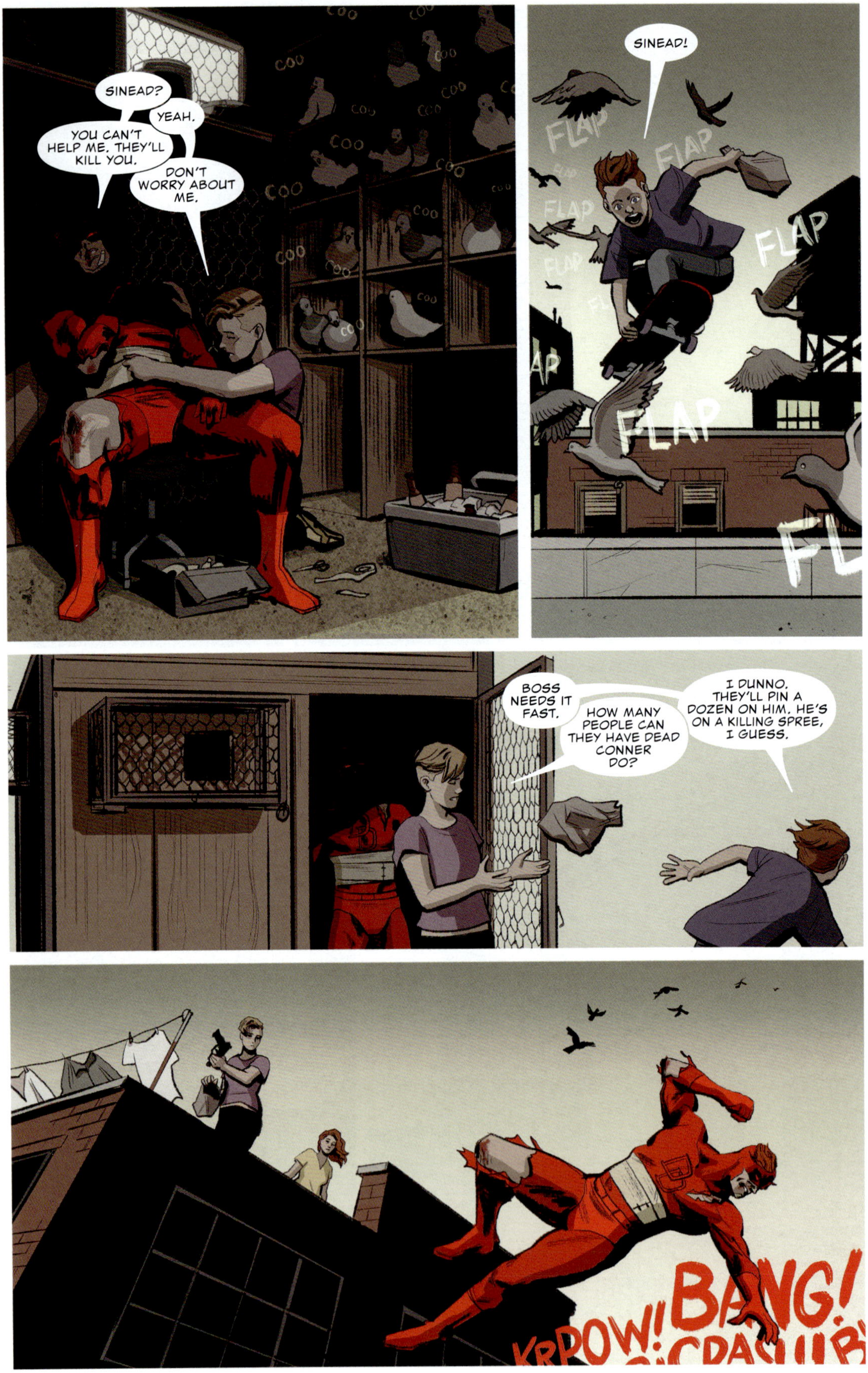
SINEAD?
YEAH.
YOU CAN'T HELP ME. THEY'LL KILL YOU.
DON'T WORRY ABOUT ME.
COO
SINEAD!
FLAP
BOSS NEEDS IT FAST.
I DUNNO. THEY'LL PIN A DOZEN ON HIM. HE'S ON A KILLING SPREE, I GUESS.
HOW MANY PEOPLE CAN THEY HAVE DEAD CONNER DO?
KRPOW!
BANG!

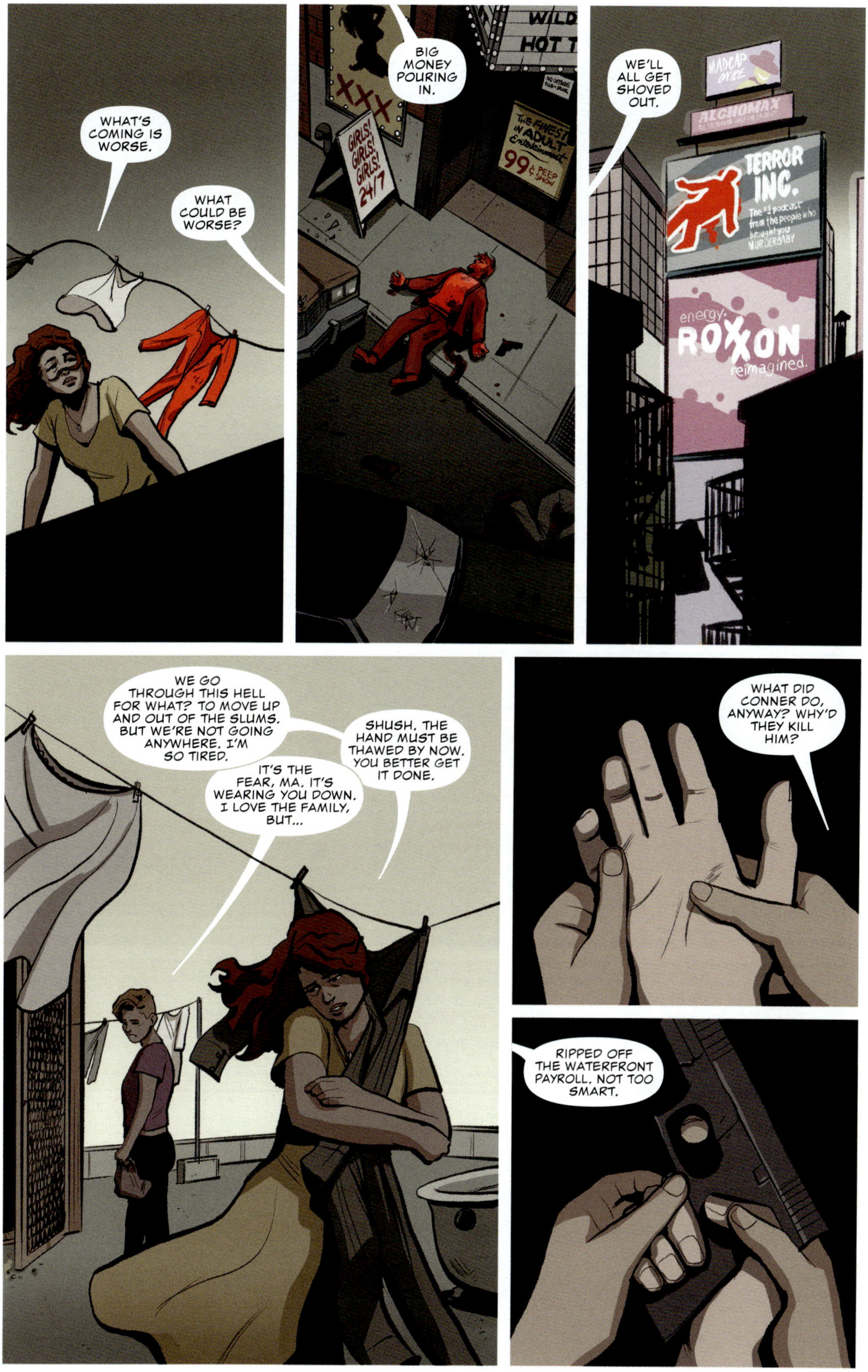
WHAT'S COMING IS WORSE.
WHAT COULD BE WORSE?
BIG MONEY POURING IN.
WILD
HOT T
XXX
GIRLS! GIRLS! GIRLS! 24/7
THE FINEST IN ADULT Entertainment 99¢ PEEP SHOW
WE'LL ALL GET SHOVED OUT.
ALCHOMAX
TERROR INC.
The #1 podcast from the people who brought you MURDERBABY
energy. ROXXON reimagined.
WE GO THROUGH THIS HELL FOR WHAT? TO MOVE UP AND OUT OF THE SLUMS. BUT WE'RE NOT GOING ANYWHERE. I'M SO TIRED.
SHUSH. THE HAND MUST BE THAWED BY NOW. YOU BETTER GET IT DONE.
IT'S THE FEAR, MA. IT'S WEARING YOU DOWN. I LOVE THE FAMILY, BUT...
WHAT DID CONNER DO, ANYWAY? WHY'D THEY KILL HIM?
RIPPED OFF THE WATERFRONT PAYROLL, NOT TOO SMART.

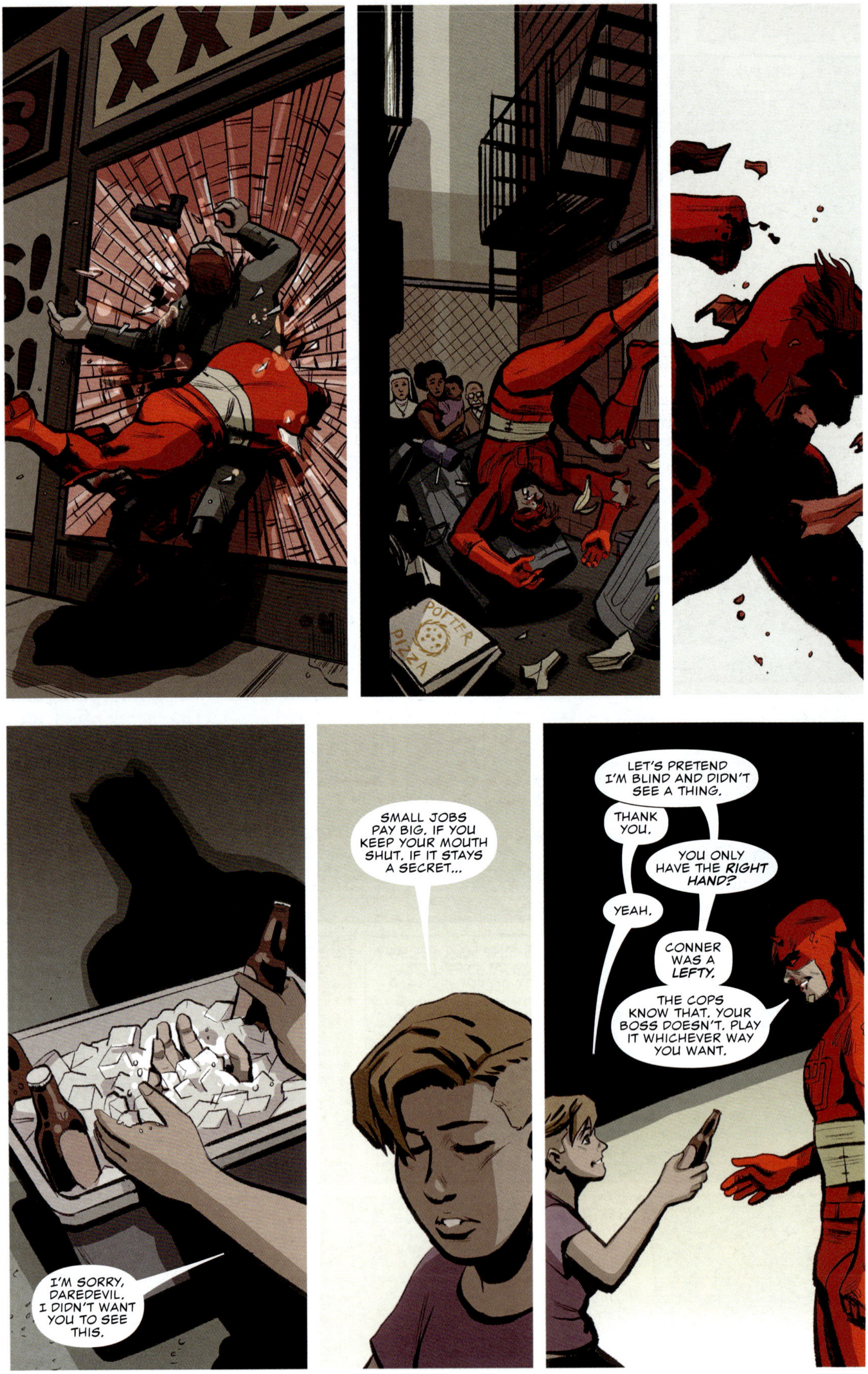
XXX
POTTER PIZZA
I'M SORRY, DAREDEVIL. I DIDN'T WANT YOU TO SEE THIS.
SMALL JOBS PAY BIG. IF YOU KEEP YOUR MOUTH SHUT. IF IT STAYS A SECRET...
LET'S PRETEND I'M BLIND AND DIDN'T SEE A THING.
THANK YOU.
YOU ONLY HAVE THE *RIGHT HAND?*
YEAH.
CONNER WAS A *LEFTY.*
THE COPS KNOW THAT. YOUR BOSS DOESN'T. PLAY IT WHICHEVER WAY YOU WANT.

MINI MARVELS

by Chris Giarrusso

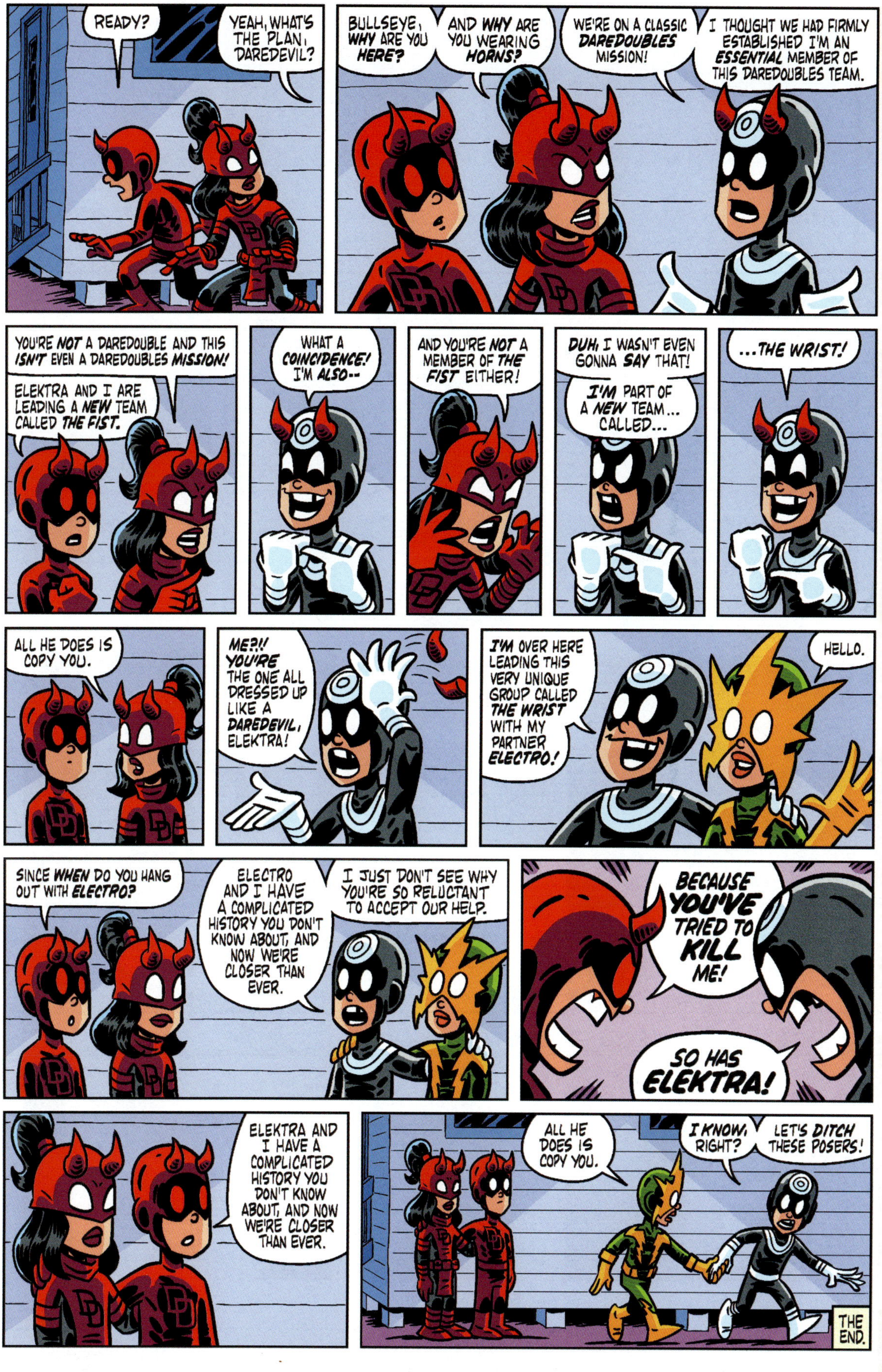

READY?
YEAH, WHAT'S THE PLAN, DAREDEVIL?
BULLSEYE, WHY ARE YOU HERE?
AND WHY ARE YOU WEARING HORNS?
WE'RE ON A CLASSIC DAREDOUBLES MISSION!
I THOUGHT WE HAD FIRMLY ESTABLISHED I'M AN ESSENTIAL MEMBER OF THIS DAREDOUBLES TEAM.
YOU'RE NOT A DAREDOUBLE AND THIS ISN'T EVEN A DAREDOUBLES MISSION!
ELEKTRA AND I ARE LEADING A NEW TEAM CALLED THE FIST.
WHAT A COINCIDENCE! I'M ALSO--
AND YOU'RE NOT A MEMBER OF THE FIST EITHER!
DUH, I WASN'T EVEN GONNA SAY THAT!
I'M PART OF A NEW TEAM... CALLED...
...THE WRIST!
ALL HE DOES IS COPY YOU.
ME?!! YOU'RE THE ONE ALL DRESSED UP LIKE A DAREDEVIL, ELEKTRA!
I'M OVER HERE LEADING THIS VERY UNIQUE GROUP CALLED THE WRIST WITH MY PARTNER ELECTRO!
HELLO.
SINCE WHEN DO YOU HANG OUT WITH ELECTRO?
ELECTRO AND I HAVE A COMPLICATED HISTORY YOU DON'T KNOW ABOUT, AND NOW WE'RE CLOSER THAN EVER.
I JUST DON'T SEE WHY YOU'RE SO RELUCTANT TO ACCEPT OUR HELP.
BECAUSE YOU'VE TRIED TO KILL ME!
SO HAS ELEKTRA!
ELEKTRA AND I HAVE A COMPLICATED HISTORY YOU DON'T KNOW ABOUT, AND NOW WE'RE CLOSER THAN EVER.
ALL HE DOES IS COPY YOU.
I KNOW, RIGHT?
LET'S DITCH THESE POSERS!
THE END.

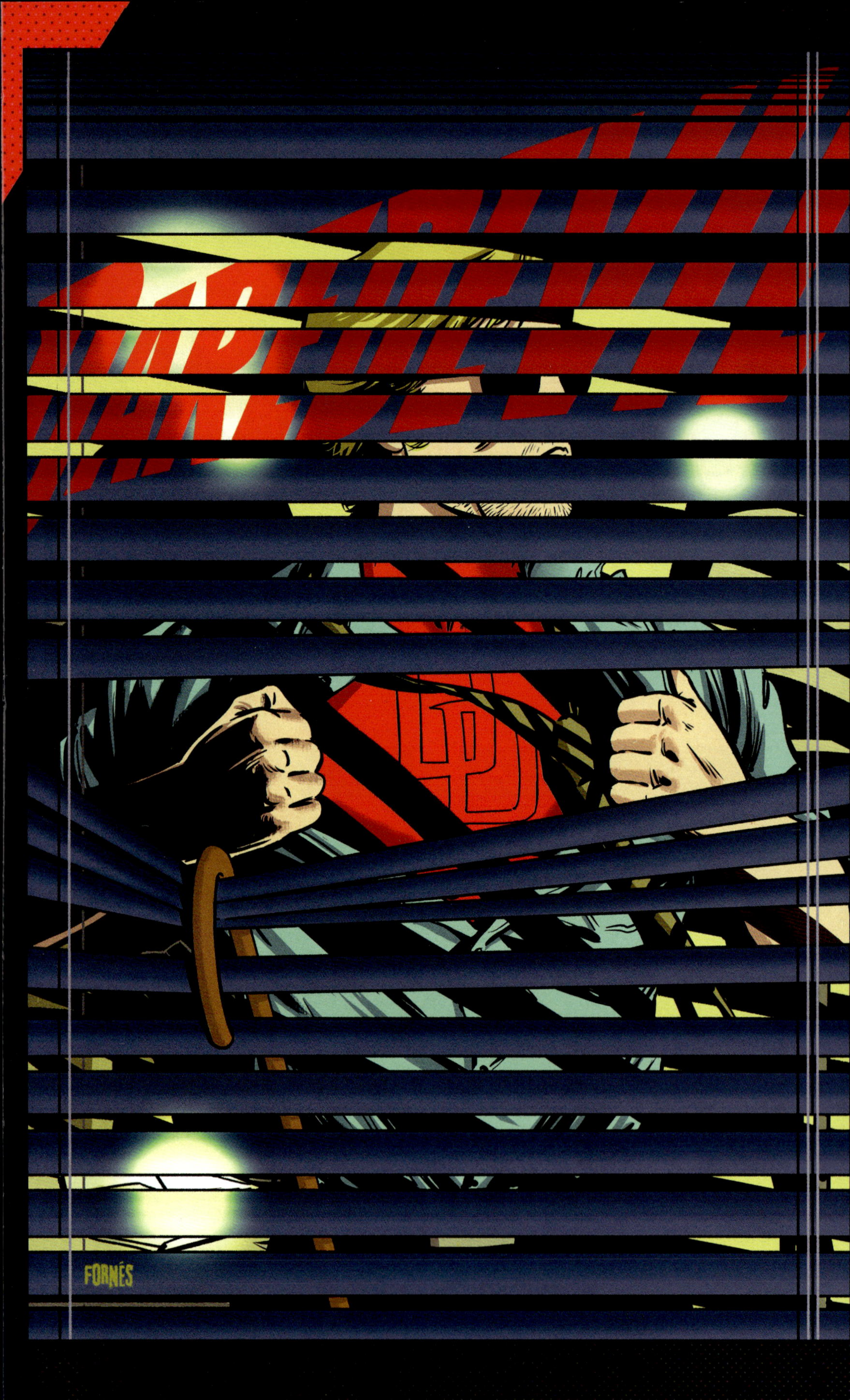
FORNÉS

#1 VARIANT BY JORGE FORNES

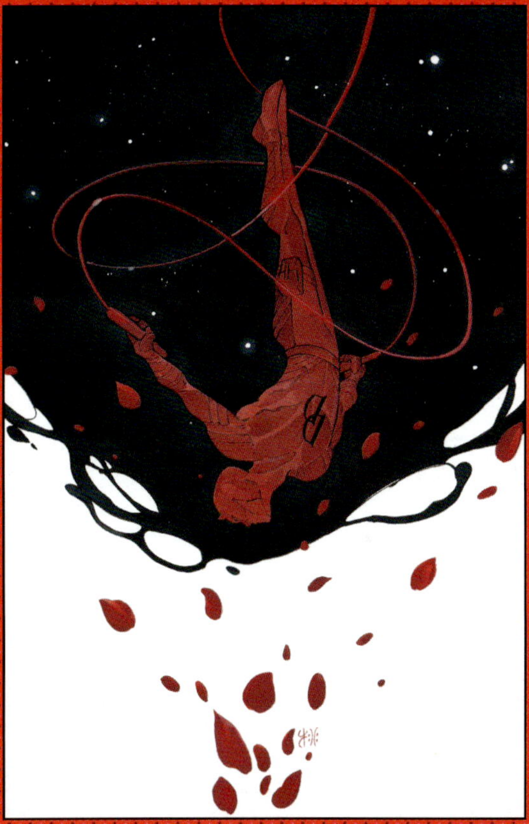

#1 VARIANT BY
PEACH MOMOKO

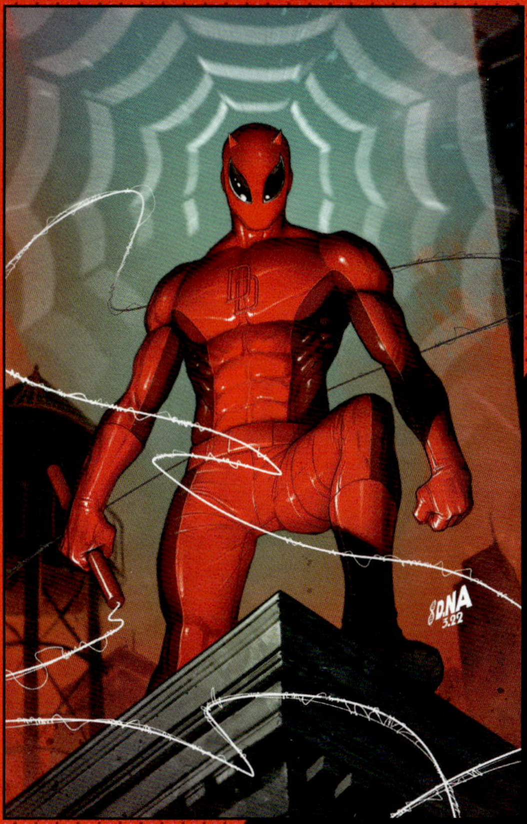

#1 SPIDER-MAN VARIANT BY
DAVID NAKAYAMA

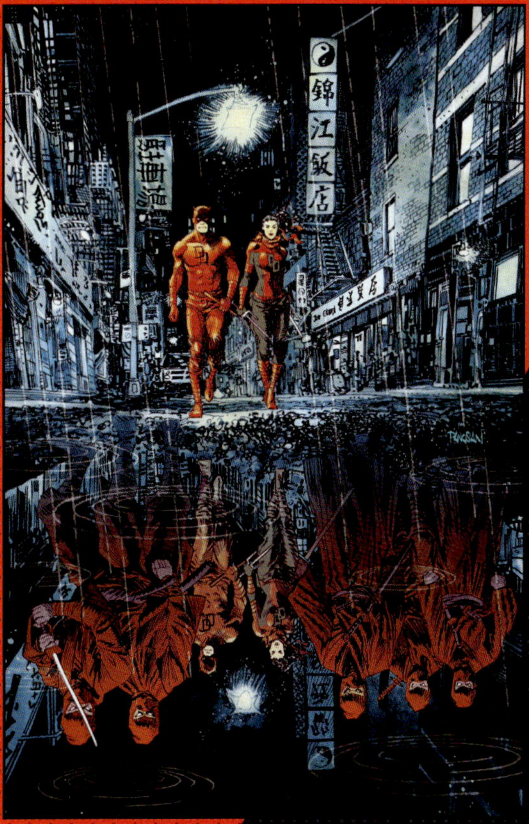

#1 VARIANT BY
DAN PANOSIAN

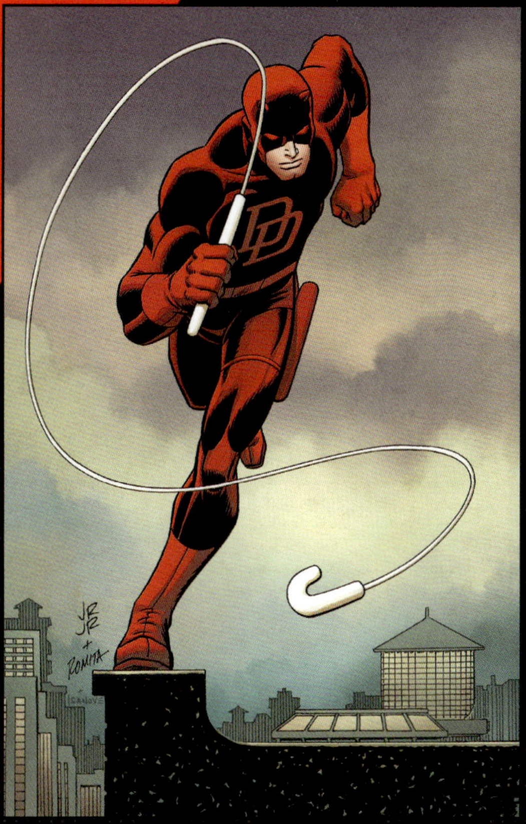

#1 VARIANT BY JOHN ROMITA JR.,
JOHN ROMITA SR. & RICHARD ISANOVE

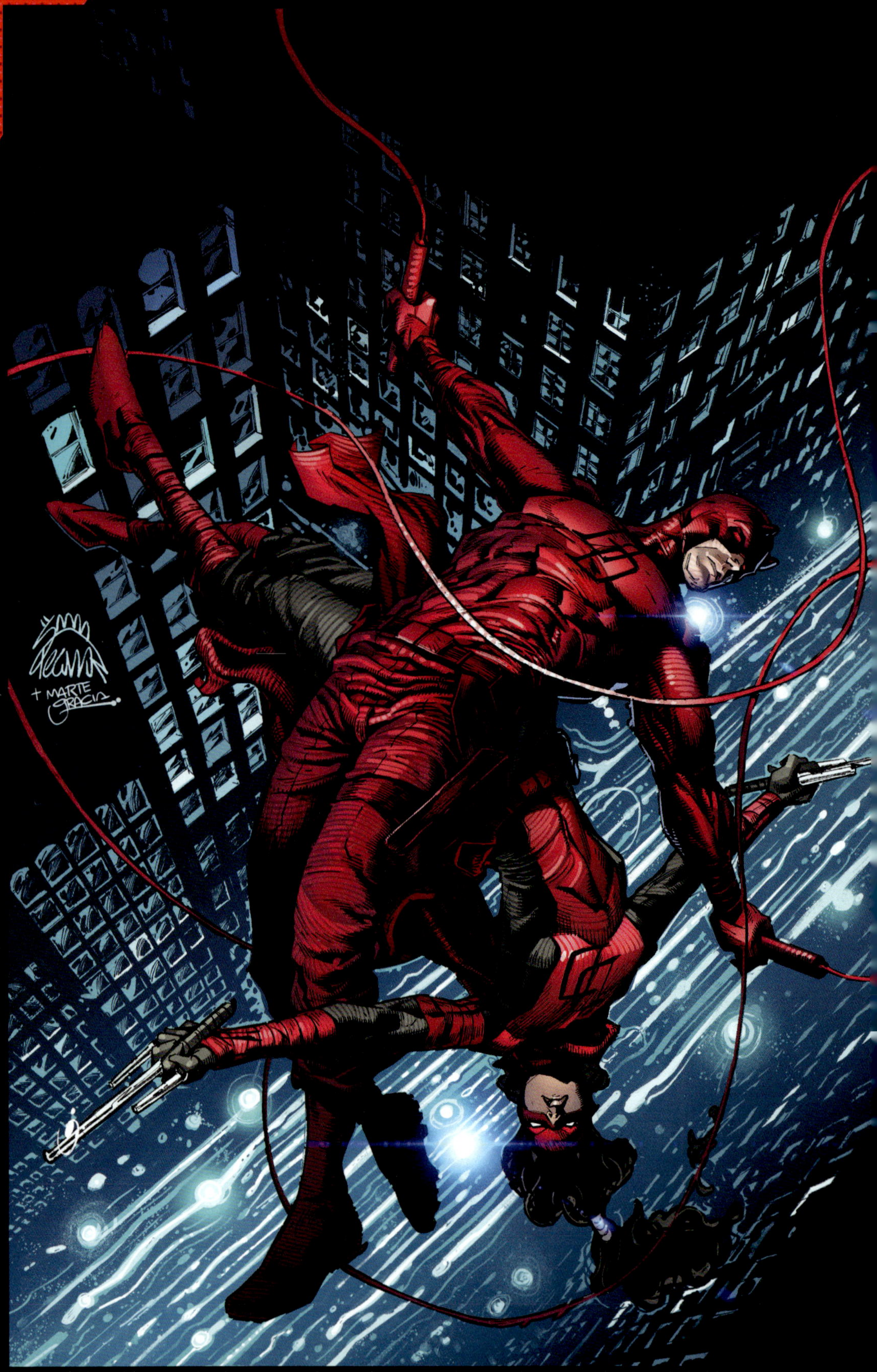
RYAN STEGMAN
+ MARTE GRACIA

#1 VARIANT BY **RYAN STEGMAN & MARTE GRACIA**

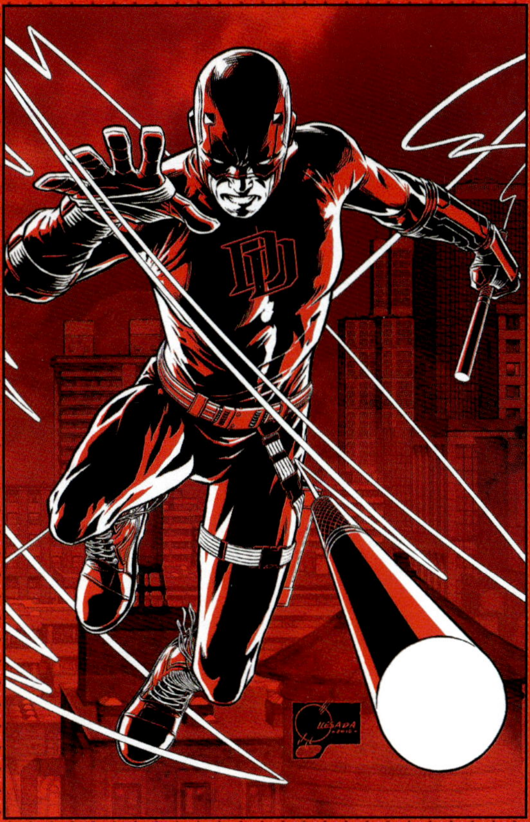

#1 HIDDEN GEM VARIANT BY
JOE QUESADA

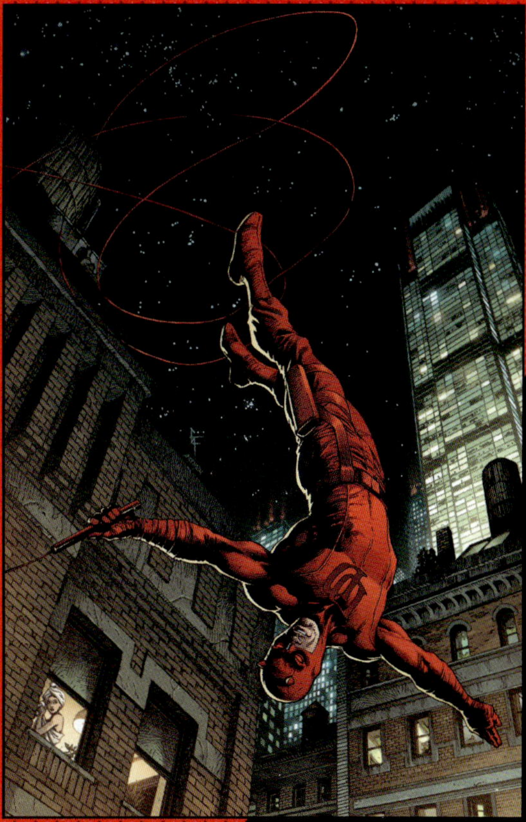

#2 VARIANT BY
GARY FRANK & BRAD ANDERSON

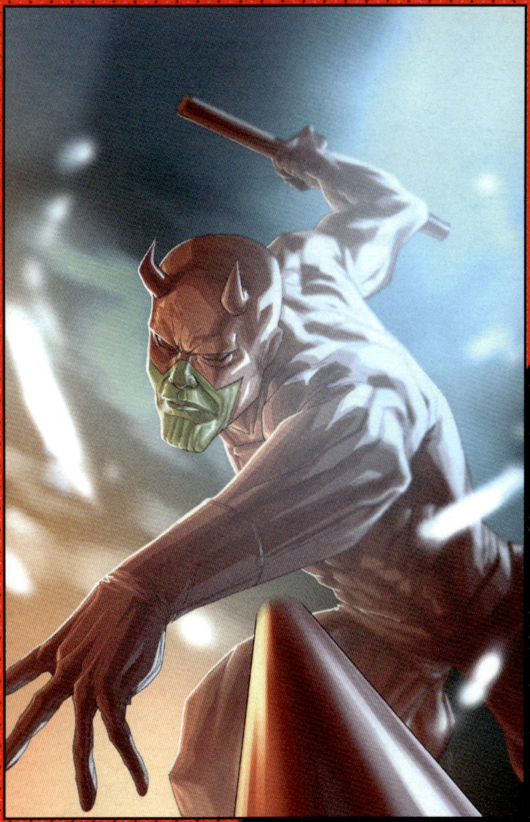

#2 SKRULL VARIANT BY
PETE WOODS

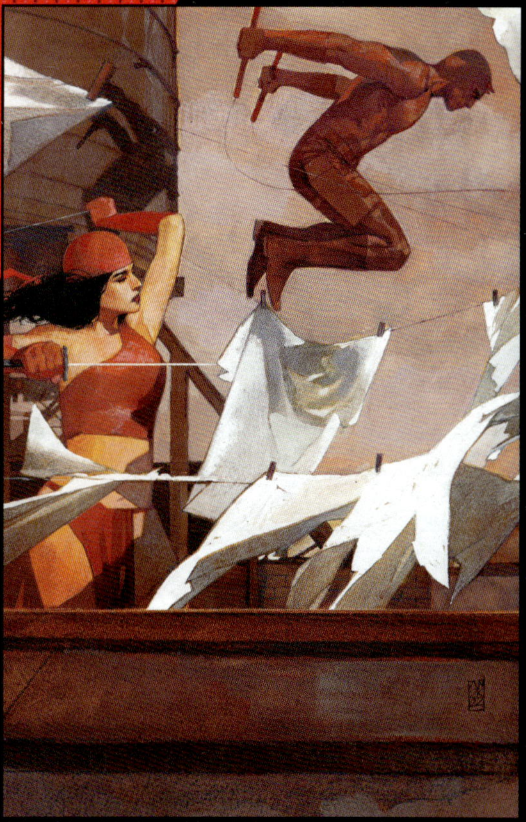

#3 VARIANT BY
ALEV MALEEV

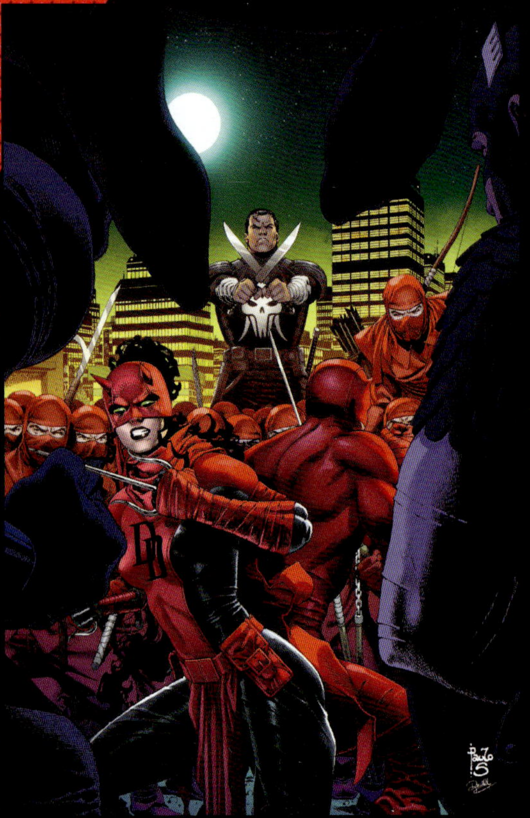

#3 PROMO VARIANT BY PAOLO SIQUEIRA & RACHELLE ROSENBERG

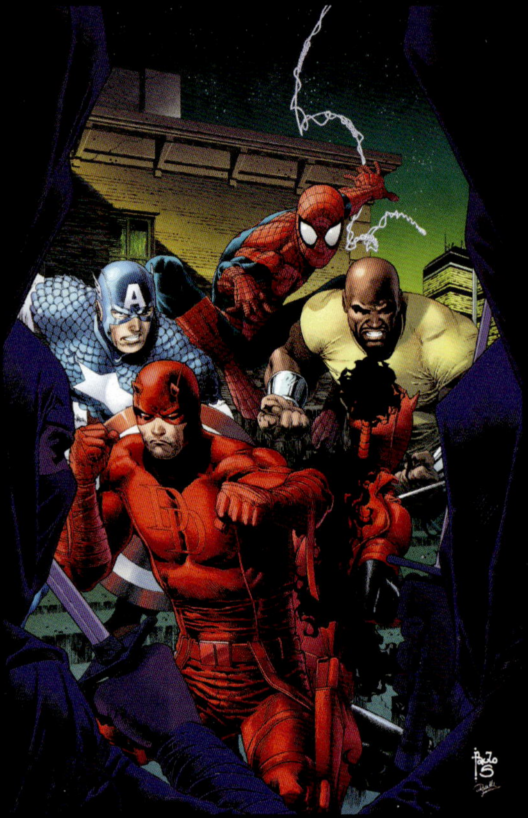

#4 PROMO VARIANT BY PAOLO SIQUEIRA & RACHELLE ROSENBERG

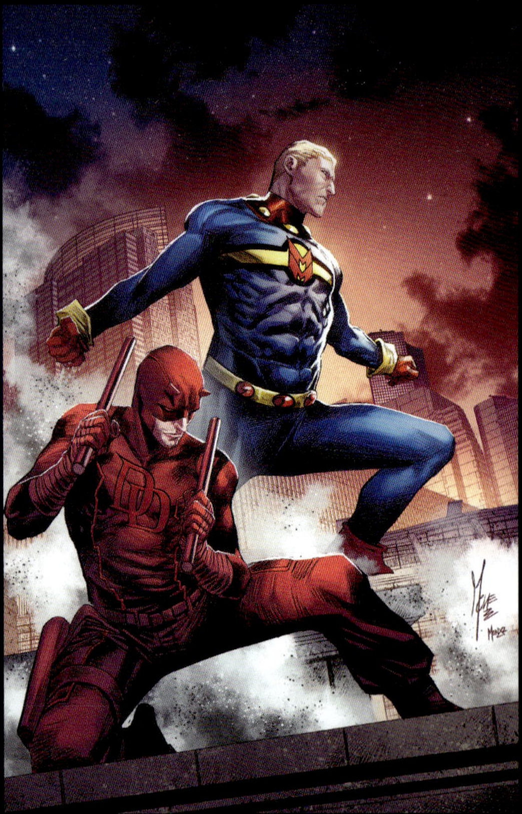

#4 MIRACLEMAN VARIANT BY MARCO CHECCHETTO & MARCIO MENYZ

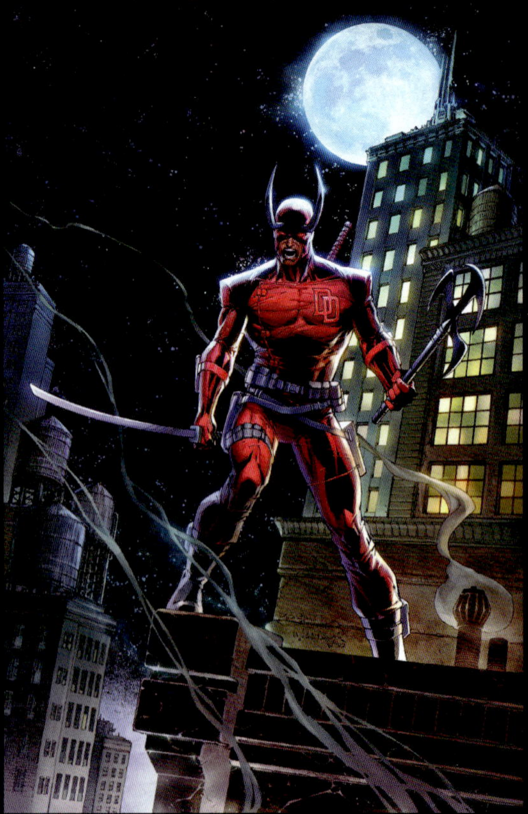

#5 X-TREME MARVEL VARIANT BY SCOTT WILLIAMS & SEBASTIAN CHANG

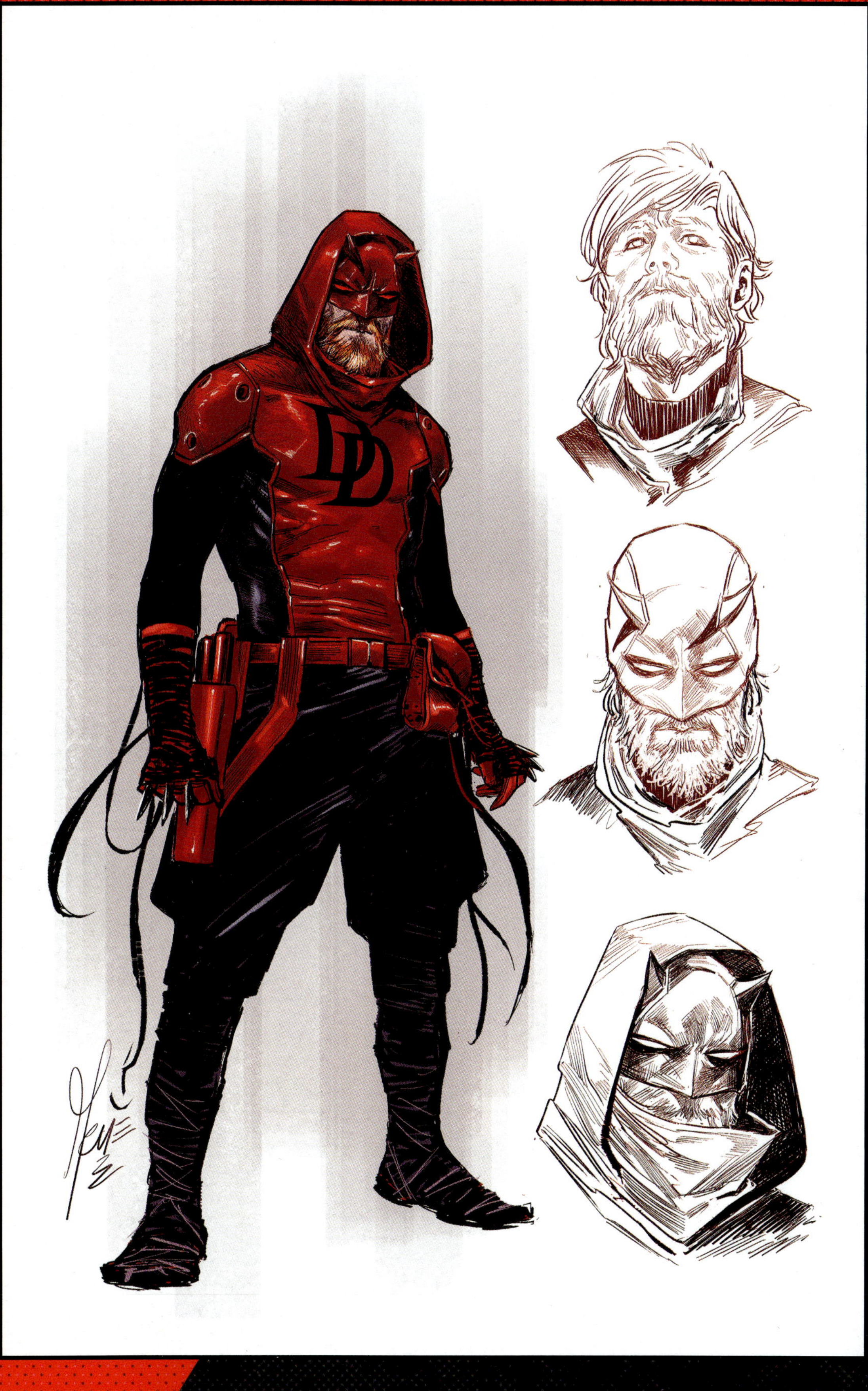

#5 DESIGN VARIANT BY MARCO CHECCHETTO